Also by Ann Aguirre

Fix-It Witch Series
Witch Please
Boss Witch

BOSS Witch

ANN AGUIRRE

sourcebooks
casablanca

To Lilith Saintcrow,
for so many reasons.
I truly cherish our friendship.

Published by Sourcebooks Casablanca, an imprint of Sourcebooks
P.O. Box 4410, Naperville, Illinois 60567-4410
(630) 961-3900
sourcebooks.com

Cataloging-in-Publication Data is on file with the Library of Congress.

Printed and bound in the United States of America.
VP 10 9 8 7 6 5 4 3 2 1

CHAPTER 1

CLEMENTINE WATERHOUSE HAD BEEN FIXING problems for as long as she could remember.

As a kid, when she heard her mother, Allegra, sobbing, she'd be the one to magic up a cup of tea after the latest knock-down-and-drag-out fight that ended with furniture broken and her bio dad, Barnabas Balfour, abandoning them. *Again.* Somehow, that pattern continued with her cousin. Clem was the one who ended up sweeping up the wreckage and trying to piece together whatever was broken.

For the past month, she'd had an ominous feeling about Danica's growing attachment to Titus Winnaker, the mundane baker who was stirring up family drama during a time already way too fraught with it.

A quiet throb started in her right temple as Clem waited for Danica to come home and carpool to their coven meeting. Her cousin dashed in, out of breath, radiating anxiety. Clem didn't push for details, knowing that whatever was wrong, her cousin would explain at the meeting. So Clem headed to the car and drove over to Kerry and Priya's place, two coven sisters who were among Clem's closest friends. They were also a committed couple who'd just moved in together. Kerry Quarles was an angular woman with blond hair and sharp features while Priya Banik was softly rounded, her bronze skin a glowing complement to her river of silken black hair.

Clem and Danica greeted their hosts with hugs and a bag of yogurt-covered pretzels. Then Danica beelined into the house. With growing concern, Clem watched her cousin pace the cozy living room, chewing her thumbnail as she went. It had been a while since she'd seen Danica this agitated, and Clem swapped a look with Priya while Kerry set out drinks and snacks. In silent reply, Priya lifted a shoulder.

Looks like she doesn't know what's up either.

Kerry and Priya lived in a two-bedroom town house with a good-sized living room decorated in a pale palette with splashes of color and set adjacent to an open kitchen. The furniture was comfortable, and Clem took a seat to wait for the rest of the coven. Margie Bower tended to arrive first. She was a quiet woman in her forties with brown hair and circles under her eyes. Vanessa Jackson got there next; she wore her hair in beautiful braids, and today, she was glowing in a yellow sundress that was the perfect foil for her dark skin. Since they lived on the same street, Ethel Murray came in with her, a plump woman in her sixties with silver hair cut in a pixie style. Leanne Vanderpol rolled in last, a redhead in her late thirties with warm olive skin who favored pencil skirts to show off her curves and who always had on a pair of heels.

Ethel took one look at Danica and grinned. "You got laid. And it was *powerful*."

At the old witch's words, Leanne took a closer look. "Damn. So she did."

"It's been ages for me," Margie said with a sigh. "I demand vicarious satisfaction."

For fuck's sake, she was navigating family interference like it was an active land mine, while her cousin was off boning. Clem's eye twitched as Danica made a shooing motion.

Then Danica said, "I'll take questions about my sex life later. Something big might be looming. Titus told me a big, scary guy barged into the bakery and started yelling about witches. He made threats and flipped the cash register and spiked his coffee on the floor when they asked him to leave."

Fear swirled inside Clem, exacerbating her headache. Though witch hunters weren't usually so overt in their actions, she couldn't assume it was a mundane with mental issues. The safety of their coven depended on staying hidden.

Kerry cursed quietly, addressing Danica. "You've made two service calls there recently. If this guy's a hunter, he could have followed your energy trail."

Danica let out an unsteady breath. "Exactly what I'm thinking. I haven't bothered using a dispersal ritual in ages. I got comfortable. And careless."

Of course she did. She's obsessed with the baker and his buns.

"The hunter hasn't got us yet," Ethel said with a pragmatic air. "My mother told me about one who came sniffing around in the thirties. They didn't find us then either. Try to calm down."

Breathe, Clem told herself. *Stuff like this happens. It'll be okay. I'll find a way to keep them safe.*

Seeing how upset her cousin was, Clem moved to comfort Danica, but Priya got there first. She rubbed Danica's shoulder. "It's not your fault. I suspect that none of us have been as careful with our magic as we could've been."

Vanessa nodded. "It could have been any one of us that pinged on his radar."

With a sigh, Danica shook her head. "But I'm the one who's spiking like crazy. My output is off the charts lately."

"At least you admit there's a problem." Clem tried to sound neutral, but she was angry and scared in equal measure.

How the hell do I put this cat back in the bag?

If anything happened to her coven sisters, she wouldn't be able to live. Clem loved all of them so much, even if she wasn't the most demonstrative, and the idea of anyone hurting them exacerbated her headache. Visceral fright lodged in her brain like a rusty railroad spike. To make matters worse, her cousin didn't even acknowledge her words.

Danica turned to Ethel. "You said there was a hunter here in the thirties. Did your mother tell you how they got rid of him?"

"First, we protect this place so he can't sense our workings," the old woman said. "And then we do a joint casting to confirm if he's the real deal."

"Divination is your forte," Vanessa said.

Ethel nodded. "That's why I'll be taking the lead. Priya, can you lock the apartment? You've lived here for years, and your imprint is stronger than Kerry's."

"Understood. I'm on it." Priya bolstered her wards in each

room, creating a secure site that shouldn't leak any sign of their workings.

Leanne confirmed the seal was solid, then Kerry and Priya procured the implements Ethel requested, white candles and purified water in a copper bowl, along with various ceremonial herbs. The old witch took the lead, intoning softly as she scattered the carnation and mugwort, finishing with sea salt for purity. Without prompting, they joined hands around the table, allowing Ethel to pull from their energies as she peered into the glimmering water.

At first, it was cloudy as she whispered, "Tell us, spirits, true or false, false or true. Him we seek and him we find. Let none hinder this quest of mind. Hunter, the water reveals the truth of you."

The liquid roiled inside the bowl, gentle bubbles that slowly clarified into the image of a large man reclining in a vinyl chair. A leather jacket was slung over the back, and he was drinking a beer in a cheap motel room. He was big, but more, he radiated intensity and determination. At his feet lay a battered leather satchel. He wore battered boots and torn jeans. From head to toe, he promised danger, and if that wasn't enough, he was ruggedly appealing too. Strong jaw, dusted with dark stubble, a shock of hair so black, it gleamed, and his eyes were an eerie silver gray. And though it was impossible, he *stirred* as they gazed on him, glancing around as if he felt the invisible weight of their attention.

Gazing at him, Clem felt...something straightaway. Not fear. Not exactly. It made no sense, but it resembled...inevitability. *Clearly, I need to sleep more. I'm hallucinating.*

Carefully, Ethel drew back, and Danica rubbed her hands together nervously. "Well?"

The old witch stared into the now-quiescent tureen. "We're in it now, my darlings. He's the real deal."

Her coven sisters sat quiet for a bit, each likely wrestling with their own fears. Diverting him might require something of Clem she didn't want to give, but so be it. *I have no plan, but I'm the fixer, right? I'll figure something out.*

Clem squared her shoulders. "No worries. I'll handle him."

A few days later, after doing some legwork, Clem came to O'Reilly's dressed to slay with the witch hunter in her sights.

In a slinky black dress, she was too much for a wannabe Irish pub in a tiny Midwestern town that mostly succeeded at being a dive, but she still walked the room like a runway, making the most of her entrance. Multiple heads swiveled in her direction, likely because of the fuck-me shoes and the length of leg she was showing.

She took in the room without seeming to do an obvious inspection—wide-open bar with a standard layout, square counter in the middle with multiple bartenders, tables and booths surrounding it, pool tables on one side. There was a stage near the back for local talent on the weekends, which was not currently in use, and the lighting was industrial. They didn't have the budget to get burnished wood to make the place authentic, so the decor was more like a TGI Fridays threw up a bunch of Irish memorabilia, with signs like KISS ME, I'M IRISH and a framed poster of a leprechaun about to bare his ass.

Clem clocked her target in a booth near the restrooms, where he had a good view of the whole place. The witch hunter held a bottle of beer, glistening with condensation, but from the look of it, he hadn't enjoyed more than a sip or two. His posture seemed to be relaxed, but even in her peripheral vision, she could tell that he was watchful. He was smart to start the recon here. People got loose in bars, with liquor greasing their wheels, and the hunter might learn something valuable while listening to gossip.

However, she didn't make the rookie mistake of appearing to notice him. Instead, she sauntered to the bar and ordered an old-fashioned. The bartender asked, "Do you have a preference on the whiskey?"

"Got Jameson?" It was a solid choice, good for mixing, not too expensive.

"What kind of an Irish pub would we be if we didn't? Coming right up."

In short order, she took her drink and sipped at it. Better than she might've expected, considering the source. It took real talent to arrange herself on the barstool and cross her legs without flashing her panties. Clem glanced toward the door like she was waiting for someone who was late then checked her phone, ostensibly looking for a text that wouldn't ever arrive. She crossed and recrossed her legs twice before the first hopeful sidled up.

A tall, thin man in his forties with the sad eyes of a basset hound settled next to her. "Looks like you've been stood up."

"I won't give up yet," she said in a dismissive tone.

A little flicker on her nerves, like the spark of fireflies on a summer night, told her she'd attracted the hunter's attention. He was watching her sporadically but not with the sort of fascination she needed. Under no circumstances could she go to him, even if this meet-cute took all night. He had to think everything was his idea, or her half-baked gambit would fall apart. She hadn't even risked using a charm to make herself more alluring because that might've pinged his radar. No, her natural appeal had to do the job. Hopefully, he wouldn't register the fact that her necklace was quietly enchanted to dampen her aura as a witch.

"Buy you a drink?" Basset Eyes offered.

She lifted her old-fashioned. "Thanks, I have one."

The lack of eye contact and her flat tone discouraged him, and he eventually went to ask for the next game with some random guys shooting pool. Clem tapped furiously on her phone; to the casual onlooker, it probably seemed like she was angrily texting, when, in fact, she was bingeing the next big thing, more addictive than Candy Crush. It was a game where she played as a pop singer, and currently she was juggling three love interests, and she hadn't yet decided who would get the happy ending, so to speak.

Another wannabe interrupted her gaming, this one far less subtle than Bassett Eyes. The guy wore a plaid shirt, a CAT cap, and had a fine farmer's tan. "Waiting for someone?" At Clem's reluctant nod, he added, "Well, stop. I'm here, baby. Let's have us some fun!"

"I'm good, thanks," she said.

He leaned in, offering her a whiff of his imitation Axe body spray. "Don't be like that. Finish that drink and loosen up a little bit."

The opportunity couldn't have been more perfect if she'd hired this asshole to hassle her. He put his hands on her, and just as fast, his arm was twisted behind him, and the witch hunter was suddenly there, though she hadn't seen him move. Towering over both of them, he was hard-faced and silent, smelling slightly of leather and asphalt. Inky-black hair fell in disheveled waves on either side of a strong, bony face. The hunter wrenched the other man's wrist a little more then let go. His face didn't reveal his emotions, but gray eyes glittered with a febrile light, like there was an ocean of darkness beneath the surface just waiting for the chance at release.

"Sorry to keep you waiting," he said smoothly. "You won't bother my friend again, will you? I thought not." His accent was crisp but not posh, a bit rough at the edges.

Clem was American enough to get a bit goofy over any English accent, even those that weren't considered attractive across the pond. Sternly, she locked down that response. It didn't matter if he was tall or chivalrous or had biceps as big as her head. He wasn't handsome, but there was something deeply compelling about the directness of his gaze. At some point, his nose had been broken, maybe more than once. The witch hunter looked like he was comfortable with violence.

Nerves tried to get the best of Clem. *What am I doing? This is bananas. He'll know.* With great effort, she steadied her resolve.

Clem swiveled on her stool as Farmer's Tan mumbled something and darted away like his plaid shirt was on fire. "My hero?" She let her voice drift upward on the last word, making it a question instead of a statement.

"Sorry if I overstepped. He looked to be the handsy sort, and it's not my nature to overlook a wrong being done."

"Yeah, that's hero territory." With a little sigh, she tucked her phone into her bag. "Looks like I've been stood up, but I want to buy you a drink in thanks before I head out."

"Are you in a hurry?" he asked.

He didn't take a seat without asking, but he did prop up against the bar like a living pylon dedicated to scaring away weirdos. Clem shook her head, swirling the melting ice in her old-fashioned, and tilted her head at the seat nearby. "You're welcome to join me. I need to drink this slowly." She gestured at the beer he'd abandoned. "Want another one of those?"

"Please, no." His smile shouldn't be this charming.

If she didn't know who and what he was, she might be taken in by the easy humor that didn't touch his eyes. No, he was still on guard, still skimming the room for goddess knew what, without realizing he was already chatting up the only witch in the place.

Clem firmed her resolve and let out a quiet laugh. "Then what'll it be?"

"I should take it easy as well, or I'll be in no state to ride."

"Was one of the motorcycles I saw outside yours?" she asked, signaling the bartender. "Can I get a sparkling water, please?"

"Right away."

She turned to the witch hunter with a teasing smile. "Gin and tonic, hold the gin. Will that work? If you hang out a little longer, it should discourage the rest of the populace from messing with me. Tonight, I'm really not in the mood."

"Something bad happen?"

Clem lowered her gaze so her lashes would hide the triumph that must be sparking in her brown eyes. "You could say that."

You happened. Now I'm on damage abatement.

"Want to talk about it? Sometimes it's easier to unload your problems on a stranger." His voice truly did shocking, possibly unlawful things to her insides.

"You're moving too fast," she joked. "Maybe tell me your name first."

"Gavin."

"Clementine." She lifted her glass in a mock toast.

"As in 'oh, my darling'? Should I sing it?" Teasingly, he hummed a few bars.

"Only if you want a punch in the mouth."

———

Gavin Rhys thought the woman beside him might not be joking.

"Feisty" was the word some would apply to her, but he loathed that description, best saved for small dogs. He probably shouldn't have gotten involved, but it seemed obvious that with her date doing a runner, he'd be watching a slow progression of prats pestering her for the remainder of her sojourn. She might think he was an arse as well, but he wouldn't prevent her from drinking in peace, at least, or put his hands where they weren't wanted.

He shook his head lazily, sipping the tonic water she'd kindly procured. "Let's save that for our second date, shall we?"

"Is this supposed to be our first?" she asked.

"I do believe in capitalizing on opportunities as they arise. Why, do you want to see me again?" Flirting was simple, barely distracted him from focusing on the magical eddies.

There was...something in the room, but he couldn't get a read on it. The whole town registered this way, as if there were lots of witches working low-key magic behind imperfect warding spells. That trickle of energy—interspersed with incredible magical spikes—had drawn him to St. Claire in the first place. He'd just finished a job down in the Florida panhandle, and he was fucking tired.

So far, he'd been unable to tell his father the truth: *I hate our legacy and want nothing to do with it. I'd rather go back to teaching.*

"Maybe," she said, surprising him. "I'm a sucker for a good hero complex, and I can't resist a British accent."

"I've noticed that. The American weakness for the accent, that is. Back home, I'd be decidedly average, but over here, I seem to set hearts aflutter."

She grinned. "Glad to hear you've kept your modesty, at least."

"Are you accusing me of being vain? You bet I think this song is about me."

Clem laughed, a surprise since "You're So Vain" was *not* playing. He was impressed she even knew the song. His mum had been a Carly Simon fan back in the day, which was the main reason he'd made the joke, fully expecting it wouldn't land. Gavin savored the delight as he registered genuine amusement in the curve of her lush mouth.

She appeared to make up her mind suddenly. "You've got that heroic vibe, and I'm up for some fun with a guy who doesn't stand me up. So do you want to see where that goes?"

Suddenly, Gavin was fully present in the moment, no longer using the conversation with Clementine to cover scoping out the bar. She was gorgeous, with a foxy face, glittering dark eyes, a full mouth, smooth skin, and chestnut hair cut in a short, casual style that made him wonder how it would look once he'd kissed her and run his fingers through it a few times. Her body was sleek, like a sports car that elicited admiring looks, enough that a maddening number of men would've taken a crack at her if Gavin hadn't put a stop to that nonsense.

"Unless that means something quite different here, you're asking…" He let the sentence trail off because, despite his grungy exterior, he couldn't quite bring himself to say the words.

While he wasn't untouched, his experience didn't match the biker persona either. Most often, he blew into town, did his job, and got out. The nomadic lifestyle didn't leave room for attachments or even many hookups, though there had been a few. Gavin waited to see what Clementine would say.

"If you're DTF," she finished.

Down to fuck.

"Right now?"

He hadn't been contemplating it until she put the offer on the table. Then it was *all* he could think about. Probably it was a terrible idea since she'd seemed upset over being stood up. Revenge sex might sound like a brilliant idea tonight, and in the morning, she'd be a sack full of regrets. He'd rather not leave her feeling worse.

Her lazy smile roused an answering spark dredged from some primal part of him that didn't give a shit that somebody had stood her up tonight, about the witch hunter order, or his family's honor.

Clementine traced the rim of her drink then lifted her finger to her mouth. He might not be practiced, but he recognized certain signals when they were obvious.

Then she said, "Maybe not. We're in the middle of the bar, and we'd get arrested if you lifted my skirt and had me against the counter."

Utterly without warning, her tease had him hard as a rock. Because he could visualize it perfectly, only in his white-hot lightning strike of a mental image, he ripped her knickers clean off and fucked her from behind, her hands spread on the bar top, moaning each time he sank his cock into her. The flash of attraction exploded so quick and hot that the aftermath left him slightly dizzy and disoriented, like they really had fucked.

Somehow, he got a hold of his end of the conversation. "I'd rather not be detained, and I'm not an exhibitionist either."

"Neither am I, so I suppose that's out. But you didn't answer my question."

"I'm...interested," he said at last, feeling the pull of attraction as if it were a fishing hook caught in his cheek, tugging him inexorably toward her.

Gavin set his hand on the counter, wondering if she'd mirror his movement. After a brief delay, she did, flattening her palm next to his. *Why does not touching her hand, just seeing hers next to mine, feel so fucking sexy?* Already he could imagine what her skin felt like, how soft and smooth it would be. He even wanted to look at the whorls on her fingertips, minutely scrutinizing the patterns. Chemistry had never hit him like a cosh upside the head, his body rioting to get closer to her.

"That's direct," she said, knocking back the last of her drink. "Then let me make you an offer. While you're in town, I'll be your local guide. Let's see where that leads."

"You drive a hard bargain. If I agree, where would you take me first?"

Clementine grinned. "Is this a test?"

"It might be."

"I've never been graded on my ability to come up with a fun date on the fly, but I'll have you know that I'm competitive by nature."

"You're stalling," Gavin said.

She pulled up a glossy site on her phone, but Gavin couldn't see the details from this angle. "Bluestar Farm is waiting for you. Admission to fun! Open daily, weather permitting. We can have a picnic, walk the grounds, see the animals. They have Jersey cows, Belgian draft horses, Shropshire sheep, and Nigerian dwarf goats!"

"Are you quite serious?" he asked.

Ridiculous, how charming he found this suggestion. *Did she seriously suggest a farm tour for a date?* Certainly, they were in the middle of America, with the closest major city an hour away, but she had the most delightful twinkle in her eyes, as if she grasped that he was reluctantly delighted with the way she'd leaned into these regional charms.

"As a heart attack. We can roast marshmallows in the firepit after it gets dark, and if you play your cards right, I might even take you to a 1930s-style barn dance."

"Must I bring my own coveralls, or will they be provided for me?"

She surveyed him from head to toe, and Gavin felt the skim of her gaze like she was touching him. "If you lose the jacket and change your shirt to something plaid, you'd fit right in without the need for more costuming."

He laughed. The way he looked, cultivating that frightening air, so few people made eye contact, let alone joked with him. "I don't know how I'm meant to take that. Is it a compliment? An attack on my wardrobe? Both?"

"I can't answer all your questions on the first night," she said. "It's better for our relationship if I maintain some mystery."

"Relationship? I thought this was meant to be a bit of fun."

Clementine slid from her stool, signaling that she was done with the conversation, all too soon for his liking. "Relax, English. It's a word, not a bouquet of flowers with a ring hidden in it."

His heart pounded a little too fast over the idea of letting her walk out without making concrete plans to see that dratted farm with her. "In all honesty, you had me at Nigerian dwarf goats. By all means, let's go. If I offer my mobile, will you call yours and save my number?"

"I'll add myself to Contacts. Give." She held out a hand in a playful, imperious gesture.

After some deft fingering—and didn't that put all sorts of delicious filth in his head—she soon passed the device back. Gavin saw she'd saved herself as CLEM ♥, and because he was a cynical bastard, he immediately hit the call button. Her mobile lit up at once.

"Did you think I gave you a fake number?" she asked, with a hard-to-read look.

"I did wonder. It's not every day that a beautiful woman offers to take me on a farm tour. Something too good to be true usually has a catch."

"What's too good to be true, me or the farm?"

"An excellent question," Gavin said with no intention of answering it.

"You might enjoy being cagey, but you'll soon learn that I prefer not to waste time. I have every intention of seeing you often, at least until I get what I want." The smoky intensity of her look went right through him, making him feel naked.

God, I want her. This is madness.

"And what's that?" he asked.

On her way out, Clem delivered the answer like a grenade lobbed at an enemy, one she was determined to conquer. "You."

CHAPTER 2

OVER THE NEXT FEW DAYS, between her usual workload, coven business, and family matters, Clem did so much juggling that she considered enrolling in clown college.

Three days after Clem met Gavin at the bar, she was creating social media graphics for Fix-It Witches when Gram dropped by to give her an iced vanilla latte with a shot of hazelnut, a container of chilled melon and pineapple, and tuna salad in lettuce cups. Apart from the latte, everything was homemade, crafted with a grandmother's love. Since it was a nice gesture and Gram hadn't said a word about Danica's relationship status, Clem dug in.

"Thanks, this is delicious."

"My pleasure. I miss cooking for you, but I don't feel right about inviting everyone over to Gladys's place."

"You can always use our kitchen," Clem said.

"Maybe I will. If you're sure. I don't want to step on any toes. That's why I don't stay with you girls when I'm visiting."

She laughed. "Please, you just want to live it up with Gladys."

"Speaking of which, she needs my help in the garden. Hug Danica when you see her."

Clem braced herself for a heavy-handed suggestion from Gram about Dania's dating profile on Bindr, but Gram only waved and rushed out, hailing the rideshare driver who pulled up to the curb soon thereafter. Clem ate her lunch standing at the counter in between responding to inquiry emails and answering the phone. The repairs in the back could wait for her cousin, who dashed in an hour later.

"You missed Gram," Clem said.

Danica's shoulders immediately came up. "Crap. Did she nag you?"

"Surprisingly, no. She just brought me lunch." Clem held up the fruit container. "Want some?"

"See, this is why I say she likes you best. I get endless pressure about possible dates; *you* get packed lunches."

With effort, Clem managed not to roll her eyes. "That's because she knows you're a viable target. She could send me texts all day long, and I wouldn't budge unless I was genuinely interested. And she also knows that if she pushes me too far, I'll draw the line. I mean, I blocked Barnabas's number, and he's my biological father."

Danica blinked. "You did not."

"I'm serious." Producing her phone, Clem showed her cousin the log, revealing four blocked calls today alone. "That's his number."

"He's persistent," Danica said. "Are you sure it's okay to ignore him like this? It seems like it might be important."

"Well, it's also important for you to get to work on time," Clem snapped, not wanting to discuss Barnabas.

She was trying not to be grumpy, but her cousin wasn't

carrying her share these days, and that made it tough because Clem had to work longer hours. Seeming to read Clem's mood, Danica murmured an apology, but she didn't promise things would change. *Saying sorry doesn't fix a problem, does it?* Clem nodded and let it go.

As she headed out, she exchanged flirty texts with Gavin:

Clem: Be honest. How long have you been waiting for me to text?

Gavin: Hold on, checking my papers. I'm 35. When I was a tyke, I didn't have a mobile, so let's call it 25 years, give or take.

Clem: Wow, no pressure. I hope I'm worth the wait.

Gavin: Something tells me you will be.

Operation Witch Hunter wouldn't be getting off the ground until Sunday when she'd finally carry out her threat to take him to Bluestar Farm. They'd missed the window for the barn dance she had mentioned, but the other stuff was available.

———

Sunday afternoon, Clem met Gavin at the café near the shop because if he registered the wards layered all over her house, it was game over. He would probably take it as the natural caution of a single woman who didn't want to invite a relative stranger over to her place just yet. If they kept hanging out, there would come a point when her reticence became an issue, but that was a problem she could put off—and she would.

Today's outing didn't lend itself to sexy dresses or stiletto heels, so she rolled with it, dressing in khaki shorts and a white sleeveless top that laced up the back. She completed the look with a pair of walking sandals, pleased with the coral polish that still looked decent on her toes. She arrived at the café ten minutes early and bought a bottle of water. Gavin showed up five minutes later, and he'd heeded her instructions. Today, he still had on the ripped jeans and battered boots, but he'd opted for a plain, blue T-shirt in place of the biker gear.

"Do you want anything?" she asked, twirling her drink.

"Will you get it for me if I say yes?"

"Sure. It's all part of the service."

"The complete package," he agreed with a smoldering look. "Pity, I've never cared that much for coffee. And iced tea is just... wrong."

"Too hot for a proper cuppa?" she teased.

"Entirely. But I wouldn't decline a lemon twister."

That was essentially a fresh lemonade mixed with sparkling water; such a wholesome drink order from an intimidating man struck her as amusing. Clem nodded as she sauntered to the counter and got his beverage, then she beckoned Gavin to the door, handing over the drink when he joined her.

"Here you are. I'll drive since you don't know where we're going."

"I can't leave my bike on the street," he protested.

"You think it'll be safer somewhere else?" Clem laughed quietly. "Quit worrying. The meters are free today, and downtown St. Claire is secure as a bank vault."

Gavin sighed, seeming to follow her against his better judgment. As she climbed in on the driver's side, he folded into the passenger seat, belted in, and set his drink in the cupholder. "It seems that I'm putting myself in your hands."

"For better or worse?"

"That's not how I'd put it," he said. "Uncomfortably close to certain vows, isn't it?"

"Relax, English. I'm teasing you. Drink your lemon twister and chill. There will be Nigerian dwarf goats at the end of the ride."

"Promise?" The deep and husky intonation drew Clem's gaze as she backed out of the choice parking spot in front of the café.

"About the goats? Absolutely. Unless the farm has changed and didn't update their site. I can't be held responsible for technological neglect."

"No, indeed."

Since Clem was driving, she couldn't look at Gavin for long, and that was good since she liked his face. That part of the mission was easy; she didn't have to pretend to find him attractive, and truth be told, she *enjoyed* flirting with him.

Currently, she was fuzzy about the endgame; she needed to get with Ethel and find out if her mother had left any notes on how she'd gotten rid of the witch hunter in the thirties. Until then, if she kept Gavin's eyes fixed on her, he shouldn't be hunting her coven sisters, and that had to do. Tightening her knuckles on the wheel, she didn't let herself fret over a permanent solution.

Live in the moment.

That posed a challenge for Clem since she loved her plans and preferred keeping a schedule to being spontaneous. In fact, she was the least likely person to propose having adventures with a random stranger or go on random dates that might end in sweaty sex. She took a sip of her iced latte to cover the silent void created by her racing thoughts.

Oh no, I'm already dropping the ball.

"We're keeping it light," she said, "so I don't know if I'm allowed to ask personal questions." She cut a look in Gavin's direction and found him gazing out at the endless cornfields that surrounded St. Claire.

At this stage, the stalks were tall and green, though not as big as they'd be right before harvest time. The terrain couldn't hold much interest, as the land was flat, dotted with farms and country houses set back from the road with long driveways wending through mature and stately trees. Occasionally there was a billboard about Jesus, one promising a huge legal settlement, or a hand-painted sign offering hay, dirt, or fresh fruit in season.

"You can ask. I don't promise that I'll answer."

"What brings you to the U.S.?"

"You assume that I don't live here," he said.

"If so, you must've just moved in, because otherwise Mrs. Carminian would've gotten the scoop from Walter Reynolds. He's the local Realtor, not a gossip per se, but Mrs. Carminian has a nose for newcomers."

"The local busybody," Gavin said, smiling. "Always in every-one else's business."

"It's a universal truth. But you didn't answer my question." She expected him to deflect again, but he surprised her.

"I'm on extended sabbatical from my post as a history professor. I'm meant to be working on something I can publish, but mostly I'm roving the States in search of excitement."

"And you stopped in St. Claire?" Clem laughed, shaking her head. "Is it because you were secretly hoping someone would take you on a romantic farm tour?"

"You've figured me out. I drove nonstop from the Florida panhandle, pining all the while for this precious opportunity."

"Thankfully, you found me at O'Reilly's before disappointment did you in."

"It's a dreadful way to go," he said mournfully.

Damn it, he shouldn't be funny. Or likable.

Clem ought to be able to disregard his charm since she knew what he was hiding. Maybe he was a professor on sabbatical, but he was a witch hunter too. Did witch hunters have day jobs? It stood to reason that they might, as she couldn't imagine there was much profit in the latter. Or maybe there was. Honestly, she knew far too little about the organization or what befell witches once they were caught. Mostly, they seemed to…disappear.

That can't be good. Be careful.

She'd memorized the route to Bluestar Farm, so she made the last few turns on automatic. First, they passed a farm stand selling local produce, and she followed the signs to a gravel road with community garden plots on either side; farther on, she saw agricultural fields, a picnic pavilion, and an orchard, though it was too far for her to make out what fruit. Apples or pears seemed most likely, given the climate. She parked in the unpaved lot alongside the other cars, probably families as opposed to dating couples.

Though she'd proposed this outing as a joke, Clem had to admit the scenery was delightful. The place was film-worthy, exactly as Hollywood might envision a farm, down to the white fences and the bright-red outbuildings. The house was framed by blue flowers shaped like stars, likely how the place got its name. In the distance, the lowing of cows sounded, along with less readily identifiable animal noises.

Gavin clambered out and stretched, wearing an utterly mystified expression. "I kept waiting for you to tell me this is an elaborate joke, but no. Here we are."

"You were promised Nigerian dwarf goats," she reminded him.

"So I was. Lead on. I'll leave myself in your hands, as this is not my natural habitat."

"Mine either," she admitted. "According to the site, some activities aren't available today, but we're free to walk the grounds and visit the animals."

"No milking class then?"

"You checked the website!"

"That I did. I had to verify this was a real place and that you weren't secretly planning to abduct me and steal half my liver and one of my kidneys."

She grinned, clicking the lock button on the key fob. "Maybe I want you to lower your guard, and when you're overwhelmed with bovine cuteness, bam! That's when I'll strike. I could be quite dangerous, you know."

Gavin's gray eyes glittered beneath his heavy brows. "I'll consider myself forewarned and proceed accordingly."

"You don't want to run, knowing I'm not to be trusted?"

"That makes you even more intriguing," he said softly.

Gavin couldn't get a read on Clem.

He realized he didn't know her surname, but it seemed like an odd thing to ask when she'd made it clear she saw him as a passing fancy. Since he generally lived out of a rucksack, stayed in cheap motels, and often left town in a hurry, it shouldn't sting being dismissed as a permanent possibility. Yet it did, a bit like salt in a wound he hadn't known he'd taken.

She seemed to be joking with him about the danger, but he couldn't dismiss it entirely, for all she looked sleek and delicate, there was also a bit of steel about her. Hurriedly, he moved after her, his boots crunching on the gravel. A few children ran about the farmyard, too excited to know which direction they should turn. While he didn't share that level of glee, he had to admit this was altogether novel, not something he'd have done in a thousand years, left to his own devices. Some of the farmland here reminded him of the green expanses back home, on the outskirts of Newcastle. Without the rolling hills, of course, and there were cows here instead of inquisitive sheep.

It was most unlike him to follow her without a flicker of protest, but she guided them flawlessly to an enclosure full of wee goats. The little ones he'd spotted earlier were feeding them with great and raucous glee while indulgent parents watched from a distance. Clem procured a supply of goat treats that looked like pellets, then she filled his palm with them.

"Here you go. Have at it. Make all those dreams come true."

"You're not joining me?"

"I'm taking pictures," she said.

At first he suspected that must be another of her jokes, but indeed, she had her mobile at the ready, aimed at him in preparation for some mishap. These goats were too small to knock him down, however, and so they butted him repeatedly in the shins as they jockeyed for position. A greedy little devil shoved his fellows out of the way and devoured all the feed in record time, leaving Gavin's hand wet with goat spit. Grinning, he swiped it on his dungarees and scratched every single one of them that he could reach on top of their goatish heads.

When was the last time I did something simply for amusement?

It was terrible that he couldn't recall. A man shouldn't live without pleasure. Just then, Clem hopped down from her perch on the fence, evidently done filming him, and she drew his eyes with a compulsive power that he couldn't explain. Certainly, she was a beautiful woman, but he felt electrified in her presence, percolating with unspent energy and constantly thinking of wicked ways he could burn it.

"Cows or horses next?" she asked.

Right, this is a wholesome outing.

Truly, he shouldn't be entertaining such thoughts about a woman he'd only met twice, though she'd sown the seeds of seduction, and they showed all signs of growing into a fine and hearty sex tree one day. Her legs were smooth and gorgeous, but he probably shouldn't admire them with such alacrity. It would be humiliating if she caught him, and he'd rather not have her class him with the wankers who'd failed to chat her up the other night.

"Horses," he decided.

A pair of volunteers let them into the barn, and he stayed out of the way of the mucking shovels. The Belgian horses were beautiful animals, and he patted their noses one by one. His favorite was a dappled bay, who pleaded for treats with liquid, long-lashed eyes. Clem didn't approach, just like she kept her distance with the goats.

He cocked his head with sudden curiosity. "You don't like animals?"

"More accurate to say they don't like me. When I was twelve, I was in that horsey stage. For my birthday, my parents took my cousin and me for riding lessons. We had the same introduction, same instructions, and Danica adapted like a champion, but I couldn't get my horse to heed a signal to save my life. When I pulled back on the reins, it ran off the path. I ended up hurtling through a cornfield, completely off the marked route, and they had to send someone after me by the time the damn thing stopped running."

"You weren't hurt? Did the horse throw you?"

"No, I was too stubborn to let go," she said.

For some reason, he heard a threat or maybe a promise in that. Odd that he'd infer such a thing, but her presence had him acting entirely out of character, so what was a little more strangeness when piled up with the rest? Soon he'd have a weird hoard to sit on like a dragon.

"I don't imagine you were eager for a second riding lesson, though?"

She shook her head. "Never been on a horse since."

"Pity. You look as though you'd do excellent work astride." That came out much filthier than he intended; he'd meant it as a compliment on her being well fit, but from the way her dark eyes flashed, her mind went right down the hall and into the bedroom.

Then she smiled, and her expression nearly did him in. "In fact, I do."

For the life of him, Gavin could only picture Clem on his lap, moving with growing urgency. Riding. *Fuck. No. This is wrong. There are children about.*

Somehow he countered the natural reaction to those mental images, but it was a near embarrassment. Hurriedly, he turned away, no longer following her without question. He got himself oriented and located the Jersey cows. They were, frankly, the least interesting part of this tour, and he'd seen plenty of them ambling about in less charming fields. Funny animals that often laid down right in the mud with their legs folded.

Eventually, he faced Clem, feeling a bit less ravenous, and managed to say, "Unless you fancy a stroll in the gardens, I think that's everything, and I'm a bit peckish."

She pushed away from the fence with a smile. "Lucky for you, I found a restaurant between here and St. Claire. I can't wait to try it."

"Looking forward to the next stage of this perfect date," he said.

Walking back to the car, Gavin startled himself by looking at Clem's hand. She moved with sure purpose, her arms relaxed at her side, and he was wondering if he could manage to hold it without feeling awkward. Probably not, and it wasn't something he should want anyway. The fantasies about hard and dirty sex were bad enough, and they'd kept him sweaty since he met her. There was no way he ought to allow himself to have softer dreams, ones where he got to stick around for a change, instead of racing after the next alleged threat.

When he contemplated it, he found it ridiculous to be this age and have no control over his life whatsoever. He stifled a sigh.

"Not having fun?" she asked, popping the locks with the key fob.

Startled, he glanced up to find they'd somehow gotten all the way back to the car without him noticing. "Quite the opposite. You've the raised the bar to the point that I don't know how I'll cope with lesser experiences in the future."

Clem laughed quietly. "You're really into Nigerian dwarf goats, huh?"

And you, he thought but wouldn't say.

They drove for twenty minutes or so, listening to music, and in all honesty, her ability to be quiet was a relief. His job left him unaccustomed to the normal chat other people found comforting, so it felt restful being with her as she navigated. The restaurant she'd picked turned out to be the most outlandish place imaginable, a renovated barn decorated with reclaimed Americana. Everything was rustic or red-checkered, and he caught Clem watching him like a hawk, her amusement so strong that it was practically a third wheel.

With great trepidation, he perused the menu and found they had normal food listed, as well as some fascinating German specialties. Gavin had done some hunting in Austria, and he had a soft spot for a good schnitzel. So he ordered that while she went with the quintessential cheeseburger.

"What do you think?"

"I won't know until I taste the food," he said. "The decor is certainly...memorable." There was even a clown going from table to table, making balloon animals for the children and taking Polaroids of couples and families who wanted them.

"That's not what I'm asking." The crispness of the question drew Gavin's gaze back to Clem, and he found her leaning forward with a certain irresistible intensity.

"Then help me understand the question." Delicate barbs of need sank into him—to the point that he ached to touch her.

CHAPTER 3

CLEM SMILED, SEEING THE WAY his lips parted.

He thought she was about to ask something intimate. "About the Nigerian dwarf goats, of course. That's what we were talking about in the car, remember?"

She sat back, stifling a laugh at his expression.

Let's be honest. This is not a hardship, and the danger makes it hotter. Adds another level of excitement when life's gotten so boring. By nature, she wasn't a risk-taker, so maybe that was why this game felt so heady. Flirting with the enemy, tempting him, pushing her luck, and seeing how far she could take this without getting caught. Hell, she'd flat out told him she was dangerous, and he fucking ate it up.

Maybe there's something wrong with both of us.

"They're adorable," he declared. "I want twelve."

"That might prove challenging on a motorcycle."

Gavin sighed. "I know. I wish I could get a pet, but the traveling would be stressful."

Not for a vivimancer, Clem thought. Talking to animals was one of the coolest aspects of Priya's magic. She kept her expression neutral as she said, "My cousin's allergic to cats, and I don't get along with most dogs."

"Like the horse when you were twelve?" Gavin asked.

Just then, their meals arrived, and the food lived up to the internet hype, which was part of why she'd chosen this place. She'd also thought Gavin might get a kick out of the kitsch. And he seemed to enjoy the schnitzel and German potato salad well enough. When she'd eaten most of her burger and some of her fries, she pushed her plate back.

"What do you think? Should we do this again?"

"Visit goats? Or eat in a restaurant? Or—"

"Funny," she cut in. "Are you in or out?"

"In. If you're willing. I can only imagine what other local attractions await."

She gave him a look. "I can't promise you a giant twine ball, that's in Kansas."

"A road trip is out of the question, I take it? Distances here are so prohibitive."

Because she was ridiculous, Clem checked her map. "Yeah, that would be like ten hours in the car. I'm not driving that far for twine."

"Ten hours," Gavin repeated, shaking his head. "You can go from London to Edinburgh in less than half that time."

"Keep bragging, English."

"It's a statement of fact," he pointed out.

She waved a hand dismissively, finishing her cheeseburger. "How long did it take you to get here from Florida anyway? On the bike."

"It should've been two days of travel, I suspect, but I did it all at once. Eighteen hours at a go, including periodic rest and breaks."

"That's wild," Clem said. "Weren't you sore?"

"Excruciatingly. I was also exhausted and half out of my mind, hopped up on those ridiculous 5-hour Energy drinks they sell at all the truck stops. Almost gave me arrythmia!"

That would explain Gavin's outburst at the bakery, the one Danica had reported at their coven meeting. From the time she'd spent with him, it did seem out of character. She smothered a smile over the idea of 5-hour Energy being strong enough to make him act so twitchy and out of control. He narrowed his eyes, apparently reading some of that in her expression.

"What's so funny?"

She couldn't admit that she'd known who he was before they met, but she could cover with the truth. "It's adorable that someone who dresses like a biker could be undone by something teenagers knock back during exams like it's no big deal."

"When you put it that way," he mumbled.

Clem signaled the waitress and snagged the check before Gavin could. Winning little power plays like this always put in her a good mood; she liked living with her secret motto written in all caps—BOSS WITCH IN CHARGE.

"Bathroom break?" she recommended, after she paid the bill.

"Are you asking or telling me?"

"I mean, it's a suggestion, but do what you need to," she said, smiling. "I'll be back."

"Confession, I'm slightly disappointed that you didn't attempt the Arnold accent."

"I'll do my best not to let you down you again." That shouldn't sound either slightly flirtatious or vaguely ominous, but somehow her tone made it both.

Clem headed for the bathroom before he could decide she was weird. *And I am. I totally am. There's* no way *I should be having this much fun when so much is riding on the outcome.*

When she emerged, she didn't see Gavin in the restaurant anywhere. Already, his name popped into her head instead of his title, and that...might become a problem. There was a small gift shop attached, so she headed that way to kill time and found him browsing a rack of souvenirs. He'd bought a tiny stuffed goat, and it looked absurd and adorable tucked beneath his right arm.

"This is for you," he said, handing her the plush. "A memento."

"That sounds like you're planning to leave town."

Please do. Before this gets more complicated and I do something we'll both regret.

Yet while that would be the best and simplest conclusion, better for everyone involved, a small part of her wasn't ready to let him go. In fact, she braced for his response.

"Sooner or later. I'm a bit of a nomad. But I've no immediate plans for departure."

Clem admitted privately that her reaction to that intel could be fairly divided between worry and relief. "Thanks." She ran her fingers over the tiny yellow horn. "I'll treasure it."

"Will you?"

Damn it, everything he said made her want to kiss him.

"Stop that," she said.

"What?"

"Being disarmingly sincere. It doesn't go with the rest of your package."

"At least you're thinking about my package."

Constantly.

Closing her eyes, Clem counted to ten then headed out. "Get in the car before one of us gets arrested for indecent exposure."

"And we've circled back to exhibitionism. I rather suspect we'll set the curtains on fire the moment we're afforded some privacy."

"You might be right." She followed her own advice and started the engine as Gavin folded into the other side. "I hope you had fun today."

"I did. More than I might've reasonably expected."

A bit unsettled by the earnestness of those words and the brilliant smile Gavin aimed in her direction, Clem turned up the music on the way back to St. Claire to discourage conversation. As she'd promised, his vintage Ducati was fine, and she pulled into the space next to it. If this situation were normal, she'd absolutely kiss him. This was *technically* a first date, but not a first meeting, and while she usually paid attention to the norms, none of the regular rules applied here. Because ordinarily, she'd freaking *never* ask someone if they were DTF.

Am I supposed to get out of the car?

It seemed rude not to, so she hopped out. But then she realized they were outside the café in full view of everyone going about their business. While the square wasn't bustling on the weekend, there were enough restaurants with folks walking around. She recognized Hazel Jeffords, walking her big ginger cat on a leash of all things, but their neighbor didn't wave. Mrs. Carminian did, power walking with her reluctant husband; she also threw a wink in Clem's direction, waggling her brows at Gavin.

Unfortunately, he noticed because he was always watching, even when it seemed like he wasn't. He appeared to find the interchange amusing. "Was that tacit approval? I do think she was silently egging you on."

What the hell. Now that they'd been spotted by Mrs. Carminian, gossip was assured, and she might as well live dangerously. *The setting doesn't matter. I'm doing this.*

Stretching onto her toes, Clem grabbed Gavin's shirtfront with both hands and went for the kiss.

Gavin didn't have time for anything as sophisticated as a thought.

No, this moment demanded reaction instead, so he dragged Clem close without hesitation, dipping his head to meet her halfway. On some level, he'd been envisaging this kiss from their first meeting at the bar. *Scorching.* The top of his head tingled when her lips parted. She bit his lower lip gently, sinking her fingers into his hair and tangling them as if to hold him precisely where she wanted. When he deepened the kiss, tasting her, she made a sound into his mouth, a gasp or a sigh. He took it in, along with the darting tease of her tongue. His hands framed her hips, and he was already on fire, thinking only about how he could get closer—

Then he registered the wolf whistles and people cheering.

Right, there are people watching. That must've been quite a show.

It was a wonder he hadn't forgotten himself entirely and done even more. Heat washed over his entire face. Inwardly he felt singed like a charcoal briquet as his natural reticence kicked in. Gavin's breath hitched, and for a moment, he looked everywhere except at Clem.

"I'll...er, I'll message you, shall I?"

Instead of a verbal response, he got a wave and a wink. Then she got into her car and drove away. Only after she'd gone did he realize he still didn't know that much about her—not her last name or what she did for a living. Gavin also sharpened to the awareness that he'd lost sight of the reason he'd charged into St. Claire in the first place.

The thought of rooting out the witch who had spiked on his magical radar held no satisfaction. That was all his father, Jason Rhys's mission, and Gavin was sick of the obligation. He'd been reared on the move, never allowed to play or see his mum. When he called her, he got punished. Same with Nan. As a kid, he'd hoped someone would save him—that Grandad might come back, or that his father would change.

But nothing ever did.

I could leave. But if he catches me...

Gavin didn't know what happened to hunters who refused to work, but based on whispers he'd heard, it wouldn't be good. The thought of returning to the crapulent motel where he'd been making do—so much like the other places he hadn't called home over the past few months—depressed the shit out of him. Before he could talk himself out of it, he dodged into Java House and bought a bottle of water so he could make use of their fine free

Wi-Fi. Gavin pulled up a few short-term rental sites, and to his astonishment, like it was fated, he found a decent place straightaway, an over-garage flat with a private entrance, offered at a shocking discount—50 percent off for reserving the full month and another 10 percent since the site was running as a summer special. When he did the mental conversion from USD, he widened his eyes in shock. For this, he couldn't rent a room back home, let alone a whole flat.

Dealing with the issue might not take that long, but he could fudge the timeline, delay the order with claims that the investigation was more complex than he'd thought initially. Normally, he'd never try to trick his superiors, but Clem made him want to stick around for a while. If he dragged it out *too* long, they would send backup, and then his father would raise blue hell over Gavin's moral failings.

Like it's not normal to crave connection. Permanence. Things I'm not permitted to have.

Allowing temptation to take root, he input his details and rented the flat, starting tomorrow. His motel room was paid up for a few days yet, but he didn't mind losing those funds. Within moments of completing the transaction, he had a stream of messages telling him how to get inside, where everything was located, and advising him that he could park on the right side of the garage on the extended driveway pad.

With housing handled, a more decent place for private time with Clem, Gavin ought to stop mucking about and get to work. Reluctance weighted his feet as he chugged the last of his water and dropped the bottle in a waste bin. The moment he got serious about the work that had brought him to town, it also meant running down the clock on his stolen moments with Clem.

Outside, the day that had been muggy enough to leave him breathless—and grateful for the abbreviated outfit she'd worn— had cooled slightly as the sun sank. He had no enthusiasm for the task, but he decided to head for O'Reilly's again to continue his observations. Little as he relished the chore, it was still less dispiriting than ordering takeaway and sitting in that vinyl chair until the walls closed in.

There were other bars in town, but this one seemed to be the busiest. He passed the night nursing one beer, played a random game of billiards, and didn't sense even a whisper of magical energy. Odd, ever since his arrival, things had been eerily quiet, though the prior spikes had drawn notice from multiple hunters. *But I got the call, lucky me.*

Still, it was truly mystifying.

Possibly the witch had experienced a crisis of some kind, realized they were in trouble, and left town? If that were the case, other hunters in some other part of the States would pick up the trail. Eventually. But delays in communication would likely mean that Gavin could hang out here for a month and just…breathe. Enjoy the unexpected pleasure of a summer fling.

Hell. Yes.

Around midnight, he decided there was no point in loitering any longer, and the waitress was starting to give him the evil eye over his light drink order. He headed out and reveled in driving the Duc on the dark and silent roads between the bar and motel. Nighttime was a goddess to him, and it felt like he could see forever with the pavement glowing beneath the beam of his headlamp.

As he hopped off the bike and removed his helmet, his phone pinged. New message. He hoped it was Clem, but no such luck. Back home, it was six hours later, which meant his father had chosen to give him hell directly upon awakening. *Story of my life.* Until he left home, Gavin had never been allowed to sleep past five. He sighed at the avatar blinking on his home screen, but aggravation wouldn't make the notification go away. Tapping the screen, he read, You should have sent your first status update by now. What's the situation?

The elder Rhys hadn't wanted Gavin to accept the assignment across the pond, but by then, Gavin had been desperate to get a little slack in the line. Time difference and great distance should be enough, but as soon as he saw his dad's text, his lungs constricted, suffocating him. The old man could suck the air out of a space like nobody else.

> Do you know how big this country is? It took two days to get here from Florida. I'm investigating carefully and methodically. As I'm supposed to.

Fuck, Jase must've sensed that Gavin experienced an emotion adjacent to happiness, and all Da's alarm bells went off.

> Don't bollocks it up.

He ignored that charming bit of advice and sent back: It's gone midnight here. I'm going to bed. With great effort, he restrained the urge to tell his father that he had no right to be checking up on him. Here, Gavin didn't fall under Jason Rhys's chain of command, exactly why he'd quietly requested the reassignment, because even the stint in Germany didn't put him beyond his father's clutches.

Sometimes, in his bleakest nightmares, the ones that left him shaken and sweaty, he feared he'd die before the old man, never having done a damn thing of his own free will.

CHAPTER 4

SIGHING, CLEM LET GO OF her magic and set down the waffle maker.

Since Allegra and Dougal, Clem's stepfather, would be arriving soon, she couldn't dodge calls forever. Mom might need to talk to her about travel plans or something. Hopefully, she didn't need a ride from the airport. They usually rented a car while they were in town, but she could never be sure what Allegra would do. The woman could be unpredictable.

Maybe they're not coming after all?

"Hey, Mom," she said, picking up on the fifth ring.

"I finally got you! Is the shop swamped?"

No, there's a witch hunter in town, Gram is trying to set Danica up with someone while she's dating a mundane on the down low. And I have no idea where to go from here while pretending I've got it all figured out already.

"It's a busy time of year." That wasn't really an answer, but fortunately, Allegra had other items on her personal agenda.

"I see. I wanted to ask you—we found the cutest cottage on a little lake, and it's a good rate—but I'm afraid the photos are deceptive."

"Let me guess, you want Ethel to check the place out before you commit." There were diviners in Florida too, but Allegra believed that nobody could match Ethel for accuracy.

And maybe Clem was biased about her coven sisters, but she had to admit Ethel was incredibly skilled. She mentally added this task to her growing list even as Allegra said, "You guessed it! I'll send you the property listing. If I message Ethel, she might ignore me, but I know she won't turn down a request from you."

"I need to go see her later anyway," Clem said. "I'll take care of it."

"Thank you! Call me when you know about the cottage." Allegra hung up quickly then.

Which was good for Clem, but...it would be nice if Mom called when she didn't need something. She couldn't remember the last time they had a conversation and Mom just wanted to know how she was doing. But that wasn't how their relationship worked, and Allegra didn't even seem to realize how backward it was.

Feeling low-key bummed wouldn't change anything, though, so she got back to work on the waffle iron. Her phone pinged with a message from Gram, but instead of asking how Clem was doing, she sent:

> Have your cousin call me. Feeling a bit hurt. I've hardly seen you girls this summer. Normally, you'd have invited me over for a movie night by now.

A while later, Danica arrived—late again—and three light bulbs popped overhead. Clem changed them without a word, jaw tight. *I will not fight with my cousin. Her life is her own.* She didn't feel great about leaving the shop, however, so Clem stuck around long after she would've normally bailed.

Until Danica glared at her. "Would you get out already?" she asked, sounding exasperated. "I've got this. I'm calm."

"Don't forget to call Gram," Clem said. "She texted me looking for you."

It would be nice if one of my relatives contacted me without needing me to do something. Right now, the only relatives not getting on her nerves were Danica's parents, Auntie Min and Uncle Laurence.

Danica scowled at Clem for passing on the message. "I'll handle it," she said.

Yeah, okay.

Clem headed out, the witch hunter problem taking precedence over her family issues.

What am I doing with Gavin? What can I do?

Really, she should learn from Allegra's mistakes, because once Clem had been Daddy's little girl, endlessly charmed by his Scottish accent and the variety of houses he owned all over the UK. But then, his girlfriend came to the house, demanding that Mom free him from marital imprisonment and stop using his daughter as a shackle. That was apparently what he'd been telling the girl behind their backs, then he said she was nobody in front of her—that she meant nothing—and he didn't want to lose his family over an indiscretion.

That was the beginning of the end, though the divorce didn't happen right away; there was a lot more pain to come. At one point, Allegra and Barnabas fought over Clem like she was a toy they didn't mind breaking. She was so tired of being in the middle of that.

While Danica seemed to envy Clem for allegedly being Gram's favorite, she wished she had a happy family like Danica. Clem always had two sets of parents, along with a series of ex-stepmothers and stepsiblings across the pond, some of whom tried to stay in touch, and fuck, it was all so exhausting. She ignored Barnabas's latest nonsense when it pinged her phone in email form. Since she'd blocked his number, maybe she should blacklist his email too? He would probably try from another account, though.

Meanwhile, Danica was staring at her with her arms folded across her chest, a sure sign she felt defensive. "Are you okay? You look more stressed than usual."

"Of course, I'm stressed," Clem snapped. "There is literally a witch hunter in town..." She managed to swallow the "because of you," though she thought it would be reasonable if she had said it. "Gram is demanding attention, I've got my own family stuff to deal with, and I'm taking up the slack at the shop. I'm *tired*."

In all honesty, the game she was running on Gavin offered the only real respite from a whole slew of problems. *How screwed up is that?*

"Things are tough for me too," Danica said. "You don't understand—"

"What you're going through?" Clem finished tightly. "I think I understand pretty well. You're putting all of us at risk, and for what? A fling? A chance to rebel? The rest of the coven won't call you on your bullshit, but *I* will."

Her cousin flinched. "That's not fair. I didn't intend for any of this to happen."

"You know what they say about good intentions. I broke up with Spencer for you when you were crying over Darryl, remember? The asshole you dated to make Gram happy. And I was there to pick up the pieces when things went sideways, like I *always* am."

"Don't hold back, tell me how you really feel." The sarcasm was thick enough to be spread on a cake.

Given Danica's tone, Clem figured there was no point in dragging this out. "Lately you don't listen to a word I say, so I'm probably wasting my breath."

Her cousin hunched her shoulders, and tears spilled down her cheeks. Yeah, this was why Clem seldom opened up: Danica thought her frankness bordered on mean. And maybe she was right. But Clem saw no point in lying; if someone close asked how she was doing, she'd give an honest answer.

"You should go," Danica said in a subdued voice. "I'll take care of the shop."

Possibly I'm an asshole, but if you don't want my real opinion, don't ask for it.

Clem convinced herself that Danica was fine. She had errands to run, starting with a visit to Ethel. To figure out how to throw Gavin off their scent, she needed more data. She usually had the car, though she ostensibly shared it with her cousin. Danica liked riding her vintage bike around in lieu of more taxing exercise, and that worked out for Clem. The best thing about being a technomancer was taking some absolute piece of junk and transforming it to mint condition via magic. She'd suggested they expand their business to include cars, but Danica feared that such big-ticket items would draw unwelcome attention in addition to offering a higher profit margin, and she was probably right.

Clem put her worries about Fix-it Witches aside and backed out of her parking space. A ten-minute drive from the shop, Ethel lived near Vanessa at the end of a cul de sac. Most of the houses were typically Midwestern, a variety of ranch style with attached garage or Craftsman with parking detached. A few had long, Southern porches, sporting wooden swings and the ubiquitous American flag.

Ethel lived in a cozy bungalow painted forest green and trimmed in white. The elder witch had a rattan patio set on her front porch instead of a swing, complete with floral cushions. She'd also installed netting so she could enjoy summer nights without getting eaten alive by mosquitoes, and she had a profusion of plants she kept alive through a natural green thumb with occasional infusions of vitality courtesy of Priya or Kerry. At this point in the summer, they were blooming wildly, red and yellow, white and purple, long vines streaming from clay planters, metal pots, and hanging baskets.

After parking in the driveway, Clem jogged up to the house and rang the bell. When nobody responded, she guessed Ethel might be gardening out back. Ethel was a crafty sort of person— knitting, crochet, furniture DIY projects, a vegetable patch, and goddess knew what else. Clem thought Ethel made jewelry as well and had an online store for it. She also sold various charms, though she called them scented sachets. It amused the older witch to market small blessings to mundanes who then used them to mildly enchant their underwear and scarves.

Muttering, she circled around back and found Ethel puttering around her tomatoes, checking the wire frames and removing weeds. The afternoon sun was still bright as hell, and Ethel had on an over-the-top straw gardening hat with humongous silk flowers on the side, oversize gloves along with a flowing purple tunic, black spandex bike shorts, and a pair of yellow rubber boots. Immediately Clem decided that the biggest draw about aging was the freedom to dress like this and not give a damn.

"You're my hero," she declared.

Ethel blotted away some sweat with the hem of her top and peeled off her gloves. "That goes without saying. I suppose you need something and that's why you're here without calling."

Pointedly Clem got her phone out and dialed Ethel's number. The older witch's cell phone rang inside the house, as she'd known it would. "See, that's why I didn't bother. I figured you'd be out here messing around."

"I'll give you that one. Let's go inside and talk. I made some lemonade earlier, and I have some watermelon cut up. Is this a private sort of chat, or can we sit on the porch?"

"Probably better inside," she said.

The risk of being overheard was low, but since she needed coven history, it was better not to risk a leak. Honestly, most people in St. Claire were so prosaic that witches could talk about anything out in the open, and if questioned, claim it was related to a supernatural TV show they were watching. With all the new streaming services, even international ones, nobody would blink twice at hearing things that once would've gotten them put on trial and executed.

Inside the house, it was blessedly cool, thanks to multiple ceiling fans and an old-school air conditioner. Ethel hadn't sprung for central air yet, and she coped by moving the portable unit around to whatever room she was using. Right now, it was chilling the front room, which was adjacent to the kitchen. Clem took the icy glass of fresh lemonade and a bowl of watermelon cubes then headed into the living room to wait.

Ethel's pet parrot greeted her with a squawk. "Tell your fortune?" Percy offered.

Percy was a green Amazon parrot with yellow and blue bands. The bird was like thirty years old, amazing when Clem considered that they belonged to the same peer group.

"Okay," she said. "Let me have it."

In response, the bird wolf whistled at her and said, "Stone-cold fox. Getting lucky!"

Clem blinked. "Is that my actual fortune, or are you hitting on me?"

The parrot danced along his perch bar and made clicking sounds, as if avoiding the question. He was probably good company for Ethel since she lived alone, but it must be freaky when he shouted obscenities in the middle of the night. Funny part was, Ethel had a TikTok channel devoted to her parrot, and she got thousands of hits when Percy went on a rant.

I don't even have a TikTok channel.

Soon Ethel joined her, carrying her own bowl of watermelon and a tall, frosty glass of lemonade. She ate a piece of juicy melon with obvious relish. "Tastes like summer," she said, smacking her lips. "Now then, my young apprentice, what's the big issue?"

———————

Despite the late night, Gavin got up early, glad to be getting out of the fleabag motel.

He traveled light out of necessity, so it didn't take him long to collect his things and stow them on the back of the Duc. The flat he'd rented was easy to find thanks to his mobile. American homes were so large compared to the ones in the UK, even normal single-family dwellings. This one was a split-level, judging by the exterior and number of upper-story windows—a white house with black shutters that didn't close, so far as he could tell. Ruggedly trimmed hedges lined the front walk, offering some privacy when he pulled into the drive. The landscaping did add a sense of separation to his own entrance, and he parked on the cement pad on the right side of the garage. Sturdy wooden stairs behind the parking area led up to a modest deck with a couple of Adirondack chairs and small side table covered in flowering plants. Gavin devoutly hoped he wasn't expected to take care of the foliage while he was staying here.

The door had a keypad, as promised, and the code he'd been given granted him access. Inside, the flat resembled the pictures enough that he didn't feel cheated, though the flooring looked like wood in the pictures. Up close, it was a vinyl tile that probably was much easier to maintain and clean, along with throw rugs scattered here and there.

There was a blue futon in the sitting room, placed beside a

comfortable-looking armchair, a small coffee table set in front, facing the compact entertainment center. It looked like a smart TV, with the remote offering buttons for various streaming services. A short user's guide on the side table gave him a rundown of amenities, including the Wi-Fi password and where various cleaning supplies were kept. No central air-con, but he wasn't used to that anyway. There was a window unit in the bedroom and a ceiling fan in the sitting room. Everything was dark blue, cream, or misty gray, a cool and neutral decor choice.

Gavin continued his exploration.

Calling the cooking space "a galley kitchen" would be kind, as there was a mini fridge, two induction burners, a shallow sink, a microwave, a toaster, and that was about it. An efficiency island separated the living area from the kitchenette, offering a combined work top and eating area. Perfectly fine; it wasn't like he planned to prepare gourmet meals. There was basic tableware for two settings, and he did locate the kettle, a box of black tea, sweeteners, and powdered cream. *Need to do some shopping.* That was a first; he couldn't recall the last time he'd been to a market that wasn't attached to a petrol station.

The bathroom was behind the bedroom, not ideal for long-term living, but this wasn't designed for permanent habitation. Considering the price, everything was much nicer than he expected. Gavin felt quite odd as he unpacked his meager belongings; there was plenty of space in the small wardrobe and tall, slim dresser tucked beside it. In fact, he had drawers to spare when all his things were tucked away.

When was the last time I unpacked anywhere?

His father would be screaming about how he needed to live at a high state of readiness, always prepared for hostile engagement with the enemy. But hell, Gavin was dead tired of living like he was at war. He meant to make the most of this stolen interlude. And he'd try his best not to hurt Clem when he inevitably got called away.

With a careful hand, he touched the linens, a higher thread count than he'd seen in years. The whole flat smelled fresh, meticulously cleaned, and there were little touches that made him think a woman had some input, infusions of clean cotton on freshening sticks. The bathroom had dispensers mounted full of body wash, shampoo, and conditioner, and there were two sets of towels and washcloths. Everything was clean and white, not expensive materials, but efficient and well maintained.

No toiletries needed.

He poked through the kitchen a bit more and found a small fruit and cheese plate prepared in the mini fridge in addition to a six-pack of bottled water. The owners had included a friendly, handwritten note inviting him to ask if he had any questions or needed any information on local attractions. That gave him an idea.

While he didn't *want* to work, he needed to pretend he was putting in some effort so when his old man demanded an update, he wouldn't be caught unprepared. Cheerful note card in hand, he retraced his steps and headed around to the front of the house. After ringing the bell, he heard a dog barking, furious as anything. But when a plump, middle-aged woman with light-brown hair swung open the door with an inquiring look, he didn't see the massive hound he expected. In fact, he could hear the dog woofing, but it must be too small to see out of the screen frame.

"I was expecting to be eaten by a Great Dane," he admitted.

"You must be our tenant." She offered a smile and bent to pick up an adorable mini dachshund who *sounded* much more ferocious than she looked.

"Gavin Rhys. I just wanted to thank you for the little touches in the flat. The fruit and cheese plate is lovely."

"Mina Rodriguez. Before you ask, no, I'm not Mexican American. My husband is, and I took his name."

Gavin blinked. "I...wasn't planning to ask that, though you did offer to answer inquiries related to area attractions."

Snuggling the little dog to her chest, she quirked a smile. "Sorry, force of habit. I'm proactive in forestalling the 'you don't look Mexican' thing, which pisses me off, because it's a nationality, not a physical genotype. Anyway, you had questions?"

"I do. If this isn't a good time, I can come back."

"No, it's fine. I work from home, so now is as good a time as any. Do you want some tea? It's the cold kind, not—"

"That sounds lovely," Gavin said, though it was practically a criminal offense to serve it over ice.

He followed Mina through the house, which was as comfortably decorated as the upstairs flat. After setting the dog down, she poured a couple of tall glasses of iced tea and set out some boxed cookies. Her kitchen was large enough to house a small dining set, and he took a seat opposite her, sipping the drink to be polite. It was far sweeter than he'd prefer and laced liberally with lemon; that part he rather liked, but drinking tea cold would never be his first choice.

The mini dachshund wasn't barking, but the animal eyed him with major concern, sniffing at his boots and dancing away. Mina noticed and said, "Leave him be, Trixie. He's a guest. Don't bark at guests." She smiled slightly. "Tiny dogs can be so territorial."

"How much does she weigh?"

"Around nine pounds."

"So cute." He wasn't saying that to be polite.

"Thank you! My children are grown, so she's my baby now. I spoil her shamelessly. Anyway, you said you had questions about the area?"

"I'm a bit of an oddball, so I was curious what you'd recommend for someone with a penchant for quirky entertainment."

Mina appeared to ponder briefly. "You mean like the giant peach in Georgia or alligator wrestling in Florida? That sort of thing?"

"I've been told there's a giant twine ball in Kansas," he said. "But I'm also into nature, so those recommendations would work as well."

Witches, if they were deeply entrenched in St. Claire, would need privacy to celebrate their seasonal rituals. And it wasn't like he could ask his congenial hostess, *If you were pagan, where would you go to dance naked beneath the light of the silvery moon?*

Suppose I could. *Probably wouldn't get my deposit back when she kicks me out.*

"Pretty scenery or kitsch," she said thoughtfully, tapping a manicured fingertip on the kitchen table. "I love the latter myself. There's just something about visiting a weird site and wondering what the heck that person was thinking. Have you heard about the bottle cap house?"

"I can't say that I have."

"There's this woman—think her name was Olga—in the Siberian taiga who collected like thirty thousand bottle caps and used them to create mosaics all over the outside of her house. It's kind of amazing. Search and check out the pictures. But you want something like that locally...oh! We have a farmer, well, Dale's family *used* to farm, but he's built something quite strange on the homestead. He claims it's so aliens who are about to invade will know to spare him. His farm is worth a look, if you can manage to peek without getting shot. For the nature, you can take a stroll in River Park, or there's the..." She went on in extensive detail, giving him a whole list of parks and preserves he might enjoy. "Is that enough to get you started?"

"Most definitely," he said, smiling. "Thanks so much."

Now I have a wealth of useless local knowledge to keep the old man off my back, and I can finally take a break.

CHAPTER 5

CLEM HAULED A WHOLE CARTON of journals home from
Ethel's place, all written by Etta Mae Goode, the other witch's
mother.

Most weren't related to the hunter from the thirties, but as
Ethel had said, "You're the one who promised to deal with this.
I'm not wading through the minutiae of Ma's life. If you're deter-
mined to solve this mystery, Velma, then do the legwork." When
Clem had complained, Ethel added, "Let this to be a lesson to you
about volunteering for stuff."

So here she was, rooting through journals penned in crabbed
writing with incredible attention to detail regarding the prices
of various food items. This would've been during the Great
Depression, so on some level, that made sense, but it made
for tedious reading: 1 pound of bacon, 38 cents; 1 pound of
hamburger, 24 cents; 1 pound of butter, 25 cents; a loaf of bread,
8 cents. Clem didn't have the mental energy to run the numbers to
compare what those prices would amount to today, but pennies
were a lot harder to scrape up back then.

Normally, she'd ask Danica for help with a job like this, but her cousin was a fritzing stress ball, and Clem couldn't bring herself to add to Danica's problems. They'd talked about the situation a bit, but from Clem's perspective, nothing had been resolved. With a sigh, she put aside the journal and went to sleep. Things should be brighter in the morning.

The next day at work, Clem jumped at shadows, afraid Gavin would somehow sense her magical repair work and storm in to confront her—when she still didn't have even the flicker of a plan. *The wards will hold. He won't be able to tell.* That was from the outside, though. If he came in, he might detect residual magic, and if he took a close look at the back room, he'd have no doubt they didn't repair things through physical effort.

Sometimes it felt like she was learning acrobatics on a tightrope and some joker had stashed away the safety net. After taking a deep breath, Clem didn't say much when Danica relieved her. They usually joked around, and often her cousin brought her some iced coffee or another treat, but lately, things had been fraught between them.

When they fought, Danica always got teary and quiet, making Clem feel like shit for speaking her truth. They'd snapped at each other a fair bit this summer, and more than anything, Clem wanted to get back to their supportive sisterhood.

She sighed. Tonight her cousin had a date with the baker, and Clem had a choice between digging through those journals and hanging out with the rest of the coven. Yeah, that wasn't a tough decision; she deserved a fun night before she got back to research and derailing Gavin. First, though, she needed to bait the hook and reel him again. It worried her how much she enjoyed weighing her word choices to create the perfect, irresistible text.

Finally, she thought she had it right—flirty, fun, and a touch challenging. Miss me yet? If you're ready for round two, meet me at Java House day after tomorrow at 7 AM. If you dare.

Clem didn't wait for a response. She offered Danica a halfhearted wave, silently dispirited by the distance growing between them. *Do I have to apologize? She's probably still upset, but really, did I say anything wrong?*

After she'd hung out with Kerry and Priya for their impromptu housewarming, Clem had a standing invite to chill with them whenever she wanted. They lived in one of the newer developments, uniform rows of houses with similar landscaping. When she arrived, Leanne and Vanessa were already there—no Ethel or Margie, though. Just being around her coven sisters eased her tension a fraction. Clem skimmed their faces one by one and took satisfaction in knowing she was keeping them safe. It no longer mattered that she was stressed.

"Looking fantastic," she told Vanessa, who was sporting a new hairstyle.

Vanessa had gotten an angled bob with a touch of purple ombré that deepened into violet tips, and she tossed her head with a brilliant smile. "I'm looking good, but it's nice to get acknowledged. Everything okay with you?"

Clem lifted a shoulder in a halfhearted shrug. "Things are tense at home. I think I pissed Danica off with my frankness."

"You have a tendency to be tough on her," Priya said.

"Whatever. I didn't come to talk about my problems." Clem passed the bottle of wine she'd grabbed on the way over to Kerry. "What are we watching tonight?"

"It's a Mexican show—kind of a murder mystery wrapped around a telenovela," Priya called across the kitchen island. From the sound of it, she was making popcorn on the stove.

Vanessa settled onto the couch with a happy wiggle. "That sounds excellent. Are we doing drinks when somebody gets slapped?"

Kerry brought out bowls spilling over with buttery popcorn, and everyone settled in for the first episode. The actors were all ridiculously gorgeous, and they all had perfect houses and shiny cars. It was even more fun doing this with her coven sisters because Vanessa and Leanne kept everyone giggling constantly with their running commentary. They binged several full episodes while devouring an entire kettle of popcorn, and by the time they decided to call it a night, Clem was feeling much better. She hugged everyone in turn then said, "Thanks for having me over. This was exactly what I needed."

"We're always here for you," Priya said.

The rest of her coven sisters echoed it, and Leanne even gave her a second hug, unusual because she wasn't the most demonstrative of Clem's friends. As she headed out, her phone rang. She hadn't heard from Gavin, but she needed to know if their second date was happening the day after tomorrow. Surprisingly, despite the late hour, he was calling—so retro.

"Hey," she said softly, hurrying to her car so the others couldn't eavesdrop.

And they totally would.

"You're a little out of breath. Did I catch you at a bad time?"

"I'm about to drive home, but it's fine. What's up?"

"Sorry I didn't respond earlier. I'd set down my phone, and I've been getting settled in at my new place."

"You're staying?" That was... Hell, she didn't know how to feel. Gladness had terror in a headlock, and the two responses were throwing down in her brain stem.

"I've let the flat for a month. Even a rolling stone yields to inertia now and again."

"Is that a fancy way to say you're sick of traveling?"

"You've no idea," he said quietly.

"So tell me."

"Perhaps when we know each other a bit better. I don't want to put you off by dumping my complaints on you straightaway."

"That's fair. I figure you're not only calling to apologize for ignoring my text, though..."

"True. I'm taking up the gauntlet. I'll see you day after tomorrow at 7:00 a.m. Any tips regarding how I ought to present myself?"

Clem thought he was asking about a dress code. "Just wear comfortable clothes, nothing you mind getting dirty."

"Now there's an intriguing statement and one that's likely to keep me up tonight."

There were *so* many ways she could respond, and she damn well deserved a prize for not rabbiting down the path of filth immediately. "I refuse to take responsibility for disturbing your sleep." Clem paused judiciously before deciding to acknowledge the heat flaring between them. "Though there may come a time when I will."

"Tease," he whispered in a deep, deep voice.

She hung up before she could say something *highly* ill-advised.

The next morning, Clem remembered what Gavin had said about wishing for a pet and decided to surprise him. *If he doesn't want it, I'll keep it.* As distractions went, this one should be top-notch, but she would need Priya's help to pull it off. The local pet store opened at eight, so she had time before work. Clem headed in and picked out a white mouse with coal-black eyes, along with all the necessary accessories, then she headed over to Priya's place, hoping Kerry would already be at work, because she'd likely view this as a ridiculous idea.

Thankfully, Priya answered her knock and widened her eyes at the bags Clem was carrying. "What's all this? You know I need to leave in like fifteen minutes, right?"

"The witch hunter wants a pet, but he travels all the time, so most animals are out. I thought maybe a mouse would work, but they're easily stressed. If you talk to the little guy…" She'd gotten a male mouse because she read they could live alone happily and would form a deep bond with their caregiver. "Explain the situation and bolster him a bit with magic, hopefully he won't mind all the traipsing about as much."

"I can do that," Priya said slowly. "But…how does this factor into your master plan?"

At that gentle question, Clem's bravado collapsed. She didn't burst into tears, but it was a near thing. She squeezed her eyes shut, breath coming fast, and Priya pulled her into the apartment, hugging Clem as she nudged the door closed behind them.

"I don't even have one," she admitted in a rush. "I have absolutely no idea what I'm doing, and I'm scared to death."

"Oh dear. Let me call the office. I don't have a nine o'clock appointment anyway, so let's talk this through."

"Will you still help with the mouse?"

"Absolutely," Priya promised.

Gavin didn't see Clem or hear from her for a whole day.

That shouldn't bother him as he went about his business. Yet it did.

The following day, he parked his bike in front of Java House at ten minutes to seven, silently amused at his own eagerness. Nothing was open at this hour except the convenience store, and she deserved better. He couldn't even grab Clem a drink to earn a few brownie points. Not that he needed them.

Or do I?

A few minutes later, Clem arrived in a rideshare, surprising him. He'd expected her to drive again, but it seemed like she trusted him to take her out on the Duc. Gavin liked that idea a hell of a lot. He never let anyone on the back of his bike, but for her, he'd make an exception. Briefly he pictured her snuggled up against his back, arms tight around his waist.

Fuck yeah.

"Morning," Clem said.

She had on a backpack, a pair of gray jeans, trainers, and a sleeveless top in bright blue, revealing the graceful curve of her arms. Her skin held a faint sun bronze, making her dark eyes even prettier in contrast. Clem's short hair looked as if she'd simply run her fingers through it—endearingly spiky, but somehow instead of looking untidy, she gave the impression of sexy dishevelment.

"Slept well?" he asked.

"Not bad. Hand me your phone."

It came across as an order, and he complied before it occurred to him that he might not want her poking around in there. But she only pulled up the map function and input an address then handed it back.

"You're driving today, fair is fair."

Gavin couldn't contain a smile. "But you won't tell me where we're headed, I gather. You certainly do enjoy your surprises."

"You'll like it. Probably. Maybe." With that ringing endorsement, she jerked her chin toward the Duc.

He got on, clipping his phone to the front of the bike as she settled in behind him. "Ever ridden behind before?"

"Do I look like I have?"

"That's not something I can tell at a glance," he said, firing up the Duc.

"In that case, the answer's no. Anything I should know?"

Gavin gave her a few tips regarding the fine art of balancing as a passenger. For him, it was all theoretical, things he'd heard from other riders but had not tested personally. Their destination was a bit closer than the last, and he enjoyed putting the bike through its paces. Having Clem on the back turned out to be every bit as delightful as he'd imagined. Summer clothing did little to hide the heat and softness of her breasts against his back, and he fought a sharp spike of arousal.

This is why people risk death to ride these things. Well, that and the freedom.

The morning sunlight and the fresh breeze made for an

excellent ride. Twenty minutes later, he saw handmade signs for a U-Pick berry patch. *That can't be it, right?* He followed the GPS, and sure enough, the journey terminated in a roughly paved drive that widened to a parking area liberally spread with pale gravel. As before, there were a few cars, early birds out to catch a worm, or pick some berries, as it were.

"We're seriously going berrying?" he asked. "Did I use that word correctly? Sounds wrong as a verb somehow..."

"Never mind the grammar, English. You have some exciting choices ahead. We have our choice of raspberries, blackberries, or blueberries, and they're all in season. Which is your favorite?"

"Can we go for the trifecta or is that against the rules? I make a delicious fruit parfait, if I do say so myself, and my kitchenette is barely up to the task."

"We can pick by container or by weight, if you don't want a pail of each," she said.

"It's not that I mind the idea, but I doubt three of those buckets full would fit on the Duc," Gavin said, stifling a smile.

"We don't have to fill them. Don't you have storage under the seat or something?"

"Please, I didn't buy the Duc at IKEA."

Actually, there *was* a storage compartment, but he was curious about her ability to adapt. Some people got irritated if things didn't go to plan, but Clem didn't seem overly fussed as she selected three of the smallest containers.

"These will go in my backpack. Don't think you're getting out of this," she added. "I expect parfaits in my future."

"I'm a man of my word."

He understood why she'd suggested casual clothing; picking berries inevitably left juice on the fingertips. On impulse, he carried her right hand, red with raspberry juice, to his lips, and licked the pad of her index finger. Her brown eyes went molten, and he carried on, tasting each in turn. She gazed at him until his head went fuzzy with the need to kiss her, and it was difficult as hell to get his mind back on berrying afterward.

He'd honestly had no notion that there could be thousands of berry bushes spread out over a vast distance. There were others out collecting their own fruit, but the space was sufficient that they had plenty of privacy. Not quite enough for him to risk stealing another kiss, though he desperately wanted to.

Eventually, they had enough berries, but instead of leading him back to the bike, she headed over to a copse of trees offering shade from the morning sun. In the cool shadows, there were several picnic tables along with a notice telling them to HAVE FUN, LEAVE NOTHING BEHIND.

Clem opened her backpack and set out three plastic containers. One held cut fruit, another was full of mini quiches, and the other one had toasted wedges of bread. She also produced a thermos with hot tea in it. Not prepared correctly, of course, but he found himself unaccountably moved by the fact that she cared about his preferences. Gavin couldn't imagine that many Americans drank hot tea on a warm summer morning.

"How is it?" Clem raised her brows, as if challenging him to complain.

"I've never had a breakfast picnic before. This is lovely," he said softly.

Everything could be eaten with his fingers, including the clever little quiches. The food was delicious and the tea quite passable. When they finished, she dusted the crumbs off the tables for the birds and packed away the empty boxes. By nesting the containers and removing the lids, she made space for their berries as well. Silently Gavin admired that problem-solving spirit. He could use a bit of that logic for dealing with his father.

"Sorry there were no goats, but I thought you might enjoy getting some fresh air, a little exercise, and—"

"Spending time with you? Yes, I adored it. Sign me up for the macramé class next."

Clem grinned. "It would serve you right if I found one accepting new students. Maybe I'll ask down at the coffee klatch if any of the seniors can hook me up."

All of Gavin's instincts sharpened. "Coffee klatch?"

If he knew anything about pensioners, they had the sharpest eyes in town and certainly had plenty of time to watch their neighbors and gossip about them. This could prove invaluable for when he inevitably had to put some energy into the job he loathed, if only to appease Da. Even thousands of miles away, the specter of his old man and his damned honor had the power to cloud Gavin's mood.

"You okay?" she asked.

"What?"

"I don't know, it was like your face was about to rain or something."

"If you bring me to tears, I'll let you know," he said, quietly startled. "But you didn't answer. Coffee klatch?"

"Right, sorry. The seniors meet up Monday through Friday at the fire station from eight to ten in the morning. It's a quarter for a cup of coffee. The stories are free. I stop by before work sometimes as a form of community service. Old folks are a hoot."

"I imagine that they would be. Is it open to anyone?"

Clem smiled. "Anyone with a quarter and a modicum of patience."

"Good to know."

Whatever else he might've said was forestalled by the buzz of his phone. His father's icon flashed, and he stifled a sigh.

He made a "hold up" gesture in her direction. "Just a moment. Duty calls, I'm afraid."

CHAPTER 6

WHILE GAVIN MOVED OFF TO speak quietly on the phone, Clem interpreted his expression.

She couldn't read lips, but she could tell this was a prod to do his job from whoever oversaw the witch hunters. Everything about this situation sucked, but the aching tug in her chest sucked the hardest. It was so unadvisable to care what made him look like that, to wonder why his face was suddenly a storm cloud when he'd been all smiles before.

You have to stop nagging Danica if you catch feelings for a damn witch hunter.

Maybe it was too late for that since she'd already gotten Gavin a pet mouse, one specially coaxed by a gifted vivimancer to adapt to new people and situations. *It's a strategy, that's all.* Clem tried to give herself a pep talk as he wrapped up the conversation and she checked her backpack to make sure she'd stowed the berries securely. Eventually, he headed over, but she could tell the date was done. She pulled the straps over both shoulders and secured it. Her wallet was in there along with the U-Pick berry haul and the empty breakfast containers. It wouldn't do for it to launch onto the highway on the way back to St. Claire.

"Ready to go?" she asked, not giving him a chance to call an end to the interlude.

For some reason, it mattered a lot that the power stayed in her hands for this moment. Hell, this man—no, this *witch hunter*— had too much influence over her emotions already. Gavin nodded. Then he floored her by lacing their fingers together, matching his pace to hers as they strolled toward his bike.

"Sorry for the interruption."

"It's fine. I need to be at work soon anyway. I'm glad you could indulge me with a weird, early date since I open the shop every day but Sunday."

"Doesn't it get tiring?"

"Sometimes," she admitted. "But I'm more of a morning person than Danica, and I sometimes take time off to attend conferences. I just got back from a marketing seminar, and she worked from open to close all four days."

Gavin laughed quietly. "You don't have to defend your cousin. I didn't mean to imply she's taken advantage in any fashion. I was ruminating on the monotony of a day job."

"Is that why you took a sabbatical? Tired of students pestering you?"

"Partly," he said.

Clem read the ambivalence in his expression, but she chose not to press. She told herself she was being judicious with her questions so as not to arouse his suspicions, but deep down, even she didn't believe that bullshit. The truth was, she didn't want to poke at his sore spots when she ought to be looking for any weakness she could exploit. Instead, she threw her leg over the back of his bike and snuggled against his warm back, pressing her cheek to the firm muscle before he laughingly tossed her a helmet.

"Right, I should wear this. Safety and all that."

"Trust me, I'd rather have your pretty face as well, but I don't want to be responsible for mucking it up." With that, he fired up the vintage Ducati, and they roared off in a spray of gravel.

Clem watched the countryside zip by through the filtered lens of the tinted helmet. It was weird not feeling the wind on her face when she could hear it rushing past. She tightened her arms on his waist, furtively glorying in the soft tingles of arousal that spread through her entire body. *Holy shit.* Sex with the witch hunter would most likely blow off her figurative doors. Possibly the bike vibrations were giving her some of these good feelings, but the excitement couldn't be explained entirely that way.

By the time he dropped her off in front of the café, she was almost ready to drag him off into an alley to finish any way she could, even dry humping against the wall like a teenager.

Fortunately, Gavin didn't seem to realize how much he turned her on, so he didn't tease or offer one of those thick thighs for her use.

With a light tremor in her hands, she pulled a foldable shopping bag out of her backpack, willing her body to settle down. *Fuck, this is bad.*

But fucking would feel so good, her wicked side argued. *And I bet it would distract him even more.*

Oh, hell no. What was she supposed to do if her magic flared in flagrante delicto? *Bad brain. Think about something else. Like, when should I give him the mouse I'm hiding in my room?*

Mentally scolding herself, she put the berries in the sack then handed them over. "Here you go. I expect you to keep your promise," she joked.

"I'll definitely make a delicious parfait for you."

Okay, now "make a delicious parfait" would take up permanent residence in her brain, replacing "Netflix and chill" as a euphemism for sex. Maybe she ought to put it on Urban Dictionary so others could enjoy the update. Belatedly, Clem realized she needed to stop thinking about fucking Gavin Rhys and make some sensible response.

"When?"

"Lunch today?" he suggested, silver-gray eyes bright as moonlight and just as hopeful.

Clem wished she could green-light the suggestive promises she saw flickering in his eyes like summer lightning, but Gram had sent her a message because she wanted to talk about Danica. *I'm so fucking tired of family drama.* She didn't enjoy being used, whoever was trying it on, not even when it was her beloved grandmother.

"I wish I could. I'm meeting Gram this afternoon." That was a wholesome activity, right? Nothing suspicious about a woman hanging out with her grandma.

No witches here, no sir.

"Tomorrow then? I'll take you to a late lunch after work and to my place for dessert."

Clem had already turned, ready to hustle over to the shop,

but the husky tone of his voice stopped her in her tracks. His stare was so heated and intense that she bit her lip, and his gaze focused on her mouth. Her heart kicked into overdrive, making her a little light-headed. If she accepted, it meant sex was certainly on the table, and she wasn't sure if her self-control would allow her to leave without—

"Yes," she said.

"Yes to...the whole plan?"

She nodded. "Lunch wherever you like, and then dessert at your house. I'd like to see your rental anyway. I'll text you the shop address later. Meet me at two. That's when I hand things over to my cousin."

Yeah, she was outright avoiding him finding out the name of their business because she didn't entirely trust her own poker face where Gavin was concerned. He might be able to tease out some hint of the secrets she was desperately trying to conceal and that could *not* happen. Her coven sisters were counting on her.

"You work from nine to two, Monday through Saturday, off Sunday."

"Yep. Are you memorizing my schedule?"

"Would it be weird if I said yes?"

"A little, but it's also flattering, so I'll give you a pass on the excessive interest. It only shakes out to around thirty hours a week. Danica puts in more time overall because she closes out the accounts, deals with the financial angle, and handles invoicing for all clients. I do online stuff and manage our social media. Often, I'm trying to think of funny stuff to post related to the business even at night, and I count it as work too."

"Definitely," he agreed. "Never thought of it before, but running a small business requires you to wear a lot of hats."

And that's not even counting the witchy one.

Not that she owned the sort of thing that generally made up a mundane-inspired witch costume for Halloween. No black hat, no bell-shaped dress or pointy shoes either.

"Thanks for noticing. Now I really have to get to work." Impulsively, she kissed his cheek, and holy shit.

His skin felt incredible, sun-warmed and rough with stubble. It required all her self-control not to nuzzle a path to his mouth and just start making out in the middle of the square. Another bad idea, as businesses were opening all around them.

"I'll message you," he said.

Clem lifted a hand and sauntered off without revealing how tough it was not to turn around and blow kisses like a lovesick kid.

Since she was a few minutes late, she had a pair of customers waiting, both elderly women who often fritzed their devices without having a clue what they'd done wrong. Fortunately, they loved gossiping with each other, so Clem set them up out front with two cups of coffee and left them to chat while she got to work. At Fix-it Witches, they tried not to keep gadgets overnight because often people would lose patience and buy a new one. That led to a semilucrative side hustle where they sold refurbished items online, but overall, it was simpler to fix stuff straightaway and return it as fast as possible.

Hopefully, Gavin won't feel me power up my magic. A chill swept over her. It would be fine; the wards should hold.

Here goes nothing.

After parting from Clem, Gavin figured he ought to stop by the coffee klatch she'd mentioned and start making contacts.

The pensioners who attended such gatherings would be starved to share their stories with a new and willing listener, so he should learn a lot about St. Claire in a short time. It wasn't like he could come right out and ask, *So who do you peg for witches, right?* Doing that at the bakery had been a wildly incompetent move, fueled by exhaustion, rage, and too much 5-hour Energy. Normally he didn't ride into town and make a complete arse of himself.

Probably ought to swing by that bakery and apologize.

Otherwise Gavin could get in trouble with the law, and he couldn't afford to rely on his father's connections to get him out of trouble. *After the mess in Austria—*

Well, best not to test paternal love, at any rate.

Sometimes he wondered whether there was any love at all. It did seem that the old man saw him as a means of settling an old score and proving Rhys hunters were true to the bone. No divided loyalties. For Gavin, it would be nice to feel that, for once, he had done enough, no need to belabor a point he'd already devoted his whole life to.

Before he could tumble headlong into grim thoughts, he got back on the Duc and pulled up directions to the fire station. He had just under an hour to make some new friends, and he planned to make the most of those forty-seven minutes. On impulse, he brought the berries with him. Back home, the pensioners loved it when people brought gifts. Fruit or cheese were big favorites, wine if they were still allowed to drink. Fresh berries seemed far more appropriate for a breakfast gathering, though if he got them bosky, they'd likely open up even faster.

Must invite a few of them to some rounds on me over at O'Reilly's.

Gavin had never been in a firehouse before. Most of it was devoted to a garage that connected to a wide communal space. He could see what looked like lockers and a gear area, and there was a sign pointing the way to the conference room that had big, clear windows, a long table with sixteen black, padded office chairs, most of which were occupied by a diverse group of elderly people. Against the wall, there was also an entertainment center, but the TV was off since everyone was chatting.

"Hello, hello," a little old lady with brown skin and a froth of white curls said, flashing him a wink.

The old fellow sitting next to her scowled. "You lost, son?"

Normally, he'd get irked at being called that by a stranger, but his mission was to charm these folks, not antagonize anyone. "Not in the slightest! I'm precisely where I'm meant to be this morning."

"That right?" the man grunted.

"Don't be grouchy," his lady friend said. "Ignore Leonard. He's always like this until he's had a full cup of coffee. Speaking of which, it's twenty-five cents. Help yourself and pull up a chair."

Gavin didn't have any coins in his pocket, so he dropped a wrinkled dollar bill in the ceramic pot labeled COFFEE KLATCH, poured himself a cup of plain black coffee—honestly, he didn't enjoy the stuff no matter what was stirred into it. To him, it tasted the way ashtrays smelled. Then he settled across the table from Leonard.

"Gavin Rhys," he said, extending a friendly hand.

The older man shook it, and he even managed a smile. "Lenny Franklin. Only Gladys calls me Leonard. Well, and my mother, God rest her soul."

Gavin offered what he hoped was a sufficiently pious expression, echoing the sentiment. "A pleasure to meet you."

The woman Leonard had indicated as Gladys gave him a bright smile that made him homesick for the mum he barely remembered. *How many years has been it now?* His father had been brimming with bitterness over her supposed betrayal, and he'd repeatedly told Gavin how little she cared, otherwise she wouldn't have abandoned them both.

Is that true, I wonder? Did you never try to reach me at all, Mum? Or did Da stop you?

Unable to help himself, he smiled back at Gladys. Though he'd just met the woman, he thought she radiated an incredible air of sweetness, like she was the type to bake pies and bring tea and lemon drizzle cake when neighbors were sick. Or whatever the American equivalent was.

"What brings you here?" Leonard asked.

Gavin couldn't bring himself to use an informal nickname for an older gentleman, even in his own head. So Leonard he would remain.

"To the firehouse or St. Claire?"

Leonard shrugged, sipping at his coffee. He looked like a strong man, even at his age, though his shoulders were a bit rounded, as was his belly. But he had fine, fierce eyebrows that were still more black and gray and steady brown eyes that said he'd tolerate no nonsense.

"Either," he finally said.

"I'm on sabbatical. History professor," he added, forestalling the question. "I'm writing about American history for a change."

"Book or article?" Gladys asked, as another woman said, "Oh my, how fascinating."

That lady was round like an apple with a poof of permed white hair and a fine hand with lipstick. Her puce tracksuit was rather memorable as well. Gavin quickly learned that her name was Hazel Jeffords, she had a recalcitrant cat named Goliath, and she was a talker. The introductions came fast and furious after that: Angelica, Ethel, Stanley but "call me Stan," Howard Carruthers, "used to own the hardware store, my son runs the place now." Sometimes they spoke so fast that the words overlapped, and his brain whirled.

Don't let this opportunity get away from you, he scolded himself.

"Before I forget," he cut in.

He made a show of finding a plastic bowl in the coffee supplies and apportioned a generous amount of berries, while saving enough for the promised parfaits, then washed them, sprinkled them with a packet of sugar, and carried them to the table.

"I brought these to share with everyone," he said. "They're fresh this morning, picked with my own hands."

"Did you ever do that over in England?" Howard wanted to know.

"Never," he said.

Others who'd had a less rigorous and isolated childhood likely had different experiences. But his father had kept far too sharp an eye on him for there to have been many moments left to spare for leisure. He had only vague memories of his mother, who had left when he was four. That was what Jason Rhys claimed, and then they moved. Soon, the only people in his life were Grandad and Jason Rhys, who insisted on training Gavin every hour that he wasn't in school. Most children loathed sitting in classes, but for Gavin, it had been a respite.

Impatient with himself, he shunted aside those grim and lonely memories.

As he'd hoped, the berries smoothed the path and the pensioners warmed up to him. Now they saw him as a nice boy, someone they might set up with a grandchild once they got to know him better.

"That explains St. Claire, but it's a bit odd that you're here at a senior meeting," Gladys said, when the chat came to a natural lull.

Fortunately, he was good at sweet-talking when he had to be, came from rolling into a new town repeatedly and needing to get good at ingratiating himself. "I heard this is where all the hot people hang out."

The curvy silver-haired woman with the pixie cut—Ethel, he thought—laughed and said, "He's got you there, just look at the lot of us. We're about to steam all the paint off this table."

Both Hazel and Howard smirked, and the old folks traded jokes for a little while as they sipped on their coffee. He didn't want to wear out his welcome, and it looked like time was almost up for this gathering. So he got to his feet.

"Thanks for making me feel so welcome. This was fun, so I'll definitely be back."

"Aren't you going to ask for my number?" Ethel teased. "I saw you eyeing me up, don't even act like you weren't."

Gavin grinned. "There's no law against looking."

That got a hoot out of Hazel, and on that note, he headed out. "Take care, everyone. See you soon."

There, that was some good groundwork. Next time he showed up, he could ask a few questions, acting like it was related to maybe relocating here because the town was so dang charming. Appeals like that always went over well, because people loved thinking their hometown could enchant anyone who passed through. But as he strode out of the firehouse and got on the Duc, one thought burned in his brain like it was written in fire:

I wish I could be free.

CHAPTER 7

THE NEXT MORNING, CLEM WAS at the shop early, determined to clear all the devices that people had insisted on dropping off because they were far too busy to wait.

Arguing was a waste of time, and it would also be suspicious if they never appeared to order parts. Outside of magic, it was impossible for a repair shop to have every possible replacement already on hand. So even though she didn't like the risk that clients would get impatient and abandon their stuff, she usually acceded and filled out the paperwork, including a rider that said if they didn't pick up their belongings within fourteen days, the owners of Fix-It Witches were free to dispose of said goods as they saw fit. Still, she was nervous as she worked, constantly reaching out with a magical touch to check the integrity of the wards.

It was most likely Danica's power spikes that had attracted attention in the first place, but damn, had Gavin really sensed her all the way from Florida? *Nah, how could he?* It seemed more likely that another hunter had detected Danica going haywire, but then, for reasons known only to witch hunter internal politics,

Gavin caught the assignment instead. Maybe Gavin was the equivalent of a teacher's pet?

"Fuck," Clem muttered, catching a shock from the phone she was working on.

Her own magic sizzled and sparked, and she knew damn well that was nerves. Taking a deep breath, she centered herself and found that the battery was shot. Normally that would be it for a smartphone like this, as batteries weren't designed to be replaced, but she nudged it slowly, charging it with her magic and then tweaking so it would hold a charge. In this case, it wasn't a permanent fix. She could coax it to do her will for a while, maybe another year, and then they'd have to bring it back. After four or five fixes, it might even be cheaper to buy a new unit, but she'd never say that. In time, the client would decide that on his own, as nobody kept phones around forever. Well, unless they had something special saved on them.

Before she knew it, it was nearly two and Danica wasn't here yet. Clem sighed. The one time she had plans, and her cousin was off doing goddess knew what. Though if she was taking bets, it had something to do with Titus. Muttering a curse, she grabbed her cell and called, but Danica didn't answer. Then her heart leapt into her throat because she saw Gavin stride up outside. If he came in, the wards might ping him. That, along with the name and—

Clem hurried outside, her heart beating so fast that it made her slightly dizzy. "Hey!"

She wasn't normally like this, but she wound her arms around his neck and squeezed him, hoping a sudden hug attack would divert him. Gavin returned the embrace, his big hands splayed to cradle her close. For a long moment, she breathed him in: soap and leather oil, a hint of mint, and just a whisper of citrus. *Wow, he smells amazing.*

"Missed me, then?" he asked, a thread of amusement lacing his tone.

"You got me."

She registered the moment he saw the sign. His body tensed and he stepped back, eyes flat and shadowed. "Cute gimmick," he said.

Clem forced herself to grin. "Yeah, my cousin came up with it. She searched online, and apparently, there was a witch in the 1600s with our same last name or something."

"What's your surname, Clementine?"

It couldn't be good that he was using her whole name. "Waterhouse. Why?" Goddess, she hoped her innocent look was convincing. This was the first major hurdle.

"Your history is off a bit. Agnes Waterhouse was hanged in 1566."

She widened her eyes, trying her best to look awed instead of terrified. "Whoa, how do you know that off the top of your head?"

"History professor, remember?" Gavin smiled slightly, but the look still didn't reach his eyes. He seemed wary.

No, no, no. Think fast.

"Oh, right. Listen, I hate to ask, but would you mind riding around the square to look for my cousin? She's supposed to be here by now, and I can't go to lunch until she arrives." Would he let her play it off?

Gavin blinked. "I've never met your cousin. How am I supposed to track her down?"

Quickly Clem brought up a recent selfie she'd taken with Danica. "She'll be riding a retro green bicycle with a basket on the front, festooned with plastic flowers. I promise she's impossible to miss."

His gaze warmed, lingering on the silly pose she and Danica had adopted for the shot. "No lunch until I find her or she answers her mobile, I take it?"

"Yeah, I'm stuck here until she shows. Do you mind?"

This errand made sense, thankfully. Because otherwise, it would be logical to invite him into the shop to wait with air-conditioning. Normally, she'd never freaking ask for a favor like this, let alone from someone she was dating. In fact, old partners had complained she didn't lean on them enough, didn't let them in or ask for emotional support when she was suffering.

That's what my coven sisters are for.

It was also the reason she'd considered long and hard about asking Priya out. From one angle, it made perfect sense because Priya was already inside her circle of trust. Letting down her defenses would be easier in some respects. But if things went sideways, it might've made things incredibly awkward as well. A moot point, as while Clem weighed the pros and cons, Kerry came on like a tropical storm.

"I'll take a look," Gavin said. "If she's about, I'll find her. Try ringing her again, yeah?"

"On it." Clem raised her phone in emphasis as she headed back inside.

About fifteen minutes later, he returned with her cousin in tow. He must've left his motorcycle wherever he found her, and Danica was walking her bike as well. Cheeks flushed, she hurried in. "Sorry! The time got away from me."

"I can see that," Clem said, swallowing a more acerbic retort.

"He's waiting to take you to lunch. Will you be home tonight?"

Clem simply shrugged, gathering her purse and the surprise for Gavin from the back room. She was in no mood to talk to her cousin. Clem got that falling in love unexpectedly could throw somebody off-kilter, but she didn't like how Danica was acting. A relationship that edged out all other aspects of a person's life—that shit wasn't healthy. And she couldn't support it either, not when she'd seen her mother constantly put Barnabas first. If her mom knew how to be happy alone, Clem had certainly never seen any evidence of it. And now here Danica was, repeating those mistakes.

"Don't wait up," she said. "I'll leave the car keys for you."

She placed them on the counter and then left without looking back. Gavin greeted her with a bright smile, and some of the resentment faded. Normally she didn't mind being the one who had everything under control, but some of that containment might be failing. The seams around her emotions were about to burst, especially when she gazed at Gavin Rhys.

"Any requests for lunch?" he asked.

"We can go to Java House. It's close, and they have a chicken BLT wrap that's surprisingly delicious."

"I gather you're more interested in dessert," he said.

"It's time to put your parfait where your mouth is." When the words came out, they sounded way filthier than she'd planned.

His lips quirked. "That can be arranged, though it might not be wise."

He had to be talking about food and sex and yeast infections, but Clem pretended she had no clue what he meant and gave him a wide-eyed look that he probably didn't buy. She led the way to the café, and they placed their order. They both got the wrap she'd suggested, along with icy Italian sodas. The place was crowded, and they were lucky to snag a table.

"So did you introduce yourself to the coffee klatch gang?"

Gavin laughed. "I certainly did. Next I hope I'll get to hear the stories you mentioned. I popped in yesterday, but there wasn't time for more than basic, chaotic introductions."

"Ten bucks says Hazel Jeffords mentioned her cat, if she was there."

"I refuse to take that wager."

"She did," Clem said, laughing, as the server delivered their order.

"What's in the box?" Gavin asked.

"You'll see. It's a surprise for later."

He studied the carefully wrapped carton with holes cut in the sides. Though Clem couldn't speak to the mouse like Priya had, she did get a sense of his emotional state, and he seemed to be okay since his habitat was getting air from the holes and the box provided some insulation from the restaurant's noise and bustle. Hopefully, the little dude didn't freak out too much about the brief motorcycle ride to come.

The talk was light and fun while they ate, but she noticed Gavin couldn't keep his eyes off her. It was flattering, but she had the same problem. Lately she couldn't stop checking out his hands and forearms, which was a new obsession for her.

Once they finished, he offered a lazy smile. "To mine, then?"

Oh no. Oh yes.

If this was a test, she'd fail it.

It must be a coincidence, yeah?

Gavin had been telling himself that ever since he saw the name of Clem's shop and learned her last name. *Remember, you were the one who approached her first.* If nothing else, it was certainly proof the universe had a sense of humor. What were the odds that an actual witch hunter would hit on someone who carried the family name "Waterhouse"? In his shoes, his father would immediately begin the tests, most of which would be painful and degrading.

Gavin had been told it was for the greater good and hunters no longer killed witches. They severed their power and blurred their minds, allowing them to live as mundanes. He'd heard rumors that the order also seized assets as a penalty, and he honestly didn't understand the reasons or the histories. In his childhood, he'd sometimes ask, "But *why* are they so dangerous?" and he never got a satisfactory answer. Only talk about pride and tradition. Then he'd often get starved or beaten until he stopped questioning.

More and more, he didn't feel good about continuing this work. Certainly, the hunters above him in the order said these witches were wicked and dangerous, that they hurt others with their powers. *We're protecting the helpless mundanes, don't you understand that?* But there remained a niggling core of doubt, and it had only grown as he aged, until it was more of a thorn lodged permanently inside him, and he bled each time he followed what might be a bad order.

It's a coincidence, he told himself again.

Clem had a parcel she was being mysterious about, but he didn't question her as he secured the box inside the storage compartment on the back of the Duc. Thankfully, the ride offered him an excuse for this brooding silence, as it was damn difficult to make conversation on the Duc, so he luxuriated in the clasp of Clem's arms about his waist, taking pleasure in her closeness. He parked on the pad closest to his flat entrance and let her hop off the bike first, then he followed, squaring away their helmets for next time. She was delightfully flushed from wearing it in this heat, and he barely restrained the urge to kiss her. He retrieved the carton, and she clutched it to her chest.

"This way, the stairs are around back," Gavin said, instead of indulging in a quick kiss. After climbing the steps, he input the code and gestured for her to precede him. "After you."

"It's nice," she said, smiling as she surveyed his flat.

She headed inside and set the box on the coffee table.

Gavin followed, moving past her to get started in the kitchenette. "Quite adequate for one person. It might be a squeeze if two of us were shacked up for an extended period."

"I heard so many stories about people trapped in an Airbnb that they thought would only be for a couple of days, and then—"

"Been there," he cut in. "Let's not talk about the dark times, shall we?"

"Good idea. Shall I keep you company while you prepare?"

He nodded, and she took a seat at the small island that doubled as a work desk. "I'll have you know that I was inspired by the trip to the berry patch. I'm not anything like experienced at it, but I found a recipe for stovetop granola, so everything in these parfaits is fresh."

Clem grinned, and he loved the mischief in her sparkling eyes as she prepared to tease him. "Even the yogurt?"

"I bought that at the market. But it says 'natural, unsweetened, organic' right here."

She peered at the label. "That's a local brand. Good choice."

The kitchenette had mason jars, presumably for iced beverages, but they served perfectly for layering. He'd already washed and sliced the berries, so he made quick work of the parfaits, not about to admit that he'd watched multiple instructional videos and then bought organic raw honey. Why? Because he wanted to impress her. Which was ridiculous.

Yet here we are.

"And voilà," Gavin said, nudging the parfait toward her.

The desserts were beautiful, if he did say so himself. It boosted his ego tremendously when she angled the jar and took a photo. "This is going right on Pictogram."

"Thank you. Nothing but the best for you." Before she could dig in, he grabbed her spoon. "Wait. This isn't nut- or gluten-free. I should've asked before I offered to make food."

"Lucky for you, I don't have any allergies. Can I have my spoon back?"

He relaxed, abruptly aware of how nervous he'd been. "I was afraid this date might end badly if I didn't check."

"Have there been a lot that did?" she asked, taking her first bite.

Gavin sampled his as well, and everything tasted amazing. "I should probably be flippant but...that feels deceptive. There have been hookups more than dates."

"Well, since we agreed that this"—she gestured between them with her spoon—"has an expiration date, I won't pry into your commitment issues if you don't poke at mine."

Why does it bother me so much to hear it stated plainly? Everything she said was true and correct, but it also pissed him off something fierce.

"Fair deal," he muttered, stuffing his mouth with fruit and yogurt so he wouldn't immediately push the boundaries of what they'd agreed on.

And ask her, *Why is someone as amazing as you looking for dead-end encounters?* Relationships with a best-by date didn't seem like they'd be Clem's style, based on what he'd learned so far. She was a hard worker, a loyal friend, and she cared about her grandmother. In fact, she also—

For fuck's sake, man. Stop it. Stop now.

In a lucky break, she seemed far too absorbed in the quality of the fruity treat to notice his preoccupation with delving her mysteries. As she finished the parfait, she licked the spoon, and it went right to his cock. "I'm going to need that granola recipe. It tasted incredible. But I hope it wasn't complicated because I'm not much of a cook. If it can't all be dumped in a Crock-Pot and called food, then I can boil pasta or scramble eggs."

"How does one fail at salad?" he asked.

"That's not cooking, it's assembly." She narrowed her gaze, flattening her palm on the counter like she was about to lay something deep and serious on him. "It's one of my pet peeves when I'm trying to make something, usually because my grandma is coming over, and I'm looking for a recipe online, right? So I click the link and it's something like, 'for minestrone soup, buy a can of minestrone soup. Open can, put in pot, heat for five minutes, eat.' That's not a recipe, it's instructions!"

Gavin laughed. He couldn't help it; she was so adorably outraged. "You've run into this problem a lot, have you?" He heard his own voice, a tone he'd literally never produced before— all softness and delight. Even her ranting seemed endearing.

"More than I'd like. It's not funny," she added with a glare.

"Right. At any rate, the granola was easy. Oats, oil, and honey in a pan, cook a couple of minutes, add nuts and dried fruit, and Bob's your uncle."

Clem propped her chin on her hands. "I have never heard anyone say that before. You're adorable, you know that, right?"

"It's the accent, isn't it?"

"It's...everything." From the way her face froze, she hadn't meant to say that.

Does that mean she's struggling with the lines we've drawn as much as I am?

"Is it now?" Gavin heard the deep rasp in his voice, but he couldn't control it.

Clem smiled, a flirtatious cast to her expression. "Have you looked in the mirror lately? You're hot."

"Thanks for noticing. It's quite early, and I can't imagine that you want to spend the whole day cooped up in this little flat. Any suggestions?"

"Yes, as a matter of fact." She got up and fetched the mystery box. "This is a surprise for you. If you don't like it, I can—"

"Why don't you let me see what it is first?"

He opened it with caution and found a small, wire cage with a solid yellow floor. There were shavings and shreds of tissue and a gnawed-on toilet paper tube, along with a wheel, a water bottle, and a little house with a ramp leading up to it. This had to be a rodent habitat of some kind, but he saw no sign of the little chap, even after he settled on the floor by the cage.

"I got you a pet," Clem said in a rush. "He's probably nervous since mice don't like being moved. If you're patient, once he calms down, he'll come out and let you have a look at him. Since you're here for a month, that ought to be long enough for you to bond with him, then he won't be so stressed when you travel, and maybe you won't be so lonely."

Before Gavin could respond, a wee white mouse with black button eyes popped his head out of the mouse house, his pink nose twitching, and a wave of tenderness deluged him—for Clem, for the mouse—and damned if he didn't nearly tear up.

"Thank you," he said. "I shall call him Benson."

CHAPTER 8

"THAT'S AN ADORABLE NAME," CLEM said. "What's your inspiration?"

"You'll laugh if I tell you."

"Now you have to." She settled on the floor next to Gavin, careful not to make a lot of noise or any sudden motions that could frighten Benson.

"The gumball machine from the *Regular Show*."

By compressing her lips, she contained her amusement. "I loved that show. Was Benson your favorite?"

Gavin hesitated and eventually said, "Honestly, the character reminds me of my father. Love the name, though."

Clem nodded, watching the little mouse edge toward the ramp. He had probably been hiding since she boxed him up, and he must be hungry and thirsty. She could only imagine how terrifying it must be to be hauled around and strapped to a motorcycle, even if she'd done her best to tone down the frightening aspects.

"I did a little reading, and it's easier to bond with him if you offer treats. Sunflower seeds and millet are good options. Everything I bought to set up the cage is in the box, along with food and treats. Make sure he has tissues for nesting and cardboard to chew. The habitat will need to be cleaned periodically, but don't be *too* thorough or he'll get upset, as mice mark their territory."

"I'll do my own research, then, don't worry."

"Does that mean you're keeping him?" Clem asked.

"Absolutely. I might need to look into a travel kit for him, as I wouldn't feel good about treating him like luggage for a long ride, but the habitat is quite portable." Leaning forward, he kissed the tip of her nose. "Thank you...from the bottom of my heart."

She went gooey inside and cleared her throat to hide that reaction. "We should leave him be for a bit, so he can move around and eat. Does your Netflix work?"

"It does. I'll pick something, shall I?" Without waiting for her to respond, he queued up a show on the TV.

She migrated to the sofa, and as Clem settled into the crook of Gavin's arm, she was surprised to find he'd chosen a Turkish show about a guy who was apparently a guardian who had to defeat an immortal to save the city. "I've been looking at this one!"

Gavin shot her a surprised look. "I thought most Americans didn't like subtitles."

"Generalities are dangerous," she said. "And I'll have you know that watching international entertainment is a great way to train your ear in different languages. Plus, you get to learn cool stuff about other cultures."

"Are you trying to learn a second language?" he asked.

"I have several on my language app. I'm not the most dedicated, but I'm pecking away at Russian, Mandarin, and Korean right now. My Spanish is conversational. I forget my tenses sometimes, and it's tough for me to remember what gender inanimate objects are. There may be a pattern, but I'm not finding one. So the sun is a dude, and the moon is a lady, which sort of tracks in mythological terms."

"I thought if words end in 'a,' they're feminine," Gavin said.

Clem noticed he was looking at her more than the show. Since she was doing the same, she couldn't say much. "It's not that simple. Words like 'agua' throw everything into disarray. It's 'el problema' and 'el agua,' making life difficult for me."

He laughed. "That's unfortunate, isn't it?"

"Still easier than English as a second language. I'm sure you're familiar with the 'fish' spelled G-H-O-T-I example."

Gavin shifted to face her, seeming fascinated. "I am. What made you start studying languages? There can't be too much use for it in your work."

"One day I'd like to travel," she confessed. "Take a year and visit as many countries as I can, live out of a single suitcase. And I don't want to be an annoying visitor who doesn't even try to communicate, demanding everyone else speak English or whatever."

"They speak those languages in the countries you want to visit?"

She nodded. "I'd love to spend like a month traveling all over Europe by train. And did you know Russia is connected to a lot of places by ferry? You can sail from St. Petersburg to Estonia, Finland, Sweden—" Suddenly she realized she was practically gushing with enthusiasm. "Sorry, I got a little carried away."

"I loved it."

"Loved what?"

"Seeing you so excited."

Somehow Clem doubted that he'd meant for those words to sound so fucking sexy, but they sank into her, all the way down to her core. And she thrummed with excitement of a different sort. She became aware that they were alone in his apartment, and nobody would be interrupting anything she chose to do.

Nobody has to know.

"I'm usually the calm, logical one," she said.

"Perhaps I elicit the wildness in you."

She pressed her lips together, heroically resisting the urge to grab his shirt and kiss the hell out of him. "That's indisputable."

"I'm not following the program. And I'm really struggling with the urge to kiss you. We have all this privacy, so things might get…heated."

Taking a deep, tremulous breath—utterly unlike her, she whispered, "Go ahead with the kiss. I'm good with fooling around, orgasms are excellent. Let's draw the line at penetration."

"Just as well, I haven't stocked up on condoms."

In all honesty, Clem had no need of those. She couldn't get pregnant unless she timed it right and did some purposeful magic. Witches were luckier than mundanes in that regard. And thanks to her coven sisters, she couldn't acquire unfortunate human-transmitted diseases either, another advantage of the Waterhouse legacy. But there was no way to explain any of that without giving herself away.

"Then fondling, kissing, dry humping, and hands on junk only," she said decisively.

Gavin bit his lower lip hard, gray eyes sparkling, but in the end, he appeared to lose the battle and let out a sharp chuckle. "Never in my life have I had the terms set out so thoroughly beforehand. You truly are a delight, Clementine Waterhouse."

Normally, she felt a bit tense and awkward when people pointed out how fully her brain ruled the rest of her, but in Gavin's case, it seemed like he meant it. This wasn't a backhanded compliment in the slightest. She smiled a bit.

"Isn't it better to have it all understood up front? Then we just...enjoy ourselves. No need to worry or guess where we're headed, as we're on the same page."

"I can't argue with that."

He moved so swiftly that it startled her a bit. The TV was still playing in Turkish as Gavin swung her into his arms and carried her into his bedroom. Nice linens, still a bit rumpled. He tossed her lightly on the bed and started stripping. She knelt on the mattress, taking her cue to do the same. He left his boxer briefs on, so she followed his example and left her green panties. Briefly she wished she had on better underwear, but he didn't seem interested in her lingerie at *all* when he pounced.

"I've been obsessing about this for days."

"Getting me in your bed?"

"That, yes. But also kissing you again." He claimed her lips hungrily.

And her whole body lit up, pleasure spiraling through her sharper and more intense than anything she'd ever felt. Clem dug her fingers into his back, urging him closer as Gavin toyed with her mouth, alternately nibbling and nuzzling. She teased his tongue with hers, stroking in little darting movements. The stubble on his jaw abraded her cheek, and his mouth was soft and hot, just a little rough. Somehow, it was even hotter that she could feel his experiences that way, just as she tasted the sweetness of berries on his tongue.

Gavin groaned into her mouth, one hand roving down her side. "You beautiful treasure," he whispered, his mouth hot and open on her throat.

When he covered her body with his, she reveled in his heat and hardness, widening her thighs so he could settle between them. *Goddess, he feels good.* He was hard already, throbbing against her pussy through the thin layer of their underwear. She hadn't done this since high school, but there was something indescribably hot about it, knowing this was the line they wouldn't cross.

He nuzzled her throat, her shoulders, planting kisses and softly tantalizing her with the occasional graze of teeth. Maddeningly, he still hadn't touched her breasts, her ass, or her slick, aching pussy. Clem shifted forward and repaid him in kind, sucking on the side of his neck. The sudden reciprocation made him jerk against her, pushing uncontrollably with his hips.

She moaned. "That's a hot zone for you, huh?"

"Anywhere you put that mouth feels amazing," he gasped. "But yes. I'm sensitive there."

"Shall we make this more interesting?" With a seductive wriggle, she lifted her hips, angling them so she could feel every inch of him slowly grinding against her.

"I'm already riveted, but...what do you have in mind?"

"First to come has to grant the winner a wish."

"Challenge accepted," Gavin said.

If he didn't get off her, it wouldn't take long, and that would be embarrassing at his age. It wasn't like he was in form one and had never seen a pair of actual tits. He had to admit that Clem's were spectacular. Rolling off her, he lowered his head to kiss the tops of them, licking down toward her nipple. She made an incoherent sound when he wrapped his lips around the tip, sipping delicately. Clem sank her fingers into his hair, and when she massaged his head in rhythm with the tugs from his mouth, the sharp blaze of desire that streamed through him felt...supernatural. That was an odd word to pop into his mind, but his whole body was trembling, just from the touch of her fingers on his scalp and the delicious, honeyed-melon scent of her.

Her skin felt incredibly soft and smooth beneath his mouth, and he licked down her stomach for the sheer joy of it, even knowing that he wasn't allowed to taste her pussy. That restriction only made him crave her more—to the point that his mouth was watering. Gavin kissed her belly just above the line of her knickers, and she tensed, her hips pushing upward. The green cotton gusset was dark, soaked through with her excitement. Deliberately, he touched her through the damp cloth, stroking a fingertip back and forth over her clit.

"I want to taste you so badly."

"Fingers only," she reminded him.

Then she pushed him. Not away, exactly, but he landed on his side and didn't resist when she nudged him onto his stomach. And then she was kissing the back of his neck, biting and sucking. *Fuck, I shouldn't have told her my weakness.*

There was something sexy as hell at having her hot, wet pussy grinding into his ass while she pressed her teeth into the side of his throat. He jerked against the mattress, and before he knew it, he was practically fucking a hole into it, pushing forward as she rubbed against him from behind. From the sting on his throat, she was leaving marks.

And he fucking loved it.

"Please let me touch you."

She was breathless when she dismounted, landing beside him with a little bounce. Gavin rolled onto his side, his cock so hard that it hurt a bit, and it was leaking like mad. If they kept going, he'd cream in his shorts, and he could tell she wanted him to break first. Though he didn't know why, he had the sense that this little bet was important to her, and he rather wanted to grant her a wish in any case.

Anything you desire, anything at all.

"Only if I can reciprocate," she murmured.

"Have at me."

His gaze stayed locked on hers as he teased a path down her abdomen and into her knickers. Looking away from her wide, dark eyes with pupils blown proved impossible, so he navigated by touch, stroking her labia and swirling the juices around until she chased more contact, angling for him to graze her clit. Her hand was trembling when she stretched the elastic band of his boxer briefs and dragged his cock out. In his experience, women often had no idea what to do with their fingers. Most rubbed him too lightly or their angle was off, so he didn't think he'd come before she did.

But Clem surprised him by settling beside him, shifting her body so she could jerk him just as he would do it—firm grip, palming back to front—and since she was lying beside him, it felt...right. So fucking good that his breath immediately quickened to a pant and came out as a groan. His balls tingled and tightened as she found her rhythm. At this rate, it would only take a few minutes for him to spurt all over her hand and his stomach. His cock swelled as she pumped, throbbing with each tug.

"Hard nipples, deep flush. Getting close?" She kissed his shoulder, seeming more focused on his pleasure than her own, despite his fingers swirling on her clit.

"You're too good at this," he managed to say.

"Let go. Gush for me, Gavin." She squeezed a little harder.

"*Clem.*"

He lost it, fucking her fist like a beast until he grunted and came, long, satisfying pulses that ended with his semen on her hands, his belly—messy and delicious. He panted, eyes closed, while she petted him through the aftershocks, care he didn't normally receive from his casual fucks. Clem finished with a soft kiss, her lips toying with his as his heartbeat steadied.

"I win," she whispered.

"Feels like *I* did. Give me a couple of minutes, and I'll make your toes curl, love."

"I'll go wash up."

Probably he ought to do...something, but for the moment, he felt boneless. When she came back, she had a damp washcloth she used to complete the cleanup. "Now you're spoiling me," he said.

Then, to his amazement, she settled on his left thigh with a determined look. At her urging, he bent it a little, and she rubbed against him frantically, her cheeks flushed, eyes glittering. He caressed her back and held her hips, but it didn't take long at all for her to grind herself to a shuddering orgasm. He felt the sudden wetness on his thigh, even through her knickers, and he cuddled her close as she shivered.

"Next time, let me give it to you."

She wore a strange look as she snuggled into his side. "That was just...faster. I was beyond my tolerance for a slow build. I needed to get off."

"You're saying I turned you on that much."

"That orgasm face." She fanned herself.

He thought she meant it, and his heart quivered in his chest. Had anyone ever been that excited just from touching his cock? How much stronger would her response be when their mouths—*oh, it's when. I see.* Already he was planning to get tested so he could find out.

"Would it be ridiculous if we took a long nap and then ordered delivery for dinner? Maybe we can take another shot at that show we didn't watch and check on Benson. I know he has food and water, but I don't want him to be frightened."

"Sounds perfect," she mumbled sleepily.

After pulling the covers over them, he settled her close, taking her scent in with deep, delighted breaths. Now she smelled of honeyed melon, pineapple, and sex. It was possibly the most delicious perfume ever invented, and he wanted to lick her from head to toe.

"Are you staying over?"

I shouldn't have asked. Flings don't get overnight privileges.

If she stayed over, if they had dinner and spent the night cuddling and watching TV, then took things back to bed for round two, they'd be entering relationship territory. So he braced himself for the inevitable refusal. He shouldn't want more than he was allowed.

This is enough. It must be. Then her answer broke over him like an unexpectedly bright sunrise, shades of undeserved joy spilling through him in emotional pinks and golds.

"I'm staying."

CHAPTER 9

TWO DAYS AFTER CLEM SPENT the night with Gavin, she reached her limit with Gram's criticism regarding her cousin Danica's poor judgment.

She'd been reading texts and listening to voicemails until she was good and pissed. Today, they were having it out, as she was tired of being asked to report on Danica like she'd been recruited as a double agent. Families shouldn't be like this. It wasn't the first time she'd had such a thought, and anger boiled inside her like water in a tea kettle.

She couldn't deal with the pressure of distracting Gavin while Gram carped and complained. Now the old witch stood outside the shop, staring at Clem pointedly. Resisting the urge to roll her eyes, she beckoned in silent invitation. There were no customers in Fix-It Witches, and Danica hadn't come in yet.

No time like the present.

Clem didn't waste time on pleasantries as the bell on the door tinkled, signaling Gram's arrival. She did put down the old-fashioned radio she was working on, though.

"If you're here to talk about Danica, you can turn around," she said, firing from the hip.

"Why are you so hostile, Clementine? I only want the best for Danica...and for you as well. But if you'd rather, we could talk about your mother."

She sucked in a breath. *So that's how she wants to play, huh?*

"Mom can manage her own life. So can I. Danica can too. If you're bored, since you frittered your power away on that grimoire, take up a hobby, or get married again." Clem smirked. "Want me to find you some good Bindr profiles? You're an attractive woman. I'm sure somebody would be interested."

Gram narrowed her eyes. "I see what you're trying to do here, and it won't work. Truly, have you no care for this family at all? You're the only one who has any hope of talking sense into your cousin. She loves and respects—"

"So you want me to weaponize the love and respect Danica has for me, is that it? Does that *feel* right to you? I wonder what goes on in your head, I seriously do."

"She's dallying with a mundane. Such naivete will ruin her life!"

"You say it will, but Auntie Min and Mom seem happy enough."

It cost her to pretend nonchalance, as Clem had internalized too much of her grandmother's prejudice to be fully sanguine about her mother's remarriage to a mundane. Allegra seemed brighter, though, and there were no tumultuous arguments, no dishes smashing or sobbing fits after Barnabas dropped some particularly vengeful magic. Never to do physical harm, but he'd often ruined her mother's things to exact punishment for her expectation of loyalty and devotion. Clem had her own conflicted feelings about monogamy, but she did know one couldn't simply decide fidelity was for chumps without having a conversation with their partner first. If a relationship stopped meeting someone's needs, they should end it if a new normal couldn't be negotiated. In her opinion, both her parents had failed in various ways, but Barnabas had been more of a dick about it.

Gram stared at her as if Clem had unexpectedly stuck a knife in her chest. "I thought you missed your father. Goddess knows, the man could be a trial, but have you forgotten—"

"Have *you* forgotten how you tried to patch things up between them, and we caught him in bed with two of my friends?"

Mundane girls, barely eighteen. And they were *former* friends now. Though it wasn't their fault, not even slightly, Clem couldn't get past the awkwardness. Now, whenever she saw Ashley and Tara, she flashed on them bracketing her father, naked, and that was not a scene she cared to revisit. It was also when she'd stopped engaging with him because she'd understood then that he accepted no boundaries on his own pleasure, and he believed himself to be so important that it didn't matter who he injured, so long as his desires were fulfilled.

Gram grimaced. It seemed that even pure witch blood didn't absolve Barnabas in this situation. "Such a thing would be impossible to forget."

"That was the last straw for Mom," Clem said. "And yet, you learned nothing from forcing her into a hellish marriage that stripped away all her dignity and self-respect."

For once, Gram didn't have a quick answer. She flattened her hands on the counter, and Clem noticed the trammels of time on them—wrinkled, crepe thin, and the faint dotting of age spots. A slow sigh escaped her, as if she acknowledged Clem had a point.

"Then you think it's better for her to lose her magic slowly, until she's as mundane as Minerva. I fear for the future of all witches, truly I do. Hunted and hated by those who remember, our power stolen by those who have forgotten."

"It's not black and white. Nothing ever is. People should make their own choices."

"What would yours be?"

Clem considered the matter seriously. "I would rather be alone than lose my power. When the time comes, I'll use a witch donor and rely on my coven sisters to help with parenting when I need a break. Over the years, I'm sure I'll take lovers, whoever they may be, but I won't give them any control over me."

Gram reached for her hand, nodding with sharp approval. "That's a strong choice, one I endorse completely."

That's not the point. But she didn't say it aloud. She'd witnessed too many of her mother's tears to feel safe turning over the keys to her innermost heart.

What if I choose poorly? I could end up with someone like Barnabas.

"But I'm not the problem, am I? You came to nag me about Danica, and I'm sick of being in the middle. Take your issues directly to her from now on. I'm not intervening and I'm done meddling. It's her life, do you get that?"

"Fine," Gram snapped. "Curse me up and down for caring, then."

Clem half expected the old witch to deploy some version of

"you'll be sorry when I'm gone," but evidently she had some measure of self-control. From the way Gram was tapping her nails on the glass, she had something else to say, and Clem wished she'd get on with it. She missed the simpler times when she'd enjoyed the illusions cast for their entertainment: a garden full of fairy lights and fireflies, tiny dragons dancing on the fold of a flower petal. She loved her grandmother, and on some level, it was endearing how much she cared. Clem just wished Gram could learn to be a little more patient and a lot more tolerant.

"What is it?" she asked.

"I'd hoped some of your resentment toward your father would've died away by now. Because you see—"

The bell chimed, alerting them to a couple of new arrivals. Gram turned; Clem didn't have to. Both her hands curled into fists as she recognized her biological father with a woman younger than Clem clinging to his arm, gazing at him as if he held all the brightness of the sun in a summer sky.

"Clementine," Barnabas exclaimed. "How lovely to catch you on the first try. I've come to present your new stepmother."

————————

Gavin was at the coffee klatch again.

He'd wanted to bring Benson along, but it wouldn't do him any good if the mouse popped out unexpectedly and made the little old ladies hop on chairs and scream. Most likely, the noise would traumatize the little chap.

Amusingly enough, Clem had been right about this gathering. The same faces greeted him today as the first time, allowing him to bypass awkward introductions. Gladys seemed glad to see him, as did Hazel and Howard. Leonard appeared to be withholding judgment, and perversely, that made Gavin want to win the codger over more than ever.

"You're looking lovely today," he said to Ethel, who swept in right behind him.

She bustled past with a bulging sack, like he imagined Mrs. Claus would look, if she were also a fan of hippie chic and handmade bracelets. After plunking her bag on the table, she set out the same sort of jewelry she was wearing, and the ladies all leaned forward eagerly.

"Oh, these pendants are new! They're so pretty. I wish I had your talent," Hazel said, peering at them wistfully.

Ethel scowled. "Talent is an excuse, and you know it. I'm not naturally gifted. I got better at this because I worked at it, so it's a pet peeve of mine when people act like I've been blessed by the heavens—that I suddenly started making perfect projects with no effort at all."

"It was a compliment," Hazel snapped.

"Sounded more like an excuse," Leonard muttered, but he quickly crammed a cruller into his mouth, likely not wanting to get sucked further into the bickering.

Gavin found himself oddly charmed by the whole tableau. Because his family was a fractured wreck, he'd spent relatively little time around pensioners like this. Mostly, they'd shouted at him in the village back home or shaken their sticks at unruly teenagers, muttering how the realm was falling to rack and ruin.

"You couldn't get enough of us," Gladys cut in. "I'm glad you're back. Are you looking for work?"

"Not officially," he said. "I've no work permit, so I couldn't take on a position formally, but if you need help, I'd be happy to turn my hand to whatever job might need doing. Provided I can manage it."

Suddenly, he had ten pairs of eyes locked on him with varying degrees of interest. Then Howard said, "What are the parameters?"

"Pardon me?" Gavin had the feeling he'd committed a faux pas somehow, but for the life of him, he couldn't figure out how.

"You just made an open offer," Ethel pointed out. "Didn't set any limits. So they could ask you to trim hedges, mow yards, drive them to doctor's appointments, dredge sewer lines, clean gutters, date their grandchildren—"

"That's not really a chore, is it?"

"You've never seen my grandbaby," Howard joked.

"Megan isn't that bad," said Hazel. "Though I'll allow that I find all those piercings distracting. How does she eat corn on the cob?"

Ethel laughed. "That's what you're worried about? You should support Megan's right to do as she pleases with her own body."

He decided he ought to set those limits. "Garden work is fine. I wouldn't mind driving but we'd need to use your car, as I can't imagine any of you would enjoy a ride on my Ducati."

"I would," said Gladys.

"What about your bad hip?" Leonard looked like he might physically wrestle Gavin to keep him from absconding with the pretty little apple of his eye. "You have rheumatoid arthritis, for God's sake!"

She scowled at Leonard, a surprisingly fierce expression.

"Clam jamming me won't get you in these granny panties any faster, old man."

Gavin choked on the sip of coffee he'd inadvisably taken, just before Gladys went *off*. "Did you say—"

"Clam jamming. Also called 'twat blocking.' It's the equivalent—"

"Yes, I understood you, though 'twat' means something different where I'm from."

"That's why I said 'clam jamming' first," Gladys said, like he was a bit thick.

He laughed until tears gathered at the edges of his eyes. "Understood. But Leonard has nothing to fear from me. I'm seeing someone already."

"You work fast," Ethel noted.

"Who is it? What are they like?" Hazel served herself from the box of pastries, eyes avid as the old woman prepared for some fine and proper gossip.

And he appreciated the fact that she'd chosen a general pronoun, not assuming anything about his preferences. The fact was, Gavin had always been more attracted to personality traits. He liked people who were mentally strong, a bit stubborn, prone to giving him a hard time. Submission did nothing for him, and he liked a bit of conflict—

Suddenly he realized everyone was staring at him, expecting an answer. He had no reason to hide the fact that he was hooking up with Clem, so he said, "Clementine Waterhouse. She runs Fix-It Witches, the repair shop near the café."

For some reason, Gladys and Ethel swapped a look. Gavin

intercepted it, but he couldn't interpret what that glance meant. Neither of the women spoke.

"She's my neighbor!" Hazel said. "Nearly, anyway. I live four doors down."

Good to know.

He might be able to pump Hazel for information about Clem if it became necessary, as he still had a low-key thread of… something. Not quite misgiving, but it tugged at him over time. Her surname. The name of her shop.

Certainly, his task couldn't be that easy, and he'd never sensed any magic on her, but—

No.

More likely, she was a mundane using the history of witchcraft as a gimmick because she had no idea of the truth. Defiantly, he shoved that unease to the back of his mind.

"Yard work and driving," Gladys said, guiding the discussion back to what work he was willing to do. "What about cleaning out attics or basements? Maybe moving furniture if we want to rearrange the house?"

"That's doable," he said. "I've never done any painting, and if you wanted anything planted, I'd need supervision, but I'm willing to provide muscle as needed."

"Have mercy," another old woman said, fanning herself as she came into the meeting room to overhear his comment.

"This is Judy Carminian," Ethel said.

"Nice to meet you. Anyone who might need some help while I'm in town, hand me your mobile. I'll input my number."

Unsurprisingly, all the women sent their cellular devices to him. The men responded more slowly. Their generation found it difficult to ask for help, he suspected.

"Hit me up if you'd like to get a pint," he said to Leonard. "I'm in the market for some drinking mates too."

"Wouldn't you rather make friends your own age?" the old man demanded.

Gavin shook his head. "Haven't you heard? We're a generation of wankers."

Startled, Leonard let out a sharp bark of laughter. "Some of you are okay. But you never know, might take you up on that."

"I'm looking forward to it."

CHAPTER 10

WITH ALL HER HEART, CLEM wished she could hit the reset button on her life.

Back when everyone was quarantining, she and Danica had offered online tech support for a nominal fee. She'd said, "Is it plugged in? Have you tried turning it off and on again? Factory reset didn't work?" so many times, but unfortunately, witches couldn't be reset like a malfunctioning phone.

No matter how long she stared in silence, her father was *still here*, and Gram was smiling at him, like she knew something about his arrival beforehand. That pissed Clem off, frankly. Gram knew exactly how shitty Barnabas had treated Clem's mom, yet she saw only his proper accent, his old money, and the superficial good manners that glossed over his many defects.

"Tell me you didn't invite him," Clem said.

She suspected that her complicated life was about to get worse. And she couldn't take more pressure when she was already struggling to clean up her cousin's mess. Guilt immediately assailed her for thinking of Gavin that way, and she reminded herself that it was a fucking *con*.

I'm not supposed to feel anything for him. He's the enemy.

Into the fraught silence, Barnabas declared, "How rude. You haven't greeted your stepmother."

Clem extended her senses and realized this young woman registered as a null. *She's a mundane. Did he run out of witches willing to overlook his history and marry him?* While he'd messed around with mundane girls before, this was a new development, one line her father hadn't crossed.

Until now.

Still, though she wanted to snarl, this woman wasn't her enemy. Most likely, she had no idea what kind of man she'd married. It wouldn't be long before she found out—in the most painful way possible—so Clem restrained her urge to lash out and tried to smile. The expression felt weird on her face, probably looked even stranger.

"I'm Clementine Waterhouse. Clem. Nice to meet you," she said grudgingly.

"Pansy Balfour."

It was a sweet name, and it matched her ingenue aspect. Clem had to hand it to the old man; no matter how much he aged, he never lost the ability to pull. Pansy must be in her late twenties, several years younger than Clem, and she had huge dark eyes and fair hair, a contrast that probably wasn't natural.

Gram spoke, her thin face wreathed in smiles. "Once you acclimate to the idea, you'll be glad that both your parents will be here to…spend time with you this summer. How many years has it been?" she added in a fond, wistful tone.

That had to be an oblique reference to the Lughnasadh. Clem

stared, utterly aghast. "Tell me this wasn't your idea. Mom and D-Pop will be here soon!"

Barnabas immediately took offense. "You're acting as if that disreputable layabout is your father? You never address me directly, and you use my first name when you speak of me to others. Do you think that's appropriate? It's so disrespectful that I..."

Yeah, tuning him out.

Briefly she closed her eyes, wishing her magic could poof her somewhere else. Teleportation would be a super awesome power, one she unfortunately didn't possess. When she opened her eyes, her three unwelcome guests were still in the shop, but at least Barnabas had finished his lecture, and Pansy was trying to chat with Gram.

Good luck, she hates mundanes.

Just once, Clem would like for Danica to show up early and help her out of an awkward situation. Their relationship didn't work that way, however. Not that it was her cousin's fault—Clem tended to ice others out when she was most vulnerable.

"I'll take the guest room at your place," her father said, because the conversation had evolved to discussing where everyone would stay. "It's only fair. I never get to see you, and you grew up with your mother. I want us to be closer, Clementine."

You don't even know that I hate being called that.

"Like the song?" Pansy asked with a slow blink that made her look like a baby deer.

Ugh. Why?

"If I let you stay at our place, Mom will be hurt," Clem said flatly.

"It's childish of Allegra to ask you to take sides," Gram put in, like she didn't do the same thing constantly where Danica was concerned, as if she wasn't taking Barnabas's side over her own daughter at this moment.

Goddess, I'm so done with everyone.

"Telling everyone to make their own housing arrangements is hardly playing favorites," she snapped.

A headache started behind her eyes, throbbing at her temples and tightening around the back of her head. She recognized the symptoms—tension and repressed rage, manifesting as pain. In this moment, she just wanted—

Gavin.

Oh no.

But she couldn't dispel the mental picture of how comforting it would be to nestle into his chest and whisper, "Make them all go away." He'd do it too. Despite how gentle he was with her, she sensed he'd tolerate no nonsense that disturbed her. He might be British like her father, but they had nothing else in common.

Pansy put a gentle hand on Barnabas's arm. "If you don't mind, I'd rather stay at an Airbnb or a hotel. Right now, I'm a stranger to Clem, and I want us to start off on the right foot."

Most of her stepmothers had been more like the ones from the worst fairy tales. It figured that Barnabas had snagged someone genuinely nice this time, who might be wrecked when he cheated. Clem would never understand why he bothered getting married when his inclinations were so clearly polyamorous, but she suspected he wouldn't enjoy sharing his partner with other people; he just wanted to get more than he gave. Maybe that was even part of the fun, the addictive thrill of sneaking around and feeling like he was getting away with—

Shit.

Clem realized she was intimately familiar with that sensation. That described the rush she got from playing with Gavin precisely. Sickness turned her insides upside down, leaving her a trembling mess.

I need them to go before they notice.

Dammit, I don't want to have anything in common with Barnabas.

On some level, perhaps she'd sensed this flaw in her own makeup, and that was why she preferred her relationships brief and light. Better not to commit than to make promises she couldn't keep.

Fucking hell.

The long silence built until Gram finally said, "You're kind to make allowances for Clem. She's always been a bit stubborn and temperamental."

Okay, that's it.

"This has been all kinds of fun," she said, "but I have work to do."

"We must get together for a meal," Barnabas said.

She had zero desire to do that, but if it would get them out of here... "Sounds good. Send me a message."

"You blocked me!"

"Email me, then." Clem refused to let his complaint get any traction.

Gram made that scolding noise Clem hated. "Clementine Odette, that's reprehensible. Whatever issues Barnabas has with your mother, he's still your biological father. And I've long said that her relationship with Dougal crossed certain lines long before they officially—"

"Get. Out," she gritted through clenched teeth.

Pansy seemed like a natural peacemaker, tugging Barnabas toward the door.

Even Gram must have realized it would be highly unwise to linger, because she murmured a farewell and hurried out. Clem sucked in a shuddering breath, white-knuckling the counter with all her strength. Her magic surged, creating a wave that powered up all the machines on display out front. Blenders whirred, a waffle iron clanged, and an old iPod blasted "Breakin' Dishes" by Rihanna while the dial on a radio across the room spun wildly. It took all her focus to shut each one down before someone noticed the gadgets going haywire.

Forcing the magical focus helped a little, though her head still hurt like a bitch. And of course, fifteen minutes later, Danica finally showed up to relieve her, but she was a damn mess.

Clem couldn't bring herself to confide in her cousin when Danica looked like microwaved shit.

But that left her carrying the weight alone, just like always.

———

Gavin never thought he'd find himself pruning shrubberies instead of following his old man's edicts, but he liked Leonard substantially better than this own father.

In some ways, he reminded him of the grandfather he hadn't seen since he was thirteen.

Once, they had been close.

With an emphatic snip, he severed an unruly branch. If only his thoughts could be controlled so easily.

He was almost finished, and the hedges looked level, though he hadn't checked by measuring. If Leonard wanted military precision, he could pay someone for this.

A short while later, the older man brought two icy bottles of beer and gestured to the patio furniture on the cement pad that passed for a terrace in these parts. "You said you want a drinking buddy. Here I am."

"I meant at O'Reilly's, but your back garden is nice too."

Leonard laughed. "I can't figure you out, son. You don't look like any college professor I ever met, and I get a funny feeling about you." The old man narrowed his eyes. "Yep, you're definitely keeping secrets."

That was astonishingly on the mark, but Gavin lifted a shoulder, accepting the amber bottle and tracing the cool condensation down the side. "If you like, I can bore you to tears with a lecture on the War of the Roses. Would that make me seem more professorial?"

"It probably would," Leonard allowed. "And it would also conceal that fact that you just deflected, instead of addressing my original point."

"You're relentless," he said with a bewildered sort of admiration.

"Oops, you did it again, just like that poor Britney Spears."

From the gimlet gaze fixed on him, Gavin could tell he had to say something, and that his usual jokes wouldn't suffice. Neither would the truth. So he decided to obfuscate with a different version of it.

"If you must know, it's highly probable my sabbatical from university will become permanent. I can't find any joy in academic writing these days, and it's a rather ruthless prestige system. If I don't produce, they'll hire someone who will. Which leaves me unemployed and wondering what to do with the rest of my life. I have some savings, but…"

"They won't last forever," Leonard said. "You're looking at an early midlife crisis, then. Is that why you're touring America on a motorcycle?"

"Perhaps. It cost me three hundred pounds to send it over, but it has sentimental value." Gavin sipped his beer, knowing this meant he was committed to hanging out at Leonard's house until he metabolized it. "But enough about me. I suspect you're nursing a crush on Gladys. How's that coming along?"

The old man glared at him. "That's none of your business. And slow. I keep telling her that we're old and we shouldn't waste time, but she enjoys keeping me wrapped around her adorable little fingers."

Right, that's too cute for words.

He concealed the smile with some effort. "Shall I write her some love poetry you can Cyrano her with?"

"Mind your own business!"

"Understood."

They drank for a bit in silence while he tried to figure out a subtler way to seek information about the weird residents of St. Claire. As usual, he had been using detection snares here and there, but nothing had popped so far. Sometimes he ran across a tingle of old magic, but he couldn't get a lock since it was faded and weak.

Eventually Leonard said, "What's on your mind? You've got a serious thinking face on, so you might as well spit it out."

"I was just curious who the interesting people are around here. There's a pensioner in the village where I grew up who knits sweater vests for cats." That was a lie.

He'd read about that woman on the internet. There was no cozy home village or heartwarming story from his past, just hard lessons from Da. When he looked back, his world kept getting smaller, with Da winnowing away those who loved him—first Nan, then Mum, and finally Grandad.

Wonder if they're safe and happy, if they think of me at all.

"You're curious about our local oddballs, huh?" Leonard laughed. "First one that springs to mind is Dale the Prepper. He lives out at the old Oswald farm, only comes into town twice a year. Never met anyone who hates people more, and he's constantly ordering supplies for when the world ends. And..."

Come to think of it, Mina had mentioned this character as well, something about an unusual installation he'd built to communicate with aliens. "What?"

"This is only what I hear, of course, but apparently, he's out at all hours, mucking around in other people's fields. And Roger Stevewell says that John Farmer told him this... Whenever Dale's been creeping around, strange things happen."

All his instincts perked up. "What sort of things?"

Just then, the other man's mobile rang. "I'm taking this. It's Gladys."

Sprawled in the chair, Gavin enjoyed his beer until his own mobile pinged with an alert. Your Hotmail account has been locked after multiple failed login attempts. Please check to ensure the safety of your account and change your password if you suspect your information has been compromised.

What the hell.

It had been years since he'd even looked at that email, one his grandfather had helped him make when he was like thirteen. Before…

Yeah. Before.

Mildly curious, Gavin completed password recovery because hell if he could even remember what it was back in the day. Probably something he'd thought was clever as a sprat, like *sexparty6969*. He got the text via code, and in a few moments, he was in the formerly abandoned inbox, scrutinizing ten thousand spam messages. An embarrassing number of them were porn related. With a wince, Gavin searched how to delete a Hotmail account.

Then a new message popped in at the top, and he stared at it, frozen in shock.

Kevin Rhys.

Nobody in the order talked about his grandfather. His name had been stricken from all the records, and his father had hammered it home that if Grandad wasn't dead, he would be if the order caught up to him.

Gavin took a breath. Another.

And opened the email.

Dear Gavin,

First off, I'm sorry. Not for the choice I made but for leaving without saying goodbye. You must've been so hurt, angry, and confused, but I made the call to save someone's life, someone precious to me. I'm not saying you mattered less, but he needed me more.

You see, I learned some things that made my heart shrivel, and I couldn't walk that path anymore. I don't know what your father's said about me, so I'll just say that I think of you every day, and I look at old pictures of you often. It's hard for me to imagine that you're a grown man. You might even have a family of your own by now.

That's the hardest part of this separation. Missing you and knowing that any contact between us might put you at risk too. I happened to remember this old email address—remember the day I helped you set it up? You've changed the password since then, sorry about locking your account.

But me failing to login proved this email was still good, so I had to take a chance. I want you to know that I'm proud of you, no matter what you're doing.

But I do have some cautionary words. The order can't be trusted.

If they find out I've gotten in touch with you, neither one of us will be safe.

I love and miss you, Gavin.

Love always,

Grandad

Head whirling, Gavin stared at his screen, hardly able to think. *He's alive. He remembers me. The order can't be trusted?*

CHAPTER 11

AFTER THE DAY CLEM HAD, she should've been texting her coven sisters demanding comfort.

And yet, she stared at the message she'd sent Gavin, wondering if the witch's council would accept temporary insanity as an excuse for her behavior. It worked in mundane courts sometimes. Rereading the sentence didn't change anything.

Had an incredibly shitty day. You free tonight?

He replied right off. Had a bit of a day myself. Would help to see you.

A few seconds later, That's a yes please, if it wasn't clear.

Dammit.

Now she had a date, and she couldn't pretend this was about distracting him. She'd reached out because she liked him and she took comfort from his presence.

And it's all based on a lie. Doesn't that figure.

She sent the message back with a mental shrug. I'm taking tonight as a mental health day. Clem did have some mild concerns that if she banged him, her magic might spark up, and of course he'd notice. *What the hell, might as well live dangerously. If I get caught, I'll try to convince him I'm the only witch in town.*

She'd known volunteering for this might end in sacrifice. The others hadn't worked it out yet, but when they did, it would lead to another pointless argument. But maybe she could find something in Etta Mae's notes.

When she left Fix-It Witches, she didn't tell Danica that Barnabas and his current wife were in town. She just waved and went, playing her cards so close to the vest that her cousin probably didn't even know Clem *had* cards. She headed home to shower because sometimes that let her symbolically scrub away stress and annoyance. Today she wasn't so lucky. The day's irritations clung to her like burrs tangled in a dog's fur.

Beneath the lukewarm spray, she finished washing up and then chose her outfit with care: a white dress patterned with yellow flowers, light enough for summer with spaghetti straps, a deep V on the neckline, and an adorable tie front and a peekaboo cutout. This dress even had pockets. Next, she laid out accessories—a delicate necklace on a gold chain that had been a birthday gift from Allegra, chunky white sandals, and a yellow clutch. As she smoothed the lotion on, her signature scent of honey melon and pineapple, she got another message from Gavin. Don't know if I can live up to the precedent you've set, but I'm having a go. Hope you like surprises.

She gazed at her phone with guilt and excitement duking it out. "You mean like a witch hunter showing up and turning out to be sexy and fun and…" She stopped herself, exhaling in a controlled burst. "Nope. Enough of that."

Short hair was awesome in summer; she put a little gel in her hands and tousled her pixie cut, leaving it to do as it pleased. The result was usually playful and adorable, just as well because Clem lacked the patience for a higher-maintenance style. She wouldn't get ready yet, though, because her clothes would get wrinkled lounging around.

As she pulled on a robe, she sent a reply. Where should we meet?

Gavin answered, The café? In a couple of hours.

Sounds good. See you then.

Clem dedicated over an hour to reviewing the notes she'd gotten from Ethel, but they were infuriatingly detailed on matters unrelated to witch hunters. She paged through them, but since she didn't know the exact dates involved, it was slow going. When the alarm on her phone went off, letting her know it was time to go, she hopped up with alacrity and got dressed. She rarely wore much makeup, and today she only used a touch of bronzer and a tinted lip balm. There were two reasons that was a good idea. The weather was hot and muggy, so she'd sweat through a heavier paint job in no time, and it would be smeared during sex anyway. No point in pretending she didn't know how this would end. Finally, she rubbed on a tincture Ethel had made, something that should permit intimacy without allowing Gavin to sense her magic.

There wasn't much of a breeze as she made her way downtown at a leisurely pace. Gavin was already waiting for her, propped against his bike, and his smile—*oh goddess, his smile*—crinkled his eyes at the corners, giving him a rakish air. He stepped toward her like he absolutely couldn't help it and extended his hand.

Without even a second's hesitation, she wrapped her fingers around his, and it felt as if a low-wattage current flickered between them. If attraction could be measured in voltage, they surely had enough to wreak havoc on the grid.

"You take my breath away," he said, low.

Damn, it was too much, considering the look and sound of him and the delicious cologne he was wearing. She breathed in a smoky, salty scent that made her mouth water—notes of wood sage, grapefruit, a whisper of hibiscus accentuated by a suggestion of the sea. Like a bonfire on the beach at sunset, he overwhelmed her senses, pushing Clem ever closer to forgetting her mission and indulging herself in him. Gavin Rhys was an ocean she wanted to dive into, and it didn't much matter if she drowned or swam.

He pulled her in gently, touching the tip of her nose in a teasing caress. "Nothing clever to say? You haven't called me 'English' in a while, and I rather miss it."

"It wasn't meant as an endearment," she muttered.

"You can't stop me from taking it as one. Ready to go?"

She'd forgotten that this dress might cause her to flash people on the back of his bike, and she slid on behind him quickly, tucking the skirt in as best she could. Once she felt sure she wouldn't stop traffic, Clem settled close and wrapped her arms around his waist. It really shouldn't be legal for anyone to smell this good.

"Does that answer you?"

"That's lovely. Don't forget the helmet."

She complied, and as soon as they took off, the breeze boosted her mood. It didn't matter where she was headed, but each mile he put between them and St. Claire, she felt lighter, like the burden of keeping her coven sisters safe was melting away. The pressure of Barnabas's arrival lifted too, giving her space to breathe. That was an illusion, of course, a lie she was choosing not to disbelieve, just for this stolen moment. Clem tightened her arms around Gavin's waist, and he glanced sideways at her, though not for long. He drove the bike like he was part of it, or vice versa, and she reveled in the wildness she always repressed.

Until now. Until this moment.

The ride didn't last as long as she wished. Soon, they pulled up outside Bulldog Brewing Company. It was a charming choice, and she'd bought their beers at the market before, but it had never occurred to her to check out the place in person. Gavin pulled his helmet off, his inky hair spilling around stubbled cheeks, and a flare of heat lanced through her so fiercely that she had to tighten her thighs.

He bit his lip, adorably boyish. "I've booked us a tour and a tasting in one of the private rooms. There's a park nearby where we can walk, afterwards."

"Responsible," she commended.

"How is it?"

"The surprise?"

He nodded. "Does it measure up? I realize there are no goats, but—"

"I'm looking forward to it," she cut in. "Thank you for finding this place and making arrangements. I really needed the getaway."

Gavin laughed. "This is hardly a vacation, love."

Love?

It wasn't the first time he'd called her that, but hearing it now, it didn't feel...casual. A happy thrill rushed through her because she did feel precious, and—*crap, this is bad.*

Clem forced that response away and decided to believe it was an English thing. "Let's do this. If it's good, we can take some home."

"Home," Gavin repeated, a wistful twist to his sexy mouth.

"Figure of speech."

"It's been longer than I care to recall since I had somewhere I belonged."

Oh hell.

That was way more personal than the parameters of their relationship allowed. This was supposed to be a fling, and now he was sharing his feelings. Making *her* share them, setting a fire of curiosity that might well burn her alive, if she fed the flames. Yet she didn't shut down this conversation like she should, not when she sensed her words had the power to injure him. *Fuck, he's my enemy. I should shoot to kill.*

But Clem couldn't even bring herself to raise the figurative gun.

———

Gavin probably shouldn't have said that.

He could see in her expression that he'd edged past the line they'd drawn, but Clem only smiled slightly and linked her fingers with his.

"Right now you belong on this brewery tour."

If it wasn't the declaration he wanted to hear, at least it wasn't chastisement or a recommendation to mind his place. They arrived right on time as the brewing company employee was looking for them to take the tour. Gavin had done such things before, so he only paid half attention to the information being provided. Instead, he focused on Clem, watching when her interest sparked. Sometimes she asked pertinent questions, and the man guiding them around seemed to enjoy the exchange.

The whole place was infused with a lovely aroma, if possibly an acquired preference—yeast and hops and the sour-mash scent of fermentation. It was all exceptionally clean, properly impressive, and he followed their guide into the private tasting room, which was like a pub in miniature, all gleaming wood with tall glasses set out.

"Which of our craft brews would you like to sample? You can try three," the guide said.

Gavin privately admitted he'd already forgotten the man's name. Louis, perhaps, something with an "L" anyway.

"Honey Brown Lager for me," he said, glancing at Clem. "You can choose the other two. I'll have a sip of each."

She stared at the listing for over a minute before finally saying, "Let's try the Storm Cloud Porter and the Underground Pale Ale."

Lester or Leroy beamed at her. "Fantastic choices. I'll pour your drafts. You have the room for half an hour. Enjoy your drinks, and thanks for coming to Bulldog Brewing Company."

Once the guy left, Gavin settled at the table with his drink. It was a quality brew, just a touch sweet, but not so much as to be cloying. Mostly, it was simple and pure, a sipping lager, not something a college student would shotgun to chants of "chug, chug, chug." The porter had chocolatey notes, and the ale tasted dry and crisp. Everything they tried, he enjoyed, though the porter was his least favorite. Clem finished it happily enough, and they drank mainly in silence. He could tell she had something on her mind, but hell, so did he.

The order can't be trusted.

His grandad's unexpected email popped into his head. Gavin had been trying not to think about it, but it was proving impossible. He got up before Lazlo came to eject them to make room for the next private tour group. Clem preceded him, beelining for the park he'd mentioned.

It was late enough that the sun was setting. Not fully, because the days were long here during the summer. Just starting to drop, so the heat gave way to a softer warmth, and the sky was aglow with pink and orange, shades of gold from the falling sun.

She chose a path that led through an avenue of carefully manicured trees with whitewashed trunks. Gavin had always wondered about the purpose of painting the bark. Did it discourage pests? When they'd walked for a few minutes, she sighed and stretched, raising her arms heavenward.

"You want to tell me?" she asked without looking at him.

"About what?"

"Whatever has you so distracted. I'm not taking offense that you can't give me your complete attention, but you seem quite agitated. Your hand's been curled into a fist for the last five minutes, and that's after drinking the beer. I bet your whole body's tied in knots."

He was surprised to find that she was right. Deliberately he uncurled his hand and rolled his neck, but he couldn't pop it. There were hard limits on what he could share with her, but maybe he could provide some semblance of an explanation.

"When I was a lad, my grandad fell in love with someone... unsuitable. Da disapproved, and they quarreled. I've not heard from my grandfather in twenty years. Today, out of the blue, I got an email from him, and the news was...unsettling. Not sure what to make of it yet. I suppose you'd say I'm still processing."

Clem stared at him, eyes wide. "Twenty years, wow. Were you close before...everything happened?"

"We were." He appreciated her for not requesting more information than he'd provided, because it would be impossible to articulate why Grandad's partner was inadvisable.

Possibly, he could've let her think his dad was homophobic, but it wasn't the fact that grandad ran off with another man that bothered Jason Rhys. Of all things, the man was a sodding witch, one Kevin Rhys had been sent to deal with, complicating matters further. And Gavin had spent his whole life proving there was nothing wrong with the Rhys line of hunters; they weren't collaborators or traitors.

"It's not okay when parents get their children involved in issues like that," she said. "My parents are divorced, and I feel like they're constantly trying to get me to pick a favorite or validate their questionable life choices."

Gently Gavin cupped her chin, tilting her shadowed face up so he could see her expression. "Did something happen?"

"Just more of what is, unfortunately, my normal. My dad's in town with my fourth stepmother, and she's younger than I am by four or five years."

"Yikes."

She lifted a shoulder, feigning indifference so well that he almost believed her. "Divorce is the gift that keeps on giving."

"How many times has your mum been down the aisle then?"

"Twice. Once with Barnabas and again with Dougal. There's no arguing that it's Barnabas's fault—he's a serial cheater—but sometimes I blame her for picking him in the first place. If my mom was a better judge of character, my life would be less messy. I know that's not fair, and I'd never say that to her, but—"

"It's how you feel. I can understand that. Feelings don't have to be fair as long as we're not hurting others with them."

She smiled fully for what might be the first time since he'd picked her up. "You're a good listener, English."

"Ah, there it is. I'd almost forgotten where I'm from, but now you've reminded me and it's all good."

Clem laughed, pointing out, "You don't say 'bloody' or 'bollocks' nearly as much as I feel like you should. Isn't there a quota?"

"Would it make you feel better if I called you a—"

"Nope," she cut in.

"You don't even know what I was about to say," Gavin objected.

"True. And let's keep the mystery alive. Are you hungry?"

"I am. Shall we soak up some of the liquor so I can drive us back?"

"Sounds awesome." She patted her bag, and he had no idea why, until she added, "I have clean underwear, a toothbrush, and a box of condoms in here. Just so you know."

He blinked. "I collect that means you're planning to stay over."

"It's not really a plan, per se. But I'm ready and willing if you want me."

If *I want you? What nonsense is that?*

"I want you," he said huskily. "In a little while, I'll prove precisely how much."

CHAPTER 12

CLEM WISHED THIS MOMENT DIDN'T feel so right or so inevitable.

They'd both gotten tested in their spare time, and they showed each other the results after placing their food order. She'd also told him she had an implant, since she couldn't exactly confess she was on witch birth control. Their seats on the terrace offered a charming river view, and it amused Clem to prove they were both safe to smash under such romantic circumstances. Once that hurdle was cleared, they enjoyed a delicious meal of spinach and artichoke dip followed by chicken Caesar salad, and then they headed to his place.

Hers was too well warded and contained too much trace magic for her to invite him in casually. The place would need to be fully prepped and cleansed before he crossed the threshold. But...she didn't want to think about witch stuff. Not now. Not when she needed the pretense that this was like any other fling.

"How's Benson?" she asked as she walked into his front hallway.

Gavin brightened immediately. "He's acclimating much faster

than I expected. I've been talking to him and giving him treats. Little chap climbed into the palm of my hand earlier."

I'm glad Priya's spell is working. Likely it wouldn't occur to Gavin to do any tracking in the heart of his own home, and the small magic the vivimancer had used on the mouse would fade quickly. She glanced over at the cage, where Benson was running on the wheel like mad.

Clem smiled, wondering what the mouse was thinking. Pets that received an infusion of vivimancer magic tended to be smarter and to live longer. "Glad you're bonding."

"Mind if I wash up?" Gavin asked then.

"Not at all."

With a smile, he vanished into the bedroom, leaving her to listen to him shower. If they were in a proper relationship and this wasn't their first time, she might have squeezed in there with him, despite it being an efficiency unit sized for one. With sufficient enthusiasm, such issues could be overcome, especially if the participants didn't mind making a mess.

When Gavin stepped out of the bathroom, clad only in a white towel, she licked her lips reflexively, imagining how incredible it would be to catch the water droplets glistening on his abs. He smiled at her, a deep and heated look that warmed his eyes to molten silver and curled his lips in a way that expressly invited a kiss.

"That look is going right to my head," he said. The towel tented, demonstrating his meaning clearly.

"Good enough to eat. But first, let me shower. Try to keep that level of eagerness."

"It won't be hard," he said. "Or shall I say 'difficult'? It's more accurate."

Clem grinned. "Five minutes, max. Then I'm climbing you like a tree."

Flashing him a smile that showed none of her inner turmoil, she sauntered into the bathroom. Maybe she didn't need to rinse off since she'd showered earlier, but she had ridden his bike and walked around in the summer heat. Since he'd bathed, she should as well. In intimate matters, it seemed better to err on the side of smelling fresh and fantastic.

She removed her pretty summer dress carefully and hung it on the hook on the back of the door, left her panties on the bathroom floor. Then she hesitated. She'd applied the tincture, and she shouldn't get her entire body wet. Clem satisfied herself with a quick spot wash. There was a peculiar intimacy in using the same shower gel as Gavin. Sure, it hadn't been personally selected by him but still, they'd smell the same, just with the products given a slightly different twist by personal pheromones. As promised, she was quick and wrapped up in the other solitary towel offered for use.

When she emerged, she found Gavin hadn't budged, still waiting for her in the living area. On impulse, she launched herself at him, and he caught her. They kissed like a tsunami making landfall, a wet and messy wave that had Clem touching every part of him she could reach while their lips clung and tongues tangled. He carried her easily, though they both lost their towels on the way to the bedroom. She dug her fingers into his back as he kissed a scorching line down her throat.

This didn't feel like a hookup so much as life support, as if she'd die when Gavin stopped. Pleasure coiled deep inside her, growing more powerful with each graze of his mouth. The attraction broke briefly when he dropped her on the bed, but he came down to her immediately, and she wrapped herself around him, conscious that her magic wasn't sparking wildly as it sometimes did when she fooled around with a mundane.

Instead, it rolled inside her in a steady purr, as if it was well content with this decision. And if that seemed strange, Gavin didn't allow her to dwell on it. His lips and hands were everywhere, and it seemed as if he had psychic tendencies because each touch, each kiss, felt better than the last, until she was squirming and breathless.

"You are breathtaking," he whispered against the soft skin of her belly.

Her knees came up and splayed wide, a silent invitation for him to keep going. Clem tangled her fingers in his shaggy hair as he teased a path lower until her whole body quivered with anticipation.

And when he finally went in, she let out an incredibly needy sound, one she'd never made before. His lips on her, his tongue working slowly, softly, circling her clit with exactly the right pressure. He was gentler than he looked when he pulled her legs over his shoulders and buried his face between them like he never needed to come up for air. He played with his lips and fingers, his tongue surging softly, and she lifted her hips to chase the feeling building in long pulses and tingles.

With enough patience, she'd come this way, and he coaxed

her to the edge several times before pulling back on the pressure, teasing her with swirling licks on her thighs and belly instead. Just enough for the need to recede, and then he started again. The cycle continued until her pussy throbbed, and she couldn't take anymore.

Clem yanked on his hair, hard. "Finish me with your mouth. Or your cock. Even your fingers, I don't care. But please."

She didn't beg. She never begged. Yet he had her desperate, the most turned on she'd ever been in her life.

"Greed looks good on you." Despite her death grip on his hair, he was smiling, and she took a certain pride in the juices glistening on his mouth. Gavin crawled up her body, and he sheathed himself smoothly in a condom and then settled between her thighs. She raised up to kiss him, her breasts brushing his chest. A current ran between them; to her it felt like magic, but hopefully he'd register it as potent sexual chemistry, thanks to Ethel's tincture. With any luck, Gavin wouldn't have banged any other witches, therefore he'd have no basis for comparison.

Even knowing this was an extreme form of risk, she couldn't stop. Didn't even want to. *If I get caught, it might even be worth it.*

The moment her mouth touched his, she tasted herself on his lips, and she sucked her own flavor from his tongue. He finally groaned, as if he found that to be irresistibly hot, and then he was tongue fucking her lips, long strokes that echoed how he craved to claim her. Gavin lined up his cock and slid into her in one thrust, holding still when he was fully seated.

She rolled her hips, delighted to finally be getting to him. He grunted when she squeezed her inner muscles around him, his eyes fluttering closed. Goddess, she'd love a photo of his face, precisely like this, enraptured and agonized at the same time. She wrapped her thighs around his hips and moved, enticing him to do the same.

This time, he groaned, seeming unable to resist. "You're so hot," he breathed.

"Because of you." To punctuate her words, she bit his shoulder, nuzzling a path to his neck, where he was most sensitive, and he jerked in immediate response, pushing faster, harder. "You liked that."

She sank her teeth into his throat, just a little nip, and he let out a growl. "Stop goading me. It's been a while, and I want this to be good for you."

"And I want *you* to lose control. We can't both meet our goals."

Another slide of her teeth, followed by the sweep of her tongue. She sucked hard on the bite, and he gasped, hips moving in a quick and jerky rhythm, the sign of him unraveling for her, exactly as she wanted.

Wanted. Hell, she needed it.

After the way he'd teased her, her own orgasm no longer seemed as important as seeing the look on his face when he yielded to her utterly, giving more of himself than she could admit that she wanted. Clem worked herself on his cock, trying to nudge them both past the point of no return. He kissed her to stop the torment her mouth offered his neck and shoulders, but when she pulled his tongue into her mouth and sucked it, his cock pulsed. More magic crackled between them, and his cock swelled, like the pleasure and the energy drew a response from the deepest and wildest part of him.

"That's it, love. Just like that. I can't hold it. Christ, you feel good."

"Don't even try. If you come, I will. I'm so close. Fuck yes."

———————

Gavin went off like a rocket from her hot whisper in his ear.

He didn't even know when he'd lost his grip on himself. He pushed deep and held, hot spurts rocking him from head to toe. In all honesty, he couldn't be certain she'd gotten off; he was so lost in his own pleasure. Normally, he wasn't like that. Being inside her did something to him, lit him up in a way he couldn't articulate or explain. If he didn't think he would sound absurd, he might even say she felt...right, in a lock-and-key sense, akin to coming home.

Yeah, I can't tell her that.

Clem held him through the aftermath, stroking his back until he recovered enough to dispose of the condom and return to bed on shaky legs. Though he'd known sex between them would be intense, he never could've predicted it would leave him feeling oddly hollowed out yet complete at the same time, as if they'd exchanged more than bodily fluids.

"I can't believe I have to ask," he muttered, sliding back into bed to curl himself around her. "But did you..."

Her eyes laughed at him. "Definitely. There's nothing sexier than feeling you lose it."

"I'll remember that."

He wrapped his arms around her and snuggled her to his

chest, breathing in the clean smell of her sweat-damp hair mingling deliciously with the scent of sex. She cuddled up without resisting and trailed her fingers down his chest, creating faint sparks of excitement, even though they'd just finished.

Is that normal? It's not.

At least she wasn't immediately scrambling to put her clothes on. Since the terms of their arrangement only accounted for hookups, she didn't have to spend the night, even if he wanted her to. Now that he'd gotten her into bed, he didn't think he could let her go willingly. She did pack an overnight bag, so perhaps he had hope of keeping her for a night anyway.

We'll have to get up for food eventually, I suppose.

It came to him that this was the happiest he'd been in longer than he could recall. His vocation had never given him any joy, only endless tension with bonus emotional blackmail. He'd enjoyed being a lecturer at university, but he wasn't allowed to stay in the position long enough to form attachments. Now it offered a convenient excuse for him to be traveling. And even while he was teaching, Da didn't let up on the pressure, reminding him that no matter what job he chose as his "cover," it would never be the reality of who and what he was. It had been like living as a secret agent, in some respects, only he remained unconvinced about the sanctity of the mission.

Sometimes, even before his grandad reached out, he'd wondered...*if it's so vital, why did he leave?* And now, he had the warning added to his own quiet doubts. There was so much secrecy in the order, so much that mustn't be asked about or spoken of.

"You seem conflicted," she said, tracing a fingertip down his nose instead of his chest.

"I wonder if you know how unsettling it is for you to notice such things so swiftly."

"Should I apologize?"

"No, it's rather nice when I get over the shock of it."

"You deflected." She called out his evasion without hesitation. "It's your choice, of course. There's no need to tell me anything if you'd rather not."

She rolled over and kissed his left cheek and then his right, taking advantage of his slow, startled blink to press her soft lips to each eyelid as well. That unexpected tenderness created a well of longing in his chest—to widen the terms of their relationship so she might offer more, like long, lazy Sundays in bed or being willing to receive his call any day, any hour, to listen to his troubles.

"Who knew an orgasm would make you so gentle?"

"You'd rather I bite you?" Clem joked. "Why not, you seemed to enjoy it a lot before."

"Vixen," he breathed.

Truthfully, he'd loved the hint of viciousness in her teeth, soothed by the incredible heat of her sheathing his cock. The twin sensations practically did him in. Just remembering it had him half ready to go again, and she must have felt the little nudge against her because her lips curled in a beautiful, knowing smile.

"Damn, look at you."

Heat flared in his cheeks, and he buried his face in the curve of her shoulder. "It's entirely your fault, I assure you."

"Hmm. Normally I'd argue against an accusation, but I find

this one rather enticing, so I'll admit culpability this once. What's my punishment?"

"Stay the night," he said, before he could help himself. To render the request less emotional and needy, he added, "I know I'll want you again."

"From my observations, you already do," she teased.

"That's true enough. But I'm willing to let you sleep a little first."

"You think we need a nap? I'm willing. I like slow, sleepy, just-woke-up sex. Maybe I'll surprise you by putting my mouth somewhere fun as soon as you let your guard down."

An irresistible tremor ran through him. "If you're asking for my permission, you have it."

"Excellent." Closing her eyes, she snuggled into his side with every appearance of relaxation, and soon, she was breathing deeply.

At first, her ease irked him to no end, but then it occurred to him that she wouldn't be able to relax if she didn't trust him. Perhaps that ought to trouble him, as he hadn't been upfront or honest in his dealings with her. But some small part of him still reveled in being someone who made her feel safe, despite the rough image he projected. Since he often had to travel to unsavory places as part of his mission, he'd learned that sometimes the best protection was coming across like the biggest bastard, one nobody wanted to try.

Eventually, he drifted off to the sound of her deep, measured breathing. And for once, the next time he roused, it wasn't to the shrill ring of an alarm or an urgent call. Instead, just as she'd promised, Clem was burrowed beneath the covers, her mouth moving on him lusciously. His cock was hard enough to hurt, so she'd obviously been sucking him for a while. His balls were tight, tingles rolling up his spine.

Before he could say a word, he was coming, right in her mouth.

What a delicious way to wake up.

The incredible part was, his cock didn't even go soft, and he rolled her beneath him with even more need gnawing at him.

No matter how many times I have her, it will never be enough.

This time he didn't think about anything but fucking her. He drove into her with a hungry grunt, needing to feel her come all over his dick.

She let out a needy whine, and he could feel that she'd gotten absolutely soaked playing with him as he slept. That drove him even wilder.

Gavin pumped into her, lifting her hips to get deeper, and she went crazy when he grazed the right spot inside her. Clem screamed and clawed his back, already coming. A hot, tingling sensation swept over him, and it was as if he could feel himself fucking her, a layer of sensation that added to his pleasure and arousal.

Since he'd just gotten off, he came dry, so hard, he nearly blacked out.

CHAPTER 13

"I'VE MADE A TERRIBLE MISTAKE," Clem told Ethel, two days later.

"Did it involve three longshoremen and a bottle of Scotch?" the older witch asked.

Clem blinked. "What? No."

"Yes! My record holds."

For a moment, she was so tempted to ask for details, but with sheer heroic effort, she corralled her curiosity and stayed on task. "Okay, we're putting a pin in that because I need to hear that story. But can we get back to my issue?"

Ethel rose, stretched, and turned toward the kitchen. "Sure, why not? I'll get the iced tea."

"Hey, good lookin'," said Percy.

Tiredly, Clem waved at the parrot. She'd crept out of Gavin's apartment at dawn, and she hadn't contacted him since. To make matters worse, Danica had disappeared because of some impulsive decision-making. If not for the coven group chat, Clem wouldn't have known her cousin had gone to freaking Arizona while she was busy minding the shop.

With Danica gone, she was working from open to close. It was tough to make repair calls because that meant Clem had to shut down the shop to do it, and she hated hanging that BACK BY whenever sign because she might miss business while she was gone. Still, some appliances couldn't be hauled in easily, so she had no choice but to head over to someone's house to check out their fridge or maybe a washer-dryer. Sometimes there were perverts who just wanted an excuse to get her in the house.

Eventually, Ethel returned to the parlor with two tall glasses that glistened with condensation. Impossible not to think of Gavin, who would doubtless prefer his served hot. She sipped at the drink and sighed as Ethel settled in the comfy, overstuffed chair across from her.

"You've encountered a snag in your flawless plan?" Sarcasm that thick could've been cut with a knife and served on fancy cake plates.

Clem aimed a filthy look at Ethel, who didn't even flinch. Percy, on the other hand, ran up and down his perch, shouting curses. Which was pretty much how Clem felt too.

"I didn't have a plan," she admitted. "Not really. Other than trying to get his mind off witches in general and locked onto me."

"Now you're hoist by your own petard," Ethel said. It wasn't a question, and she let out a chuckle. "Always wanted to say that, so thank you. I'm ticking it right off the bucket list."

"You don't have a bucket list, you'll live to be a thousand."

Suddenly somber, Ethel shook her head. "I would never. The cost of immortality is too high, my dear."

For the second time that day, Clem found herself speechless.

The older witch certainly knew the most among anyone in their coven, and she liked to allude to certain secrets, but this was the first Clem had heard about any spell for immortality. Like the story about the three longshoremen and the bottle of Scotch, she was ever so tempted to be distracted by it. This time she failed her saving throw.

I'll kick myself later if I don't ask.

"Are you serious?" She wanted to know.

"As a late tax return. There are reasons why vampirism is tied to witchcraft in the old stories. They say witches created the first of the night children, right? But it would be more accurate to report that witches *became* the first night children. Through old magic, exceedingly difficult, exceptionally rare, and born of blood."

"Damn," Clem said. Then she narrowed her eyes, half waiting for the *gotcha*. "Is this where you admit you're fucking with me?"

Ethel shook her head, serenely drinking her tea. "It's up to you whether you believe me. But this much more I will say, the night children are part of why the witch hunters persecute us."

That was a lot to take in, dropped on her suddenly. "Witch hunters blame us because ancient witches figured out how to unlock immortality via drinking human blood?"

"That's not the whole story," Ethel said, "but it's one aspect. The order keeps its own secrets, and these days, they pretend they have a holy calling."

"Gavin is certainly not celibate," Clem muttered, still reeling from the prior revelation.

Vampires are real. They're really old witches.

That might blow out the back of her head if she thought about it for too long. On some level, it shouldn't be that shocking—she was a witch after all—but this was how she imagined a mundane would feel if they accidentally learned that magic and witches were real—shocked, awed, and mildly overwhelmed.

"I'll refrain from asking for the steamy details. Let's get back to your issue. You said you've made a terrible mistake, and then I derailed you. Sorry about that."

Clem let out a shuddering breath. It was early evening, just past moonrise, and she gazed out at the night sky, stars slowly shimmering into sight, with the small amount of light pollution St. Claire offered.

"You were right, more or less. I had too much pride when I started this because I'd never met anyone who…" What were even the right words?

"Could take your breath away? Make you forget everything except—"

"Yes. That. All of that. I'm talking to you about it instead of the rest of the coven because I can't stand the teasing. It's too fresh. You're usually a bit more measured even with mockery."

Ethel gave a crooked smile. "Thanks?"

"You are so welcome," Percy shouted. Then he added, "Who's a pretty bird?"

"I'm guessing that's rhetorical," Clem said dryly.

"Are you here for sympathy or advice? I can offer both."

Clem sat forward in her chair, setting down the iced tea. "Then I'll take both. I need some guidance because I'm over my head, and you're the one I trust the most."

The other witch laughed softly. "Are you flattering me on purpose? Never mind if you are. I'll take it. First I need to ask you something."

"Go ahead."

"How far are you prepared to go? Is there a line you won't cross?"

She closed her eyes, knowing what Ethel was truly asking. "I don't want to hurt him. Hell, I don't even want him to leave, not anymore, but he must. For the coven to be safe."

With a nod, Ethel seemed to process that and file it away for future analysis. "Have you read through my mother's notes yet?"

Clem shook her head. "Not entirely. It would help if I knew the dates. There are so many journals…"

"You must've expected that when you carted off a whole bunch," Ethel said tartly. "Writing longhand in journals was the blogging of the thirties."

Clem grinned at that. "Fair enough. But you promised both sympathy and advice, and so far, I've seen neither."

"Fine." The older witch crossed the room and perched beside her, encircling her shoulders with a gentle arm. "We've all done things we know are unwise. You're not the first, and you haven't shared anything that shocked me."

"Now that's a good effort." Clem leaned into the hug.

Since her family dynamics were profoundly fucked up, she found it easier to accept comfort from someone unrelated to the whole mess, easier to let her guard down too because she knew Ethel wouldn't use her vulnerability as ammunition in some private war.

"It's not my first time. As to the practical advice, that is a little more difficult."

"It's a hard-knock life," said Percy.

Clem sighed. "You got that right."

"Give me a few. I'll do a little scrying and see if the dead have any suggestions."

A shiver ran down Clem's spine. No matter how often she saw Ethel thread the needle and whisper across the veil, it always creeped her out. Even for a witch, there were some boundaries that weren't meant to be crossed.

But since this was so important, she got to her feet. "Are your supplies in the same place? I'll help you set up."

"Of course. I'm too lazy to reorganize."

"Then I'll fetch everything and back you up." Clem headed to the crafting room that was bright explosion of fabrics, spell components, half-made jewelry, and charms in progress.

Ethel brought out her copper scrying bowl and said, "Let's discover what the spirits have to say about you and that handsome witch hunter."

She settled across the table from the older witch and lit the candles. Since this wasn't her first time, she borrowed Ethel's athame and used it to inscribe protective sigils around the casting circle, and then she sat quietly feeding Ethel energy through the flickering flames. More than most witches, Clem tended to use the candles as a focus.

Slowly, the room built up a soft charge, and the water in the bowl roiled, but instead of producing a vision, milky shapes appeared in the liquid, rising from the tureen in smoky wisps that chilled the air around them. Gooseflesh rose on Clem's arms. *Hell, I hate being surrounded by spirits.* This wasn't something Ethel did lightly, and Clem made sure not to look directly at the spirits because sometimes they took offense to it, as they didn't look as they had in life.

"We seek to divert a hunter from his course. Can you offer aid or guidance?" Ethel asked.

Sibilant whispers hissed all around them, and Clem experienced an icy shock on the nape of her neck. Hunching her shoulders, she clung to her courage, knowing how dangerous it was to break the circle. Finally, the disparate murmurs resolved into an intelligible response.

"There is a lost spell. One may find it to buy enough time to save you. But what must be, *will* be. Only love can turn the blade aside."

With every breath, Gavin hated this obligation more.

He was crouched in a cornfield in the middle of the night, watching Dale the Prepper enact an incredibly baffling ritual. The man had been running laps outside his house since the sun went down, dodging through a makeshift obstacle course built of rusty barrels, scaffolding, barricade signs, netting and rope, and a lot of metal tubing.

Is this what Mina meant when she mentioned the man's strange construction project?

It was hot as the fires of hell crouched in the ripening rows of corn. The wind whistled through the field, carrying a dusty tang that filled his mouth with grit, and sweat rolled down his back. So far, Dale hadn't done anything that suggested magic, but he could see why Leonard had called this bastard weird.

Once he finished his extended workout, Dale was shouting at the top of his lungs—in no language that Gavin had ever heard. To the outsider, it might even seem like the man was possessed. Honestly, it was a wonder no Catholic priests had come to try their luck.

Who knows, maybe there are a few hiding out here with me.

The mental image of a stern father in a cassock squatting in the corn nearly made Gavin laugh out loud. He had no idea what he'd say if Dale caught him. At best, this was trespassing.

To avoid potential problems in town, he'd taken the baker out for a beer to make amends, and everything seemed fine. St. Claire was overall very welcoming. Gavin doubted that would hold if he got caught doing something as sketchy as lurking in a cornfield to spy on the town oddball. And hell, Gavin didn't want Clem thinking he was gonzo. That wasn't a normal concern either. Usually he planned to leave as soon as he accomplished his assignment, nothing to hold him back.

On impulse, he crept closer until he managed to record a fragment of Dale's shouting. In fact the man was starkers now and shaking a fist at the heavens, the most jaw-dropping display Gavin had ever witnessed. Dale returned to running laps, which went on for over an hour. He was sweaty as hell when he finally stopped yelling and stumbled back into his house.

With a muttered curse, Gavin retreated through the cornfield, hoping the Ducati was still where he'd left it. Otherwise, it would be a long hike home. Even riding the Duc, it was still past 2:00 a.m. by the time he got in. He'd turned his phone off before he went on the recon run, and when he turned it on and plugged it in to charge, he had no new messages.

Surprising on one hand, normally his father would be berating him by now. Disappointing on another, because he feared Clem was already tying up the loose ends on their fling, like a package with a bow on it, ready to be presented to someone else. Dammit, he didn't want anyone else getting their hands on Clem. She was his gift to savor.

The truth irritated him fiercely. *No. She's not. She's not your anything.*

In a foul mood, he stalked into the bathroom and scrubbed a night's sweat off his skin, along with the dirt that clung to it. His sheets still smelled faintly like Clem, and he couldn't gather the fortitude to wash them when he might finish his mission and get orders to move out at any time.

Maybe it's for the best.

Settling on the bed, he closed his eyes and extended what he thought of as hunting senses. But the night was quiet; he sensed none of the magical spikes that had gotten St. Claire on the order's radar in the first place. From what he could tell, nobody was casting spells tonight, whatever the hell Dale had been doing. Which reminded him...

He played the sound bite for his phone assistant, and when it identified the language, Gavin couldn't hold his laughter. He laughed until his sides hurt.

"Klingon? He was shouting in Klingon."

Since it was a poor-quality recording, he couldn't produce an actual translation, so for all he knew, Dale was demanding that the Trek universe come to collect him immediately.

Probably not a witch.

Sadly, to rule it out entirely, he would have to observe Dale multiple times to make sure his more eccentric behavior wasn't a cunning ruse to throw off someone like Gavin, sandwiching actual magic between wild fits and starts. He sighed, not looking forward to more nights in the cornfield. That was special punishment, even for a bastard like him. It was like a scene from a horror film, and if he'd been attacked by a maniac with a hunting knife, he wouldn't have been shocked.

It was nearly three by this time, far too late to think about texting Clem, who had to be up to open the shop. He forced himself to listen to a book instead, playing it until dawn crept across the floor on little mouse feet. Eventually he drifted off and dreamt of her, curled softly into his side, leaving blissful traces all over his bed.

Gavin woke with a start, someone rapping on his door. Since he rarely got visitors, he stumbled out warily, dressing in haste in a T-shirt and a pair of athletic shorts.

To his surprise, it was Mina, the landlady who had given him advice about the area. She wore a bright smile, offering a piping-hot plate of cinnamon rolls. "I picked some up at the bakery, and they're too delicious not to share. If you don't eat sugar or—"

"I'd never turn those down," he cut in. The pastries looked incredible, large and golden, dark with cinnamon, and drizzled liberally with a glass sugar glaze.

Mina grinned. "I feel the same way. We don't indulge often, but sometimes I'm shopping downtown and can't resist the smell."

"These came from Sugar Daddy's?" he guessed.

Despite making peace with Titus after his 5-hour Energy fueled outburst, he doubted the baker would be glad if he popped in even as a patron. He'd stormed in because the traces of magic were strong there, but he didn't sense anything from Titus or his sister. Ranting about witches—*ugh*, he cringed just thinking about the loose hinge on his mouth that day.

"You've already heard of it?" She seemed delighted, like a proud auntie boasting of her relative's achievements. "Mrs. Carminian says there are people who drive an hour to try these."

"And all I had to do was get out of bed. You're truly an angel to think of me."

She glanced at his presumably rumpled hair with a teasing expression. "Sorry to wake you. Since it's past ten, I thought you'd be up. You must've been burning the midnight oil."

That was clearly an invitation to gossip, but he wasn't about to admit what he'd been doing. "Working on my paper," he offered.

"Understood. I won't keep you. Enjoy the rolls. I'll stop by tomorrow to get the plate."

She went back down the stairs with a wave, and as Gavin settled in to enjoy the unexpected baked bounty, his phone rang. *Da never fails to find the perfect moment to step on my joy,* he reflected. *I didn't even get a take a bite, dammit.* The moment was spoiled because he had no doubt his father would ruin his mood and his ability to savor the treat. He answered the call and waited in silence for the complaint.

"You haven't found anything yet? Are you even looking?" came the snappish words. "I'm warning you, don't faff about. You won't like the results."

I never fucking do.

CHAPTER 14

SINCE THE SPIRIT CONSULTATION WITH Ethel, Clem slept with Gavin four more times.

I can't stay away.

She crept into the house in case her cousin was finally back from her extended vacation with Titus "the Rebound" Winnaker, and when she reached the stairs, Danica called, "Busted!"

Clem jumped. She was edgy as hell these days, but she was in no mood to be teased, considering how much slack she'd taken up for her cousin.

Folding her arms, she tilted her head, trying not to act defensive. "Okay, let's go. You're in *no* position to comment on anything I do. You fucking *left the state* without talking to me about it. You disregarded our promise like it was nothing and didn't even have the courtesy to text me. And you left me minding the shop for *how* long? Cousins who are like sisters, my ass."

Danica didn't even try to mount a defense. "You're absolutely right. I'm pleading temporary insanity. And scientifically speaking, falling in love creates a similar—"

"Oh no, you don't," Clem cut in. "If you make me laugh, I have to forgive you, and I'm not ready to do that yet."

"I'm so sorry. The way I handled everything was shit. In hindsight, I'd have done so many things differently. But I have something important to tell you, and I think it might affect your commitment to the single life when you hear it."

Exhaustion swept over her as she sank into an armchair with a sigh. "Start talking."

"I visited my mom yesterday, and I happened to see one of her old journals. Apparently, there's no Waterhouse curse. We don't have to keep our witch lines pure, and I'm not losing my magic. Gram made the whole thing up. My mom is so mad, she said she'd 'deal' with Gram."

"Holy fucking shit," Clem breathed.

"My thoughts exactly. It was a way to control us, to keep us fearful and from going against her wishes."

Clem snarled another curse as the implications sank in. Oh, she'd known Gram could be manipulative and prone to passive-aggressive behavior, but she'd put up with it because she never doubted the old witch loved her family. Even so, she'd never imagined this depth and breadth of duplicity.

"Aunt Min really said she'd take Gram on?" she finally asked.

"Shit's about to get heated." Danica made a ridiculous face.

A chuckle escaped her. "I mean...it's summer, so it's already—oh crap. I laughed."

"Yes! Does that mean I'm forgiven?"

"You're cooking in my place for two weeks, but yeah. There's no reason for us to worry about taking sides anymore. She's still our grandmother, but she's—"

"A hateful, manipulative old witch?"

Clem closed her eyes. "Yeah. It's so hard to reconcile with how awesome she was when we were kids. Guess we have to remember that just because she was nice to us, it doesn't mean she didn't hurt other people."

Danica nodded, pulling the blanket up around her shoulders. "Agreed. I haven't decided if I'm cutting her off entirely yet. I probably need to talk to Mom more. That's where the problem started. Gram raised us believing that our mothers were weak—that they didn't have anything of value to teach us. Maybe she didn't say it outright, but..."

"It was insidious, this slow and careful indoctrination. Fuck!" Fists clenched, Clem leapt to her feet. "I need a shower."

Danica opened her arms. "Hug it out? We'll always be best friends, even after we mate for life."

"Ugh, fine."

"Something you want to tell me, Clementine Odette?" Her cousin seemed to be looking at the side of Clem's neck.

Irritation practically overwhelmed her. "If you *ever* drop my middle name again, I won't be responsible for the consequences."

Danica shook her head. "You didn't answer the question."

With a groan, Clem buried her face in her hands. "I'm in so much trouble."

"What's wrong?" her cousin asked.

"I can't stop sleeping with him!"

"The hunter him? Gavin Rhys."

"Yeah," she muttered.

"Fuck," Danica said.

"That's precisely the problem. It's like I'm bewitched."

"I guess that's one way to distract him. Not the path I would've chosen, but maybe…"

Clem sighed. "I'll figure it out. And for the record, you're forgiven. We're good."

It was easy to say that, not so much to mean it deep in her heart, but she had to be the bigger person so they could get past this. *Damn, I have a lot to process.* On the plus side, however, at least she didn't need to feel guilty about disregarding Gram's bullshit about giving Barnabas a second chance. With the Lughnasadh approaching, she was waiting for that shoe to drop. So far, Barnabas had tested that she still had his number blocked—four calls today and counting. He'd proceeded to sending emails; Allegra and D-Pop would be arriving soon.

Won't that be fun?

She'd worked nonstop while Danica had her mini breakdown and now, finally, she could take some time off. Danica offered to let Clem rest at least, and she took her cousin up on it. Clem's brain hurt from fretting, and she was no closer to deciding a course of action than she had been. Priya and Kerry had been calling, asking why she wasn't down to hang out. Same with Vanessa, Leanne, and Margie. The only person who had the full picture was Ethel, but the older witch wouldn't say a word until Clem was ready to do it herself.

Hell if I know when that will be, though.

With a tired sigh, she called Priya, knowing she was the least likely to ask difficult questions. The other witch picked up on the second ring.

"I've been so worried about you! The stories the squirrels tell me are most alarming." Priya probably wasn't joking either.

"Nosy bastards," she muttered.

"Your lights are on at all hours, it's to be expected. Now what's up?"

"I need to reapply the sigils that keep my power on the down low," she said.

She had been using a combination of Ethel's tinctures combined with life magic runes, and goddess knew what would happen if she relaxed her precautions even for an instant. *Calamity. Mayhem. Calm down, you're coping. It's fine.*

"That, I can assist with. Do you want to come over?"

"If you can, it'd be better if you came over here. Danica wants to have a party to mingle the coven with Titus's pals, and if Gavin finds out, he'll think it's weird if I don't invite him."

Priya was silent for a long moment. "That...is a big risk."

"I'm aware. I have to completely dismantle the wards for the night and cleanse the premises." Exhaustion swept over her just thinking about it.

"We'll *all* need some of Ethel's dampening charms so we don't trigger his witch hunter senses," Priya pointed out.

Clem sighed. "I know it's complicated. Ethel told me she and Gladys are already carrying them, and that they socialize with him at the coffee klatch. So far, so good."

"You're asking us to assemble as a coven," Priya said in a cool tone. "And socialize with a hunter. Please think about what you're suggesting for a second."

Since Priya was normally quite easygoing, it highlighted the recklessness of her plan. "It's the best way to throw him off the scent. If we pass this hurdle, I suspect he'll decide the magical signature belonged to a witch traveling through."

"And then he'll leave town." Priya fell quiet again, probably weighing the risks against the potential rewards. "Fine. I'll help you, but it's against my better judgment. This might be the most nerve-racking party any of us have ever attended. For multiple reasons."

"Thanks. What time can you make it?"

"I'm still at work. Be there in two hours. Have everything set up for me," Priya said briskly.

"On it."

Clem was about to take a nap when someone knocked on the front door. She was half expecting Hazel Jeffords with some complaint about Goliath, but instead, she found her mother, Allegra, and her stepdad, D-Pop. Allegra was thin and graceful; she took after Gram in appearance more than Minerva, and she favored the same classic style: simple color combinations instead of patterns, natural fabrics, and elegant accessories. Today, she had on sand-linen capri pants, polished coral toes, and sandals with a wedge heel, paired with a lemon-yellow sleeveless blouse. And from how fresh Allegra looked, nobody would ever guess that she'd flown in from Florida that day. D-Pop was a little grubbier in a wrinkled polo shirt and cargo shorts, sporting a beard that suggested he'd never heard a Jimmy Buffett song he didn't adore.

No wonder Gram doesn't like him.

D-Pop radiated a sort of scruffy chill and tended to greet everyone with egalitarian aplomb. Even now, he joined Allegra in the hug, but where her mom was careful not to muss herself, Dougal gave Clem a big squeeze and patted her back.

"Good to see you, darling Clementine."

Normally, she'd hit anyone who called her that, but for some reason, she didn't mind it from D-Pop because he always smiled beatifically, eyes crinkled up, his face leathery above the beard from twenty years without sunscreen under the Florida rays.

"You too, D-Pop." She'd never been able to get herself to call him "Dad," but she didn't say that to her sperm donor either. He beamed at her and offered a fist bump. At least he didn't object to D-Pop, just as she let him get away with "darling Clementine."

"You look pretty," she said to Allegra, because Mom loved hearing that.

And frankly, it was true. Allegra looked ten years younger than she was, even though she was a bit older than Dougal. His lack of skin care and the graying beard added years to his face, but his bright-blue eyes remained ever the same, always a hint of a twinkle, like life was a joke and he knew the punch line. He was also steady as a rock, unflappable no matter what crisis (real or imagined) riled Allegra up.

"Thank you!" Mom said, beaming. "I had a facial treatment, exfoliating and revitalizing, the day before we left. It's so sweet of you to notice."

Shit. I have to get rid of them in the next two hours.

"Come in." She stepped back and beckoned them inside.

They settled in the front room while she poured three glasses of fresh lemonade. Allegra wouldn't touch cookies, so she also cut up some apple and added cheese chunks for Dougal. He ate like he was hungry, maybe starved by mediocre plane food.

"Did you have a good flight?" she asked.

That gave Allegra space to vent while D-Pop inhaled cheese and apples. When her mom paused, Clem had to act fast. *Best to make things clear.*

"Did you get the cottage I had Ethel check out for you?"

Allegra brightened. "Yes! It's a delightful little place on the lake, half an hour away. There's a hot tub and all the privacy we could want."

Some of Clem's tension drained away, and she relaxed her shoulders, relieved this wouldn't be a big deal. "Sounds like a fantastic getaway."

Her mom nodded. "I'm excited to see everyone."

That was code referencing Lughnasadh rites that were coming up. As far as D-Pop was concerned, this was a combo trip meant for catching up with friends and family while taking a break from Florida in summer.

Swallowing a sigh, Clem braced herself. "It's better if you find out from me. Barnabas is in town, and he brought his fourth wife, Pansy."

Then she winced in sympathy for the neighborhood dogs as Allegra went sonic.

———

It had been too long already.

In truth, Gavin should've written back to his grandad straight-away, but he'd been so shocked at first, and then he couldn't decide what to say. If his old man found out—

"But how would he?" he asked Benson, who was currently nestled in his palm, allowing Gavin to run a gentle finger down his spine.

To Gavin's knowledge, Jason Rhys had no idea about this old Hotmail account, and if he learned about these communications, it meant he had spyware on Gavin's phone.

"Oh hell, maybe he does. Does that sound like something Da would do?"

The mouse twitched his whiskers, and for some reason, it looked like a "maybe" to Gavin. On impulse, he searched for the nearest store where he could buy a cheap netbook, as all his electronics had been provided by the order. Doing this constituted a fundamental breach in everything that had been drummed into him for as long as he could remember.

Witches are evil. Evil must be eradicated. The order will serve.

Even now, he could recite the code in his sleep, and while he *knew* there were trackers in his electronics—in case he was taken—this was the first time he'd wondered if there were actual keyloggers or if they were looking at his search history back at headquarters. Given his old man's tendency toward paranoia, it wouldn't surprise him.

Making up his mind, Gavin carefully placed Benson back in his cage, and the little chap promptly dashed to the exercise wheel; he genuinely seemed to enjoy running. Then Gavin headed out to quietly begin his rebellion. Getting on the Duc and driving to TeqMart felt revolutionary. He pulled cash at the ATM and paid with it for the netbook, earning a sideways look from the clerk. Even if it was a cheap laptop, it had to seem sketchy as hell for him to drop a bundle of notes for it, especially with the image he cultivated.

It's not too late. I could back away from this. Go back to being a good soldier.

But frankly, he'd never been a happy one, even if he had been obedient.

Why is it wrong for me to have electronics that aren't issued by the order?

The rationale was that unsecured devices could be charmed by a technomancer; a plain, store-bought unit lacked protective measures granted by official ones, and order secrets could be stolen. Now it seemed like more of a leash than any necessary safety measure.

Since this was a plug-and-play unit, it was ready to go within fifteen minutes of unpacking. Then he logged manually into his old email account without even syncing the browser on his other laptop. Just in case the order had planted something that would alert them to a secondary device.

A fresh wave of spam had buried the email from his grandad, but he pulled it up via search and reread the message. Then he clicked COMPOSE and started typing.

Dear Grandad,

I've taken the leap and I'm writing to you outside of official parameters. You know as well as anyone what that means. I was young when you left, but not too much to understand the scope of it. Da made it clear there was no going back. They erased your name from the rolls, and he caned me each time I mentioned you. Until I stopped.

But I never forgot your toad in the hole or the taste of the tea and toast you made for me. It was the best in the world, I reckon. I hope you've kept well and happy all these years. The boy in me just wants a hug and to tell you that I've missed you dreadfully. The man I've become knows it's not that simple. I can't ask you to tell me where you are and trust that I won't betray you immediately to the order.

They say a man can't row two boats, and you'd know best how I feel right now. Did you have doubts too? Did they nibble away at you, whispering questions we're not allowed to ask? I've wondered how long it went on, until you couldn't follow those orders any longer. And I've wondered what's wrong with the rest of the hunters—that they don't feel as I do.

At any rate, what I can do is ask how you've been. I'd like to hear about your partner if you're willing to share. I know little about the…

Here, Gavin hesitated. Typing the word seemed like blasphemy. But then he went on with the email.

I know little about the witch for whom you risked your life, the one you left us for. Pardon if that sounds bitter because I know it was grim choice, a snap decision. And I hope you're safe and happy. Truly.

If you're able, I'd love to learn more about your life, any details you feel safe sharing.

As for me, I'm well enough, if plagued with uncertainty. I'm starting to want to follow your path, Grandad. But I'm scared of what it would mean and what that choice would do to Da. Real men aren't afraid to admit fear, right?

Here I am, admitting, if only to you.

And finally, leaving the best—or worst—for last, what did you mean that the order can't be trusted? I read the sentence, but it's swollen to ten times its size in my head, and I need to know more. Please, tell me what you discovered, what made you run.

Please.

Love always,

Gavin

Whew. He rubbed at his eyes, mildly surprised to find tears standing in them. Immediately he wished that Clem were here because he could really fucking use a hug. As if he'd conjured her, her icon lit up his phone screen, indicating a new message.

Tomorrow night, we're having a party. Will you be my date?

Startled, he stared at the text. That…it sounded like a function that she'd invite an actual partner to, a significant other, not a hookup. Her friends would be there, most likely her cousin, and people who were permanent fixtures in Clem's life. He should refuse. He should—

No, this was exactly the sort of occasion he must leverage. And Gavin hated that thought because it came straight out of his father's playbook. *Infiltrate. Identify. Eradicate.* Briefly Gavin closed his eyes, beyond conflicted. There was no way in hell he could miss this party. He rang her up, figuring if she had time to text, he ought to get to hear her voice to offset the awful swirl of guilt in his wretched gullet.

"Hello, love. You're free?"

"But not cheap," she shot back.

Gavin laughed. Despite the awfulness of his situation, her voice always boosted his spirits. "When and where?"

"You're asking about the party? Just clarifying that this isn't a booty call."

"Well, it wasn't..." He drew the last word out as heat shimmered within him, never needing more than a spark where she was concerned.

"Not tonight. I have family stuff to deal with," she said on a sigh.

"Me too." The words came out before he could stop them.

"Want to talk about it?"

I want to get lost in you.

He substituted another truth. "I miss you. It's becoming a problem, what should I do?"

"Endure until tomorrow," she said, delicately heartless. "Do your best, English. I'll make the wait worth your while."

"Promise?"

"Cross my heart and hope to—"

"No," Gavin cut in sharply, suddenly alarmed and he didn't even know why. "Not that. Don't ever say that."

CHAPTER 15

SOMETIMES CLEM WISHED SHE COULD strangle Danica.

She'd dropped a breezy, "let's have a party!" type message in the coven group chat and left everyone else to sort out the details. Since her cousin wanted to host, all the prep fell on Clem's shoulders. *Sure, I said I'd handle it, but I didn't mean* every *damn thing.* Thankfully, Kerry, Priya, and Margie pitched in with the cleansing, and Ethel lent a hand with removing the wards. When the day of the party dawned, it should be impossible to detect any abnormalities.

Yeah, just a totally normal house party.

Full of witches. And a witch hunter.

She glared across the room at her cousin. Seriously, how could Danica not even *ask* what Clem had to do to make this happen? Clem tried not to be high-maintenance, but there was a line between stepping up for people you cared about and being taken for granted. Despite this being Danica's idea, Clem had done all the wrangling to make sure people brought food and drinks, set up the sound system, and plugged in the silly little disco ball.

"Is a word of thanks too much to ask?" she muttered.

Priya put her hands on Clem's shoulders. "Breathe. When she realizes how self-centered she's been lately, she'll feel really bad."

"And then she'll cry, and I'll become the bad one for upsetting her." Clem spoke beneath the thrum of the music.

The whole coven was already assembled, and some of them were tense—Margie, Vanessa, and Priya among them—while Leanne giggled with Danica. Neither of those two seemed to realize or care how much was riding on their preparations holding up. Clem didn't have a read on Ethel, but the other witch was relatively laid-back, capable of adapting to problems on the fly. *Glad she's on my side.*

Clem peeped out the front window in time to see Gavin roll up on his bike. Parking wasn't an issue for him, and she noticed he was wearing a surprisingly decent outfit: jeans with no holes, a button-up done properly, and his usual boots. No jacket because it was hot. *And oh, hell, so is he.*

"Showtime," she said, loud enough for the other witches nearby to hear.

Then Clem threw open the front door and greeted him with an enthusiastic kiss. It had been a few days since she'd seen him, and he smelled amazing. Felt amazing. For a few seconds, she genuinely got lost in the magic of his mouth and forgot they had an audience until someone cleared her throat. A quick glance back showed Vanessa standing there, her head cocked.

"Really? You're just gonna have at him without introducing him to the rest of us."

Clem laughed. "I'd say it's not like that, but you witnessed it.

Sorry, that's my fault. Everyone, this is Gavin Rhys. He's a history professor on sabbatical."

"Seems like you're trying to make some history with our girl Clem," Vanessa joked.

Gavin laughed. So far, he didn't seem to find anything strange about the house. *Thank the goddess.* But the night was young, and all kinds of shit could still hit the fan. Quickly, she introduced everyone by name, sharing a few facts so he could get to know them.

"And how do you know everyone?" he asked.

"Book club," she blurted before anyone else could. "We made a group online looking for local members and here we are."

"What's the last thing you read?"

Luckily, they were prepared for this, and Margie launched into a discussion of their latest romance pick. If he said a damn derogatory word about romance novels, she'd pinch him. Hard. But he only listened with evident interest, and before long, Titus arrived, diverting Danica right off. Clem watched in amusement as Leanne locked onto the blond, surfer-looking guy beside him immediately and threaded through the room like a hunting hawk. Clem wasn't sure, but she thought the blond guy's name was Trevor.

She opened with, "I'm Leanne. Want to be my third husband?"

Trevor blinked. "I mean…maybe? Because I could get on board if you're looking for a low-key, no-ambition type to look after the house. I cook and clean, do most general maintenance as well. Ask Titus, I've got references."

"As a handyman, not my third husband," Titus clarified.

Danica slipped up beside him, kissing his cheek. "Are we letting this happen?" she whispered. "Leanne may destroy him."

"Live and let live. He looks…intrigued, which is higher energy than I've seen from Trev in a while."

Some of Clem's initial nerves settled, and she guided Gavin toward the kitchen, intending to offer him something to drink, but Titus intercepted them. She'd only spoken to the guy a few times, and he was always bringing her stuff to eat. While she didn't get the appeal at all, she understood that Danica was serious. Likely, this dude would be joining her family. She could get with the program or end up losing her cousin entirely. While they still had shit to work out, that didn't mean she planned to torch a lifetime of sisterhood.

So she forced a smile when Titus put a bakery box in her hands. "Here, red velvet cupcakes. Hope you like them."

Honestly, she had no idea why his thoughtful gestures irritated her, but it came off like the kid who followed the teacher around, offering apples. Like, settle down, Timmy. We get it, you want the teacher to like you. For Clem, it was too much, and it made her itchy.

She tightened her knuckles on the box, trying to force some enthusiasm. "Okay, you win. You've earned my seal of approval. Love my cousin and make her happy, but stop stuffing me with treats. They're going straight to my ass."

"Thanks for that," Gavin said. "I'm rather a fan."

She nudged him. Hard.

"Of my baking or Clem's ass?"

"Both."

At that, Clem stifled a chuckle, trying to stem the rising tide of her nerves. She caught Priya and a few others eyeing her skeptically, but at least Titus's friends didn't know how critical tonight was. Then Gavin distracted her when he leaned in for a kiss that curled her toes. She laced her arms around his neck and forgot all the reasons why tonight was stressing her the fuck out. They finally broke apart, and he leaned his forehead against hers, a move that secretly made her melty on the inside.

She surveyed the scene. It seemed like everyone was staying calm. If they didn't stress their sigils, they ought to be able to pull this off. *And then he'll get orders to leave.*

That's the endgame.

Leanne slapped her own ass and then whacked the surfer guy on his butt too. With half her brain, Clem was curious about that conversation, but since the dude wasn't crying for help, he'd be fine. Probably. A few minutes later, she broke away from Gavin to answer the door. It was a bunch of guys she didn't recognize, must be Titus's friends, as Gavin only knew old people from the coffee klatch. It'd be funny if Leonard, Howard, and Gladys showed up, though.

It surprised her when Titus stepped up as a host, facilitating the mingle magic. Danica didn't notice certain behind-the-scenes necessities, but the baker did. And instead of leaving it to Clem, he helped. Which...she appreciated. Titus shepherded his friends around, making intros until the groups mixed on their own. Vanessa chatted with Cal while Dante asked Margie for advice on being a single parent. Miguel seemed to be offering recipes to Ethel, and everybody had a drink in their hands.

A while later, Gavin came up behind her, wrapping his arms around her in a classic back hug. "Having fun yet?"

She closed her eyes, savoring the sensation. "I am. What about you?"

———————

Gavin buried his face in Clem's hair, breathing in the delicate scent of her shampoo.

Mmm. Yes. Fantastic.

But he spoke lightly. "Nobody's called the constable—cops—on us yet, so I feel like we could do better."

"What did you have in mind?"

"Let me think on it. I can be a bit laddish, you know."

"Do I even want to know what that means, English?" She seemed to be teasing him, but sometimes he wasn't sure with her.

I fucking love that.

"Dance with me," he whispered, discarding the idea of trying to make things rowdier.

The party could fend for itself. Her friends were nice enough, the few he'd spoken with, but he hadn't come to socialize. At some point, he had to get clear and test the premises. He still had some lingering doubt about her shop name, her surname, and this would be the quickest way to clear it up. Unless he decided to follow in his grandad's footsteps, he still had a job to do.

"Give me five minutes. I'll circulate and be right back."

"That's fine. Is there a downstairs lavatory?"

She grinned and kissed his nose. "You're so cute. Five bucks to call it a 'loo.'"

"How dare you, madam. I cannot be bought. For that price."

Clem laughed and then pointed. "Over there. Also we have a bathroom right up the stairs if the other one's occupied."

"Ooh, you trust me, do you? I could have some nefarious scheme to sneak upstairs and prowl through your underthings."

Rising on her toes, she whispered, "You already do that when I'm wearing them."

Quick as that, he was hard, straining against his denims and imagining a fast fuck, someplace close and secret. He'd love to find out what knickers she was wearing and, more importantly, whether she was wet beneath them.

Stay focused.

He grazed a kiss across her temple and turned. The downstairs loo *was* occupied, and it rather sounded like the redhead who had dragged the bewildered blond man in here a while ago might be devouring him alive. From his enthusiastic yelling, it didn't appear as if he minded. Gavin didn't knock; they'd likely be a while.

Casually he sauntered upstairs and overheard what sounded like another couple getting lucky. Based on his observations downstairs, it must be the cousin and her boyfriend. With great resolve, he resisted the urge to spy on Clem, not for any official reasons but out of sheer bloody curiosity. What would her room even look like?

I'll find out when she shows me.

Gavin headed into the bathroom and locked the door behind him. Likely he didn't have long because someone would guzzle too much beer and need the room, so he closed his eyes and focused, extending his senses as he'd been taught. And—

There was a flicker.

Not strong enough for him to accuse anyone, but faint and definite. It could be a fading trace from someone who had visited, possibly the same witch who'd been in the bakery. *Dammit. I still can't entirely rule it out.* He'd wanted to find an inert space that offered no sparks at all, and this was worse somehow. The whole house was vaguely suffused in a way he couldn't explain. But it was old energy, only trace amounts.

Maybe the witch lived here before Clem moved in?

Swearing beneath his breath, he used the toilet while he was up there because it never hurt to cover one's tracks. As he stepped out, he found one of Titus's friends waiting for a turn. Dante, he thought the man's name was.

He wouldn't win any points acting like an arse, so he greeted the man politely. "Gavin Rhys. I don't think we met earlier."

"Dante. You mind?" The bloke gestured at the lavatory.

"Sorry, not at all. I'll clear out." His mood was considerably more somber when he went downstairs to rejoin the party.

While he was upstairs, they'd shoved the sofa and chairs out of the way and pulled up the rug, revealing lovely hardwood floors. Clem was pleading with people to take off their shoes so as not to mar the finish. *Why do I find her nagging so delightful?* Possibly it was because he understood, on some level, that the requests came from a place of deep concern. She wanted things to be just so, and it frustrated her when she fell short of perfection.

Soon, Dante came back down, and he went for the retiring type, it seemed, because he started smooth talking the quiet woman Clem had introduced as Margie and didn't rest until he got her to dance with him. The oldest lady at the party had a wild streak and gods above, could she drink. Gavin decided he didn't give a damn about the elusive witch he was starting to think might be a figment of his imagination.

He headed straight for Clem. She'd moved on once everyone kicked off their shoes, dancing in their socks like some fifties film, and now she was in the kitchen, stacking dishes into the dishwasher. From what he'd seen, she hadn't relaxed for a second tonight, laser focused on everyone else's good time.

While her cousin gets lucky upstairs. That didn't sit right with him, not even slightly.

"Come here," he said huskily.

He picked her up and perched her on the kitchen island, framing her hips in his hands. Now they were on eye level, and he could see how fretful she was, how unable to relax. Gently, like she might bite him, he set his hands on her shoulders and kneaded away the tension. At first she mumbled a few protests, and he sensed the moment when her intent to resist melted. She tipped her face up and closed her eyes, soft and warm beneath his hands.

The kiss, it was inevitable. He didn't give a damn who was watching or what they thought. This moment belonged to the two of them, and when he touched his mouth to hers, even the music faded away. She tasted sharply of lemon from whatever she'd been drinking, and he kissed her until her tongue went from tart to sweet, slipping into his mouth again and again. He pulled her to him, lost in her heat. She wrapped her arms around him, her legs too, until they were a tangled fusion of need.

Eventually, one of Titus's lads barged into the kitchen looking for mini corn dogs and dashed back out again, practically falling over his feet in embarrassment. "He thought we're about to finish what we started, here in the kitchen," Gavin said.

Clem shook her head. "Not a fan. I only forgot my aversion to having my ass on the kitchen counter while you were kissing me and now—"

"It's fresh in your mind again?"

"Got that right. Dance?" she suggested.

"Thought you'd never ask."

That led to more delicious grinding, leaving him more frustrated than he'd been as a teenager. *I really need to fuck her.* They were practically doing that anyway, slowly rolling their hips together, with his hands blatantly on her arse. Thankfully, everyone was sozzled by now and making their own bad decisions. Otherwise, the blond surfer chap certainly wouldn't be twirling those knickers on his index finger.

"Is there any chance of you showing me your room?" he whispered. "Any chance at all?"

CHAPTER 16

CLEM SHOOK HER HEAD, AMUSED by the obvious way Gavin's face fell.

Then she offered some sweet to offset the bitter, kissing his cheek and his stubbled jaw. She loved the tang of his skin; he tasted like summer, the bite of salt on top of an iced melon, though he was much hotter when he pulled her into his arms. He nuzzled his face against the curve of her shoulder, one of his favorite spots.

"Might I know why?" he whispered.

"Because if we go upstairs, the house is still full of people. They might bang on the door, bother us until they pass out. I'd rather go to your place."

It was also safer because her room would have the highest concentration of magic since that was where she slept. They'd cleansed the space, but she didn't feel sure enough of their preventive measures to take that risk. If Gavin noticed something off, the night could go from high risk to utter downfall while her guard was down.

I had him over, hopefully allayed any suspicions, and now I'll distract him again while I keep searching Etta Mae's journals.

"You'd rather be alone." He seemed surprised. "What about the party?"

"Danica can clean up. She let me deal with all the prep, so it's fair to leave the rest in her hands. Besides, I suspect Titus will stay over, and he might be annoying, trying to sneak out at baker's hours." She peered into his eyes, trying to gauge how sober he was. "Can you ride? My car is currently blocked in the drive."

"I've been nursing the same beer all night, love. These days, I prefer being the one sober enough to take incriminating photos."

"Had enough of being caught with obscene Sharpie drawings on your forehead?"

Gavin grinned. "The consummate uni experience. But yes, I'm sober as a vicar. Do you want to say good night or...?" He turned, and they both surveyed the uncontrolled chaos.

"I doubt they'll know the difference. Let me grab a few things upstairs, so I can go straight to work from your place, if you're okay with it."

"Are you planning to leave any of those things at my place? You've already got a toothbrush," he added.

Clem paused halfway to the stairs, aware of a terrible, inevitable warmth building in her chest. It felt suspiciously like happiness. Under the circumstances, it made no sense, but she savored the feeling nonetheless. This must be how it felt to exist in the eye of a hurricane, aware the storm could level her at any time, but for the moment, everything was tranquil.

"I can..." Clem let the sentence trail off because she couldn't bring herself to ask for his input. Since he was the one who'd brought it up, it seemed like something he wanted, though.

"Why don't you bring the basics? That way, if you sponta-neously decide to spend the night, you'll be set."

She was the sort of person who bought spares before the origi-nal ran out, so she did have extra lotion and deodorant. His tooth-paste and other toiletries were fine for casual use. And she already had a small pack of cosmetics she kept in her purse—BB cream with sunscreen, eyeliner, a simple shadow palette, a compact, and tinted lip balm. That just left her packing up a couple of outfits, one to wear tomorrow, another to leave with Gavin.

Surprisingly, she caught Margie making out with Dante as she came out of her bedroom. They were so into each other that they didn't even notice when Clem went past. *Huh, that's more Leanne's thing.* Margie must be seven or eight years older, but they were both single. She mentally gave Margie a thumbs-up as she hurried downstairs. Since she didn't spot Gavin anywhere, she guessed he must be waiting with his bike.

And he was, helmet already in hand. He handed hers over, and she put it on then checked to make sure her backpack was secure. When she settled behind him and wrapped her arms around his waist, he pressed his hands over hers briefly, a fleeting but signifi-cant touch. *I'm getting too close to him—on more than one level.*

Without another word, he started the bike, and they zoomed into the sultry heat of a summer night. The stars went liquid overhead, filtered into lines of light, tinted amber by the helmet. She reveled in his heat, the way he smelled of leather oil, wood sage, and soap. His back felt strong and hard against her chest, wide enough to shield her from the wind. In no time at all, they reached his rental. Lights were off at the main house, so he cut the bike off half a block away and pushed it the rest of the way, more considerate than one would expect.

"That's nice of you."

"You needn't sound so startled. I'm a prince, haven't you noticed?"

You'd be perfect if you weren't committed to hunting people like me.

As fatal flaws went, it was an insurmountable one. And Clem wished she could make herself hate him as she had before she got to know him. Before, she'd heard the excuses people gave—*he's not a bad person, he just—*

Has this horrible, inexcusable view. Hates others for no reason.

She loathed herself for falling into a trap she'd laid. There was no point in pretending this was completely a ruse anymore. Packing an overnight bag, choosing to stay with him? Those were things she wanted to do, despite her better judgment. At best, the sex between them should be hate-fucking. Because even if he didn't realize it, Clem did.

And hell, she shouldn't be falling for him, knowing exactly who and what he was. *What is* wrong *with me?*

Those bleak thoughts nearly made her change her mind, but when he extended a hand, she still took it, even while wondering what this hand had done to other witches. Gavin led the way up to his apartment without ever letting go, keyed in the code with his free hand, and as soon as they stepped inside, he barely gave her time to shrug off the backpack, and then he was kissing her fervently, pressing her up against the door.

Clem dug her hands into his hair, wanting to lose herself—to stop worrying for one more night. Gavin parted her lips gently and took the kiss deep, his hand cupping her cheek. With a soft caress, he traced her jaw as he kissed her, drinking in her quiet cries, and she wanted to make him feel as she did, drawn and conflicted, anguished and aroused. As they kissed, he rolled his hips against her, deliciously shameless.

"Take it to the bedroom?" Despite his obvious excitement, he was still asking, giving her the chance to change her mind.

Maybe she should.

She didn't. Instead, Clem took his hand and led the way. His room was dark and shadowed, exactly right for her mood. She didn't even want the moonlight shining on them tonight. In silence, she stripped off her clothes, catching vague glimpses as Gavin did the same.

"Glorious," she whispered, tracing a fingertip down the center of his chest.

He shivered. "I'm wild for you. Come to bed?"

Gavin didn't have to ask twice.

In seconds, Clem tumbled into his arms, more of a tackle than a hug, and he fell backward in a cooperative spirit, letting her take the lead.

From her aggressive start, he expected her to follow up on that ferocity, but instead, she came to him like hot silk, draping her body over his. She kissed his neck and shoulders with teasing, delicate pecks, echoing his favorite places on her body. And perhaps it was intentional, a demonstration of how it felt when he made love to her.

The words should've frightened him. This was never supposed to be a forever sort of arrangement, but now the idea of leaving her felt like the threat of an open wound, one that might never heal. Her mouth was soft, tracing over his collarbone like liquid fire. She kissed a zigzag path between his nipples, darting lower with willful sweeps of her tongue, then raked her teeth over his sides. It tickled and it felt good, and he ran a hand down her back, simply admiring the supple curve. It was strange how much he wanted her but also how patient he felt, as if they had a lifetime and not these stolen moments.

I can't even rule her out as a witch.

That ought to alarm him.

If he had any doubts at all, he shouldn't have her here in his flat, in his bed. The moment he fell asleep, she could sabotage his belongings, but that wasn't even in the forefront of his mind. No, it was fear. For her.

That can't be true. Fate wouldn't be so cruel.

Gavin arched as she kissed the curve of his hip, nuzzling her face into his pelvic bone. He wasn't remotely prepared for her to taste him from all angles—the knob of his knee, his ankle, his inner thigh, teasing him to a painful extent. It was like she wanted to paint herself over his body, a quiet claiming, and his cock jerked over the idea, even if it was only in his head.

At last she came back over him, thighs bracketing his hips, and ever so slowly rubbed her slick cleft against his hard length. Since he'd barely touched her other than the kissing by the door, this was proof of how much she craved him.

"Am I meant to keep my hands to myself?" he asked, partially teasing.

Clem smiled. The moon glazed her skin in silver, making her seem half a mythical figure, more seductive than should be humanly possible. From the slope of her shoulders to the angle of her chin as she gazed down on him, everything about her spoke—no, everything about her *sang* to him, like a siren song from olden days that led ships to smash upon the rocks.

She dragged her blunt nails down his chest, alternating light and heavy pressure, never enough to hurt, always enough to send delicious shivers through his entire body. Tenderly, she brushed the hair from his brow and bowed her body to kiss him in the same moment that she grasped his cock and plunged down, taking him fully, like she meant to consume him.

I'd let her.

At first Clem set a leisurely pace, riding him in smooth undulations. She felt incredible, and he kissed her until he lost his breath, their lips sliding nearly apart as he gasped with each plunge of her hips. She tugged lightly on his lower lip, working in ever-tightening circles, and he touched her everywhere, unable to credit how amazing this felt.

The sex between them had been incredible before, but tonight, there was another layer, a fullness that he couldn't place. Now, he felt connected to her completely, no longer solitary but joined and basking in the starry brightness of her soul as well as her body. With each push, he went a little deeper, glimpsing secret parts of her that she'd never shown anyone else.

How alone she felt sometimes.

How she found it impossible to ask for help.

How she feared not measuring up and that no matter how

loyal she was, no matter how hard she tried to connect, she'd turn out like her father, a man who couldn't be true or faithful to save his own life.

What the hell is happening? How do I know these things?

The connection snapped and he was alone in his head, coming hard, arching up into her body as she shook on top of him. Her pussy clenched and tightened, increasing his pleasure, but the loss of emotional intimacy was jarring, so fierce that he cried out, and not from the pleasure. No, this orgasm had teeth, clawing out of him on a wave of impossible, inexplicable loneliness.

Gavin held her, but he had the eerie feeling that it was only her body—that her mind had gone, detaching from what they'd done. And he had no inkling why he felt that way, stroking her sweat-damp spine until her skin dimpled with gooseflesh, either from his touch or the night air.

"Are you all right?" he finally asked.

He sensed that she wasn't, but she also wasn't the sort of woman who confided easily. *Maybe I'm not the person she would talk to either.* Just because she'd invited him to one party, it didn't mean he had a place in her life. Hell, this might've been good-bye. *Maybe that's why it felt so intense but also heart-wrenching.* Gavin had heard of good-bye kisses, but if he was right, this would be his first farewell fuck.

"I'm okay," she answered readily enough.

Gavin didn't fully believe her, yet he had no grounds to make an issue out of it, so he tried to press a kiss to her temple. She let him, but it didn't soothe the unease growing inside him like a chemistry experiment gone horribly awry.

There was nothing overtly wrong, but heaviness settled into his spirit, even as she felt ever more insubstantial in his arms, like she was made of air and would soon drift away. It wasn't the sort of fear he could articulate without sounding strange, however. In the end, he went to sleep without saying another word.

Gavin woke alone.

CHAPTER 17

THE WEEK OF THE LUGHNASADH was bright and clear.

Clem hadn't seen Gavin since she'd spent the night after the party, and it had been radio silence on his end too. The bell rang out front, drawing her out from the back, and she frowned when she recognized Pansy standing in front of their display of refurbished items. With a smile, the younger woman turned, approaching the counter.

"Barnabas told me about the tension between you," she said, gazing at Clem with big, brown eyes. "And I was hoping I could mediate. I have a counseling certificate and—"

"That's kind of you," Clem cut in. "Can you let me think about it?"

She couldn't bring herself to set fire to Pansy's good intentions, but if Clem knew Barnabas, he was manipulating Pansy, trying to use her to pull Clem to his side in the family feud. While she didn't know that much about family counseling, she suspected it was better not to be related to the counselor, and whatever her qualifications and despite her age, Pansy was Clem's new stepmother. *Fucking yikes.* Pansy made conversation for a bit longer, and Clem was relieved when the woman finally left.

People didn't leave Clem be at all that week. The next day, Gram stopped by—on a beneficent mission; she brought an herbal remedy she'd whipped up, something that was supposed to restore energy and boost immunity, along with healthy snacks. She gave Clem a hug, brimming with enthusiasm.

"Did you know Gladys has Mina keeping an eye on that witch hunter for us?"

Astonished, Clem shook her head. Mina Rodriguez wasn't part of her coven; she belonged to Gladys's. At one point, there'd been a single coven in St. Claire, but the group split twenty years ago because Ethel wanted to go her own way. Having Mina on watch took some of the pressure off Clem, not that she wanted Gram to know how pressured she felt. She'd asked Danica to leaf through the grimoire, and her cousin had said there were several spells they could try, but if anything went even slightly awry, Gavin would know. Instead of diverting him, the spell would lead him right to the people Clem loved.

In ninety years, there had never been such a risky Lughnasadh festival. To Clem's knowledge, they'd never hosted one with a witch hunter in town. She forced a smile for Gram.

"Thanks. I'll enjoy this," she said, pulling the care package across the counter.

"See you soon," Gram called, rushing off to another meeting.

With the Lughnasadh around the corner, she must be busy. The rest of the week, Allegra stopped in with D-Pop, and Barnabas came by as well. If Gavin hadn't given her some space, with her family acting up, Clem might've snapped.

By the time the night of the festival rolled around, Clem was perilously close to losing her patience. But as she gazed around in wonder, she made up her mind to enjoy the occasion. The usual site had been secured with blurring charms and ten other layers of protection they didn't ordinarily bother with. Tonight, so many lives hung in the balance, and it would be prudent to cancel, but if they did that, it not only dishonored the goddess but also betrayed their holiest of sabbats and the generations of witches who came before. Gladys would've hexed anybody who even suggested it, as she had some amazing plans.

Even to Clem, who had seen such festivals so many times, she had to admit the committee had exceeded all expectations. A few tents had been built, magical, billowing ones that caught the night air like a pirate ship's sails. Multiple stalls filled the wind with delicious scents—that of homemade wine and fruit tarts and fresh baked bread. Every witch within a hundred miles was in attendance, and Clem felt halfway guilty that she wasn't with Gavin right at this second to continue distracting him, even though the task cut into her as if she'd mistakenly grabbed a knife by the blade.

A dedicated troupe of neuromancers, none of whom Clem recognized by name, were casting illusions to charm and delight those celebrating the harvest. Flowers came to bud in the blink of an eye, unfurling into improbable colors and configurations, racing across the ground in a carpet that led passersby to a booth where they could receive charms for prosperity or luck, provided by Ethel, who gave a jaunty wave when she spotted Clem. Percy was perched on top of her stall, offering colorful commentary to witches who stopped to check out her selection.

"Doing well tonight, my dear?" Ethel called.

Clem lifted a hand and jerked her chin in a nod. Mostly, she was still unsettled by what she'd experienced in Gavin's arms. She'd only heard of witches connecting at that level; that was why Gram was so hard-core about finding a proper witch partner to complete the magical match, all the gross bloodline stuff aside. It was impossible to understand how or why it had happened with Gavin.

The illusionists stayed on their craft, casting fireworks that wouldn't be visible outside this little bubble. Hopefully. If the committee had done their work properly. Still, the risk niggled at her, and she wondered where Gavin was. If he were close by, through some awful coincidence, no wards would be able to block all this energy at close range. Green and yellow bubbles tumbled by with the whimsical images of fairies dancing inside, more cunning spell work by those casting for the sheer joy of it.

Apart from necromancers, who gave other witches a bad rep, every type of witch had a role to play tonight. The diviners had set up a fortune-telling booth, and the vivimancers were crafting beautiful custom houseplants on demand for those who always wanted tulips that smelled like roses. Enchanters had a variety of charms for sale, and technomancers like Clem got to enjoy the festive mood celebrating a rich and fruitful harvest, for their work took place before the party, ensuring all necessary devices ran silently and endlessly without electricity. Even if witches didn't live off the land as they had in the old days, it was important to keep the link alive. Clem believed these rituals and celebrations kept the farmland fertile with energies released throughout the year.

As a technomancer, Clem's part of the rite was small, more symbolic than anything else. She usually paired with a vivimancer to offer a surge of power to fuel the blessing they offered the earth. A few of the local witches did farm, and Clem would enchant their machines when possible, so they didn't break down or run out of fuel before the harvest was in.

She wandered the festival, taking in the sights. Her entire coven was here. Leanne was sampling all the wine while Margie walked around with her son, Chris, another fledgling technomancer, though Margie specialized in neuromancy. Clem spotted Priya and Kerry holding hands, feeding each other bites of a blueberry tart. And Vanessa was strolling around with Danica; they seemed to be gossiping hard, laughing every other step.

Her stomach rumbled, reminding her she hadn't eaten in a while. She got a cup of wine and a sampling of pie, arranged beautifully on a plate that had been transmuted from a handful of twigs. Once the Lughnasadh ended, all the repurposed goods would return to their original state, sort of like the pumpkin carriage after Cinderella's ball.

Everything will be fine. I'm sure Gavin's in town, too far away to notice anything.

Midwestern witches were so crafty that even the locals who lived a mile away had never noticed anything going on under their noses. *Everything will be fine*, she repeated the silent litany.

"Why so glum?" Suddenly Leanne stood beside her, offering another cup of wine.

From the tingle in her fingers when she took it, the drink must be charmed, but she didn't even ask. She trusted her coven sister not to feed her anything that would harm her.

"Just a general bad feeling," she said.

Mustering a smile, she downed the wine and let Leanne convince her to join the games, laughing with the rest of her coven and admiring the unique flowers Priya had developed especially for the occasion. Lilies that bloomed bright red like the deepest rose and then faded to pink as they aged, smelling of jasmine.

Eventually she crossed paths with Danica, who looked happier and more at peace than she had in years. Apparently confronting Gram was like slaying her personal dragon, so she was no longer spiking magic like an untrained wizard in a storybook. On some level, Clem was still mad at her cousin, but she needed to get over it because she hadn't been lying when she said she forgave her for going off on her own and forsaking the pact.

The whole thing was pointless anyway.

Soon the drink fizzed in her veins, lightening all her burdens, and Clem threw herself into the celebration, funneling her magic for the big ritual that always capped the night. The collective power of all the witches fed into a beautiful whirlwind, snapping with energy in all hues, like a rainbow spun into the shape of a tornado. It broke over her in a glorious wave and it carried a soft fusion of the hopes and dreams of every witch present.

That we're safe and happy.

That we continue to prosper.

That my garden grows well.

Those wishes whispered in her until she couldn't help but

smile, connecting fully to her community—more than sisterhood; this was the truest of unions. Slowly, gradually, the power trickled back into the ground, falling into the connecting lines to feed and replenish the earth.

"That was fucking awesome," Leanne said, wrapping an arm around Clem's shoulder to give her a one-armed hug.

"So it was," she said.

She spotted Barnabas across the way, and he was about to become Clem's problem, headed in her direction. Thankfully, Mom was walking around with Gram and Gladys on the other side of the festival, but if Barnabas and Allegra crossed paths, there would be drama. Leanne stroked a fingertip down Clem's face, ever so subtly glazing her with the illusion of being someone else. Barnabas passed by without a second look, and Leanne grinned.

"You deserve a break tonight," her coven sister said.

Clem wrapped an arm around Leanne in silent gratitude. Choosing to celebrate and affirm life had been a big fucking risk, but some things were worth it.

This *is worth it.*

That night, Gavin had a beer with Leonard, who was quickly becoming his best friend in St. Claire.

The old man had a hundred funny stories, and Gavin rather loved listening to how his pursuit of Gladys was going. It seemed the woman had private plans tonight, and Leonard was quite worked up about it.

"I asked her two weeks ago," he complained. "But no, she's

busy. I ask you, how long in advance do I need to set up a date? I swear to God, I find out Howard's trying to get her first, I'll punch him in the mouth."

Privately, he'd put money on Leonard if the pensioners truly decided to scrap. "That might be excessive," he murmured.

Leonard scowled at him from beneath thick salt-and-pepper brows. "Have you seen Gladys? She's adorable!"

"But quite often, the git who gets punched receives sympathy and cuddles while the offender is scolded."

"That's so true." Leonard knocked back a good portion of his beer, sighed, and shook his head. "I don't want to get on her bad side. Gladys sure can hold a grudge."

"Better to exercise restraint." It was right at twilight, street-lights coming on. Children streamed home down the sidewalks, shouting to each other as they darted into their houses.

He'd never known anything like that freedom. And maybe it showed, because Leonard said, "What's eating you, son?"

Instead of voicing the inchoate dissatisfaction that had been gnawing at him for ages, he asked something else. Something equally important.

"How do you know it's love?" he asked.

Maybe Leonard could provide a primer for someone who'd never had the time or freedom to discover for himself.

"Why the hell are you asking me that at your age? Are you yanking my chain?"

"I'm not. It's fine if you don't want to answer."

"Eh, well. With my late wife, it's embarrassing to tell this story, but...she was working in a diner when I first spotted her. I sat down at the counter, she poured me a cup of coffee, and I was a goner when she smiled at me."

Gavin grinned, picturing it. "Love at first sight, yeah? Like in all the old romantic films. Didn't know that really existed."

"People would make fun of us now. We got married after dating for only a month, but we were together thirty-five years. Fought like cats and dogs sometimes, but she always said she was sorry and made my favorite dinner when she meant it."

He laughed. "Sometimes she didn't mean it?"

"Oh, that woman could steam the paint off a wall if she set her mind on it. So sometimes she'd apologize like this: 'Sorry you're so thick, Leonard Franklin. You couldn't buy a clue at the clue store!' And that's when I knew I'd really messed up and I better make it up to her, fast."

"That doesn't answer my question," Gavin said.

Leonard smiled. "Yes, it does. The person who makes you feel like you want to be with them all the time, no matter how mean or how mad they are? The person whose face you want to see every morning, and you don't care how it changes over time? That's love, son."

Oh shit. I truly didn't want to hear that.

"What about Gladys? I guess it wasn't love at first sight."

"No, we fought for about five years after my wife died. Bickered about anything we could disagree on. I caught on eventually that she was provoking me on purpose, making me mad when I couldn't feel much of anything else. Truth to tell, she saved my life. That love came on slow, an inch at a time, until she made a home in my heart too."

"Thanks for sharing what it's been like for you."

"My pleasure. Irma and I weren't blessed with children, so I'm glad to know somebody's getting the benefit of my wisdom." Leonard flashed a grin and finished his beer. "Now I'm off to shoot some pool. You interested?"

Gavin shook his head. "Unfortunately, I have other obligations."

A few hours later, he was crouched in the cornfield again, keeping an eye on Dale the Prepper, just in case. He wished he could muster the courage to bail like Grandad. Gavin was waiting for another message from him, but so far, he hadn't gotten a reply, despite checking every day. As he fretted, the biggest burst of magic he'd ever experienced swept over him like a tidal wave. The power of it raised the hair on his arms and the nape of his neck. This…it wasn't one witch. It had be…hundreds. Way more than he could handle on his own.

Fuck.

He should immediately be on his mobile, dialing for backup. Because there was no chance in hell he could manage this situation. The order thought they were winning this war, but given what he'd just experienced, witches had secretly bolstered their numbers, growing careful and cautious, much better at hiding.

He straightened, realizing Dale had nothing to do with this. If Dale were a witch, he'd be participating in whatever the witches had just done. Strangely, the energy wave hadn't felt malicious or baneful. Rather, it brightened his mood and energized him, filling him with an emotion he could only compare to anticipation. Which made absolutely no sense.

It was difficult to ride while tracking, but not impossible.

Splitting his focus like that gave him a throbbing headache, but he rode through the night until he reached the general area where the magic felt strongest. He pushed his bike to the side of the road. Hopefully, no drunken farmers would swipe it into the drainage ditch. Gavin vaulted the ditch and crossed through the field. Rows and rows of corn surrounded him, all lightly suffused with a golden glow. At night, it was eerie, though he didn't think it would be visible to anyone without his unique training.

He tracked the fading energies as fast as he could, taking several false paths and cutting across directly whenever possible. Eventually, he came to an open space in the fields, still humming with that incredible power. It felt like a holy site, and a lot of people had been here recently.

Scores of witches, just as he'd sensed at a distance. The timing was right for this to be the remnants of one of their pagan rites. Kneeling, he flattened both hands on the ground and opened his mind. The truth burned into him like a branding iron. Some of these traces felt familiar; he'd met these witches, mingled with them. But one presence, dear God, he recognized this impression like his own face in the mirror. His soul caught fire, the worst agony he'd known since his grandad left without looking back, since his father forsook all joy in favor of duty.

It's true. I didn't want it to be.

Clementine Waterhouse is a witch.

CHAPTER 18

LAST NIGHT AT THE FESTIVAL, it had been like living through the Cold War, condensed into one frigid evening.

Clem had avoided trouble by nudging different coven sisters to distract Allegra from fighting with Barnabas. At least Pansy and D-Pop hadn't been there, and she felt a little sorry for her mom and dad. For Danica too, because she could never share that with the CinnaMan. No matter how much they loved their mundane partners, witch doors would remain forever closed.

Now Clem had a day of work to look forward to, and afterward, she was meeting up with Mom and Gram. *That ought to be a fucking riot.*

Just before 2:00 p.m., Danica blew in, all wind-blown and flushed, glowing from head to toe. Clem fought the urge to roll her eyes. "Are you still coming tonight?"

"Wouldn't miss it," her cousin said in a monotone. Then she broke up laughing. "Seriously, you had my back when Mom and Gram had dinner at our place. And let's not even mention all the shifts you've covered for me lately."

"You already apologized." She knew she sounded a bit grudging.

Yeah, I forgave her silly ass. That doesn't mean I'm glad about it.

"Okay, so..." Danica propped her elbows on the front counter, in no hurry to get to the backlog of appliances waiting for repairs. "I'm not sure how much you caught at the party, but did you know Leanne hooked up with Trevor in our downstairs bathroom?"

Clem laughed. "Everyone at the party knew. Damn, Hazel Jeffords probably does too."

"How did you know she showed up? You'd already ducked out by the time she came over to complain about the noise!" Danica seemed to be amazed by Clem's acuity.

"Duh, you cleaned for hours, whining about that ginger cat the whole time."

"Can you blame me? You took me for an allergy shot the day I petted him, remember?"

"True enough." It felt good to chat with her cousin like they used to, before needy, try-hard bakers and smoking-hot, bike-riding witch hunters complicated both their lives.

That's not even mentioning the family stuff that just won't fucking leave us alone.

Like Danica could follow along with her silent thoughts, she took Clem's hand. "I saw Uncle Barney last night. You okay?"

She choked on a laugh. Nothing pissed off Barnabas Balfour more than being called Uncle Barney. Already, she pictured his frozen smile and the muscle tic in his jaw. That was part of why Danica would never desist, a petty revenge and one Clem approved of entirely.

"The fan has been sighted and we are in the vicinity of shit."

Danica giggled. "I love how you put things. You think Gram's up to something?"

"Hell if I know. It honestly wouldn't surprise me if she's scheming to get my mom and Barnabas back together."

Danica blinked. "After all these years? That's highly ill-advised."

"My thoughts exactly. And she didn't have to live with all the screaming, crying, and occasionally telekinetic manipulation of small appliances." One time, her mom had launched a freaking toaster at her dad's head when yet another of his affairs was revealed.

Danica came around the counter to hug her. "I was there for some of it, but you must've been so scared when you were little and it was just the three of you."

"Ugh." Briskly Clem squeezed her cousin then stepped back. "I don't want to talk about ancient family drama. I'd rather unload a coven scoop on you instead." She even made use of a dramatic pause.

"No way! How did you get the deets before me?" Danica sounded positively aggrieved.

Clem indulged herself with a self-satisfied smirk, knowing it bothered her cousin something fierce. Of the two of them, Danica was by far the most social, always in their coven group chat and trying to stir up some in-person hangouts. While Clem enjoyed chilling, she preferred smaller groups, even within the coven, so when she had her first choice, she rotated who she spent time with. Margie was great for marathoning dance movies, while Ethel was her favorite auntie. Leanne was always down for girls' night out, and Vanessa still liked to go clubbing. Kerry and Priya were natural for Netflix nights in, and Danica…

Yeah, she's still my best friend. Even if she drives me out of my mind sometimes.

We're still family.

Sisters for life.

This time, the thought didn't form grudgingly. She let go of the lingering resentment. That pact would never have worked for Danica; she got attached a lot easier than Clem.

Her cousin stomped her foot. "Seriously?! You're just gonna stand there and smile? Tell me already!"

She grinned. "You might've been busy at the time, but I caught Margie making out with Dante. I don't know if anybody else saw, and I kept it quiet until now."

Danica stared, her eyes widening. "Oh my damn, that *is* major. I want to tease her, but—"

"Don't you dare," Clem cut in. "She's so tentative, even if she's halfway thinking about having some fun with him—which she deserves—you might scare her away from the idea. She'll start talking about how she's too old for this and about setting a good example for Chris."

"Yeah, I don't want that. I swear you tell me these things to test my ability to keep a secret," Danica muttered.

"Maybe I do. Anyway, I left the callbacks in the log, and all the drop-offs are in back. I'll see you at six thirty."

"At least we don't have to host this time," Danica said, apparently trying to look on the bright side.

Clem waved on the way out. The bad feeling she'd been nursing fluttered within, somewhere between worry and dread. Her phone had been ominously silent, and all her instincts warned her that something was about to go catastrophically wrong. *Maybe I'm on edge because Barnabas is in town. He always makes me cranky and goes out of his way to insult D-Pop.* Which was frankly like kicking a friendly puppy.

Clem headed home, vaguely keeping an eye out for Gavin, but she didn't see any sign of him, and her phone was still quiet. Nevertheless, her nerves only got worse, not better, as she let herself in the house. She passed the time showering and taking special care with her makeup, thinking of it like battle armor to bolster her for whatever the night held.

A few hours later, she swung by the shop to pick Danica up, then they headed over to an upscale place that specialized in vegetarian fare. Gram ate lean meat and fish, but Allegra didn't, and she preferred not to see it on people's plates. Clem parked the car, and they headed inside.

The restaurant was called Heart of Artichoke, and it was decorated all in cream and silver with posh touches and flowers on the table. The understated elegance would appeal to Gram at least, and Allegra should be happy with the menu.

Danica reached for her hand, giving her a steadying squeeze. "Whatever this is about, we're not putting up with any shit tonight, got me?"

Clem offered a fist bump. "Agreed. If Gram came to fight, we came to win."

Gavin didn't sleep a fucking wink all night.

In the morning, he didn't eat and he barely drank. Already, he'd betrayed the order by not instantly reporting his discovery. But instead, he found himself frozen. Nobody he'd met in St. Claire was evil; he'd stake his life on it.

In prior jobs, he never spent this much time in a town. The witches had been unprepared, and he was a tracker. He located them and then turned them over. That was literally his purpose, and as soon as he had confirmation the enforcers were incoming, he moved on. The rest was handled by the enforcers, or so he'd heard; they severed witches from their magic so they could do no more harm. Darker stories were whispered, but it never went well when he asked about them.

His old man dismissed them with gruff outrage. "We're bloody heroes, not monsters!"

Confusion ripened like autumn apples, darkening toward despair. Gavin raked his fingers through his hair and finally fired up the netbook, so small that it felt like a toy in his hands. There was still no response from his grandad, but he wrote another message out of desperation, outlining his circumstances fully and the choice he was currently facing.

If anyone will understand, it's you. Tell me what to do, Grandad. I'm so fucking lost.

His head felt strange and overfull, and he had no memory of closing the laptop, but he found himself standing in front of Benson's cage. Gavin opened the door and placed his palm in front. In time, the little white mouse scampered onto Gavin's hand and perched there. Perhaps he'd been alone too much, but the mouse seemed to wear an expression of concern, eyeing Gavin with black button eyes.

"What should I do?" he whispered.

The mouse cocked his head then darted into Gavin's shirt pocket, nestling in like he meant to stay. He lost the plot after that, and the next time everything snapped back into focus, he'd left the flat at some point and had wandered all the way downtown on foot. It was a significant hike in the summer heat, and sweat trickled down his spine. He felt faintly light-headed, probably because he couldn't remember the last time he ate. His feet had carried him toward the Fix-It Witches repair shop.

Gavin laughed, the sound edged in sardonic bitterness. While his brain might be bewildered, his body had no doubts.

The name's not ironic. It's factual.

Now that he understood everything, he figured the Waterhouse cousins were technomancers and their quaint little shop served as a front for the magical repairs they performed. And that fact alone...it was so prosaic. The St. Claire witches were using their power to...repair microwaves and toaster ovens?

That hardly amounted to the vicious, wicked danger he'd heard about his entire life. But...if he stepped off the path, he'd be burning bridges with his father and the order. It would mean walking away from the only life he'd ever known.

For a while, he stared at the shop, and in the end, he didn't go in. Gavin didn't get out his mobile either. Still in a daze, he ambled to the café and paused before the counter.

"Did I even bring my wallet?" he muttered.

"If you didn't, I've got you," Howard said.

Gavin patted his pockets as he turned. "Good thing you're here."

He couldn't manage a smile, and Howard tilted his head. "No need to look so offended. I'm aware you've come down on Leonard's side in the Gladys Games, but I don't have any hard feelings as long as you don't actively sabotage me."

Despite himself, Gavin laughed. "Does she know you call trying to date her 'the Gladys Games'?"

"No, and you'd better not tell her. What'll you have?" Howard asked, stepping up to place their order.

He got a simple hot tea and a random sandwich. The older man paid and seemed to take it for granted that they'd have lunch together. *Is it lunchtime?*

Gavin didn't drag out his mobile, afraid that if he did, his old man would know somehow and there would be more texted demands or worse, a call that left him floundering, since his mind remained uncertain as English weather. Surreptitiously, he pinched a bit of tomato from his sandwich and dropped it into his pocket for Benson. The slight movement told him his little friend appreciated the treat.

"How's your paper going?" the older man asked.

Right, the alleged reason he was here in the first place. *God, I'm so sick of the lies.* A torrent of emotions swirled inside him, and he sat quiet for too long.

Howard chuckled. "That bad, huh? You must have writer's block."

It was far worse than that, more like coming to a crossroads with no sense of what lay down either path. But what the hell, in absence of wisdom from his grandfather, maybe Howard Carruthers could sub in.

"I might not be cut out for the work I'm currently doing," he said.

Howard had a cup of black coffee and a bagel he was spreading with cream cheese. "Looking for career advice?"

"If you don't mind."

"Not at all! Old people love being asked for opinions, means they're not offering them unsolicited. And it makes us feel like we still have something to contribute."

"That was never in question," Gavin said, forcing himself to eat the turkey sandwich.

"What's the issue then?"

"All along I've been living for my father, following what will make him proud and happy. But it's never been enough. Not once. No matter how I behave, he's never said, 'Well done, son, I'm proud of you.'"

"Now you think maybe it'd be better to walk your own path and see where that leads."

"I'm wondering," Gavin admitted. "But the problem is, I don't know anything about that road. I've never even glanced in any other direction until now."

"Then the conflict is certainty versus risk, known versus unknown." Harold was surprisingly astute for an older man in horn-rimmed glasses currently sporting cream cheese around his mouth.

"Precisely."

"I don't know what relationship you have with your father, so I'll talk about the one I have with my son. When he was in high school, we fought constantly about him taking over the hardware store. I was dead set that he had to, because it was my life's work, right? But then I thought long and hard about that."

"And?" Gavin prompted, becoming slightly interested in where this was going.

"It's not right, trying to force your children to fulfill your hopes for them. To me, that's a form of greed. It's enough for him to be happy. So I told him that, and he left St. Claire for a while. Started a travel blog and had some adventures in the world."

"Did he come home?"

"In time he did—with a fine young man as his partner. They've got two precious babies now, and they're running the hardware store. Not because I made it happen, but because he wanted to plant his roots here." Howard paused to cram the rest of the bagel in his mouth, then he continued in a muffled tone, "My son does the daily operations, and his husband handles publicity. Business is booming. To my mind, things worked out exactly as they should."

"It sounds like you think Da ought to cut me some slack to figure things out."

"In the end, it's up to you whether you stick to the route he mapped for you or if you go off course to see what might be waiting if you're brave enough to take a chance."

"You're an adventurer at heart," Gavin said.

"Maybe I am."

In pensive silence, Gavin finished his sandwich and his tea, mulling over what Howard had said. Eventually he pushed to his feet with a nod.

"Thanks for lunch. And for the advice."

"Do you know what you want to do now?"

I can't hurt Clem or anyone she cares for. Can't look away and allow it to happen either.

"I believe so," Gavin said. "Now it's a matter of marshaling my courage."

CHAPTER 19

THE FIRST PART OF DINNER went fine.

Allegra was slim and elegant like Gram, so Clem didn't have to listen to her grandmother pick at her. She did get a little passive-aggressive a few times over Mom's tendency to chatter, but they managed to eat their entrees and were sipping coffee when the real purpose of the evening dropped, like petals from a dying flower.

"It's not too late," Gram said. That was the opening salvo.

Clem didn't know who she was talking to, but she balled up a fist, ready to defend her mother with a rude mouth since she couldn't hit the old witch. *Still can't believe she flat-out lied to us over the years.*

"For you to apologize?" Danica cut in smoothly. "Honestly, you're lucky we agreed to meet you at all after what you did."

"What did you do, Mother?" Allegra had a good poker face, and Clem stifled a grin.

Her mom knew damn well what Gram had been up to because Clem had filled her in over the phone as soon as she found out. But pretending to know less than she did had served Clem's mom well over the years; she'd pretend to be distracted until she clocked a lie and then bam! Interrogation central. Barnabas had been caught more than once, exactly like that.

"Don't try that with me," Gram snapped.

Allegra simply shrugged, smiled, and sipped at her coffee. Every gesture was dainty as she replaced the cup in its saucer. "Oh, are you referring to the failed scam you ran on my daughter and niece?"

Raising a brow, Allegra cut a look at Clem, who rather enjoyed when her mom got serious and fucked with Gram. Danica defiantly ordered a slice of cheesecake, knowing that would piss the old witch off. They sat in silence for a few minutes, nobody wanting to be the first to crack. In time, the server delivered the plate and Danica picked up her fork.

Clem shared the dessert, smirking the whole time. "So what nonsense do you plan to attempt this time?"

As if on cue, Barnabas entered Heart of Artichoke without his Pansy attachment, and Gram lifted a friendly hand, brightening as his lean figure wove through the tables. Now Clem really wanted to punch someone.

"You didn't," she muttered.

Mom glanced over her shoulder, then her whole body tightened. "Unforgivable," she whispered.

The lights flickered overhead, proof of Mom's agitation. *Shit. Oh. Shit.*

The whole coven was wearing Ethel's dampening amulets or using her tincture, but with all the confusion, she'd forgotten to get one for her mother. And Barnabas was sure to provoke her into a magical spike that would broadcast their location unmistakably to Gavin. Quickly she jumped to her feet, grabbing her mother's arm.

"Thanks for dinner, Gram. This was your last chance, and you burned it. Enjoy dessert with that asshole because you won't be welcome at our tables after ambushing us like this. I'll let you get the bill, it's the least you can do."

Leaving Danica staring because Clem couldn't take time to explain, she dragged Allegra past Barnabas and ignored his shocked and offended expression. *To hell with you, asshole.*

She hoped Gram's plan hadn't seriously been to push for reconciliation between her parents—both married to other people—but at this point, it didn't matter. *Where, where can I take her to calm down? We stripped the wards from our house for the party and—*

Ethel.

Ethel's place would be safe.

"Stay calm," she whisper-yelled.

Allegra took a breath and rushed with Clem, seeming to realize she was about to cause a scene in a way that would force the witch's council to take action. "Deep breaths," Allegra repeated, all the way to Clem's car.

"I know you hate him," Clem said, "but things could go sideways fast. Did you not hear there's a witch hunter in town?"

"I heard you're dating him," Mom shot back.

That shut Clem up for about five seconds as she buckled in and started the car. "Not the point. You're not carrying a dampener, and you spiked like you're trying to light up the skyline."

Unsurprisingly, Allegra ignored that part as Clem drove away from Heart of Artichoke with a heavy foot on the gas pedal. Her mom stared out the window like she was being abducted. "Where are you taking me? Your dad will be worried!"

For once, Clem didn't even make the usual correction and say, *D-Pop's not my dad.* Because in all honesty, she knew him better and had lived with him longer than her biological father. *Maybe D-Pop is my dad.* At least he was a good guy who treated Allegra like she was his entire world. And to Clem's knowledge, he'd never cheated on Mom or broken a promise.

She spared Allegra a hard look for her overreaction. "Please, you take three-day trips to Vegas with your coven and leave him in Florida. He's watching TV right now or napping on the couch, so he won't notice if you're an hour late. Besides, you love Ethel."

Allegra brightened immediately, settling back in her seat. "You should've said so sooner. How's Percy doing?"

"Foulmouthed as ever."

Clem kept glancing back as she sped through town, half expecting to find the lights of Gavin's motorcycle bearing down on them. It sucked to be so scared, and her own magic rose in response to her fraying grip on her emotions.

No, no, no.

I can't let this happen. Have to keep Mom safe.

She took one hand off the wheel and gripped Allegra's slim fingers, joining her in the deep breathing. The streets were quiet at this hour, little traffic to slow her down. She made all the turns, glancing back every few seconds, and then as she turned onto the cul de sac that led to Ethel's bungalow, a single bright beam shone in her rearview mirror. She'd ridden on the Ducati so many times that she recognized the roar of the engine.

He's here. He's found us.

Clem flattened her foot on the gas pedal and then reconsidered. *This is a residential street.* Trembling from head to toe, she eased off and braked when she got to the end of the road.

The bike behind didn't make any move to pass, but it stayed with her as she parked the car. Allegra didn't seem to realize what was happening yet. Closing her eyes, Clem steadied her nerves as best she could.

He knows. Oh fuck, he knows.

I feared this was coming. Distracting him was a stopgap at best. Time to have it out.

"When we get out of the car, walk straight into Ethel's place," Clem said without looking at her mother. "Don't stop, don't look back."

"You're scaring me."

"Good. Then maybe you'll take this seriously. Promise me, okay?"

"No! You think I'm a scatterbrain, but I won't leave you to face trouble alone."

Urgency spiraled through, sharpening her tone. There was no time for this. "*Please*, Mom. If it's just me, I might have some chance of talking him down. Two witches will escalate the situation. Let me do this."

Allegra glared at her for long, dangerous seconds, then she finally nodded, her eyes silently furious. "Fine."

For once in her life, Mom listened to instructions, and as Clem swung out of the car, she rushed up the walk to Ethel's house, leaving Clem to this personal reckoning. She turned slowly, watching Gavin pull off his helmet.

"Caught you," he said.

———————

Gavin gazed at Clem, limned in the light from the Duc's headlamp.

He couldn't make out her expression, but judging by the way her fists were balled up, she knew exactly who—and what—he was. *How long has she known?* Narrowing his eyes, he saw she was trembling, not with anger but fear.

What...does she think I'm going to do to her? I'm not an enforcer, I'm a hunter.

But Clem didn't realize the distinction.

"You must think I'm rubbish at my job," he said, because it was clear she couldn't or wouldn't speak first.

When he glanced over her shoulder at the woman rushing into the house behind them, she raised a fist and snarled, "Don't even think about it."

"That's your mother, isn't it? You favor her quite a bit." He didn't mean it to sound threatening, but she took it that way.

Clem stepped forward, squaring her shoulders, and for the first time, he felt raw magic streaming from her, too powerful for whatever she had been using to block it from his senses. The engine on the Duc revved behind him, and it sounded vaguely threatening. If she wanted to, she could turn every vehicle on this block against him, including his own.

Yeah, definitely a technomancer.

"Walk away," she said quietly. "Get on the bike and don't look back. Whatever you need to tell your bosses, make them believe it was a false trail. That's the only way we both get a happy ending."

Hearing that hurt when it really shouldn't. She'd been clear that this relationship could never go anywhere, so her words shouldn't lodge in his chest like splinters, making him bleed. And now, at long last, he understood why. They stood on opposing sides of an archaic war.

"Walk me through it," he said, ignoring that for the moment. "What did you know, and when did you know it?"

She put her hands on her hips, crackling with magic and defiance. "Want me to put my cards on the table, English?" With the mocking inflection, the word didn't feel like an endearment this time.

Every moment that he stood here, he put himself at risk. He put the order at risk. That was what he'd been taught, but she hadn't tried to hurt him, even knowing he'd come to paint a red mark on her door, so to speak. And he wanted to hear her answer.

"Indeed," he said.

"Since you stormed into the bakery with those wild accusations. We checked you out that night. So I've known from the start."

"From that first night."

She gazed at him squarely. "Now you get it. I volunteered to distract you to keep everyone else safe. Don't feel bad, I enjoyed the game."

A band tightened around his chest, snapping into place with

a suddenness that stole his breath. Deliberately, he turned and switched off the Duc, blanketing the night in quiet.

It was difficult to get the words out because they revealed how fully she'd fooled him. "You're claiming that none of it was real? Not a single moment."

"Does that scuff your pride? I'll salvage some of it by admitting the sex was excellent. Now, unfortunately, we're on opposite sides, and there can't be any fraternization."

"Are you declaring war?" Gavin asked.

"You came to my town, hunting the people I love," Clem snapped. "I'm not the one who started this fight. I didn't want it. I still don't. I was hoping you'd admit defeat and move on. Why couldn't you just *leave*?" Her tough facade fractured a little, trembling on the last word.

Fuck.

He fought through the first wave of outrage and anger—the sense that she'd fucking played him. *Yes. She did. It started as a lie, but—*

No, that might be ego talking.

Why couldn't *I just leave?*

The usual response nearly burst forth. *Because it's my job. It's my father's pride. My family name.* But those reasons no longer even seemed sufficient to him, let alone her.

"Because of you," he said then. "Because you made me want to stay, even when I knew I shouldn't."

Clem sucked in a sharp breath, and he thought she swayed toward him, drawn by the same pull that made it feel like they were one soul while they made love. "Shouldn't stay or shouldn't want to?"

"Both," he said tiredly.

Some of the magic died away, lessening the low-grade buzz on his skin. It was strange not to need to try and sense for power being used. The air was saturated with it, and he still didn't feel threatened. His old man's voice rang in his head. *She's tricking you. The moment you let down your guard—*

Instinctively he shook his head. He couldn't imagine Clem hurting anyone. Frankly, nobody he'd encountered in St. Claire seemed like bad people. *They were kind and welcoming, even when I was picking their brains.*

"Then I guess I'm more charming than I imagined and better at pretending too."

It occurred to him that he had no right to be angry. Part of him wanted to punch something and shout, *How could you? I'm a person!* But he'd been trawling the coffee klatch in a similar way, even if he wasn't sleeping with any of them. In his line of work—as a hunter—he used people all the time, trying to find a weakness or extract information that would lead to a successful ID. Then he turned all that information over and vanished.

"You're both," he agreed.

She took a breath, dropping her eyes as if she found it difficult to look directly at him. Gavin had a powerful urge to comfort her, even knowing she wouldn't want that, now that the truth was out on both sides. *God, she's a fantastic liar.*

Until last night I had no clue.

Then she firmed her chin and raised her face with renewed boldness. "This is the end for us, then. It was stressful, but I can't say I didn't enjoy some of the adrenaline."

Is that all I am to you?

Gavin couldn't voice the question, nor should he. The last time he'd felt this sad was when his grandfather vanished. He swallowed hard, wishing the words didn't echo in his head.

This is the end for us, then.

The end. For us.

"Stay away from now on," Clem warned, taking a step back. "And please leave. Please. If you're not a monster—and I *hope* you're not considering what's passed between us—you'll take this as a personal growth lesson and walk away. You might also reconsider your life path, but that's between you and your conscience." She backed toward the house, still facing him. "Don't make me fight you, English. I have people to protect in this town, and I won't let you do anything to them." Then she spun and sprinted toward the cottage like he posed a threat.

In her eyes, I do.

Most people never came to the realization that they were the villain of the story; they never saw that they were causing others pain. *But my existence is terrifying to all those witches I sensed that night.* Sick to his stomach, he held still until Clem darted into the house. Only then did he start his bike, his heart heavy. After pulling his helmet on, he rode back to his place, his head an absolute wreck.

What am I supposed to do?

The rented flat smelled dead and empty when he keyed open the door. All the good feelings that made the place feel like home had evaporated, and he stood, shoulders slumped, breathing in the stale air.

I haven't had a home in twenty years.

He sank down heavily and might have tumbled headlong into despair, if not for the mouse running merrily on his wheel. When Gavin crouched before the cage, Benson scampered over and pressed his tiny paws to the bars, as if he sensed his human needed comfort. As soon as Gavin opened the door, Benson dashed across his hand and up his arm, nestling into the crook between his neck and shoulder, his whiskers tickling Gavin's skin.

"She gave you to me," he whispered. "Even knowing who and what I am, she didn't want me to feel lonely."

Such kindness offered to an enemy spoke volumes about those the order persecuted without a second thought. Gavin took comfort from the little white mouse, and then the little fellow ran down his shoulder to settle in his shirt pocket. He'd taken to storing a few sunflower seeds in it, as Benson enjoyed nesting there. The contact cleared his head enough for Gavin to remember to check the netbook. And at long last, he had a message from his grandfather.

Too late to solve the problem, but maybe Grandad had some useful advice.

CHAPTER 20

ALLEGRA GRABBED CLEM IN A bear hug as soon as she stepped inside.

She couldn't remember ever seeing her mother this scared, and Clem rubbed Mom's back gently. Belying her bravado, Clem was still shaking in the aftermath of the confrontation. Overall, she thought she'd done a good job of covering up how sad and freaked she was.

Ethel sighed somewhere deeper in the bungalow. "I agree, Percy. They act like my house is a Motel 6."

Clem guided Allegra past the foyer, keeping an arm around Mom's shoulders. "We'll be out of your way soon," she promised.

With a shrug, Ethel said, "You know I don't mind. Should I get cookies or...?"

"No," Allegra said at the same time that Clem said, "Why not?"

"Well, I want Nutter Butters. You can abstain, Allie." In a swish of chiffon, Ethel ambled into the kitchen to get the cookies, and she came back with the whole package, not even bothering with plates.

Yeah, it's been that kind of night.

Mom flung herself on the couch, tossing her head back with a groan. "This is why I left. Too much drama!"

Clem swapped a look with Ethel, who noted, "You left the Midwest for Florida...because of drama?"

She stifled a snort. Her mom only nodded vehemently, still doing her breathing exercises. The irony went right over her head. Hell, she probably didn't even know about all the Florida memes. Sometimes Clem input "Florida Man" and her birthday, just to see what the latest chuckle would be.

"She means family drama," Clem said, eating a Nutter Butter.

"Understood."

"I'm also trying to be a good daughter, but Mother doesn't make it easy," Allegra added in a cranky tone.

Clem raised her gaze to the ceiling. They'd just confronted a witch hunter, but Allegra planned to spend the night complaining about Gram and Barnabas. *Really?* She couldn't swallow the reluctant amusement. *Nothing fazes you, huh, Mom?*

Next, Ethel brought out a cup of milk, possibly for dunking, and plopped on the couch, her floaty lavender dress falling around her like a bridal train. "Hell. We're in it now, aren't we? How long before he calls the enforcers? How much does he know about us?"

Fuck. I didn't ask. I should have.

"What's an enforcer?"

"They're the ones who handle the dirty work," Allegra said, surprising Clem.

Mentally she scolded herself. *Way to go, genius. Remember how you promised to handle everything?* Somehow she'd fixated more on discussing their fake relationship than on acquiring critical info. Clem muttered a curse at her own grim thoughts, loudly repeated by Percy.

Ethel laughed as she ate another cookie, then she said, "Doesn't answer the question."

"True," Allegra said.

Finally Clem muttered, "I'm not sure. I...may have focused more on posturing than on fact-finding. My bad."

It was a good thing Ethel was the only one from their coven here because otherwise she'd never hear the end of this. Likewise, Allegra wasn't the type to focus on details. In fact, she didn't seem to realize how much of an emergency this was, and she was texting D-Pop with a big smile on her face. Clem and Ethel both watched her in amazement for a few seconds.

"What medicine do I take to be as carefree as she is?" Ethel asked softly.

Clem shook her head. "I've been asking myself that for years."

Seeming to set that aside, Ethel stared balefully at her phone. "It's late, but this won't wait. You want to pull the fire alarm in the group chat, or shall I?"

Since Ethel hated texting, though she read all the messages, Clem said, "I'll handle it."

"That's what you said before," Ethel muttered.

"That's what she said," Percy shouted.

Raising her eyes from her phone, Clem lifted an eyebrow that silently threatened all sorts of retaliation. Really, it was toothless because what could she do to Ethel anyway? The woman was everyone's favorite auntie.

"Are we not leaving yet?" Mom asked, glancing up from her screen.

"D-Pop can wait an hour longer," Clem said gently.

With a sigh, she sent: 911. Emergency light emoji. All hands to Ethel's place.

Soon confirmations and questions popped into the chat.

Vanessa: Shit, what's up?

Margie: Oh no. I'm on the way.

Danica: What the hell, you abandoned me at Heart of Artichoke with Gram and Uncle Barney! Also, OMW

Leanne: I was literally on Trevor's dick. This better be important.

Ethel: What did I tell you about that?

Leanne: Not to post TMI unless I'm prepared to send pics or videos.

Priya: Kerry's in the shower. We'll be there as soon she gets her pants on.

Half an hour later, the whole coven was in Ethel's front room. The older witch hadn't planned for company, so Clem had helped her set out an impromptu, eclectic assortment of snacks: Nutter Butter, grapes, cheese cubes, melba toast, almond butter, and Chex Mix. Not all in the same containers. There were also random drinks because Ethel couldn't host a quick gathering without turning it into a party. The coven helped themselves to snacks and then turned their collective gazes to Clem.

It's never easy to admit this. Clem closed her eyes briefly.

"I'm sorry," she said. "I fucked everything up."

Then she summarized what passed between her and Gavin, though she did minimize the sex stuff since Mom was in the room. Her coven sisters sat quiet, listening without judgment until she confided what had happened outside that night. When Clem finally ran out of words, she ended her narration with a weary sigh.

Danica moved first, settling beside her on the floor, and she wrapped both arms around Clem in a bracing hug. "This was too much to ask of you," she said softly. "We're here now, and we'll figure this out."

"So help me, if you say 'together,' I will pinch the crap out of you," Clem muttered.

Vanessa crowded into the hug. "Together. Now *I* said it, and you better not pinch me. You know what'll happen if you try."

Mom suddenly dropped her phone, staring in shock. Clem eyed her. "What?"

Allegra looked fit to pop like an overinflated balloon. "Okay, I wasn't paying attention fully, but I think I heard that you hooked up with a witch hunter. I knew you were seeing him, but you went all the way downtown? So how was it? I've never known a witch who—"

"*That* is what you're focused on?" Margie cut in.

Leanne grinned. "Wish my mom was more like you."

"Same," said Kerry.

"My mother has certainly never had sex," Priya said primly.

Then she swapped looks with Kerry, and they both started giggling.

Clem experienced a brief pang because Priya was so freaking sweet, and she'd missed out, but she was genuinely happy for her two coven sisters. More to the point, it wasn't the time to fixate on lost opportunities when she had a crater of a problem to fill.

Ethel rapped her knuckles on the table as Percy called, "Order in the court!"

Kerry glared at the parrot. "One of these days, I'll—"

"Don't threaten my bird," Ethel snapped.

Danica petted Clem's hair, her expression troubled. "I'm the one who started everything, so I have no room to talk, but we need to focus. The situation is volatile right now, and we're in unchartered waters. We could wake up to a war zone tomorrow."

Margie let out a little moan. "Oh goddess, should we start packing?"

"First, it's pointless to blame anyone," Clem said. "Yeah, Danica spiked first, but Mom had her turn tonight, and that's on Gram. I share the blame because I forgot to get Mom one of Ethel's dampening charms or remind her to put on a tincture. Basically, whenever we gather for our festivals, there's risk. And that's bullshit. Witches have lived in fear for too long!"

"Easy to say," Vanessa pointed out. "Not so easy to solve."

Ethel cracked open a can of beer and took a sip. "What the hell, I've got all night."

———

You must choose.

That was the first line of Grandad's email.

To protect or persecute. I wouldn't have brought this up if you hadn't mentioned it first, my lad, but as you said yourself earlier—you can't row two boats. Protecting this person you've come to care about will mean breaking with your father. He's my son, but he's not a forgiving man. To him, the world is divided by a wall, and all those who don't agree with him stand on the other side of it.

Are you prepared for that? Do you know what it means to cut all ties with the order?

They won't let you go. To keep yourself and your loved ones safe, you'll have to live in hiding, as I have. Even these many years later, they're still hunting us.

We move often. I hadn't planned on telling you this either—in case Jason is making use of you. But I live on a boat, Gavin, like in the pirate stories we used to read. I expect you've outgrown those by now. Anyway, the time is coming when you'll have to decide.

As one who's already chosen, I have no regrets. I love you, lad. Maybe one day, I'll get to see for myself the kind of man you've become.

Love always,
Grandad

Gavin didn't reply immediately.

Instead, he let the words sink in slowly. He tucked Benson back into his habitat then stripped off and went into the shower. Tonight, he didn't adjust the temperature, just let it stream icy cold, a shock to his system after the heat of the summer night. Not more of a shock than the last twenty-four hours. By the time some of the numbness wore off, he was shivering, and he stumbled out of the shower to scrub his face with his palms. *You will have to choose.*

The end of us.

For some reason, those two sentences stuck in his head, and he couldn't stop thinking about what might happen here and what he could do to prevent it.

But how?

The order was powerful enough that Grandad lived in hiding, even twenty years later. *What should I do? What can I do?*

Eventually, exhaustion won out, and he tumbled into bed, prepared to postpone the problem. Gavin slept poorly, his brain flooded with shadowy nightmares. It was late when he finally woke, and his whole body was sore. His father would probably say he'd already been cursed by one of the witches, but Gavin could tell it was the result of tossing and turning, sleeping with his fists clenched.

"I should eat," he said to Benson, though he couldn't muster much enthusiasm.

He had a few berries left, so he cut up blueberry and a bit of celery and gave it to Benson as a treat. Gavin wished he could be as excited about anything as the white mouse was to taste a bite of berry. He'd never broken up with anyone, not really, because there were only hookups in his history, but knowing she'd been using him from the start felt like knives slicing clean down to the bone.

Fuck.

Gavin had no power, no leverage, but he couldn't walk away either. That would be the easier path for sure, but he didn't think he could convince his old man that St. Claire was a dead end. Even if he admitted failure here and pissed him off, they'd send someone else. Someone who wouldn't care if Clem got hurt. Bold, beautiful, valiant Clem.

She'd been ready to fight him, even if she didn't want to, which proved witches were different than he'd been taught. Or at least *she* was. But that didn't make sense—that he'd randomly met *one* outlier in a world of dangerous, wicked witches. It was more probable that most witches were good people, demonized by those who benefited from their oppression.

I've worked for monsters my entire life. She said she doesn't want me to be one.

"Am I a monster?" he asked Benson.

The mouse paused with his cheeks full of berries and gazed at Gavin with soulful black eyes. For some reason, the look didn't feel like exoneration, though it struck him as sympathetic. Spinning the problem in his head, he scrambled some eggs and had just sat down to eat when someone rapped on his door. For a heartbreaking second, he let himself hope it was Clem. He threw it open with a smile trying to form, but it dropped when he saw Mina. Not that he had anything against her. She was nice, just not the woman he wanted to see right now.

Somehow, Mina's air seemed a bit different today; she radiated nervous energy as she bounced in front of his door. "Brought you a little treat. Oh! I see you're already eating. Well, everyone has a separate dessert stomach, am I right?"

"I do have a sweet tooth." Belatedly, it occurred to him to worry about what she'd make of Benson, but he couldn't think of a reason not to invite her in.

At his gesture, she swept into his apartment with a plate of delicious-smelling croissants. "Two are chocolate, three plain."

"Thank you for thinking of me," he said, aware that his voice sounded strained.

Fortunately, Mina didn't notice. There was something going on with her, but he didn't know what. It kept her from noticing the mouse habitat in the sitting room, at least. "It's no problem. I just buy a few extras. But if I ever bring something you don't like, please feel free to pass. I don't want to annoy you. I just have an uncontrollable urge to mother people."

Is Mina a witch? Keeping tabs on me for Clem.

He stared at her, stunned into silence by the possibility. Though he didn't sense any magic from her, he hadn't from Clem either, until the situation caught fire. Mina could be carrying some charm to help her hide.

Why...do witches have to hide from us?

His father had made it sound like a religious mission, as if the world would crumble into fire and brimstone without the service of hunters and enforcers. Without the order.

Mina laughed nervously, evidently unnerved by his stillness. Or maybe it was because she thought he might attack her?

"Why are you staring? Am I bothering you?" she asked.

Gavin rallied quickly, offering what he hoped was a believable excuse. "No, I'm just touched by how kind you've been. Do you treat all your renters this well?"

She beamed, setting the plate down on the small island. "Only the ones I like. Don't let your eggs get cold! And text me if there's anything you'd like to eat. The kitchenette is okay for small, quick meals, but for home cooking, you need a real stove."

"Thank you. Truly."

If Mina was a witch who had been keeping an eye on him, she must know what Clem knew by now. That would explain why she was uneasy around him, yet she'd still offered to cook for him. *Grandad was right; I can't trust the order.*

Once Mina left, Gavin ate dutifully: the eggs, a plain croissant, and a cup of tea. He was stacking the dishes in the sink to deal with later, reflecting on how to tackle this dilemma, when another knock sounded. *Did she bring me cookies this time?*

He ambled over, smiling slightly. "What did you...?" When he got a look at who was standing on the other side, he stopped, his mouth open.

Enforcers, one of whom reported directly to Gavin's old man. Ted was a snaky bastard with a coldness that made even Gavin nervous. The others, he'd seen some of them, not all, and he didn't know their names.

The fact that they were here could mean nothing good.

Even though Gavin didn't invite them into the flat, Ted still sauntered in, slamming into him with a shoulder as he shoved past.

"Stand down, hunter. We're here to take over." He made a shooing gesture and sprawled on Gavin's fucking sofa like he owned the place. "Seems you've lost Jase's trust."

One of the minions laughed. "Wouldn't want to be in your shoes."

Ted propped his asshole feet on the furniture. "Move along now, wee Rhys. You've served your purpose."

CHAPTER 21

"IF IT COMES TO WAR, we'll fight, but let's use nonviolent means first," Ethel said.

"Try to minimize the danger," Margie suggested.

It was the middle of the night, and they were *still* discussing the best way to handle the current emergency. Allegra had fallen asleep on the couch after being convinced to message D-Pop that she'd be back late and not to wait up. Numerous ideas got suggested and discarded, until Leanne said, "Have we covered our tracks at the festival site?"

"Shit. No," Danica breathed. "They could find more of us."

Kerry wore a determined look. "We have to get back out there. Tonight."

"It's a risk," Vanessa said.

"I'll do it," Clem volunteered at once.

Danica shook her head. "Not by yourself. A small group will be able to handle it better and faster. Since I created this situation, I'm definitely going."

"You'll do better with a couple vivimancers for balance," Kerry said, glancing at Priya. "Are you up for some midnight magic?" Somehow she made it sound flirtatious.

Priya smiled. "You know I am."

Ethel ate the last of her cookie. "It's settled, then. Our first step is to cleanse the site where we held the Lughnasadh. If the hunter goes back there, we don't want him finding any echoes that would allow him to identify the rest of us. Clem should be safe at least for a little while because she's formed an emotional bond with him. It's not easy to hurt people you care about."

Clem stood up, relieved to have a plan now that the situation had escalated. "On it. I'll drive. Margie, would you mind giving my mom a ride? It's outside town."

Margie shook her head. "Not at all."

Clem woke Mom gently, making sure not to startle her. The night had been traumatic enough already, though thankfully she'd focused more on Gram and Barnabas than on the conversation Clem had with Gavin. As Allegra sat up, rubbing her eyes blearily, Margie asked, "Where are we headed?"

Clem hugged her mother quickly, and Mom gave the address as everyone got ready to go. Ethel pressed a bag of supplies into Kerry's hands while Clem waved to acknowledge the chorus of "good lucks" from Leanne, Ethel, and Vanessa, who were the only ones not exiting en masse. Vanessa lived up the street, and Leanne appeared to be calling the surfer dude to find out if there was any chance of resuming their coitus interruptus.

With Danica leading the way, Clem headed out. When they got to the car, Priya and Kerry were in the back seat, while Danica chose shotgun. Clem swung into the driver's seat and headed toward the ritual site without saying a word. She'd spoken to many of them earlier, and they'd debated over so many plans.

"What music is good for narrowly avoiding calamity?" Danica asked, likely to break the tense silence.

Kerry held Priya's hand in the back; Clem could see the comforting gesture in the rearview mirror. Priya got her phone out and scrolled through her playlist, then Kerry seemed to take up the challenge as well. They all had connections to the car audio, but Kerry got there first. The speakers blared "Everything Ends" by Slipknot, and Clem burst out laughing.

"Maybe not quite that dark?" she suggested.

Priya punted that choice and substituted "Who Wants to Live Forever," which started Danica singing along while a pop of magic produced brightness in her hands that she waved like a lighter. In the back, Kerry joined in, and Priya offered a triumphant gesture that proclaimed her musical supremacy. From there, Danica played "Good Things Fall Apart," a proper sad boi anthem if ever there was one. A few songs later, and they arrived at the concealed and ensorcelled parking area that kept anyone from noticing so many cars in an empty field. Clem's vehicle slipped through the spell barrier without trouble, and the four of them got out of the car, trekking on foot to the festival site.

"I didn't wear the right shoes for this," Danica said.

Clem wasn't in boots or sneakers either, though Priya and Kerry had dressed for potential trouble. Kerry opened the bag of supplies she'd gotten from Ethel, and they set up for the cleansing ritual. Urgency rang in Clem's head, but she locked it down. No matter how dire the situation, it could always get worse if she miscast because of tumultuous emotions. Centering herself, she took a deep breath and forced out all thoughts of terrible consequences and the fact that Gavin already knew she was a witch.

He probably knows about Danica too. If I'm one, the rest of my family will be targeted. Mom, Barnabas—fuck. No. Stop it.

It took longer than she'd like for calm to encompass her. Priya, Kerry, and Danica were already waiting, seeming much steadier than she felt. Kerry lit the candles, and they assumed their places at cardinal positions, setting near enough to hold hands, with the candles burning in front of them. Danica held Clem's right hand with Kerry gripping her left. For a flawless spell, two technomancers worked best with two vivimancers, energies in balance, which was why she and Danica usually did their group spell work with Kerry and Priya. Sometimes the whole coven cooperated on a spell that needed a lot of power. Hopefully, the four of them could manage this since it needed to be fast and covert.

"Ready?" Priya asked.

Their power twined together in seamless strands, wending outward. Clem envisioned it carrying residual energies with it like a lint brush. The glow brightened around them, soft colors that reflected their auras—magenta for Danica, red for Clem, gold for Priya, and orange for Kerry. It created a prismatic wave that flowed outward, visible only to those with the ability to cast, but the spectacle was breathtaking, like the aurora borealis sweeping through the field. Since they were cleansing a much larger area than their house this time, the energy outlay nearly made Clem black out.

She swayed as the spell finished with a soft pop. Kerry squeezed her hand, turning to check on Priya, who was rubbing her temples. Danica was pale, trembling slightly. In the aftermath,

Clem felt shaken and drained, but she didn't detect any remaining traces here. With the last of her strength, she pulled to her feet and helped everyone else up. She and Danica leaned on each other, hiking back to the car at a snail's pace.

When they finally piled on, Clem let out a long, relieved breath. "We did it, but Allegra and Gram aren't safe. Neither are you, Danica. He might suspect everyone who was at the party too, but if Gavin meant to hurt me, he would've done it earlier."

"You can't be sure of that," Priya said gently. "I'm aware that you like him, but a good person couldn't persecute others in the first place."

Really, she had no counter argument, and that made her feel miserable and guilty. In silence, she drove them back to Ethel's house so they could collect their cars, still parked in front of the house. All the lights were out, so everyone must've left and let the older witch go to bed. Clem hugged her coven sisters and waved as they drove off. She was tempted to follow them home, but attention from her would make Kerry and Priya less safe, not more.

Danica didn't say a word until they were nearly home. "I don't have the mojo tonight, but we have to put the wards back up."

"It's on my list," Clem said tiredly. "I'm really sorry."

"Hey, I'm the one who suggested the party without realizing what we'd have to do to make it happen, and I left all of that on you. *I'm* the one who's sorry. Lately I haven't been much of a friend, let alone a sister. I'll do better, I promise. And you're not alone in this. I've got your back, no matter how it all shakes out."

She choked up, unable to say more than, "This isn't how I wanted things to go."

Her cousin smiled. "Was it John Lennon who said, 'Life is what happens to you while you're busy making other plans'?"

"How do you even know that quote?"

"Mom had a Beatles phase."

"If you tell me 'all you need is love,' I'm making you walk home."

Danica pretended to cry. "Please don't. You left me alone with Gram and Uncle Barney, and I had to listen to her complain for half an hour after you left. Isn't that punishment enough?"

"Just block her calls and don't respond to her. That should get the message across. I don't know why you find it so hard to set boundaries. Being family doesn't give her license to treat you however she wants. You've been patient and tolerant long enough."

"I hear you."

Her cousin didn't respond other than those three terse words, and Clem lacked the energy to persist. Frankly, Gram was the least of their problems. When she pulled into the drive, the headlights illuminated the lanky ginger tabby lounging on their front porch.

"Oh, look, your fan club is here."

Danica sighed. "The more things change, the more they stay the same. I don't have the energy to deal with Hazel. Think Goliath will cry if we ignore him and go to bed?"

"Without a doubt." Clem didn't feel like doing it either, but she got out her phone anyway. Somebody had to pick up the slack and—

To her surprise, Danica was already calling. "Get some rest, coz. I'll take it from here."

My flat is full of arseholes.

Gavin had fed the louts, much against his will, and he'd called his old man, who wasn't currently picking up his calls. But Ted knew the passcode Gavin had been given most recently, so he had no reason to doubt the validity of this assignment. He ground his teeth as they made free with his belongings, though thankfully he'd been using the netbook in the bedroom, and he had a chance to stash it before they uncovered it.

I'd really be in it if they had confirmation that I've broken protocol.

Ted had introduced his minions—Ingram, Alban, Echo, Joanna, and Darcy, three men, two women, all tough as nails and impatient to get started. To make matters worse, Echo wasn't an enforcer at all; he was another hunter, which meant Gavin's father must've decided he wasn't getting the job done fast enough.

That or I can't be trusted anymore. Honestly, he wasn't sure which would be worse.

"You can't stay here," he said. "The landlady lives downstairs, and she pops in quite often. You're eating the croissants she dropped off before you got here," he added to the silent, stone-faced one called Ingram, a man in his fifties with weathered features, a silver-black beard, and scars that told a sinister tale about his predilection toward violence.

Deliberately, Alban caught his gaze, taking a chocolate croissant from the plate, holding eye contact while he took a huge bite. *That's a dick move, innit? I was saving those for dessert.* Alban appeared to be in his late twenties, thin and weaselly with blond hair slicked back with altogether too much gel. He habitually flicked a switchblade open and closed, so his specialty must be knives. Gavin disliked him already; he'd shooed him away from Benson's cage because the bastard kept tapping the bars, frightening the mouse until he ran into the house to hide.

Echo was massive, even for a hunter, who tended to be burly because they often worked alone. He had muddy-brown hair and sun-damaged skin, which made it tough to guess how old he was. But Gavin guessed late thirties or early forties, and Echo had a nervous leg problem, kept jittering it whenever he sat, but more often, he paced the flat like a caged animal.

Joanna had to be sixty, a venerable age for an enforcer, and like Ingram, she had multiple battle scars. She wore her hair shorn close in silver fuzz, and she dressed like a combat veteran in olive and khaki utility gear with pockets that bulged with weapons of all types. Her muscles were a little slack, but she still looked fierce enough that Gavin wouldn't want to test her. She wasn't eating his croissants at least, but her watchful air worried him.

That only left Darcy, who looked even younger than Alban, early twenties at most. She was on the chubby side, also dressed in fatigues, but on her, it was cute rather than intimidating. That might be what they were counting on—that the enemy wouldn't realize how dangerous she was until it was too late. She had red hair caught up in a simple plait and a smattering of freckles on an upturned nose.

Ted got to his feet then, drawing everyone's eyes. "Relax, we weren't planning to move in. We've got our own digs."

"Where are you headed?" Gavin asked.

Ted's lip curled. "I think you mean 'we.' Before you go your merry way, you need to show us where that massive flare occurred. Don't tell me you didn't sense it, because we got reports from hunters all over the Midwest."

Fuck. Is he talking about what I sensed at the restaurant or the ritual site?

He didn't think either locale would be enough to let Echo learn anything that would put Clem and her family at risk, but his stomach churned over the prospect of this going pear-shaped. *If I lie, they'll know. This is probably a loyalty test.* Fighting nausea born of fear, he gambled with the truth. *Better for them to think I'm still on their side.*

"There were two," he said. "One was a restaurant, but I got there too late to catch the witch. The other was in the middle of a farmer's field. Where should we go first?"

"Restaurant," Echo said straightaway. "The traces will fade faster there with more people moving through."

The man was right about that, as humans carried energy with them, even if they couldn't use magic. Humans with a strong will could even smudge a witch's tracks, which was why witches blended in with humans and preferred to live in cities these days. Times when a witch could live like a hermit on a mountaintop had passed; that was a good way to get caught because there was nothing else around to confuse the energy signature.

"Then let's go." Gavin grabbed his wallet and opened the door, making sure he watched every last one of them leave before he shut the door.

I need to sweep the place. It wouldn't surprise him if they'd planted surveillance since he clearly wasn't in the circle of trust anymore. *How bad will this get, I wonder?*

The squad had a black SUV parked out front, a ride with darkly tinted windows that would absolutely draw all kinds of attention in St. Claire. It practically shouted "shady business," but he didn't say anything as they all piled in, leaving Ted by the driver's side.

Gavin got on his bike and put on his helmet. "Do you remember which side of the road to drive on?"

"Don't try to be funny, just lead the way," Ted said coldly.

Giving thanks that he didn't have to get in the SUV, he started the Duc and rode over to Heart of Artichoke, making no allowances for the size of the massive gas-guzzler they were driving. The restaurant had plenty of parking, so he pulled in and waited, hoping like hell that Echo wouldn't glean any insights. It was a freestanding two-story brick building with a lot that wrapped around, far more parking than one would see at a restaurant back home. Since it was summer, the patio was open and a few people were eating outside, undeterred by heat or insects.

Ted raised a hand imperiously, demanding Gavin get his arse to the entrance. Alban was already there, perusing the menu like he hadn't just eaten Gavin's chocolate croissant.

Alban made a face. "Looks like it's vegetarian," he complained.

The enforcer called Ingram scowled. "Stay on task. We're not here to eat."

"They may object to the lot of us poking around inside if we don't," Gavin pointed out.

"That's what the mission funds are for," Joanna said in an even tone. "Come on, let's get a table for seven."

"I'm a bit peckish," Darcy said.

"Eat this." Alban made a crude gesture near his crotch.

Before Gavin could hit him, Darcy did it herself, followed by Joanna and Ingram. There was a definite protective vibe going on between the oldest members of the crew and the youngest. *Any relation? Can I use this somehow?*

With an impatient gesture, Ted led the way in. A bunch of tough-looking people getting a meal together here would set the town gossip alight. Mrs. Carminian would have Gavin connected with Armenian weapon dealers in her version of the story in another hour. By the time it circulated, he didn't care to imagine how colorful it would be.

Mentally Gavin cursed. If he'd had any doubts before, he had none now.

Even if I never speak to Clem again, I can't let them take her.

CHAPTER 22

EVEN IN A CRISIS, LIFE had to go on.

Clem turned up to open the shop at her usual time, after burning the midnight oil with Danica to get their house warded again. Now it was for protection, not to avert discovery, because the worst had already come to pass.

I failed my mission. Not only fraternized with the enemy but started to care about him. Even knowing what he's done, what he's still doing. What the hell is wrong with me?

Self-recrimination didn't help at all, but Clem couldn't control the grim thoughts that circled in her head. On automatic, she magicked a series of devices, and afterward, she had to double-check the work to ensure she'd done it correctly. Around noon, she had some walk-in business, quick repairs she finished while the customers waited.

Getting through her shift took all her energy, and she was so relieved when Danica showed up early. She got in at one thirty and hugged Clem, sporting a worried look. Clem stifled a sigh and let it go because she understood she'd brought this on herself.

"You okay?" Danica asked.

Clem nodded. "It's not like we broke up. I just got caught."

Her cousin gave her a look. "You're more upset about this than you were when you dumped Spencer."

The sex was better with Gavin, she almost said, but that wouldn't do anything to win the argument. Not that she had the mental energy to care about that right now.

With a dismissive gesture, she changed the subject. "I'm heading home to review the journals. Maybe I'll find something."

Danica nodded. "Stay sharp. He may come after you now that he knows."

Clem acknowledged that with a grim look as she grabbed her purse. "You too. He's aware we're cousins. I'll call Mom later to make sure she's okay. I'll check in with the rest of the coven too. If we're lucky, maybe he'll take Gram off our hands."

"Clementine Odette!" Danica gaped at her, eyes wide.

Apparently, there were some lines her cousin wouldn't cross, even when she was pissed. But what the hell, there was a reason people agreed that Danica was the nice one. Clem didn't backpedal. She only muttered, "What'd I say about calling me that?"

Danica didn't let up on the intense glare. "She's out of chances with me too, but don't say stuff like that. No matter how awful she is, she's still family."

Clem paused at the door, frowning. "Why does that matter? Blood isn't everything. Like, it's kind of the problem, honestly. Gram's *way* too into our lineage, and it's twisted her up inside. So why does she get a pass, just because we're related? At what point do we say, 'You know what, I'm sick of this'? Personally, I think we're better off refusing to interact with her until she agrees to respect our choices."

The long pause told Clem that Danica didn't have an answer. Being nice only went so far; as far as Clem was concerned, beyond a certain point, it became self-harm.

I'm not a fucking martyr, even if I volunteered to take Gavin on.

Without waiting to hear whatever excuse her cousin would've come up with, she wheeled and stormed out, pissed on multiple levels. She didn't let anger make her careless, however, and she kept her head on swivel scanning for potential witch hunter complications all the way home. She walked at a rapid clip, but Gavin didn't show.

Don't know how I feel about that. Is he reporting in? This is terrifying.

Clem didn't feel safe until she got inside the house and the wards closed around her like a pair of loving arms. As she poured a glass of juice, her phone beeped, signaling a message. She was wound tight enough that she juggled the glass, sloshing one of Danica's green concoctions all over the floor. Her heart pounded like a jackhammer when she checked it.

Gavin: Be careful.

That was all.

What's that supposed to mean? Is he warning me or does that constitute a threat?

Dammit.

Even more confused and aggravated, Clem downed her juice like it was hard liquor and went to pore over the pile of journals she'd borrowed from Ethel. As before, the reading was slow and tedious, but in June of 1933, she struck gold.

The worst has come to pass, Etta Mae had written. *I've no idea what will become of us. We got comfortable and careless, I think, stopped worrying that anyone would be hunting for us at all. The old panics seemed so long ago, nothing a modern witch must fear.*

Clem laughed softly over that. *We have something in common.*

He's here searching. Before he finds us, we'll try a misdirection spell as a coven. The Herring spell is difficult to pull off, and it might tip our hand, but we have no other options. I hope we can send him searching in the wrong direction, though I don't feel good about it. What if he catches some other witches in our stead? We have no control over what will happen when he leaves, but we fear what will happen if he stays even more.

My misgivings don't matter. We cast the spell tonight.

She'd never heard of a Herring spell, but Etta Mae had left notes on the spell's creation, as it was designed to mimic the movement of a living creature, an incredibly detailed and high-skill working. Clem paged forward and found an entry celebrating their success. Like Ethel's mother, she did wonder if somebody else got caught in this feint, but it happened a long time ago; no way for her to find out.

More depressing, it wouldn't work this time.

Not when Gavin already knew who she was. Misdirection would have no impact in that case. Their best hope was a forgetting spell, and those were uncertain at best. They needed a powerful neuromancer; by herself, Margie likely lacked the strength of will to blur a witch hunter's memory.

Maybe if the coven is backing her? Softly, Clem swore and then reported her findings to the coven group chat.

Margie: Crap. It's on me?

Leanne: I have some skill with mind fuckery. It's why I always look like I have makeup on, even when I just woke up.

Vanessa: Why am I not surprised?

Ethel: I'll work up some power boosting charms for tonight. We're trying this at your place, Clem?

Danica: That would be best. We just laid in new wards and they're strong. If witch hunters try to push past, there will be collateral damage.

Kerry: The type of big news that ends up with a mysterious explosion being explained as a gas leak by puzzled mundanes?

Priya: Oh dear.

Clem: Yeah, that's about right.

Margie: I'll do my best to nail the spell the first time. Really hope the house doesn't blow up.

Danica: Same. We just got everything exactly how we want it.

Margie: This will be fine. Everything will be fine, right?

Vanessa: Are you hyperventilating? Do I need to come over?

Margie: I'm...good. Probably. Maybe. I'm going offline for a while.

Someone should go see about Margie, who wasn't mentally prepared to anchor this spell, but Clem had to get the house ready. Certain ritual preparations had to be done to give them the best chance of making this spell work. She spent two hours bolstering the candles and crystals that would be used, charging them with her power until they couldn't hold any more energy. Her own reserves would replenish as she rested, so she showered when she was finished, washing off the summer sweat. Her phone had been quiet for a while, and she dressed in a loose white summer dress, not archetypical but comfortable.

I miss him.

The thought crept in sneakily, like that annoying ginger cat from up the street. Suddenly she had it squatting in her head, getting bigger all the time. *I miss Gavin.*

No, you're not allowed to miss him.

It didn't matter if it had been fun hanging out with him or the sex was good. His freaking job was to hunt witches. That wasn't an ideological difference they could just agree to disagree on. *You can't compromise with someone who thinks you shouldn't exist.*

Not ever.

Gavin tried his damnedest not to laugh.

The replacement crew had been forced to eat a vegetarian meal at premium prices, but Echo hadn't found anything useful. Too much human interference. After lunch, Gavin guided them to the cornfield, hoping for the best. Since then, this pile of pillocks had spent hours going over the site, and they hadn't found a damn thing.

From what he knew of Clem, he guessed that she'd rallied her coven to cleanse the place, leaving not even a glimmer of energy to be traced. Now it was just a field, and while he could see visual signs of people moving around, there was no way to trace them. Echo was good, Gavin would give him that. He did some physical tracking and found where they'd left all their vehicles, some distance away. But a witch walking to their car didn't leave much evidence. And beyond that, the witches could be anywhere.

If you didn't already know who they were. And Gavin was keeping his mouth shut.

I made my choice.

Right now, he didn't have an active plan for escaping the order, but maybe he could live on Grandad's boat.

After several fruitless hours, everyone was hot and enraged, and Ted acted like Gavin had orchestrated the whole thing, snapping as he ordered the rest of his team back to the SUV. If the situation weren't so grim, he'd be smiling over how testy that arse was. He'd assumed Gavin was incompetent if not disloyal and that he'd waltz into town on the old man's orders, immediately righting all wrongs.

It doesn't work that way, you dozy prat.

He trailed far enough behind that he hoped they'd think he was out of earshot. That was the only way he'd learn more than they'd been ordered to share. And sure enough, Alban and Darcy hung back as the former tried to flirt. She was having none of it, but he could tell when someone was showing off to impress a potential mate. Alban was the most likely to slip up.

"How long do you reckon it will take?" Alban asked, low.

Darcy only shrugged.

"I'm betting at least six months. This will be the first official outpost across the pond. I hope I don't get stuck here permanently."

That was news. So Ted's people weren't only here because of Gavin? It seemed like they had been sent over to organize a field office in America and had been diverted from the original purpose. Now he wished he'd paid more attention to order politics.

The old man's still in charge, right?

There had been others who tried to use Grandad's defection as an excuse to enact a coup, but Da had fought them off, holding on to power like a desperate dictator.

Probably a dead-accurate analogy.

"Aren't you curious about our secret orders?" Alban persisted.

"Not even slightly," said Darcy.

Smart girl.

Poking about where curiosity was neither welcome nor advisable would only get them in trouble. Not that it appeared to discourage Alban in any fashion.

"I'm dying to have a look at the USB that Ted and Joanna are hoarding. They take turns guarding it, and I know Ingram's asked about it, but they won't even show him, and he has seniority in the team. If he hasn't earned a peek—"

"Shut it." Darcy's tone was curt, and she silenced Alban just in time, as Echo hung back, giving the younger members a stern look.

"Is there some reason you're dawdling? You're not here to chat each other up."

Darcy raised a coppery brow. "That's offensive. I'm walking at my normal pace, and he won't leave me alone. How's that my fault?" To Alban, she added, "You aren't my style at all, and fraternization is unprofessional, but if I had a mind to take someone in the team for a spin, it'd be Echo, not you. So sod off."

Gavin quickened his pace, not wanting to seem like he was

eavesdropping. Echo was frozen like a deer in headlights, evidently unprepared to hear he was more to Darcy's taste. Alban swore all the way back to the SUV, stomping like a spoiled child.

These are the ones in charge of meting out "justice."

He got to his bike just after Ted reached the SUV, where the arse paced like his boots were on fire and then chewed out the rest of his team. Generally it wasn't a good idea to take your shitty day out on the squad who might need to watch your back later. *Too much resentment builds up, and then oops, no more Ted.*

That's not my problem. Getting rid of them is.

"Head back to the flat," Ted ordered Gavin. "And sit tight until I summon you. Chances are, you'll be recalled, but I'm waiting for orders, same as you."

"In the meantime, we'll finish what you couldn't," Ingram said.

At his side, Gavin's hand tried to ball up into a fist, but he stopped it, knowing the team was trained to look for signs a hunter had lost drive and dedication.

"Write up a report," Joanna said. "You can send it to me directly. I want to know everything you've done since you got here, all steps taken, all avenues investigated. It will save us some legwork."

"No problem. I'll get on it."

"Give me your mobile." Joanna took it from him without waiting for him to respond and he hoped she didn't look at his messages.

Fortunately, she just tapped in her contact info and returned it efficiently. Trying to be nonchalant, he sauntered over to his bike and waved as he pulled on his helmet. Every nerve screamed for him to warn Clem more specifically, but his order-allocated mobile wasn't secure; he didn't dare send more than the vague text he'd already chanced. Hopefully if they checked his communications, they would assume he'd been slacking off with a local woman, getting some action instead of focusing on the mission. Not admirable or worthy of commendation, but nothing that would get him sanctioned. He didn't care about staying in good standing, but it would be easier to run if the order wasn't on high alert. As soon as he got back to the flat, he purged all messages from Clem. They might have them already, but they were flirty; that was all. Gavin would rather not put her on their radar if she wasn't already.

To calm himself, he cuddled Benson, who was getting bolder and seemed to enjoy receiving a gentle stroke down his furry spine. When the mouse showed signs of wanting to return to his home, Gavin got to work on Joanna's request, knowing his father would hear about it if it wasn't ready when she asked. Sure enough, as he typed away on his official tablet, his father rang, like a specter programmed to haunt the same house.

"Hello, Da. How's life treating you?" He put a cheerful lilt in his voice, knowing that nothing infuriated the old man like joyful insouciance.

"I didn't call to chat," Jase snapped.

"Ah, then please do tell me what you need. I live to serve." Maybe the old man wouldn't notice the sarcasm.

"I didn't call for lip either. Don't be clever with me, lad. Did the team show up yet?"

He was sure Ted must've reported in already, so what was the point of this?

"I've met with them," he said. "And they're waiting for my report. I've been ordered to stand down. Am I finally getting that holiday in the Maldives that I request every year?"

There was a long, fraught silence. "Are you quite finished?"

He pretended not to realize he was getting on Da's last nerve, enjoying himself immensely. "So that's a no on the holiday."

"This isn't funny, Gavin. Network intel advised me that there's a huge concentration of witches in the American Midwest. This is a massive undertaking, and I'm mobilizing all resources to cleanse that area. I expect your full cooperation." A strategic pause. "You won't let me down, will you, son?"

Fuck. An icy chill swept over him, and it took all his self-control not to shout invective.

Those are people, you monster. I'll stop you, if it's the last thing I do.

CHAPTER 23

"I HAVE BAD NEWS AND worse news," Ethel said. "Which do you want first?"

Clem glared at the older witch. The entire coven was convened in their kitchen, and they'd decided to scry to see if the situation had changed. Everyone wanted to know what Gavin was up to, now that Clem was no longer surveilling him. Not that her observation had been professional or dispassionate. According to the grapevine, Mina Rodriguez had eyes on Gavin, but she reported to Gladys, and Ethel preferred seeing things with her own eyes anyway.

"I don't think you understand how this is supposed to work," Leanne said. "We need good news to keep our spirits up, even if you have to invent some."

Margie added, "I'm trying to stay calm, but you're making it tough."

The rest of the coven stared, waiting for Ethel to continue. "Fine. Reinforcements have arrived, and it's not just another hunter. They've dispatched a team." To illustrate her words, she gestured, focusing on the water she'd been using to scry, and a vague impression appeared in the copper bowl.

Three men, two women, staying in the same motel Gavin had picked previously. Clem made a face. *Do they give a discount to hunters or something?* She sobered quickly.

"Does that mean Gavin called for reinforcements after he realized you were playing him?" Danica asked softly.

Reflexively Clem shook her head. Despite knowing what he was, part of her still couldn't believe he was evil. And that was awful and heartbreaking—to realize she was *this* gullible, so capable of wishful thinking. For a long moment, they gazed at the image in the water, and then Ethel swirled her fingers, letting her concentration drop. It wasn't safe to focus for too long on those trained to trace the usage of such energy. With the wards up, it should be okay, but she didn't feel good about taking big risks anymore.

Not after how that went down.

She would like to chew Gram out for provoking Mom with Barnabas, but that had to keep. Currently, her life was in a triage situation where the more dire problems had to be tended first. Leanne tapped her manicured nails on the kitchen table, gazing at Kerry and Priya. Clem guessed what the redheaded witch was thinking—these two had barely had a chance to be happy together, and they didn't deserve to have danger shadowing their honeymoon period.

Finally, Vanessa said it. "The plan won't work. Even if we make Gavin forget, we don't have the power to impact that whole team."

Despair hung heavy over the kitchen. From the coven's silence, it seemed like nobody had a solution. Recently, Clem had given too much, and overextending herself came at a high price—pain in her neck and shoulders, a low-grade headache messing with her concentration and blurring her vision. But she couldn't quit, and the solution might come from Etta Mae's journal.

"Then we pivot," Clem said. "Forgetting won't work on Gavin, but he's not the biggest issue anymore." Quickly, she described the Herring spell to the rest of the coven, adding, "If we convince one of the team members that they've caught our trail and we're running, that will buy us some time."

"It could be a permanent fix if they don't come back," Kerry said.

Priya put her hand over Kerry's as if she didn't enjoy pointing out problems. "That doesn't resolve the Gavin situation."

Thoughtfully, Clem got out her phone, studying the perplexing two-word message. Then she passed it around, curious what the others would make of it. One by one, her coven sisters scrutinized it, then Vanessa said, "What's that supposed to mean?"

She shrugged. "I'm not sure. That's why I'm asking for input."

Margie wasn't one to proffer faith when it wasn't warranted, so when she said, "I think he's worried about you," in a low voice, Clem took it seriously.

This woman had been majorly screwed over by her ex, and she wasn't prone to romanticizing bad actors. Clem glanced around the room, trying to read their faces, but for a while, nobody else spoke.

Finally Ethel said, "I don't think he called them. If he's working with them fully, why isn't he with them at the motel? That separation hints at an internal conflict, don't you think?"

Danica nodded. "Gavin knows who you are, and he can deduce your family is connected to the coven. If he'd shared that with the new arrivals, wouldn't they already be on their way here? I think he's trying to figure out what to do as much as we are."

"It's not easy to turn on someone you care about," Kerry added.

Clem made a snap decision because she'd been taking the lead up until this point. "Let's exclude Gavin for now. We can always try the forgetting spell later. For now, they're the larger threat. Let's try the Herring spell. Margie, you'll still need to take the lead."

Priya said, "Since we don't know exactly how this worked back then, I have a suggestion for an improvement."

"Go for it." Leanne sat forward, as did everyone else.

"Since we're stronger in vivimancy, why don't we tweak this spell to be more of a Migratory Bird than a magical Herring?"

Kerry seemed to understand at once. "You mean enchant a live creature, so we don't need as much pure neuromancy strength. Leanne and Margie can work that angle, Ethel and Vanessa can weigh in for the enchantment, you and I will make sure our target bird just keeps flying north while Danica and Clem lend their energy to prolong the effect of the spell."

"Damn," said Ethel. "I think this might be the most ambitious working we've ever attempted."

Clem nodded somberly. "We can't fail."

Vanessa reached for Ethel's hand. "We got this. When we're done, that will be the witchiest bird in the world."

"Any final notes before we get started?" Danica asked softly.

"When we release the spell, focus on the older woman," Ethel suggested. "She might be the team leader, and even if she's not, I suspect the boss will listen to her. With age comes wisdom. Supposedly."

"Good thinking," Priya said.

Earlier, Clem had set up folding chairs so the whole coven could gather around the kitchen table. Whether Margie was ready or not, they had to try this spell before the team tracked them down. The situation had officially escalated, which meant St. Claire was on the radar of whoever gave orders to all the witch hunters.

No idea what to do about that.

It was a threat much larger than any they'd faced previously. If it couldn't be resolved here, they might have to pack up and run, just as their forebearers had done in New England. Clem let out a shaky breath, aware her hand was sticky with nervous sweat. Kerry squeezed it reassuringly, and Clem closed her eyes, willing herself to be calm.

"Let's begin," Margie said in a firm tone.

But before the spell began, someone banged on the front door. Clem got up with a mumbled curse, anxiety rising in case it was Gavin come to prove her wrong or even worse, the other crew. To her astonishment, she found Hazel Jeffords on her front porch with a surprisingly beautiful pineapple upside-down cake.

The older woman shuffled her feet. "I thought...well, I saw you have a lot of cars parked out front, and you invited me to your last get-together. Ethel did anyway. I'm sure you meant to let me know. It's easy to forget to call people, and I'm right down the street..."

Since the woman wasn't yelling about her cat for once, Clem didn't have the heart to turn her away. "Come on in. That cake looks awesome. Why don't I cut some for everybody and make a pot of coffee?"

The whole coven played along when Clem turned this into a book club meeting, and they talked about the last novel they'd read, which Hazel hadn't. "I'm definitely going to see if the library has it," she said, as the discussion waned. "I probably shouldn't mention this to my Sunday school class because it sounds like it's racy."

"The library does have it," Leanne said. "But you'll be lucky to find this one on the shelves."

Hazel seemed to take that as a personal challenge; she got up immediately. "I know the head librarian from church. I'll get that book next, see if I don't. You can bring back the cake plate tomorrow," she called, speed walking toward the door.

"Does this mean Hazel is part of our book club from now on?" Vanessa wondered.

"Just look what you did," Danica scolded Ethel. "This is why we don't encourage Goliath or Hazel. They'd stay forever if we let them."

The older witch lifted a shoulder, unconcerned. "She's lonely. And her cakes are excellent. Shall we try again?"

When they joined hands, the energy rose between them in a practiced wave. Though everyone fed the working, Margie shaped it cleverly. In her hands, it became a twisty little red herring, and then Kerry and Priya took it from there, affixing it to a bird they sang to in magical tones. As one, Vanessa and Ethel shifted gears, nudging the spell toward the older woman Ethel had identified as the target. Here, they had to be careful. If the spell went wrong, their target could use it to trace the energy back to them.

But Margie grew in confidence, unspooling a fine tether that let the herring zip away. She offered just a flicker of energy in the distraction, and then the connection went taut and snapped as the ensorcelled bird raced away, crafted as a distraction that would lead the team astray. The movement and the dispersal of energy would seem like a careless witch, bleeding power on the move, plausible for a witch who was emotionally distressed.

Clem pulled out of the bond as everyone else did, conscious of bone-deep exhaustion. The Herring-Bird—an improvement on the original spell—would lead the crew astray for weeks, darting about the country in erratic movements that should run the hunters ragged. *Hopefully, it won't lead them to any actual witches. I'll post a warning on the forum.*

Margie groaned and stretched, raising her arms above her head. "I think we did it."

"You need to eat something," Danica said. "We all do."

She took the hint, assisting her cousin in setting out drinks and more slices of the pineapple upside-down cake. As her coven sisters devoured the dessert, Clem rubbed her temples. This headache had persisted for days, a perfect accompaniment to the low-key sadness that wouldn't let her go. She'd tried not to be that dipshit, pining for someone who was poison to her, but she couldn't wipe Gavin out of her heart, which she'd previously been able to clear like it was a dry-erase board.

"I think he's shielding you," Leanne said quietly.

She glanced up with a start. "What?"

The redheaded witch put her hands on Clem's shoulders and kneaded, going hard at the knots of tension. "Gavin. He must've covered for you. Otherwise, we'd already be fighting or fleeing for our lives."

Clem muttered, "More likely he's covering his own ass. Otherwise he'd have to explain sleeping with the enemy."

"You should talk to him," Priya suggested.

She ignored that suggestion. Priya and Danica were the sweetest witches in the coven, and they both tended to think that anything could be forgiven. Clem knew better. That was why she had no relationship with Barnabas, and she was ready to add Gram to her list of biologically-related-yet-undesirable connections.

"Let's check if the spell worked first," Ethel said. "Fill me another bowl of water."

What about the secret USB?

Pacing the flat, Gavin shook his head. That had to be a trap or another test of his loyalty. Even Alban couldn't be bird-witted enough to let that slip accidentally. No, if Gavin went poking around, it would confirm any doubts they had about him. There might not even *be* a secret USB, best to proceed as if he hadn't heard anything about it. Benson was asleep, curled up in his breast pocket, and the mouse made him feel less alone at least.

Just as well I have Benson. Might end up on the lam like Grandad with only this wee fellow for company.

As he fretted, he got a call in the middle of the night.

"We've found them," Ted said, his tone all triumphant. "Joanna got the lock on them, they're running. Sit tight and wait for Jase to deal with you. I smell disciplinary action!"

Panic fluttered wildly inside him, and he battled back the urge to demand clarification. *Clem's safe, right?* Somehow he feigned indifference.

"Understood." He didn't offer any good wishes, but that didn't faze the other man.

"Reflect on why you failed," Ted added.

Swallowing a curse, Gavin cut the call and controlled the urge to text Clem. His mobile wasn't safe, and if he contacted her immediately after hearing that the team had found the trail, it would give the game away. *I could use the netbook to email her at the contact listed on the shop website.* It might take a while for her to check it, though, and he shouldn't say anything too personal, as her cousin probably monitored the box as well.

That in mind, he headed to the bedroom and pulled the netbook out of its hiding space. He had put a password on it so if there had been any failed attempts to login, it would show on the screen. The machine appeared to be untouched. Thankfully, Ted didn't have orders to toss the place. His father was reluctant to admit he was doubting Gavin, perhaps.

Looks like there's some benefit to being Da's son after all.

Gavin opened his email, deciding to contact her from the old account he was using to communicate with Grandad. There was a message waiting from his grandfather, along with ten thousand spam messages. He opened it first. There were four attachments, poor-quality images that appeared to be snapped of some ancient text. If he peered closely, he could make out some of the words, but he didn't feel like working that hard unless he knew the context.

Dear Gavin,

I've thought long and hard about whether to entrust you with this.

At first, I wasn't certain if you'd come to entrap me as your father's agent, but the longer we converse, the more I don't believe that's the case. And if I'm wrong about you, then I lose nothing by sharing this information because I'm not sending my only copies. The truth is always the truth, no matter who attempts to cover it up.

I've attached photos I took in the archives, secrets I was never meant to know. This is what they're concealing from the rest of the witch hunters—there's no holy calling.

Around the time of the first trials, there was a schism in the vivimancer line. They hired us to hunt their rivals to extinction. Those purges came down to money and power. At some point, our predecessors decided they didn't like our origin story and they excised it. Apart from that copy I found, the original histories have all been burned or rewritten, casting us as heroes who fight against evil.

That's not the case. It was *never* the case.

At best, we were brutes and bounty hunters who sold our power to the highest bidder. You can read the details for yourself, though you may need to adjust the contrast if you try to print those pages. Camera phones were terrible twenty years ago, but it was all I had access to at the time.

They're not chasing me simply because I fell in love with a witch, my lad. They're hunting me because I know the truth, and it has the power to destroy them.

Witches need not fear us. We have no authority, no gifts they don't already possess. We've simply spent centuries honing our talents for harm. Hunters have been the hounds for the order while the enforcers sever a witch's connection to magic, taking away their identity, and they do it for profit. The order seizes a significant portion of each witch's assets after each "successful conversion."

It needs to end.

Perhaps you can succeed in this where I've failed. I have no ideas, only the certainty of what I've seen and experienced.

Please do the right thing.

Love always,

Grandad

Gavin stared at his screen, hardly able to credit what he was seeing. Then he fiddled with the images until he could make out the faded, crabbed writing in the journal. It was a personal account from one of the first witch hunters, and from what he could piece together, the man had been a vivimancer named Jeremiah, who took contracts to eliminate magical rivals.

He was a hired killer. That's our glorious legacy.

Immediately, he wondered if his father knew about this.

He must. But all Jase's power and prestige was wrapped up in running the order. It would require a certain flexibility of mind to acknowledge that he was wrong—that his worldview was bent and biased—and that he needed to make amends. *He'll never admit to anything. He'll never stop on his own.*

This changes everything.

So many emotions whirled in Gavin's head that he scarcely knew what to think or feel. Irrationally, he wanted to talk Clem about it, but she probably had no desire to ever see or speak to him again. He couldn't blame her either. Before he lost his shit entirely, he wrote the email to Clem that he'd planned to send initially.

Sending a heads-up. There are strangers in town, looking for you. I've given them nothing, but you should be watchful nonetheless. I'll do whatever I can to help. It may not be enough.

There was so much more he wanted to say, but he couldn't find the right words. His head was a messy place, too full of pain and echoes. So Gavin finally just added, *Take care of yourself.* And signed off as "English."

Half-dazed, he wandered outside. He knew about witches, of course, and their magical gifts. He'd studied the types of magic and the sorts of spells he might face if he stumbled into an ambush. Never once had he considered that his hunting senses or the powers he'd used to track them down stemmed from the same source.

Is that true?

It was late, the residential neighborhood quiet as the grave apart from a dog that wouldn't settle down. The poor fellow kept barking, signaling a loneliness that Gavin shared, as it ripened from agitation into a mournful howl. Mina had hydrangea bushes planted alongside the house, and some of the blooms had wilted in the summer heat. Or maybe it was just the natural life cycle; Gavin didn't know enough about gardening to be sure.

Feeling a bit silly, he plucked a dead blossom and cupped it in his palm. The petals were brown at the edges, fragile as a butterfly wing. He had no idea how to go about this, as it was nothing like his original training, but he wrapped his fingers around the flower and focused, imagining it flush and whole, pink as a sunrise. At first, nothing happened.

This is ridiculous. Maybe Grandad got it wrong? I'm not—

Energy swirled up some long-dormant part of him, trickling out through his fingers in a pleasurable shiver. This was nothing like the predatory and punitive skills he'd learned from his father. No, it was sweet and wholesome, like offering generously of himself to a creature in need. When he opened his hand, the hydrangea was furiously fuchsia, vibrant as the ones still attached to the shrub. It even smelled sweeter than the others, gently transmuted into a magical artifact.

I brought it back. Stunned, he stared at the fresh bloom in his hand.

"Grandad is right. I'm a witch. I'm a fucking witch," he whispered.

Finally, a tiny voice said, or rather—Gavin heard it with his mind, not his ears. Benson popped his head out of Gavin's pocket and gazed up at him with bright, black eyes.

It's been so boring and lonely waiting for you to figure things out, but now we can have a proper chat. My name's not Benson, by the way, but I've gotten used to it.

"This cannot be happening," Gavin said faintly.

The mouse went on as if he hadn't spoken. *Anyway, I'm your familiar, and I have so much to teach you.*

CHAPTER 24

THE NEXT DAY, CLEM CALLED Ethel to see if the hunter team was still gone, following the Herring-Bird with complete conviction.

They'd checked to make sure the crew had rolled out the night before, but Ethel felt the need to scan the motel in case they saw through the ruse and doubled back. Twenty minutes later, the older witch called back to confirm. "No sign of them in the area. I think they're in Michigan, but I won't risk a finding spell. That might give the game away."

"Understood. Thank you. I hope they go all the way to the Yukon," Clem muttered.

"Are you holding up okay?" Ethel asked, unexpectedly prolonging the call.

"I'll survive," she said firmly. "Talk to you later."

This will buy us some time.

She still had to worry about Gavin, but if he'd planned to move against her, he would've enlisted the aid of his fellow hunters, not let her coven turn them aside. Since he'd kept his mouth shut, maybe she had some hope of reaching him. That was a weight off her shoulders, and it let her focus on catching up on repairs at the shop, though after last night's casting, even simple spell work left her light-headed. She needed time to replenish her energy, but delays would impact customers who might take their business elsewhere. Fix-It Witches had built a reputation for prompt, flawless service, and their clients didn't care that hell had broken loose in Clem and Danica's personal lives.

Just past noon, she knocked back an energy drink and finally got around to checking the company email. The inbox was full of the usual spam and solicitations, along with a few inquiries about possible service calls. Clem answered those right away. At the bottom of the list, she spotted Gavin's name.

Quickly, she skimmed the message and froze, staring at the screen for long moments. She couldn't believe what she was reading at first. It sounded like he was proposing an alliance, maybe even like he wanted to protect her. There had to be a reason he was using an email address that was mostly numbers instead of sending a text like usual.

Has he broken away from the order?

She couldn't decide how to respond. This didn't seem like a ruse. Capture would be straightforward with so many hunters arrayed against her, no need to lure her into a trap. Odds were, this was a sincere olive branch. A frisson raced through her, illogical excitement over the prospect of seeing him again, even under these circumstances. It felt like much longer than a few days since she saw Gavin last. Finally she wrote:

Come to my place at four if you get this in time. If not, tomorrow will do. We'll talk more then.

Then she dove back into work until Danica arrived later to relieve her. She hesitated, trying to decide if she should share the news with her cousin. Hell, it felt like pulling teeth when they'd had that convo where Clem admitted her relationship with Gavin had gotten thorny and complicated.

So, this time, she took a breath and chose not to isolate herself. "I'm meeting Gavin later," she said.

Both Clem's parents had been too wrapped up in their personal drama to listen when she was having a hard time, and it became second nature for her to deal with shit on her own. Among the coven, she was the least likely to confess she was having personal problems, the least likely to ask for help even if she needed it desperately. Her can-do attitude, somewhere along the way, had become an "I don't need anyone else" lifestyle.

Danica dropped her phone with a clatter, and worry clouded her brown eyes. "Are you sure that's safe?"

"Not entirely, but judging purely by behavior, if he wanted the others to know about me, they would. He let them go off on a wild goose chase—"

"Maybe literally in this case," Danica cut in, likely trying to lighten the mood.

Clem managed a halfhearted smile. "I *hope* Priya picked a goose. That way, if they catch up to our Herring-Bird, it'll be a real battle."

"Right? I watched this video of a goose who fights everybody— wait, what we were talking about again?"

"Gavin. And how he didn't tell his cronies about me. I think that's a strong enough statement to warrant a discussion." Goddess, she hoped her faith wasn't misplaced.

After a moment, Danica nodded. "Are you sure you want to face him alone?"

This is exactly why I don't share stuff with people.

"I'm positive. Things good with the CinnaMan?" she asked, almost as an afterthought.

"We're great. I'm concerned about you right now...and the rest of the coven. I've been quietly freaking out since the new witch hunters showed up." Her cousin gave her a searching look, genuinely worried, not being meddlesome.

Gotta get better at accepting care. With effort, Clem refrained from snapping, *I'm handling it.* Because she understood her cousin wasn't casting aspersions on her capability. This wasn't subtext; it was just an emotional response.

"It's understandable. The situation is..." *What's the right word? Tense? Terrifying? Unnerving?* They all fit, so she lifted a shoulder in a shrug. Danica seemed to get it, no need to ramble on.

"Good luck," her cousin said, patting her shoulder.

Grabbing her bag, Clem headed out. The weather was scorching hot today, muggy as well, and she was soaked in sweat by the time she trudged home. Goliath was on the porch again, but he cried in disappointment over finding Clem instead of Danica and ambled back toward Hazel Jeffords's house with his tail swishing the air.

"I have no idea what your deal is," Clem told the retreating cat.

Who ignored her.

Honestly, it was baffling since they were cousins with the *same* type of magic, but Goliath only had one witch in his heart. With a mental shrug, Clem headed inside to shower. She tried not to linger, conscious that if she waxed everything and moisturized thoroughly, it would feel like getting ready for a date. With that in mind, she also dressed in the first comfortable clothes that came to hand: a pair of blue shorts and a striped tank top.

I can do this.

Four came and went, and she occupied herself by slicing some watermelon. *Maybe he didn't get my reply?* But the growl of his bike engine broke the quiet ten minutes later, and Clem peered out the front window, checking to ensure it was Gavin. He strode up the walk and sounded a firm knock, not seeming to share her misgivings. Taking a deep breath, she opened the door and stepped back to invite him in with a gesture.

What am I even supposed to say in this situation? There's no greeting card for this.

"Hey," she said finally.

Gavin stared at her intensely, seeming to drink her in from head to toe. "You've been keeping safe?"

"Yeah. Our spell worked on the others. Thanks for keeping my secret."

"I have one too," he said unexpectedly. "And I'll need your help with it, so it's only fair to offer mine in return."

He ran a hand through his hair and now that she was looking closely at him, she could see he hadn't been eating or sleeping well. His face was thin and drawn, darkly stubbled from several days without shaving, and dark shadows cradled his eyes. Even grubby and disheveled, he still made her pulse flutter, dammit.

This is so wrong.

But she found herself asking, "Did something happen? What's the matter?"

I shouldn't ask. I shouldn't even care. He's the freaking enemy. He came here to hurt us. I can never forget that.

"I could tell you what I've learned, but it's easier to show you. Wonder if you'll be as shocked as I was."

Then he glanced around the room until his gaze settled on a wilted plant set on a side table near the window. Normally, Kerry or Priya tended their greenery, but things had been hectic lately. Clem had no freaking idea where this was going when he headed that way, picked up the little pot, and closed his eyes. Incredibly, she sensed the kindling of energy, not the frightening witch hunter sort, though, and the plant brightened and greened before her eyes, the fronds spilling over in lush profusion.

"Surprise," Gavin said. "Everything about the history of the witch hunters is a lie."

———

While Clem stared in astonishment, Gavin summarized what he'd learned from his grandad's email.

He finished with, "And it turns out that the mouse you gave me? He's my familiar."

She suddenly sank down on the sofa like her knees had given out. Her eyes were huge as she stared up at him, seeming unsure how to process the deluge of information. "That's a lot to dump on me all at once, English."

It put a smile on his face to hear that nickname when he'd thought maybe they'd never be on speaking terms again. "Trust me, I'm aware. My grandfather's been on the run since he found out the truth twenty years ago. Back then, he couldn't figure out how to put a stop to this hypocrisy. I will."

"Is that what you need my help with? If what you're saying is true, then it's been witches hunting other witches all these years, driven by greed. So we'd be talking about going to war. And contrary to what you've been brainwashed to believe, most witches aren't violent. Most of us aren't skilled in using offensive magic. You do that to *us*."

Gavin dropped to his knees in front of her, bowing his head. "I don't expect you to forgive me. There's no excuse for the way I've lived my life until this point. I shouldn't have needed to learn I'm a witch to realize that oppressing you is wrong."

"Yeah, I don't want to talk about any of this right now. There's no telling how long our countermeasures will work." At his look, she waved away his silent request for clarification. She'd trusted him enough to meet, not to spill the coven's strategies. "We need to come up with a plan for when those assholes return. It's one thing to say you intend to stop this. Figuring out the logistics is the hard part."

She bent, tugging him up with hands he hadn't expected ever to hold again. Granted, she didn't linger, but the fact that she hadn't slapped him or punted him into the street seemed like a good sign. Carefully, Gavin perched on the edge of the sofa. His whole body felt strange, energized in a way that was brand new. Maybe it was related to the new ways he'd been using his abilities, old witch senses crackling to life when previously they'd only been used for violence and aggression.

Now the flicker of life was tangible all around him, ebbs and flows from every little thing in the world, from blades of grass to the flutter of the wind in the trees. Perhaps there was a way to manage the information overload, but he doubted Clem would be in any frame of mind to indulge his curiosity.

Not with people she loves at risk.

"You're right." His voice sounded rusty, and he couldn't remember the last time he'd eaten or had anything to drink.

I need to get myself together because I've made some big promises. I must keep them.

So I can start trying to heal the harm my family inflicted.

"Don't take this the wrong way, but you look like shit. Come on." Though her tone was brusque, her kindness shocked him.

In the kitchen, there was fresh watermelon sliced on a plate, and she quickly made a couple of sandwiches then poured them both tall glasses of icy lemonade. He didn't deserve such generosity from her, especially when he considered how many witches must've been traumatized because of his work. Sickness churned within him, mixed freely with self-loathing, and he forced it down, along with the food. Every bite strengthened him and steadied him as they ate in silence.

"Thanks," he said eventually.

"Did you fall apart without me or what?" Clem sounded more sarcastic than joking, but there was no cruelty.

It's more than I merit.

"A little," he admitted. "Didn't help that my entire life has been based on an elaborate, toxic falsehood. A calling? Please. They did it for the money."

"That is more honest," Clem said. "But somewhere along the way, they decided to act like there's a holy mission."

"In the beginning we were witches," Gavin said softly. "Vivimancers and neuromancers, mainly. And I won't keep this dirty little secret any longer. We just need to figure out how to wield this information as a weapon."

"And maybe the coup can be bloodless," Clem said.

"It's a long shot. But possibly other hunters feel as I do, and they'd be relieved to learn they can just...stop." He'd long wondered where the money came from to sustain operations, and now, based on Grandad's email, he had confirmation there was a seizure of assets involved whenever a witch was habituated as a mundane.

Such an innocuous word for what we do to them.

Now that Gavin was properly awake as a witch, he could imagine how it must feel. Even with mental adjustment, the former witches must live their lives with a constant sense of something being missing, a piece that had been permanently severed, leaving them incomplete.

"Do you have proof?" Clem asked then.

"I do, but you'll need to volunteer your laptop. I left my mobile back at the flat. I'm sure they're tracking me. The order might also be listening in, so it's not safe to contact me in any fashion other than the email I used before."

"Understood. Let me get my Lenovo. It's upstairs." Here, she hesitated. "You can come up if you want. The wards let you in without hesitation, so that means you're not a threat. And I don't have any secrets I'm hiding anymore, so you might as well."

Gavin blinked, but he stood and followed her up the stairs, feeling slightly less wretched. Clem threw open the door to her bedroom, revealing a sunny white and yellow space. Just looking at it made him smile because it was bold and lovely, and it perfectly reflected the vibrant energy she carried with her. Now, he also sensed the quiver of magic that brightened the room, warming his skin nearly as tangible as a touch.

The furniture was pale wood, shaped with simple lines—a chest of drawers matched with twin night tables framing a full-size bed. There was also a little vanity with a lighted mirror where he imagined her sitting to fix her hair or apply lipstick. Even the linens were full of personality, covered in big pineapples. The comfortable quilt was rumpled, as if she'd straightened it in a hurry before rushing to work that morning. Her laptop sat open on the right-hand table, snoozing, but a touch from her woke it up. She passed the computer over to him.

Gavin pulled up the email account where he'd stashed the images his grandad had sent and immediately saved them to the cloud. "What's your email?" he asked.

"You already have it." She didn't seem to be joking, but he doubted that the business box was the only one she used.

"Your personal one."

With a sigh, Clem reached over to input a different address in the email target line, and he breathed in her soft, sweet scent.

Her body lotion smells like melon and pineapple. Her sheets have pineapples on them too. One of these days, he'd ask about that.

Once she entered her email address, he forwarded the photos, and Clem pulled out her phone to check them. It took her a bit to skim the images, but he registered the moment when she got the bits he'd already shared with her. Hearing it was one thing, seeing it written in faded, old-fashioned script was another.

She let out a slow breath. "I believe you. So what's the plan?"

"That's what I'm here to figure out. With you."

CHAPTER 25

HOURS LATER, CLEM AND GAVIN had discussed and discarded at least twenty possibilities.

Frustration built, and she knocked back the last of her iced tea, scouring her tired mind. In her overheated brain pan, the kernel of an idea popped, and Clem jumped to her feet, excitement pulsing through her.

Is this the perfect solution? Maybe.

"Seems like you've got something," Gavin noted.

"First, we circulate the proof you found. We can't spread it wide on the web, but there are witch equivalents. You can do the same on hunter sites—I'm sure there are some. If we put magical bots on it, there's no way they can scrub the truth fast enough to keep people from seeing it." She cracked her knuckles. "This is *my* house. I rule the world witch web."

"That...could work."

Her excitement grew when Gavin voiced support. "Once we get the word out, then we follow up with the witch's council. They haven't intervened because they thought hunters have no connection with us, right? Not subject to their authority. But hunters *are* witches, so that means they're guilty of viciously attacking their brethren for centuries."

"The witch's council must have their own enforcers," Gavin said, seeming to realize what conclusion she'd reached.

"We don't have too much trouble these days, but yeah."

"Then let's get started. We'll need to take turns with your laptop—"

Laughing, Clem shook her head. "Tech witch. Do you understand what I mean by 'magical bots'? Write down the info for the hunter portals, and I'll weave it into a dispersal spell and cast it on my laptop. A thousand AIs will whisper the truth all over our portions of the web. The information can't be scrubbed or deleted through mundane means either."

Clem basked in the impressed look Gavin aimed her way. "How utterly tremendous. Is that something I could learn?"

"Since you demonstrated proficiency with vivimancy as your first instinct, and you said hunters were mainly attuned to that and neuromancy, I suspect it'd be challenging."

"Why?" he asked.

"All witches can access each type of magic, but the degree of success depends on their major attunement. Vivimancy and technomancy are oppositional on the spectrum… It's why we cast well together, offering both sides of the magical coin. Magics that are more adjacent are easier to learn, though. Someone who has skill in divinations might also be good at enchantments. Think of it like a wheel where the different gifts abut."

It felt strange to be educating a hunter—no, a *former* hunter—on what it meant to be a witch. She could only imagine how Gavin felt, how she'd feel to learn every horrible thing she'd ever been taught was a lie—

Actually, I do know how he feels because of Gram and her bullshit about Waterhouse witches mixing with mundanes.

"That makes sense. Degree of affinity dictates the level of adroitness in each area," he said, seeming to work it out in his head.

"I can draw you a chart if you like. But save further questions for after. I need to get this spell in motion."

Gavin nodded, and she hurriedly set up everything she needed next to the laptop. It felt so incredibly strange to be doing this in front of him, but there was no danger. Well, no danger from Gavin. The rest of the order still wanted to wrest away her power.

She lit the candles, opened her laptop, and got the athame she used for spell work. From the corner of her eye, she caught Gavin's reflexive flinch, but she didn't pause to reassure him. Clem felt sure he was braced for her to open a vein or stab him or something, but time was of the essence. They had no clue how long the other crew would be distracted.

Centering herself, she paid respect to the elements and gathered her power, shaping the spell in her head through symbols she etched into the air. In her mind's eye, she crafted little arrows framed from light, encoded with all the firmness of her intention. Then, with a graceful swoop of the blade, she tapped the edge of her laptop, and power swirled as the spell released.

"That was beautiful."

Clem opened her eyes. "Was it?"

"If even one hunter had seen what witches do, we wouldn't

need to circulate that hidden diary. We'd know we're the villains of the piece."

"Not all," she said with a tinge of bitterness. "Even with overwhelming evidence, some people will never admit they're the villains. They commit murder in the daytime and then claim they feared for their lives."

"That's certainly true."

"It's done regardless. The tide can't be stopped."

Since she had little physical control over the spell now that it had been released, she also sent a copy of the email to the witch's council, wanting to make sure they understood what was happening. Clem also included her thoughts on how they ought to proceed, not that she had any influence. In fact, she didn't even know who the current council members were. It was kept secret to eliminate the possibility of currying favor, and the representatives rotated annually, constantly shifting to keep any witch from building up too much political power. She'd heard the council members didn't even know who the others were, as they used a combination of masks and illusion to maintain their anonymity.

"Now we wait," Gavin said.

"That's the toughest part."

"My mouse familiar says his name isn't Benson—he prefers 'Algernon.' At some point, he was exposed to a sad story that made a major impression."

"*Flowers for Algernon*? It has a mouse in it. I hope Algernon Benson fares better," she said with a half smile.

"It's really odd that I can understand him. He's a tiny voice in my head now."

"Already? That's impressive. You must've formed a firm bond."

To her amusement, the mouse popped out of Gavin's shirt pocket, and though Clem didn't hear anything, Gavin was nodding. "Yes, that's true."

"I can't hear him. You know that, right?"

"He says he's guaranteed to live a long, happy life, as his energy is tied to mine," Gavin explained. "I still think two names is a bit excessive for such a small creature, but...yes, fine. I'll try to do better. He's accusing me of sizeism."

Clem swallowed a laugh, reminding herself she and Gavin were only temporary allies, nothing more. *Focus on the issue at hand.*

"The other crew will likely double back once they see the messages proliferating. They might try to take revenge—"

"They'll have to come through me," Gavin cut in. "I'll defend you and the rest of your coven."

Clem blinked at him, hardly able to believe he'd said that so easily. "You knew?"

"That you were protecting people you love? It's the only thing that makes sense. I suspect I met your coven at the party, likely a last-ditch effort to convince me you're a mundane. Otherwise you never would have..." He paused, his gaze dropping to his lap.

How did you plan to finish that sentence? Been with someone like me? Clem let it go because she had too many conflicting emotions, all swirling in a chaotic flurry.

She stood, tidying up the spell components without responding to the sentence he'd failed to finish. That encapsulated their relationship, so many things they'd never dared to say, and perhaps never would. Her heart ached over it because she'd never—

Oh. Oh no.

She'd never loved anyone like this. It made no sense. Why him of all people? Even now, she wanted to hug him because he was so weary, broken, and tormented.

I shouldn't, right?

I can't.

Even if he's changed his ways, he's still done terrible things. He should have known that hurting people was wrong even without learning that he's from the group he's been persecuting.

That's the basics of being a decent person.

Still, she wanted to cry over the awful impossibility of it, and she wanted to punch something over how irrational her heart was being. *I don't want to love him.*

"What's wrong?" Gavin asked.

"Why does it have to be you?" Clem whispered. "Why you, English?"

"What?"

"After seeing how my mother lived, I've kept my heart intact. I didn't want to end up at the mercy of my emotions, spinning from rage to heartbreak on a dime."

"Clem—"

"No, I wasn't asking for a response. We have to weather this crisis before we talk about..." *Us.*

She couldn't bring herself to say the word because her vulnerability to him was like a raw wound, and she couldn't even claim she'd gone into the situation unaware of who and what he was. No, her eyes had been wide open.

And yet, I still fell for him.

She had so many conflicting emotions because part of her understood he'd been educated in a corrupt system, but still. *Why didn't he know it was morally wrong? Why didn't he stop until now?*

"I have so many regrets," he said then. "If I could change everything—my whole fucking life—I would. I'd erase all the hate I put into the world. But I can't. It's done, and it doesn't matter how I feel about it. The only thing I can do is atone for my crimes and spend the rest of my life making it up to the community I harmed."

Clem froze. "Then that means..."

"Yes. After the dust settles and I make sure your coven is safe, I plan to submit myself for judgment to the witch's council."

Gavin had no more words after he made that pronouncement.

He didn't know what the council would do to him, and truthfully, he didn't care. It would be fitting if they inflicted on him the punishment the order had been imposing on witches for centuries. For profit.

He rose, feeling marginally better than he had when he arrived. Between the food and drink and basking in Clem's company, he felt like he could cope. He only needed to hang on for a few days longer, and then he could rest, whatever form that took.

"I should go," he said. "You said the wards will keep you safe if...something happens?"

Gavin didn't know exactly what he feared—Ted returning or his old man sending even more enforcers. He just knew he couldn't take any chances with her safety, not when he'd led everyone here, following orders like a sodding hound.

"They'll respond aggressively if someone with malicious intent tries to cross the threshold," she assured him.

"I'll buy a burner," Gavin said. "And I'll text you the new number. You can't use my old mobile, but do ring me if anything happens. I'll come, no matter the hour."

"Thank you." Her voice was oddly formal.

"I'll be in touch, then."

Though it was torture, he headed out without looking back at her, getting on the Duc. Benson had gotten used to traveling in his pocket, though sometimes he yelled in Gavin's mind about how loud it was. First, he headed to a convenience store to pick up a cheap flip phone along with a prepaid card with some airtime, then he drove back to the flat, where he let Benson take a break in his habitat to run on the wheel, eat some delicious pellets, and have a drink. Gavin installed the sim and used the Wi-Fi with VPN to place an internet call and activate the service. Perhaps he was being too careful, but he couldn't risk letting his father spy on him.

Like Grandad said, I made my choice.

Quickly, he texted Clem with his new cell number and she texted fifteen minutes later with a simple acknowledgment.

He'd been a tween the last time he sent a reply with this sort of keyboard, best for people with nimble thumbs. I'm here if you need me.

Already there would be echoes in the order from the spell Clem had cast. God, but it had been fucking beautiful, like a stream of silver minnows darting into the machine. Gavin couldn't just sit alone and brood while they waited for the next development, but he had nothing productive to do either.

It's been a while since my last visit.

The hour was off for a coffee klatch gathering, but Gavin found that he missed Leonard. Howard and Gladys too, frankly, but he was closer to Leonard. So he used the new cell phone to message him.

> New mobile, this is Gavin. Are you home? I'd like to make myself useful if you have any work for me.
>
> **Leonard:** Come on over.

Relieved to have somewhere to be, Gavin told Benson, "I'm heading out. Can you alert me if anyone comes sniffing around the place?"

The mouse paused on the wheel long enough to reply, *If you're too far away, you'll just get an emotional impression, but yes. I can and I will. Bring me a banana! No, a strawberry!* Silently amused, Gavin headed downstairs and drove the Duc, blanking his mind until arriving at Leonard's house. The old man had his arm in a sling when he met Gavin at the door.

"What happened?" he asked.

Leonard smiled and shook his head. "I tried showing off my bike skills for Gladys. Turns out, it is possible to forget how to ride one, and now I'm paying for my hubris with a hairline fracture."

"What do you need me to do?"

"The yard needs mowing, if you're willing. Good timing too, as it's getting tall, and it's best to do this in the morning or evening."

"Huh. I had no idea it even mattered when you cut it."

"It has to do with stressing the grass and moisture, I believe. Just one of those things you learn taking care of a yard." Leonard shrugged as if to say he wasn't entirely sure either.

"I'll do my best not to stress your grass," Gavin said with a ghost of a smile.

"Mower's in the shed out back. It's not locked. Push mower, though, so you'll get a workout. I prefer it that way because it helps me stay active, but I may break down and get me a riding mower in a few years. It does tire me out, even when I've got two good arms."

"Anything else I should know?"

"I'm sure you know how to mow a yard," Leonard said, but he also couldn't resist giving Gavin a few more tips. "I'll have a beer waiting for you on the patio when you're done. Maybe I'll order some fried chicken too. You willing to stay for a late-night snack?"

"Are you getting it from Gloria's?" That was a little joint he and Leonard had ordered from before.

"Nowhere else."

"Then I'm in."

Gavin lost himself in physical labor for a couple of hours, meticulously going row by row to make Leonard's garden as tidy as he could, and then he used edging shears to trim the hard-to-reach areas. He was sweaty and exhausted when he finally finished, but at least he felt marginally less miserable.

It was gone nine by the time he finished, but as promised, Leonard had a tin bucket of iced beers on the patio and a box of Gloria's fried chicken. It was the juiciest, crunchiest he'd ever tasted, and he sank his teeth into it with a hungry groan.

Leonard laughed. "You act like you haven't eaten in weeks."

"I've been struggling," he admitted.

"Financially?"

Gavin shook his head. "No, I wish it was that simple to solve."

"You want to tell me about it?"

"I can't tell you everything, but I can give you the gist if you're willing to listen."

"Always. I've enjoyed having you in town. You're a good man, and I've wished more than once that I had a son like you."

What would I have given at one point to hear such words from Da?

Just about anything. It was why he'd persisted on a path that bothered him down to his bones, after all. But that could only go so far as an excuse. *I'm a grown man.*

"Thank you." Gavin cleared his throat, trying not to show how emotional he'd gotten. "The situation is this, I've been living my life all wrong, according to what I was taught. But now I've learned that it's pretty much all hurtful and outright morally bankrupt. I've injured people by following those beliefs, and I can't stand myself."

"Bigotry is wrong," Leonard agreed. "But sometimes we don't realize how much poison we drank until someone comes along and says, 'Hey, you're hurting me.' We shouldn't need to hear that, right? We ought to *know*. But we don't because we're human and humans are made imperfect. The best part about being human is that we can learn and grow and admit fault and do our best to change. People can change up until their dying day. It's just that most of us are too set in our ways, and we're too vain to admit that we can be wrong."

"I don't want to live my life like that anymore," he whispered.

"So don't. You can't do anything about the people you've hurt, and you can't force them to forgive you either. But you can do better going forward. Listen, I grew up in a time where I was taught all kinds of things I now know are hateful and untrue. I was a real son of a bitch, and I'll die knowing that I was, but I do my best not to be anymore. It's all we can do."

Blinking, Gavin glanced up from the chicken leg he was holding and realized Leonard was probably talking about a different sort of bigotry, but the moral remained the same.

I can't change what I've done, only what I will do.

CHAPTER 26

THE NEXT NIGHT, CLEM COULDN'T believe what she was about to do, but tomorrow was uncertain.

With no guarantees about what the next day might bring, she wanted one last night with Gavin. While the future was beyond their control, she could choose how the next eight hours unfolded, and it might distract her from all the untested magic she'd unleashed. The dissemination spell Clem had created—there was no telling how fast or far the truth had spread. Already she'd read reactions in various private witch forums, branching discussions about the shocking reveal and arguments about how things should play out going forward.

Whatever, I left a few things at his place anyway. Nothing irreplaceable, but still. She used a rideshare app to call a driver, leaving the car keys on the side table by the door in case Danica needed it. Better for it to be parked here than at Gavin's place where there wasn't room for an extra car.

Howard Carruthers turned up in his sedan about ten minutes later. Clem was waiting in front of the house and hopped in the passenger seat with a wave.

"At this hour, it must be a booty call," said Howard.

That startled a laugh out of Clem. "Don't tell my grandmother."

"I would never." The older man offered a conspiratorial look. "What an adult gets up to is their own personal business. Be careful, though."

"Understood."

Howard bragged about his son and his son-in-law the whole way there, but more about his adorable grandbabies. His simple pride was restful after all the complicated crap Clem had been dealing with, so her mood improved a fair amount by the time he dropped her off. She quietly made her way along the side of the house, setting off motion-detecting lights as she went. The movement also alerted a few neighborhood dogs, who started barking something fierce. A vivimancer could whisper a charm to calm them even at a distance, but she lacked that skillset.

Gavin could learn. He's already talking to Benson.

Lightly she crept up the stairs and rapped on the door, not knowing what the hell she'd say when he opened it. Odds were, he was home, as the Duc sat in its usual place. A moment or so later, Gavin appeared in the doorway.

"I'm surprised to see you," he said. "Couldn't stay away?"

"Apparently not. I could claim that I'm here to get my stuff, but we both know that's not wholly true."

"Come in then, before we scandalize the neighbors."

The smile got away from her before she could stop it. Damn him for being so charming. "Does that mean you plan to do something inappropriate to me?"

"Would you let me?" he countered.

"Probably." Clem stepped past him into the apartment, resisting the urge to lean against him by the skin of her teeth.

I want his arms around me. Love the way he smells.

"Should I offer tea while pretending I don't know what you look like naked?"

"No, thanks." She paused while weighing the merits of laying her cards on the table. "Actually I came over because I miss you, and I don't know what's going to happen. We agreed this had an expiration date, and I think this might be our last night, so..." It hurt too much to finish that sentence.

Goddess, why him? She wondered again, without getting an answer.

"You want to make the most of it."

"I mean, it's not entirely up to me. If you're not in the mood or—"

Gavin was on her before she could complete the sentence, cupping her face in his hands and sealing their mouths together with desperate desire. He tasted like milk tea and lemon drops, a lovely flavor she sipped from his tongue. His stubble scraped her jaw as his mouth moved over hers. He smelled beautifully familiar already: a hint of leather oil and the citrus sage of his cologne mingled with the soapy smell of the toiletries that came with the apartment.

Clem wrapped her arms around him, tangling her fingers in the soft hair curled against the nape of his neck. From deep, hungry kisses, he broke into soft, searing ones, planted along her throat like he hoped they would bloom. And they did—into heat that swirled through her body, tingles that lit her up with absolute need.

She jumped him or he lifted her. Either way, she wrapped her legs around his hips, and he cradled her ass in his hands, rolling her against him like he couldn't help it. He was already hard, moaning into her mouth as she kissed him back with all the desire she'd been tamping down for days. Clem ran her hands over his back, digging her fingers into the bunched muscles.

Goddess, his feel, his smell...

Her body heated and slicked, just from the demanding press of his lips, but his hands drove her wild, the way he held her hips and caressed her thighs, dragging her against him as he staggered toward the bedroom. Every few steps they paused, and he leaned against the wall, breathing hard against her skin.

"You feel so good," he whispered.

"I've never been this turned on. Is it because we shouldn't do this?"

"Don't know," he gasped. "Not really thinking right now, to be honest."

"Excellent point."

In the bedroom, Gavin set her down long enough for her to fling her clothes in all directions while he did the same. She admired his strong body for a moment because she had to sate herself on this visual feast now. There might not come another chance. That turned the moment bittersweet, but it didn't stop Clem from grasping it—and him—with both hands. He groaned when she went straight for his cock, lifting his gaze to the ceiling like it had instructions written on it. She pumped a few strokes, working gently back to front, and he jerked his hips, fucking into her furled fingers with an animal grunt.

"I didn't think you'd ever touch me again. It was all part of the plan, right?"

"Not this," she said.

Gavin curled his arms around her with a quiet groan, the perfect mating of desire and despair. "Want you so sodding much."

She nudged him backward, but he pulled her with him, and they hit the mattress together with a bounce. The laugh escaped her at random, and it seemed irreverent to find joy in such a moment, but Gavin smiled while looking into her eyes, and she wrapped her arms around him tightly, breathing him in and feeling his heart racing against hers when he pressed down on her, covering her body with his.

Slowly, he rocked, letting her feel how much he wanted her. She spread her legs, in no hurry to move on from this slow, luscious tease. Each delicious glide raised her excitement and painted her juices all over his cock. He rubbed the head against her clit as he took her mouth in a slow, hot kiss, tongue lazily stroking hers.

She kissed him back with everything she had, caressing his back and shoulders, wanting to become part of him beyond this mingling of breaths. Panting, Gavin broke the kiss and ran his mouth downward to suck the side of her neck, nearly hard enough to bruise. Clem squirmed, moaning his name. The dual sensations spiraled through her, creating an ache that might never be sated. *It's not enough. But it has to be, right?*

Because for them, there might not be a tomorrow.

———

Gavin left rosy marks on her neck, moving to her shoulders.

Her breasts were beautiful, soft and full, spilling slightly to the sides. He kissed first one tip then the other, sucking each nipple into his mouth. Clem twisted beneath him, not trying to get away but to touch more of him, and pleasure spilled through him.

This longing had teeth, gnawing toward his center. His magic crackled to life, sparking off hers, and it tingled all the way to the back of his head, adding a layer of bliss to the ferocious yearning.

Her eyes snapped open as she registered the shifting energy, but she didn't try to reel it in. Instead, she tapped into the electrical wiring and created a bubble of light around the room. Gavin sensed the magic release as he pushed into her hot, welcoming body, just as the silver light shimmered around them.

She arched up and urged him on with her whole body, kissing and licking every inch of him she could reach. Gavin shuddered against her, struggling to contain magic he barely knew what to do with. It streamed out of him in ragged bursts, spilling around them like fireworks. With each release, another pulse of pleasure rolled over them, until sex and magic mingled in a superlative loop. His mouth, her fingers—she pressed two of them past his lips, fucking his mouth as he slowly rocked within her, gradually stoking their mutual excitement to an incredible flash point.

Gavin pulled up her up by the hips, and she locked her legs around his waist. Deep, harder, deeper still. It had never been like this; he could feel her blood racing through his body, her heartbeat thudding in his chest, and her breath blooming in his lungs.

He gathered her into his arms, his body curved over hers, and experienced *everything*. For an incredible moment, he understood what it was to be Clementine Waterhouse, joined to her whole being, as magic streamed between them unchecked.

It was too much.

He came, or she did.

Gavin had no clue how much time passed between the time the orgasm rocked him head to toe and his head went blank like an old TV screen. When he came to himself again, he was curled around Clem in a sweaty tangle, and she was gently petting his back.

"Is that normal?" he asked.

"In what sense?"

"The spell you cast. The way that felt. Any of it, really. I have so many questions."

"I cast the spell because I was afraid you'd spike and lead the other team back here before we're ready for them. The wiring will muffle the energy output since your place isn't warded properly." Here, she paused, her expression thoughtful. "Though if this turns out as we hope, we can adjust our wards. Right now, they're to protect us from detection from hunters. It would be nice to cast them only for regular threats."

"How does that work?" he asked.

"What?"

"A ward against normal danger."

"It would just deter the mundane from messing with that place. If they have firm bad intentions, it means they'd pick another house."

"There's so much to learn," he said in a wondering tone. "When you cast the other spell, there was a great deal more preparation, but this one you popped on the fly. Can you—"

"Explain how that works?" she guessed. At his nod, she went on, "Think of this way. Spells that require a lot of details also require more preparation and finesse. The one I just crafted is literally me building a box barrier using the room's wiring. I'm using connections already in place to do something more basic, so it doesn't take as much prep. But at the same time, it burns more energy, so it's more efficient to prepare properly for any casting. Just…sometimes life happens, and you have to respond."

"Like a reciprocal magic circle during sex?" Gavin wanted to ask if that had ever happened to her before, but he also didn't want to know the answer in case it had.

Even if it was wrong, he'd choose to believe it was special and rare, something that seldom happened even among witches. She stirred against his chest, tracing down his stomach, and his whole body reacted to the sensation. Gavin caught her hand and kissed her fingertips. *If we have only tonight, let me revel in her properly.*

I always knew this was temporary. Even if things hadn't ended like this, it would have ended. That's not in question.

But I'm not ready to let her go.

Reflexively, Gavin gathered her closer and grazed her temple with his lips. She angled her face up, requesting a fuller caress, and he obliged, pouring all his tenderness into the kiss. He dotted smaller kisses on her lower lip, her chin, her cheeks, and her forehead, then he drew back to memorize her face.

Pointed chin, broad cheekbones, liquid brown eyes fringed in thick lashes, and a naked mouth swollen from his kisses. Her hair was tumbled from his fingers, and he didn't think a lifetime of looking at her could ever be enough.

"Why do you look so sad?" she asked.

For the same reason you came over tonight.

Swiftly he tried to erase the expression, but he didn't know how successful he was. To cover up the desperate longing, he tucked his face into her hair. It felt miraculous when she twined her arms around him, seeming in no hurry to wrap things up. Maybe she'd even stay over before packing up her bits and bobs in the morning.

"Are you worried?"

"That's not an answer," she chided gently.

He could've said so many things. Could've chosen to be brave and told her the unvarnished truth, but instead, he hoarded it to himself, a love that would wither in the darkness like a flower starved of light. Clem was absurdly pretty with her shorts and tank top pooled on his floor, with the light spangling her skin in shadowy stars. Her eyes gleamed in the low light, and her magic purred over him in a constant ebb and flow.

I adore you.

Finally he said, "It's complicated."

"True enough. I shouldn't even be here. Not sure anyone in the coven would understand what I'm doing. There's no reason for me to be here. This isn't a scheme or a plan, but I just..."

Had to see me?

Gavin wanted that to be the answer, but he feared it wasn't. Part of him wondered if it would help for him to apologize again, but probably there was no point. Words could only go so far; actions mattered more, which was why he'd submit to judgment after the dust settled.

Gavin inhaled the sweetness of Clem's skin, all dewy wherever they touched. She smelled so good, like sex and fruity lotion, and a hint of his own sweat. It made him want to get her even messier, completely sticky from head to toe so everyone who looked at her would know that he'd put his hands and lips all over her.

I wish she was mine. Truly mine. Not for a night. For good.

"That look is X-rated." When she touched him, he felt it in his bones, the ache of a desire that penetrated like water wearing away a stone. Because of Clem, his shape would be forever changed.

"It is," he agreed. "Do you have the energy for round two?"

Her lush mouth curved in a sex-goddess smile. "Sleep is overrated, English. Let's do it until we die of dehydration."

With a growl, Gavin pulled her on top of him. "Bring it on."

Fuck me, I hope the morning never comes.

CHAPTER 27

ALLEGRA WAS ON CLEM'S COUCH when she got home the next morning.

Better her than anyone else, as Mom tended to focus on her own problems and not lecture the way Gram did. Danica would be ever so gentle and express deep concern about her emotional well-being, but it still felt like the kindest of nagging.

Clem had left before dawn broke fully, with Gavin sleeping in a satisfied sprawl. *That might be the last time I see him.* And now, her mother was here, her expression tight with unhappiness. The fact that D-Pop wasn't here as well meant something bad had happened, probably related to Gram and Barnabas. Clem stifled a sigh, wishing she could take back the key she'd given Allegra on a whim.

"What happened?" she asked.

Allegra promptly burst into tears and gasped out a broken version of how Gram had set up a meeting between Barnabas, Pansy, Allegra, and D-Pop, and Allegra's main takeaway was that Pansy was far younger and prettier, and Gram had apparently implied that if Allegra had been a better wife, taken care of herself better, and kept it tight while making herself endlessly available, then Barnabas wouldn't have strayed the first time, let alone repeatedly.

"And she said everything in *front* of Pansy," Allegra finished with a messy sniff.

Clem narrowed her eyes. "She did not."

"She did!" Allegra said, wiping at the tears streaming from her eyes.

She perched on the sofa by her mother and wrapped an arm around her shoulders. "You know that's not true, right? Blaming you for that asshole's choices is absolute nonsense. Whatever he did, it's got nothing to do with you. It's not your fault, Mom. It never was."

Allegra cried for a while, clinging to Clem, and it reminded her of childhood. *This is why I'm afraid of relationships.* At least with Gavin, she'd known it couldn't go anywhere, but she'd learned too late that even being aware she wasn't meant to be with someone couldn't keep her heart from being reckless. Finally, she understood Danica a little better.

That's a silver lining, right?

"Why is she like this? We've been divorced for fifteen years. Why can't she get over it? It's like she wants me to feel like a failure every time our paths cross and to feel inferior to Barnabas's latest conquest. She's my mother! Isn't she supposed to be my biggest supporter? Why does she break me down this way?"

Yeah, you have a point. And you were supposed to be the grown-up when I was a kid, but I ended up hiding from your moods or being an emotional bolster, so sometimes families don't work as intended.

It's a bug, not a feature.

Mom cried for a bit longer. For reasons known only to Gram, she'd apparently picked up where they left off after Clem bolted, and to exacerbate matters, she invited D-Pop and Pansy to rub salt in the wound. Clem comforted Allegra as best she could, offering whispered reassurances.

When Mom quieted, she dialed D-Pop, who had gone back to sleep, unbothered by any comparisons with his predecessor. Clem loved his calm, but it also drove her crazy because it meant he often didn't notice when Allegra was about to dissolve into a puddle of tears. He was great at mopping them up and appeasing her, not so awesome at heading off a mood. And really, he didn't need to be. Allegra was responsible for her own emotions, but often she came running to lean on Clem in a flip of the parent-child relationship.

Just once, I'd like to be able to rely on her or tell her about my problems.

But she'd never had any faith that Allegra wouldn't break down crying over whatever issue Clem was facing and wind up needing reassurance the problem wasn't because of her. Likely their dynamic had something to do with Mom's relationship with Gram. Fact was, Allegra needed a lot of therapy, but so far, she'd resisted every nudge in that direction.

Hell, I probably could use some counseling too.

But whereas Mom refused to admit she had emotional issues, Clem had a hard time opening up to anyone, and that included a therapist. So far, she hadn't brought herself to make an appointment, but she'd heard of people who did remote sessions, and that sounded more doable, better if she couldn't see the person's face.

"We have to deal with Gram," Clem said then. "This has gone on too long. She's fucking toxic, and she's hurt everyone in the family. I don't know what the solution is. We've all tried talking to her separately, so maybe we call a family meeting?"

"And say what?" Mom finally stopped crying completely, distracted by the suggestion. "'Please stop being yourself, your personality is atrocious'?"

That was a surprisingly biting comment, so much that Clem burst out laughing. "I was thinking something more constructive, but that would be pretty funny."

"I'll call Minerva and see what she says. She's calmer about these things. I wish I could just...not react. How do you grow a thicker skin, is there a spell for it?" Allegra gazed at Clem with wide, shiny eyes.

"It's not your fault," she said.

Goddess, she had such complicated emotions about saying that. On one hand, she meant it. Nobody should be shamed because they were sensitive or because their emotions were close to the surface. But at the same time, Clem wished Allegra's sensitivity didn't mean that she found it impossible to shield Clem or let her own daughter lean on her.

Is it too late to fix us?

With a sigh, she hugged her mom again. There was no denying that a thirty-plus year pattern left her feeling like she needed to protect Allegra. Before long, D-Pop showed up, wearing a sleepy, baffled smile and his usual rumpled T-shirt and cargo shorts. Today he had on a Grateful Dead tee, and he came in without knocking; such was his concern for Allegra.

"You okay?" he asked first thing.

"Not really."

"You should've woken me, hon. Why get a ride to cry on Clem's shoulder when I was right there in bed?"

Because she didn't want to make you feel bad. There was something sweet, if intrinsically messed up, about that.

"I don't know," Mom mumbled.

"Let's get some breakfast, babe. I'll buy you a big burrito."

Clem laughed. "You know she won't eat that. Too many carbs."

Allegra popped to her feet, a determined look firming her chin. "I *will* eat it! I'm sick of hearing Mom's voice in my head. I've spent twenty years avoiding bread, and I *love* bread."

A thought suddenly occurred to Clem. "You know what, Mom? I think Gram is acting out because we're all starting to live our own lives. Danica isn't listening to her anymore, Auntie Min never did, and I've been fighting her for years. That makes you the softest target. When you give her the reaction she wants, she feels like she's still in control of you at least."

Allegra balled up her fist, looking like she might punch something. "That...makes too much sense. I'm so done!" She turned to D-Pop. "Dougal, I want French toast. Let's go to that all-day breakfast place out past Mitchell."

"Anything you want," he said easily. "We'll get out of your hair now. Thanks for looking after your mom."

"You don't need to thank me for that."

I've been doing it my whole freaking life.

Twenty-four hours later, Gavin received a summons.

The message came from his dad personally, and at least this confrontation wouldn't take place in St. Claire. He packed up his stuff just in case he couldn't come back to the flat and arranged his belongings in the storage compartment of the Duc. He secured Benson's habitat, but the mouse preferred traveling in Gavin's pocket, now that they could communicate properly. Normally, mice panicked and bit when they were exposed to loud noises and rapid speeds, but as a familiar, Benson wasn't an ordinary pet any longer.

You smell worried, the mouse observed. *Should we be doing this?*

"It's my best option," Gavin said, wishing he believed it fully.

Briefly he stared at his phone, considering whether he should send a message to the coffee klatch because he genuinely felt close to some of them, especially Leonard and Howard. *I might never find out how the Leonard/Gladys/Howard love triangle plays out.* Since everything was uncertain, he didn't knock on Mina's door as he left. *Perhaps I'll be back. Or maybe the order will sever my magic and blur my mind.*

Hell no.

Without thinking about it too much, he clipped his phone to the front of the Duc. It didn't matter if the order was tracking him anymore, and it seemed fitting to turn their own tech against them. If he parked carefully and activated the camera, he could stream the footage to multiple sites he'd saved—on both sides of the brewing battle. Hunters and witches—who were essentially the same—should see how this played out.

He rode to the rendezvous with his head roaring loud enough to challenge the Duc's engine. The place his father had chosen was a truck stop some distance from the airport, plenty of pavement and no witnesses. Gavin arrived first, and he angled the motorcycle to catch the action. The land was flat enough that he could see for miles, and he spied a black SUV pulling into the car park in the distance. Gavin tapped the camera on his mobile, activated the video, connected to the livestream he'd set up prior, and swung off the bike.

"Stay out of sight," he whispered to Benson.

Do you think I'm a rodent of unusual size? I'm a mouse. If you need me to spy for you, that I can handle. Otherwise… The mouse's calm sarcasm kept Gavin's emotions in check. As he waited, the weather wasn't too hot despite the bright summer sun overhead. A minute or so later, Ted hopped out of the SUV and ran at Gavin like he meant to tackle him.

Gavin sidestepped, careful to stay within the mobile's frame. "Before you have a go, understand that there are witnesses."

"The fuck are you talking about? You're alone." Ted cracked his knuckles, but he didn't lash out. Yet. His crew emerged from the back doors, and they all looked pissed, especially Joanna and Ingram. "The only reason I'm not already on you is because I have orders to wait until Jase gets here."

"It's all pointless," Gavin said. "Hunters will make up their own minds, now that the truth can't be hidden any longer. We're all witches, understand?"

The air smelled faintly of petrol and the soft rubber of hot tires. This was such a ridiculous place for his fate to be sealed—with cars zipping by on the tollway and lorries parked across the way.

But here we are.

He focused on a weed that had tenaciously taken root in the cracks in the asphalt. The energy swirled forth readily this time, and he fed the weed, envisioning it growing tall and strong. The plant quivered and sprang up, big enough to widen the crack in the pavement.

"Witchcraft," said Darcy in a shocked tone. She took a step back, eyeing Gavin like she'd never seen him before and he might suddenly set fire to everything and everyone around him.

"You can all do that," he said. "With varying degrees of success. I suppose it's possible you'd have a different attunement."

"Don't say it," Joanna cut in with an icy tone. "You've just given us proof of your deviance and your break with all the beliefs we hold sacred. We have no choice but to—"

"Continue with the same bullshit?" Gavin guessed. "Just give it a fucking rest. It's nonsense. I'm sure you've read the journal pages I posted. Those who have access to the archives can even verify the documents, if they haven't been burned by now. But even if they have been, it doesn't change a dammed thing. You're *all* fucking witches who choose to hurt your own people. You have no jurisdiction, and if you take hostile action against your own community, the council will act accordingly."

"Been rehearsing that speech?" Ted asked in a mocking tone, twirling his keys.

Before Gavin could answer, another black SUV rolled up. *Truly, it's a big cliché.* His father, Jason Rhys, got out of the driver's seat. It was a wonder he could recollect what side of the road to drive on. Gavin couldn't recall the last time his old man had left headquarters and ventured into the field. It shouldn't surprise him that Jase punched first and spoke next. Since Gavin figured he owed the old man one hit, he didn't dodge. Gavin's head snapped sideways. It stung, but he was in the process of dismantling Da's entire life. As it was built on a secret and a malicious lie, this was the only way to go.

He spat blood and thumbed the red smear off his split lip. "I'll grant you that. Not one strike more."

"You awful, ungrateful bastard." This wasn't shock. No, it was pure, unadulterated rage.

In that moment, Gavin realized his fears about the old man were founded—and disappointment broke over him in a drowning wave. "You knew," he whispered. "This isn't a revelation to you, it's a secret you were keeping."

Da glared at him with eyes unnervingly like his own, only they were flat metal with no give. There never had been any, and perhaps there never would be. This man couldn't love. He craved power the way some people wanted a packet of crisps.

"That is—"

"The truth," Gavin cut in. "I won't listen to you posture about how you were doing God's work. I lived hearing that until my ears bled, always trying to please you, and it was never enough. I'll repeat what I told Ted. You're a self-hating witch, that's all. And the council has jurisdiction over witches who harm their own."

"Treacherous and worthless, just like your grandfather," Jase sneered.

Grandad had always been a sore spot for Jase, and it might

push him past the point of no return if Gavin admitted he'd gotten his intel from Kevin Rhys. So he ignored that insult.

"You should also know I've been streaming this whole time. Every witch in the world can access this feed if they choose. So can all the active hunters that I'm sure have no idea how filthy the order's secret history is."

Silent fury twisted Jason Rhys's features when he registered the phone on Gavin's bike, held in place for filming in the navigation dock. He lunged in that direction, but surprisingly Echo stepped into his path. His big body became the wall Jase couldn't pass.

"It's done," the hunter said. "No point in raging or breaking his hardware. I'm one who didn't know, and I'll be visiting the archives in person. You won't try to stop me, yeah?"

"He won't," Ingram said.

Startled, Gavin glanced around, and he was now flanked by Ingram and Echo, two members of Ted's crew he hadn't expected to side with him. Joanna still looked pissed, but there was an uncertainty in her narrowed eyes as she studied Jase speculatively. Alban was checking out Darcy's ass, so Gavin suspected the youngest enforcer didn't care that much about what happened here.

As for Darcy, she knelt beside the plant Gavin had encouraged to grow, staring at it hard. He knew what must be running through her head, the doubts and misgivings. Various sounds of shock burst from the witnesses as Gavin sensed the energy building. Then yellow flowers appeared, blooming up and down the stalk. They looked like tiny violets with the sunny hue of buttercups, and they smelled like jasmine.

"You're definitely a vivimancer," he said gently.

Darcy wore a stunned look, hardly seeming able to speak. Finally she managed, "I...I just thought I'd check. It's nothing like what we do, is it?"

Gavin shook his head. "How do you feel?"

She was starry-eyed, wonder slowly dawning. "It's like finding a piece I didn't even know was missing. This is what we're meant to be doing, isn't it?"

"Darcy." Joanna eyed the younger woman, and then she hugged her. "You always loved those wizard school movies."

Jase cursed and ranted, but with his strike team turning, what the hell could he even do? Joanna was watching Darcy experiment, taking pleasure in her joy. Echo and Ingram were furious, and they weren't the sort of men anyone ought to deceive. As for Alban, he was on his mobile, seeming done with the whole muddle. Ted stormed over to argue with Jase, and they couldn't seem to agree what ought to be done or even if anything could be.

We win, no shots fired.

CHAPTER 28

ALONG WITH HER ENTIRE COVEN, apart from Leanne, Clem watched how everything went down with the head of the witch hunting order.

Though she had no right to feel this way, she was so freaking impressed with Gavin. This didn't make up for everything he'd done, but it was a start. And she could see how broken up he was over what he'd learned.

"Did you know?" Vanessa asked Ethel.

The older witch shook her head. "No, that's an old, old secret. I had no idea they were witches who'd turned their power on their fellows."

"It makes sense, though. Because it takes magic to sever magic," Margie said.

"When I think about all the witches who are living with no clue what they've lost..." Kerry slammed a fist into her palm.

Priya sighed. "I wonder how the council will punish them."

"I'd be surprised if they acknowledge their authority," Danica said.

"Some will. The ones who had no inkling and feel like shit over being brainwashed for so long," Clem offered.

Ethel nodded. "Those who knew and covered it up may fight, but the council has ways to deal with witches who hurt others."

"I'm glad it's not my problem," Margie said. "And I'm *so* relieved this is over."

Vanessa didn't look convinced. "It takes time to dismantle anything this widespread. This might be the beginning of the end, but we're not safe just yet."

"Truth," said Danica.

Priya had her phone out, scrolling through their group chat. "Leanne hasn't answered since yesterday. Has anyone heard from her?"

With everything going on, Clem repressed a shimmer of anxiety, but she shook her head. To the best of her recollection, she hadn't chatted with Leanne since the emergency all-nighter at Ethel's place. The rest of her coven sisters said more or less the same, apart from her cousin.

Danica bit her lip, then she spoke up. "Actually, I drove her to the airport yesterday."

"Where in the world did she go?" Ethel asked.

Danica folded her arms, the picture of resolve. "I'm not supposed to tell. She wants to give everyone all the details when she's back."

"When will that be?" Clem demanded.

I can't believe Leanne took a vacation in the middle of all this.

But if the situation went bad, maybe Leanne would turn out to be the smart one, having already bailed on potential problems. Everyone in the coven had their issues, and for Leanne, it was commitment. Ironic, because she loved getting married, but staying married was a different kettle of fish entirely.

"Two or three days, depending," Danica said.

The whole coven was itching to ask for more details, but just then, the feed cut off. No more livestream. Whatever happened now, the world wouldn't know about it.

I shouldn't care. I'm not worried about him. Except she was. They might be beating Gavin to death for betraying the order, and she couldn't do a damn thing about it. Clem exhaled shakily, wishing with all her heart that things were different.

Instantly, Priya was beside her, offering a one-armed cuddle. "It will be all right. I bet the council will send an envoy soon to take the situation in hand."

"You got that right." Gladys strolled in like she owned the place.

Ethel slapped her knee and grinned practically ear to ear. "I knew it! You wouldn't admit it when I asked, but I had the feeling they tapped you in the last rotation."

"We're sworn to secrecy, apart from the direst emergencies," Gladys said primly. "And you know I can keep my mouth shut."

"That's right, you do know where all the bodies are buried," Ethel shot back.

The younger witches swapped wide-eyed looks while Clem asked Danica silently if she thought Ethel and Gladys were being literal. Danica responded with a bewildered shrug that didn't seem to rule anything out.

"Shouldn't you be in disguise?" Ethel asked.

Gladys shrugged, lowering herself carefully on an armchair that Kerry vacated. "The term will be over soon, and you'd probably recognize me anyway. We've known each other for fifty-odd years."

"True enough," Ethel admitted.

Gladys turned to Clem. "I hope you didn't think you were carrying this situation entirely on your shoulders, child. I've been minding the danger since that hunter first rolled into town. We always had your back, you know."

She blinked, softly delighted at hearing that from the head of the other St. Claire coven. "That means a lot to me."

"Me too," Ethel said. "I figured you'd blame me when everything went sideways."

Gladys shook her head.

"Thank goodness," Danica breathed.

That's so reassuring. A witch is never alone. We have our coven sisters and our community.

Kerry grinned at Clem. "Maybe they'll start an award and name it after you."

Clearing her throat to quiet the room, Gladys went on, "In light of recent revelations, the council has come to a consensus. All former witch hunters expressing remorse will receive education and commence a program of reparations, locating witches that have been forcibly converted as mundanes and helping restore them to their rightful places in the community. Those who resist our judgment will be visited by our...agents."

The pause made Clem think there wouldn't be much talking in those encounters. Not that she gave a shit about unrepentant assholes. The council could do whatever they liked, as far as she was concerned, including dropping those monsters down a deep hole.

"Why are you giving us a personal update?" Margie asked.

Vanessa inclined her head like she'd been wondering that too. Normally, big news came across the usual channels. Clem had never been personally involved with a council decision in her whole life; she read about such matters online like all modern witches.

"Because of the role Clementine Waterhouse played in getting these secrets exposed," Gladys replied.

Yikes, she used my whole name. At least she didn't call me Odette. For some reason, it felt like she was about to be scolded. "About that—"

"I don't want to hear justifications or excuses," Gladys cut in sternly. "You did what you thought was necessary, I'm sure. And the results were good, so we won't belabor the process."

"Does Gram know?" Danica ventured.

Gladys flashed a smirk in her direction, and Clem mentally winced. *That's a yes.*

Then Gladys said, "Your grandmother always seems to know everything, even without the benefit of scrying. So, what do you think?"

"Madam Waterhouse will descend on us like a plague of locusts," Ethel predicted.

Kerry got up immediately. "If the meeting's adjourned, I need to get back to the office. I have a client meeting in fifteen minutes."

"Coward," Clem muttered.

She'd locked the shop for this and changed the voicemail message to reflect that they'd be closed for a few days for personal reasons. *Witch hunters. Doomed romance. Family drama. Hidden secrets.* It was enough to make her wish she could swoon like an old-school heroine and wake up with someone gently dabbing her brow with a cool cloth. With everything going on, neither she nor Danica could focus on repairs. Hopefully, the dust would settle soon and life could get back to normal.

Without Gavin.

Kerry grinned. "I prefer to call it prudence. I'm out."

"Me too," Vanessa said. "I don't need more trouble, so I'm gone. Need a ride, Ethel? I'm heading home."

Ethel eased to her feet. "If you don't mind."

"Of course not. We're neighbors." Vanessa gave hugs and then walked the older witch out to her car.

That left Gladys, Priya, Margie, Danica, and Clem staring at one another awkwardly. Then Margie got up and waved, not even pretending to have a reason she had to bail. "I'd rather not be around when your grandmother shows up. No offense."

Danica sighed and scrunched her hair in both hands like she might pull it out. "I wish I could run away too."

You're not the one she'll be mad at. Hell, Clem had a lot to say anyway, so bring it on.

Priya crept out with Margie. None of the coven was brave enough to fight with Gram. And there was no reason for them to. *It was my decision, nobody else's.*

And it worked out, right? No reason to be mad, though that wouldn't stop Gram. *So many flavors and she chooses to be salty.* That was an old meme, but in this case, it still applied.

Gladys got up slowly. She moved well for her age, but the rheumatoid arthritis was visible in her fingers upon close scrutiny. It was wild to imagine the full authority of the witch's council in those hands. This little old lady made life-and-death decisions every day. She also made delicious sponge cake.

"I won't take up more of your time," said Gladys. "But in confirmation, your grandmother does know. Wouldn't want to be in your shoes for that conversation."

When the council agents came for him, Gavin didn't resist.

Unlike enforcers who worked for the order, these two could've been accountants. They sent a man and a woman with nondescript features, dressed in tailored gray suits. But now that he was sensitive to such things, they radiated energy on a level he'd seldom experienced. Their power would swamp his, should he attempt to flee.

He didn't.

And they were surprisingly humane, allowing him to keep most of his personal belongings. They did impound the Ducati, but only because if he drove it, they had no assurance he'd follow to their destination. He climbed in the back of the minivan, feeling a bit foolish. Benson opted to remain in his habitat since car travel was less stressful than the Duc and he had more space. Gavin had no idea where he was headed, and the mouse would be able to eat, drink, exercise, and use the facilities freely that way.

"All good?" he whispered to his familiar.

The woman cut him a suspicious look, but she didn't try to interfere. Benson scampered over to the cage bars and gazed at Gavin. *These two are serious business, huh? Try not to worry. It will probably be okay.*

As predicted, he didn't have a chance to say good-bye to anyone, but he had his netbook. The council agents disposed of his tracked electronics at the first rest stop in case Jase had enforcers still loyal to him. There was free Wi-Fi, so he tapped out what might be his last message to Clem.

I never got a chance to say it, but…I love you. Don't know what will happen to me or if I'll ever have a chance to see you again, but I wanted you to know. I'm not sorry I met you. Thank you for everything.

Once he got that sent, he relaxed a little, taking comfort in Benson's ease. Mice were supposed to be good at reading the room, right? The council agents didn't give their names and neither of them spoke much. It wouldn't have surprised Gavin if they'd blindfolded him and treated him like a prisoner, but this felt…different. Since they didn't do introductions, he'd dubbed the woman "Agent A" and the man "Agent B."

"Where are we going?" he asked finally.

"You've violated the first law of being a witch, and that's not to harm your fellows," Agent B said.

Agent A continued, "We're transporting you to an official hearing. Since you've admitted to your crimes, there's no trial, only judgment."

He couldn't argue with that. "Do you know what happened to my father?"

The two conferred silently, then A said, "He's currently at large. Our best agents are closing in on him."

If he were a better son, he might've pleaded for leniency, but after what he'd suffered at his father's hands, Gavin thought Jase deserved whatever he got.

After that, they drove for a couple of hours and crossed the state line into Michigan. Beyond this point, he had no expectations, only the determination to submit to whatever they required of him.

It was late afternoon when they arrived, and Gavin stared in astonishment. "It's a campus," he said.

Well, that might be an exaggeration. This was a small community college that had clearly seen better days, tan brick buildings arranged in an L.

"What were you expecting?" Agent A asked, evincing curiosity for the first time.

"I've no idea," he admitted.

"The head of the council teaches here. American history," Agent B said with a flicker of amusement. "All the others will participate via teleconference."

They escorted him into the building that seemed more like a secondary school than an institution of higher learning, and he found a portly, middle-aged gentleman waiting for him in a classroom at the end of the hall. Perhaps he'd expected more pomp and ceremony, but there were no robes or masks, nothing to add gravitas to the meeting. Yet there was a shimmer of energy in the air, a feeling he couldn't place.

"You won't recognize him the next time you meet," said Agent A.

Illusion. He's changed his appearance.

It was fascinating, even as he feared what was in store. Trying to be respectful, he lowered his head. Not easy since he towered over the other man.

"Let's get started, shall we?" The brisk tone made it sound like they were about to review some not particularly important paperwork, not seal Gavin's fate.

The man tapped his laptop, and five other faces appeared on screen, none of which he recognized. He didn't linger on them, as they were probably altered as well.

Then the witch council leader said, "Gavin Rhys, you stand accused of harming your own. Do you acknowledge these wrongs?"

"I do," he said, acutely conscious that it was a dreadful echo of a wedding vow.

"And how do you feel about your past work, knowing what you do now about the origins of the witch hunting order?"

He swallowed hard. "I regret everything. If I could take it back, I would. I wish I could undo every—"

"You can," a soft female voice cut in. "First, you'll study here and learn what it means to be a witch. There are hidden courses here, meant for people like you, who come to our heritage late. Normally, you'd have been taught by your family, but it's never too late to learn."

Oddly, the more he listened, the more he thought this voice sounded like...Gladys. *But that's ridiculous, right?*

The woman went on, "Once you've completed your education and learned what you must, then you'll begin reparations. The council will pair you with a diviner who will assist you in tracking down every witch you had a hand in harming. In partnership with a more experienced witch, you'll heal the magical connection that was severed by the order and restore the memories that were taken."

He froze, unable to believe those things were even possible. "Can I really do that? I can make it right?"

"In time," another councilor replied.

"I don't care how long it takes," he said then. "I'll devote myself to this until I mend all the hurt I put into the world. And I'm sorry. I'm so sorry."

He would probably always hate himself a bit for not stopping on his own. For following his father's edicts like he didn't have his own mind. But this might eventually mitigate some of the self-loathing.

"Do you accept this judgment?" the leader asked.

"Wholeheartedly. It's not even a penalty. This is better than I deserve."

"You're the product of a corrupt system," a new voice said. "And we believe in education, not punishment. Witches often served as teachers in the old days, before the world decided we were evil and dangerous and we had to hide."

"Are all council members agreed on this judgment?" the council leader asked.

A chorus of "aye" came across the laptop, then he asked, "Any opposed?" and they were quiet.

The leader smiled at Gavin. "Your Ducati will arrive in the next day or two. You're free to explore the area, as you're not a prisoner. Classes will begin in a couple of weeks, and you can stay in the short-term apartments nearby. To external observers, you'll appear to be a nontraditional student taking courses. I'm not giving you my name, as you may wind up in one of my classes down the line, and you're not supposed to know any of the council members. It prevents lobbying and keeps our judgments honest."

"I understand," Gavin said, unable to believe how much kindness he was receiving.

This incredible generosity only underscored how wretched his old man was in comparison. He'd lived to rob others of magic and resources, and Gavin wished he could drain that blood from his damned veins. If only it were possible.

Another council member spoke. "Don't mistake our leniency for weakness. There are spells in effect to monitor your behavior, just as we read the sincerity of your remorse. If you attempt to run or try to renege, you'll find our retaliatory measures—"

"Yes, he gets the point," the councilor who sounded like Gladys cut in. "Go on now. We truly do welcome you to the witch community, Gavin. It's been a long road, and I'm sorry you had to pass through such a shadowy vale to get here, but...welcome home."

Inexplicably, tears prickled in his eyes. "Thanks. Can't express how it feels to hear that." But before he could sink fully into this feeling of relief, he had to know. "What happened to Da? They said—"

"We caught him at the airport," B said. "We will attempt to educate him, but—"

"We don't have high hopes," A finished.

It wouldn't surprise Gavin if Da turned up as a mundane,

always feeling like he'd lost something but with no words to explain that unshakable certainty. "Thank you for telling me. My grandad, he'd want to be part of this. I have his email. Can I get in touch with him and ask him to come? He stopped hunting twenty years ago, but I think he'd want to make reparations as well, if that's still possible."

"We should offer an amnesty program," one of the council members suggested.

"Email him," the council leader said. "If he wants a home in our community, he'll have one, if he's willing to do the work."

Hearing that, Gavin's tears finally overflowed.

CHAPTER 29

NEVER HAD AN EMAIL BROKEN Clem's heart.

It was absurd, and she understood that, but her eyes still welled up reading the message. On impulse, she tried his old number, and it delivered an out-of-service message.

He's really gone.

Clem considered responding, but what would be the point? She breathed through the pain, the worst she'd ever experienced over ending a relationship. Not that she was even sure what they'd had deserved the term since she was deceiving him for most of that time. Yet her heart didn't care, not about the obstacles or all the reasons why it could never work between them. Sadness pumped through her body along with her blood, leaving her uncharacteristically glum. Clem let herself cry quietly in the privacy of her room, then she got a damp cloth and put it on her eyes to mitigate the evidence she had actual emotions.

Can't have that getting out.

Squaring her shoulders, she unblocked Barnabas and created a family chat that included everyone except Danica's dad, Pansy, and D-Pop. Mundanes couldn't be part of this discussion, but everyone else had to talk. Gladys had warned them Gram knew everything about her affair with Gavin, and honestly, she was surprised at the long silence from her grandmother. It couldn't herald anything good, so it was better to head that conversation off by creating her own agenda. Without preamble, she sent:

Family meeting. My place. Tomorrow night, 6:30 PM. This is not optional if you want me to consider you part of my family going forward.

That should get everyone good and pissed.

Gram replied at once. I'll be there, dear.

Just bet you will.

Auntie Min had questions, but she did say, I can make it. I'm looking forward to it.

Next, Barnabas weighed in. What's this about, Clementine? I have theatre tickets.

Tell Pansy to take a friend to the show instead, she sent back.

Fine. But this better be important. Barnabas sounded snotty even in text form.

Danica replied with a thumbs-up emoji.

Clem had chosen six thirty to ensure her cousin would have time to close and get home if she hurried. Danica ought to be there, because Clem needed the moral support big-time. They'd already had two blowouts with Gram this summer. Seemed like Clem needed to deal the whole family in on some comeuppance, though Gram was largely responsible for all the chaos.

Hell, it's like she feeds on it.

Finally, Allegra answered, See you then.

Mom couldn't be looking forward to another confrontation

with Barnabas, but it had to happen for everyone to be on the same page. Clem had some words for her parents as well as her grandmother, ones she'd been saving for a long-ass time, swallowing them for far too long.

I'm done hurting myself so other people don't feel bad.

For witches, it was especially harmful to suppress emotions, as it often resulted in wild, unpredictable magic. *I can either sort out my baggage or accidentally curse a small town.*

Time I handled this.

The next day and a half dragged as she missed Gavin, focused on work, and dreaded what was coming in a few hours. They had a backlog at the shop again, thanks to being closed for a few days, and Clem toiled nonstop to catch up on those orders.

Danica showed up early, another summer miracle. She seemed happy these days, dividing her time between their house and Titus's. Slowly Clem was getting over her bias against the guy, belatedly realizing some of Gram's prejudice against mundanes must've rubbed off, and she didn't feel great about that. She'd been telling herself, *It's not that he's a mundane, it's because rebounds never work out,* but she had to face her own bullshit. Her cousin had been nice enough not to call her out, and thankfully, she hadn't been a complete asshole to Titus.

I extended an olive branch at the party. It's fine, right? She couldn't apologize to him for disapproving because he wasn't a witch, so treating him better going forward had to suffice.

As Danica set her purse on the counter, she wore a bright expression, eyes dancing. "You want the hot gossip?"

"How do you find everything out before me?" Generally,

she acted like she didn't care, but it was kind of maddening how in-the-know her cousin always was. Like the deal with Leanne, for example.

"People like me," Danica said blithely, like that wasn't a poke at Clem's social skills.

She scowled. "Excuse you, I'm personable. Charming, even."

Danica paused, seeming not to know how to respond. "Yeah, okay. *Anyway*, I picked Leanne up from the airport—"

"I know you weren't about to steal my thunder," Leanne said, tip-tapping into the shop in her ubiquitous heels.

Clem had no clue how she ran around in those all day. "Then you tell me!"

"Ta-da!" Leanne flourished the ring finger on her left hand. "I got married! Third time's the charm, right?"

Clem blinked. "Uh, what?"

"I took Trevor to Vegas. Swore Danica to secrecy, she owed me one."

"Congratulations?" Probably that shouldn't have come out as a question—fortunately, Leanne didn't seem to notice.

"Thanks! I'm getting Trev moved into my place today, so I'm off." In a swirl of expensive perfume and sparkling, magical vibes, Leanne left as quick as she'd dashed in.

"How are we supposed to feel about this?" Clem asked. "She's known him how long?"

Danica shrugged, a rueful smile forming. "Let's be supportive. We can always console her if it doesn't work out."

"If," Clem mumbled. "Well, whatever. I'm off. I'll get a charcuterie platter for tonight's intervention."

"Ooh, fancy. I'd offer to bring cinnamon rolls from Sugar Daddy's, but Gram doesn't deserve them."

Clem grinned, trying to pretend she was fine, her heart wasn't aching, and she wasn't tense as hell about this situation. "True. And you know I enjoy saying 'charcuterie.'"

"It's an awesome word. See you later!" Her cousin headed toward the back.

St. Claire was beautiful in the summer, bittersweet that she wouldn't be able to show Gavin how pretty it was when the leaves turned. The town went through an awkward stage just before the snow fell, like a kid in junior high, all barren limbs and brown earth, but when everything was blanketed in white and the holiday lights sparkled, winter was magical too.

No wonder there are so many witches in the Midwest.

Clem stopped by the grocery store and set the food up. By five, she was ready. By six, she was freaking out.

Her family arrived en mass, shortly after half past six. Already, she could cut the tension with a knife, with Allegra glaring daggers at Barnabas, and Gram sending him sympathetic looks, like he was the big fish that got away.

Enough.

Clem took control of the family meeting. "I have a few things to say, so I need you all to listen without interrupting. I'll take comments once I've finished, okay?"

"Fine" and "okay" came back with various levels of enthusiasm. It didn't matter if they liked it, only if they consented to hearing her out.

"First, this is for Mom and Dad." She seldom called them

that, so they both stilled. "It's been ages, and I need you both to stop now. Stop using me as a game piece, trying to one-up the other." When they would've interrupted, she held up a hand. "I don't care if that's not your intention, it's how I feel. And I have the floor right now."

Barnabas nodded tightly, and Allegra had tears in her eyes again, but she inclined her head as well. *Good, they heard me.*

Clem went on, "Let's stop, okay? Don't let Gram stir the pot. Just ignore her."

Gram let out an outraged noise. "Clementine Odette, I'm sitting right here. I have a few things to say too! I heard *all* about what you did. How dare you—"

"Ask you to be accountable for your actions?" That certainly wasn't what Gram had been about to say, but Clem was on a roll, and she talked over the old witch. "You've hurt all of us long enough. You're passive-aggressive with Auntie Min, you cut my mom down constantly. You tried and failed to control Danica, and you're constantly manipulating us. I wanted everyone here to hear what I'm saying." She paused to let her words sink in. "Do we acknowledge as a family that there's a problem with how we interact?"

Everyone nodded, even Barnabas. Gram's face tightened, and it looked like she was about to kick off.

Danica shook her head. "Let her finish, Gram. You agreed."

"This is the end of my patience," Clem said, shooting her cousin an appreciative smile.

It wasn't easy for Danica to stand up to Gram, but she had Clem's back today, as promised. *Sisters for life.*

Since Clem had the floor, she'd speak her mind fully. "Gram, we've warned you repeatedly, yet you still pulled that crap at dinner. And for what? To shame Mom because she doesn't live up your standards of what a witch should be? Guess what, I *love* my mom. And I'm strong enough to fight, so let's go.

"If I have to, I'll cast a spell to block you. I'll even go to the mundane police and get a restraining order. Whatever it takes, I'm done letting you hurt people I care about."

Gram crumpled, her face drooping with a complex mixture of heartbreak and fury. "Where's this coming from? I can't believe you have the audacity and bad manners to speak to me like this. I basically raised you, and you—*oh*." She clenched a fist. "I'm so angry!"

"Fine, you're angry. But I don't care if you pray mad, stay mad, and die mad. That's your choice. Or you could choose to be different. To care about your family and accept them as they are instead of only giving a damn about your bloodline. How this turns out is up to you."

———

In a matter of weeks, Gavin's life became unrecognizable.

Not only did he settle into the slightly down-at-heels flat in the building across from the small campus, but he also attended classes during the day. He submitted his resignation to the university in Wales, making his sabbatical permanent. It had been difficult anyway, balancing his father's expectations against the day job, and in the end, he hadn't been able to do it.

Gavin hadn't seen his old man since the showdown in the

car park weeks ago. The council had taken him, but he had no notion if a man like Jason Rhys could be rehabilitated. At base, he trusted the witch's council would act with more compassion than his father.

It was odd to get a formal education on a part of his heritage he hadn't known about, but apparently, it wasn't unknown, as ten other witches shared his curriculum. The classrooms were warded carefully, so mundanes couldn't wander in or overhear any of the information. Gavin befriended a few of his classmates, who ranged in age from past secondary school to a man old enough to be a pensioner. Sal reminded Gavin a bit of Leonard.

"When they said I'm a wizard with machines, I had no idea they meant it literally," Sal joked one day after class.

They hadn't discussed their major attunements, but Gavin guessed Sal was a technomancer. It seemed rude to ask how he'd gotten to that age without knowing he was a witch. But maybe he'd been raised by mundanes? Gavin suspected unexplainable events must've dogged Sal's steps, odd things that couldn't be accounted for by science or logic.

Three weeks into the program, there was a knock on his door toward evening. He'd been emailing with Grandad, and he'd even provided his address, but he wasn't prepared to find him standing in the corridor outside his flat.

An older man waited beside Grandad, brown-skinned with curly gray hair and a well-trimmed beard. He wore wire spectacles and a bow tie. Gavin liked him on sight. He was as proper and put together as Grandad was scruffy. Time hadn't changed that. His grandfather still favored navy jumpers, even though the weather was too hot for it. He was tall and thin, sea-weathered from twenty years on a boat, hair gone mostly white, but his eyes twinkled as he pulled Gavin into a mighty hug.

"Surprise," he said, pulling back.

"Grandad! What are you doing here?"

"I've been missing you for twenty years, my lad. Now that the dust has settled and we made some personal arrangements, I couldn't wait a minute longer."

Delighted, Gavin hugged his grandfather again. "So glad you're here."

"As am I."

Gavin turned to the man who had to be Grandad's partner. "Gavin Rhys, it's so nice to meet you."

They shook hands, then the man said, "I'm Samuel Banks. Don't call me Sam."

"We've been together for a long time," Grandad put in. "You can think of him as another grandparent, but he might not warm to the notion of being addressed informally right away. He's a bit of a stickler for the proprieties."

"Good manners never go out of fashion," said Samuel.

Gavin found himself smiling, enjoying the interplay between the older men. Stepping back, he waved them into his small flat. The place must look a bit dingy, but they ought to be used to close quarters; their boat probably wasn't a luxury yacht.

"Are you interested in the amnesty program? You can learn all about our actual history and learn to use your magic properly. It's all been rather incredible." Belatedly he realized he was babbling. "Sorry, have a seat, both of you."

The small living room had two loveseats, a low table, and not much else. This place wasn't designed for entertaining. Fortunately, they didn't mind snuggling up while he put the kettle on. That was the first thing he'd purchased. He refused to make tea in a microwave.

I'd rather eat with my feet.

"It's so good to see you," Grandad said.

"Hard for me to believe you're actually here. Toward the end, my life was a nightmare, and it's as though I've finally woken up."

"I know the feeling," Grandad said.

"Do you think Da's doing well?" he asked.

Grandad swapped a look with Samuel. "If he doesn't cooperate, he'll receive a taste of his own medicine," Samuel said eventually.

"I can't get over all the lies he told me." Gavin let out a sigh, rubbing a hand across the back of his neck.

He wouldn't blame the other witches if they hated him for who he was. Yet they didn't, just as Samuel seemed to adore Grandad. *Maybe there's hope for Clem and me.*

"It's not your fault, my lad." Grandad patted him gently on the shoulder. "I'm sure you're confused, but the important part is you're learning the truth now."

"Come to that, I do have one question, and my professors don't know. Maybe you can answer?" It might be a long shot, but Grandad had a unique perspective from his time as a witch hunter, then later, when he bet everything on love—and Samuel Banks, who'd probably been teaching him about witches for the past twenty years.

"I'll do my best," Grandad promised.

"Since hunters and enforcers are witches, using magic to track other witches, why didn't we ever get false positives from our own?"

"Likely we did," Grandad said. "Sometimes we never found anything for all our looking and concluded that our enemies had gotten impossibly clever, but in fact—"

"We were pinging our own people?"

"It's probable. But over the years, our powers became quite different because of the way we used them. So I think—and this is just a theory—our powers turned inward, becoming almost more of an ability than true witch's magic." Grandad glanced at Samuel. "Does that sound reasonable?"

The other man nodded. "It does. And with the enforcers, what they do is localized and it's done quickly. I doubt it would've spiked enough for anyone to notice it."

"Makes sense." These theories couldn't be proven, and Gavin was glad to be done with the order. With a smile, he changed the subject. "Either of you hungry?"

"I could eat," Samuel said.

Grandad nodded as well, so he fixed three cheese-and-pickle toasties. They ate those while the tea was steeping. Gavin offered cream and sugar, which they both accepted.

That's how he used to drink it.

But it had been so long that he hadn't been sure, either of his own memory or maybe Grandad's tastes would've changed. Grandad glanced over at the habitat where Benson was running on his wheel. "Your familiar?" he guessed.

Gavin nodded. "We scored high in our affinity testing. He understands me perfectly and vice versa. I passed a 'psychic' test using Benson as my proxy."

"That's fascinating," Samuel said. "I've never bonded with an animal, but I always wished I could. And Kevin felt it would be cruel to confine a larger pet to the boat."

They chatted about the program a little more, with Gavin providing details about the sort of classes he'd taken. Unsurprisingly, he found witch history fascinating, and if possible, he might look for work teaching in the States. Online instruction might solve a variety of problems, but that would require a little more education.

"Get your online teaching credentials," Grandad suggested. "If it's a matter of money, Samuel and I have some saved. I'm sure he'd be all right with a loan."

Warmth rushed over him as Samuel nodded. It felt fantastic to have grandparents who cared about what he wanted. Gavin managed a soft smile. "Financially, I'm doing well enough. And I'm looking into it."

Grandad sat forward wearing a serious look. "That's all I need to hear, my lad."

"Is there something else?" Gavin asked.

"In fact, I *am* here to turn myself in. I'll do the educational course if they let me, and then I mean to start working on reparations."

"It's never too late to do the right thing," Samuel said, covering Kevin's hand where it rested on his thigh.

"I may not be around long enough to make up for the damage I've done," Grandad said with a quiet sigh.

There was also the chance those witches might've passed on already. Gavin's missions were more recent, so he hoped to track down everyone he'd harmed—with the council's help. According to what his counselor had said, they were already delving into records seized from the hunters, going back decades.

Most hunters hadn't known, it seemed, and they were working with the council to make up for past crimes. For Gavin, it would be six months more before he graduated from witching school—as he privately thought of it—and go into the field as a healer.

So far, he hadn't written to Clem. Nor had she responded to his final email. So that was over, probably.

It hurts more than I can bear.

No, not more. Exactly as much.

Any worse and he might die of it, but he affixed a smile, not wanting Grandad to think he had misgivings about this reunion. People were made of multiple emotions, so joy and sorrow shared space equally within him.

"Now I feel like I'm fit to make conversation," Samuel said, setting down his cup.

"Is it rude to wonder what kind of witch you are?" Gavin asked.

"Not at all. I'm a neuromancer. We're a bit rare these days. I specialize in illusions and glamours. Or I did, before I ran off with this mad pirate." Samuel smiled fondly at Kevin, his eyes full of a lifetime's devotion.

Grandad grinned back, mischievous as Gavin remembered. "Privateer."

Fascinated, Gavin asked, "Is Samuel serious? Have you been working as smugglers?"

"Nothing dangerous," Grandad said. "But yes. Quite often we're running medicine and supplies to people oppressed by their governments. A small boat can get in and out of port fast, and with Samuel's illusions, we've never been caught."

"There were some near misses," Samuel allowed. "And some plans that unraveled entirely and we had to improvise." He shuddered delicately. "I loathe improv."

"You must have the most amazing stories," Gavin said. "I want to hear them all."

Grandad beamed. "And so you shall, my lad. We're staying for a while." He hesitated, seeming unsure for the first time. "Your grandmother and your mum want to come."

Neither his father nor his grandad had managed to keep their marriages together. Before Kevin met Samuel, he had been divorced for a few years, and Gavin's old man followed in that fine tradition. Gavin hadn't seen either of the women in years.

"Are you asking or telling me?"

"They miss you, but the way Jase raised you..." Clearly Grandad feared the brainwashing had stuck and that Gavin wouldn't want to reconcile with his grandmother or his mum.

"I've missed them both for years," he said simply. "Get them on the next flight, if you can afford it. I want my family back. I want *everything* back that he took from us."

"My lad." Grandad made that an endearment, like always, and he drew Gavin into his arms, like he didn't properly tower over the old gaffer.

Samuel came over and rubbed both their backs, not quite joining the group hug but showing that he'd work up to it. Probably. "It's never too late," he said again.

This time, Gavin took the words to heart.

CHAPTER 30
18 MONTHS LATER

"I CAN'T BELIEVE YOU HAVE a kid," Clem said, staring at Leanne's baby in awe.

Nobody had honestly thought Leanne and Trevor had a shot together, but somehow, despite some messy maneuvering and a near-separation, they were making it work. Trevor would never be a high-powered career guy, but he'd taken online classes and was working at home doing web design while caring for their little one.

Leanne seemed pretty damn happy about the whole situation.

"Has Melanie shown any signs in front of Trevor?" Danica whispered.

That was the trickiest part of raising a magical child with a mundane. The witch parent had to keep a sharp eye on the situation to ensure their untrained offspring didn't spark up at the wrong time. It could be managed, but it was challenging.

"Not a problem," Leanne said. "Ethel made her some baby clothes that keep things in check when I'm not around."

They were at a coven meeting hosted at Leanne's place, and Trevor was off for boys' night with Titus, Calvin, Miguel, and

Dante. From what Clem had heard, Margie was still hooking up with Dante, and they both thought nobody knew about it.

Everyone knew, of course; they just weren't talking about it. Well, not talking to Margie and Dante about it anyway.

"Have you heard from you know who?" Kerry asked.

Clem sighed. "He's not Voldemort, you can say his name."

Given that much basic encouragement, Vanessa went right for it. "Gavin! Are you talking to him at all?"

She shook her head. "He sent me an email as he was leaving town, but what we had wasn't real, it was a trick I played on him. So what would be the point of replying?"

Every witch in the room stopped what they were doing and gave Clem *that* look. Then Ethel said, "You can lie to yourself if you want, but don't try it on us."

"Disrespectful," Margie added.

Getting it from Dante on the regular had made the woman downright sassy. Clem liked it on her. She glanced around the room, seeing nobody who was willing to back her up.

Not even Danica, who was disgustingly happy with Titus. They were even talking about getting married, now that his sister, Maya, had moved in with her girlfriend and his stepsister, Lucy, was going away to college soon. Even Gladys had a boyfriend these days. She went everywhere with Leonard Franklin from the coffee klatch.

As ever, Priya was the sympathetic one. "She doesn't want to talk about it. We already did the group casting, so that leaves books. Why don't we chat about what we're reading?"

"I have people online who want to Zoom in for this," Margie said.

Vanessa had invites as well, and thankfully, the coven meeting gracefully evolved into the book club they openly claimed it was. *At our place, Hazel would be here by now.* Their neighbor now attended every coven meeting Clem and Danica hosted. Leanne fired up her laptop and invited all their guests while her baby napped peacefully in the baby swing.

Happy endings all around, right?

Things were better for her family too. They'd fought for hours that day, but at the end of it, she'd ratified a truce between Allegra and Barnabas, who was somehow still married to Pansy, even to this day. She didn't register as a witch, but she must have super-powers or something, as she was accomplishing the impossible—keeping Barnabas Balfour in check. Gram was toeing the line Clem had drawn, thankfully, and peace had reigned for quite a while.

I should be happy. Privately, Clem admitted that she missed Gavin.

Close to midnight, Trevor came home from poker night, hosted at Titus's place, and kissed Leanne with such reverent tenderness that an ache started in Clem's chest. The two of them had beaten the odds and made their cracked pieces fit. Trevor picked up baby Melanie the moment she stirred and tucked her into the crook of his arm. The guy was a freaking natural with babies, a fact that Leanne crowed about constantly. Taking that as a cue, every-one gave hugs and said bye; Clem headed out with the rest of her coven.

She wasn't the kind of person who wallowed in her emotions. Unlike Danica, she didn't spend three days drunk after Gavin left, cry constantly, or melt into a puddle of sadness. But in her private heart, she acknowledged she'd lost someone special, the kind of connection that Gram used to justify her bias against half the freaking world.

That soul magic thing? It's real. I felt it with him.

Ethel caught Clem's arm as she was headed behind Danica to the car. "From what I hear, he's nearly done with his work for the council. And once he's released, he'll be free to do whatever he wishes. Life's too short, my dear. If you regret how things ended, you can always begin again."

"It's already over," Clem muttered.

"Not because either of you wanted it to be. Yes, you met under the wrong circumstances, but think of it this way... Gavin was essentially raised in a cult. He's been through deprogramming now, and he's made amends. Only you can decide if that's enough for you to feel safe giving him another chance. A real one this time."

With that, Ethel patted Clem on the arm and hurried after Vanessa in a swirl of filmy chiffon and floral perfume. Danica was driving tonight, so Clem hopped in the passenger side, feeling pensive. Her cousin glanced at her as she started the car.

"What was that about?"

Quietly Clem summarized what the older witch had said on the drive home, with Danica listening in silence. "Thoughts?" Clem asked, as Danica pulled into their driveway.

"I agree with her. To me, it seems like you've simply been... waiting. I didn't say anything because you get prickly when I offer unsolicited advice."

Clem brought her shoulders up, silently acknowledging the

charge. "It's because of Gram. No matter how smart or well-intended the suggestion is, I have this knee-jerk 'you're not the boss of me' reaction."

"Yeah, and I have the tendency to panic and expect you to fix the shit I've broken. We're both works in progress."

Impulsively Clem hugged Danica across the small car console. "As long as you know," she muttered.

"We'd be lost without you. Hell, you're the one in the coven we call when shit goes sideways. Like, if there was a body to be buried, you'd be all, 'Okay, we'll need a tarp, a shovel, some bleach—' and we'd follow your plan, whatever it might be."

"Love you," Clem mumbled.

She'd probably never be as open about these things as Danica. *And that's okay.*

Smiling faintly, Clem climbed out of the car, but she still heard her cousin's cheerful call of "love you too."

At the front door, Goliath was waiting for them. She smirked. "Seriously, what's your secret? What'd you do to this cat?"

"I'm a pussy magnet, what can I say?" Danica sashayed into the house, not even seeming slightly sorry about that pun.

"You've been waiting your whole life to use that, haven't you?" Clem called.

Danica grinned over her shoulder. "The last one too, probably. Do you ever wonder about that?"

"Reincarnation? Sometimes, but I have enough problems in this lifetime, so I don't linger over it." She hesitated. "You really think I should contact him?"

There was no question who she was talking about.

"Totally. If you want. If you miss him. Nothing ventured, nothing gained, right?"

Since Clem had a tendency to get in her own way, she refused to overthink this. She marched directly upstairs, opened her laptop, and brought up the last email from Gavin, the one that broke her heart, even if she'd been pretending otherwise for the last year and a half.

Time didn't heal all wounds. Some you just learned to live with.

She took a deep breath, typed three words, and hit send.

———————

I MISS YOU.

The email popped into Gavin's inbox at the perfect moment, just as he was packing up his life as a council healer. Benson was perched on his shoulder, nuzzling into his neck. *It's from her, isn't it? You already smell happier.*

"Quiet, you." The words lacked heat because Gavin *was* bursting with excitement, practically beside himself with glee.

With the records retrieved from the now-defunct order and the support of the council's best diviners, he'd not only restored every witch he'd ever located, but he'd also tracked down others who needed help as well. Finally, it felt like some of the weight had lifted from his soul, but it wasn't enough. He didn't want to live like a nomad anymore, and St. Claire had been calling from the moment he'd left.

That hadn't been a choice so much as necessity, and now that

Clem had gotten in touch, he had no doubts about where he was headed. Once again, he was riding across the country, straight to her, but this time, he didn't get hopped up on 5-hour Energy first. Instead, he took the journey slowly, in gentle increments to make it easier on Benson, who kept up a running commentary throughout the trip. *Are you going to stand outside her house with a boom box?* For some reason, the mouse was obsessed with old romantic movies. When they eventually arrived a few days later, both he and Benson were in good health.

The little town hadn't changed much, only a few new shops he noticed as he rode through. Eventually he'd figure out where to stay, renting a flat permanently, as the council had helped him sort out his permanent residency in America. But everything hinged on how Clem reacted to seeing him again. Gavin could've responded to her message, but he preferred checking the look on her face first. The surprise should show him everything he needed to know.

It was late enough that she'd be off work, might be at home if she didn't have other plans. If she was dating someone, she surely wouldn't have sent that message. He'd been too busy working for the council to think about that, even if she wasn't firmly emplaced in his heart. He'd spent far too many lonely nights in a strange bed, reliving their sparse, shared memories. But if he hadn't lost his sense of nuance, her email was certainly a "hit me up" sort of thing.

He parked the Duc in her drive and strode up the front walk to the porch then rapped firmly on the door. Within a moment or so, Clem answered. It was February, so he got to admire her winter fashion. He'd only seen her in summer clothes before, but she was beautiful in gray leggings and an oversize sweater as well. There was no snow on the ground, but the earth was damp and brown, several shades lighter than the huge eyes currently staring at him in disbelief. And then she smiled.

"You cut your hair," Clem said.

"Several times." His tone was solemn, hiding much of his joy and how much he wanted to sweep her into his arms. "You said you missed me. I'm here, so you can stop. If you'd like."

"Like what?"

"For me to stay? To stop missing me."

"Are you suggesting we pick up where we left off?" Clem stepped back while asking the question, making space for him to come in.

Now that he was fully aware of himself as a witch, he felt the warm slide of her wards as he moved past them. They felt like a welcoming hug, assuring him that people of good heart would always be safe here.

"I would rather have a clean slate," he confessed. "But it seems silly to pretend we have no history. I can't introduce myself as if we've never met."

She led the way into the kitchen, prepping a cup of tea that would warm his insides the way the sight of her soothed a part of him that had been aching and raw for over a year. After a few minutes of puttering, she sat across the table from him and peered at him over the rim of a steaming cup.

"Ethel said it's up to me to forgive you. Or not. For the things you did before we met."

That was the rub, wasn't it? Even if he'd done his best to make it right, the harm still happened. He didn't know if he deserved another chance with Clem, but he wanted one. So Gavin sipped his tea and waited for Clem's judgment with more fear than he'd felt submitting himself to the council.

"What do you think?" he asked.

"You're a witch. For a while you were a bad one. Now the council says you've paid your dues. That's enough for me, English. I want you in my life. Since you're here, I'm guessing you want that too."

"I missed you so," he whispered.

Still here, Benson reminded him.

Right.

He cupped his hand, and the mouse popped out of his pocket, hopping onto his palm. "Can we make the little fellow more comfortable while we...talk?"

In short order, Clem offered a cardboard box and placed a slice of cucumber and a blueberry at one end. Gavin shredded up some tissues for nesting, and Benson scampered into the temporary accommodations with apparent alacrity. He would devour the treats and then doze like a tiny Roman emperor.

"Will this do?" Clem asked.

"Perfectly. He loves blueberries, and he knows not to cause problems in human homes."

She caught his gaze, and the look went through him in a slash of desire. They'd only had a few sips of their drink, but now that Benson was settled, Gavin rounded the table in a fever. She stood to meet him, and his mouth was on hers with the hottest demand. Clem tasted of sweetness and tea, and he swung her into his arms.

Since she laughed and curled her arms around his neck, he raced for the stairs with only that as encouragement.

"You're taking me to bed?"

"I've been living for the memory of our last night together for over a year. I can wait if you prefer, but—"

"We've always been backward, so let's keep going. Sex first, relationship talk after."

Relationship talk. That's fucking marvelous.

Nothing about her room had changed. He gazed fondly at her pineapple comforter. "You always smell like pineapple, and you even favor them in your decor. Why is that?"

Clem blinked, seeming startled. "It wasn't conscious. I just like the way the lotion smells, and I thought the comforter was cute. But if I do some self-analysis, I was super into SpongeBob as a little kid. Who—"

"Lives in a pineapple under the sea," Gavin finished in a credible imitation of the sea captain. *I can't wait to tell her about Grandad and Samuel. For her to meet Mum and Nan.*

Her magic shimmered all around him, awakening that deeper connection he hadn't understood before he learned the truth about his nature. Now he realized they were wonderfully matched, perfectly in balance through the nature of their magics. Yet it wasn't magic but yearning and haste that made their clothes disappear.

Gavin kissed her all over, delighting in her moans and shivers, then he feasted on her with lips and teeth and tongue, until she rocked against his face and came with a scream. That wasn't enough, so he licked her through another orgasm. Finally, he allowed himself the pleasure of her slick, hot pussy. He pushed into her with exquisite slowness, marking the side of her neck with his mouth. Clem dug her hands into his back, urging him on, and he lost himself in her.

Afterward, they cuddled in the center of her bed. She ran her hands over him like she was doing an inspection. "You're thinner than you were. Was it tough?"

"Yes. Meeting people you've harmed, even to help them…it's onerous. And even though I apologized as well, it's not enough. How could it be? I'm glad I did what I could, however. And I'm relieved it's over." Gavin paused, thinking. "I may still work with the council on an on-call basis now and then, helping witches who need healing for other reasons. If you like, you could…go with me?"

She kissed his chest then his shoulder, and her affection rolled over him in a delicious wave. "I would *love* that. I've wanted to get more involved in council work, and combining social service and my secret dream of seeing the world?" Her gaze turned dreamy, as if she was peering into a future that shone with magical promise.

"Then I'll tell them to keep me on call," Gavin said.

"For now, what will you do?" she asked.

"Make St. Claire my home base. Mum and Nan want to meet you. I saw them for the first time in years, and they're talking about moving to the States. Would you hate that?"

"Meeting your family or having them around full time?" Clem seemed to be teasing with that sly little smile. Maybe.

"Both. Either."

"No, I don't mind. It sounds fantastic, honestly. Will I get to meet your grandad and his partner?"

"Assuredly. They live on a boat, but they made it to Michigan when I was in school there. I see no reason why they can't travel a bit farther south. I've told everyone all about you, until they're sick of hearing it."

"That's sweet," Clem whispered. "Any other plans then?"

Gavin gathered his courage. "I just want to be yours. To live for you. I said it in the email, and my feelings haven't changed. I love you endlessly. I thought the feeling might fade—out of sight, out of mind and all that."

"It didn't?"

He shook his head, gazing into her piquant face. "If anything, it got stronger as I mourned what I thought I'd lost forever."

"Not lost," she said softly. "My cousin said I was waiting. Not consciously, mind you. That's not my style. But even someone as unromantic as I am knows."

"Knows what?"

"When they meet the one. I love you, Gavin Rhys. Let's date for a while and eventually have magical babies and grow old together." That declaration was fabulous, but she made the moment her own with a saucy grin. "Or not. Whatever."

It was a hilarious proposal, and so Clem. "Yes, please," he whispered against her mouth. "I'll give you some time to buy me a pretty ring."

"I'll save up," she promised.

In time, he'd tell her all about his plans for their future, but for now, he had in mind another romp on the mattress. After that, they'd build a life together, loving, laughing, chasing white mice, and helping other witches. Hell, whatever she wanted, he'd ensure she had it.

From now until forever, this Fix-It witch filled his heart with love and his soul with magic.

Don't miss Danica and Titus's story
in *Witch Please*. Available now!

CHAPTER 1

IF DANICA WATERHOUSE EVER DECIDED to write a how-to
guide for other witches, the first rule would be: *Do not cast when
you're hungover.*

It would be right up there with *harm none* for important
tenets. Unfortunately, she was known for having great ideas but
not so fantastic about following her own good advice. Which was
why she was unlocking the door to the Fix-It Witches shop at 8:57
a.m. when it opened at nine, though a thousand angry goblins
were kicking her brain stem.

Despite the gargantuan headache, the shop's logo always made
her smile—two witches on broomsticks, both wearing tool belts.
Her cousin Clementine had said the design was too risky, considering their nature, but Danica enjoyed the irony. Plus, people in
the Midwest were too pragmatic to take such things seriously.
The first Waterhouse witches had fled the Old World due to the
persecution of poor Agnes, and then with that dustup in Salem,
they had quietly slid a bit farther west to settle in and keep a low
profile. At this juncture, the chance of discovery was minimal.

Clementine usually took the early shift, but she was out
of town, and they had a backlog of work orders. Danica had
promised herself she wouldn't drink too much at the bachelorette
party last night, but she had been trying altogether too hard to
prove she didn't care about the wedding.

With a groan, she got the door open and stumbled in, flicking lights on as she went. Not magically, although the light switches might've responded. The alarm system did, disarming with a flick of her fingers.

Danica had a knack with all machines, and sometimes it extended to various modern conveniences. Not reliably, however, and it was best not to get in the habit of leaning on small magics. Otherwise, she might slip up when she was surrounded by mundanes. And while she didn't think they would dunk her in a pond or tie her to a pyre before the council could intervene, it was still best to be cautious.

Before she tackled the gadgets waiting for her attention, she got a bottle of water and two strong painkillers. This hangover might scramble her ability to magically repair malfunctioning machines, and it wouldn't do to give someone back a toaster oven that now served as a shortwave radio. That would raise entirely too many questions, and it wouldn't help the business either. She could imagine the reviews online already.

When some of the goblin noise subsided in her head and she could see without a corona of light, Danica flipped the sign on the front door to open and settled in back at the workbench. In films, they always showed witches working around cauldrons, dressed fully in black, sacrificing small animals and whatnot, whereas she was wearing a pair of ripped jeans, ratty sneakers, and a fleece sweatshirt with cat ears on the hood. Not because cats were her familiars; she just thought they were cute.

Sadly, she also had a terrible allergy to them. Which didn't stop cats from sticking to her everywhere she went. Danica had no idea if that was witch-related or if cats were just assholes with a tendency to gravitate toward those who would rather pass. But the minute she set foot on the street, if there was a cat within five blocks, it would present itself, rub all over her legs, and follow her home sometimes too. It was bad enough with strays, but it got awkward when she had to call people to inform them that their beloved pets were on her porch and wouldn't leave.

She took another sip of water, and it stayed down. Good—she figured she was only *slightly* hungover, so it should be fine to get to work, as she was only breaking the *no casting while impaired* rule a little bit. So many inventions designed to make life easier, so many gizmos that needed fixing—Danica couldn't throw fireballs or heal the sick, but she *could* fix a television pretty damn quick. Tech magic had run in the Waterhouse family for generations, but she and Clementine were the only ones with real power these days.

Gram had poured her magic into a precious gift—a spellbook that would help her when she needed it most—to Danica when Gram retired, and her mother... Danica sighed. Minerva was married to a mundane, and she had squandered her magic, let it trickle away as she led a trivial life in Normal, Illinois, of all places. Sometimes Danica thought the name of the town where she'd grown up was a little on the nose.

Before Danica could get to work, the phone rang, and she grabbed the extension in the work room. "Fix-It Witches, this is Danica. How can I help you?"

"Just calling to make sure you made it to work on time. Raquel posted some pictures of the party, and I saw enough to wonder if you'd even hear the alarm." Clementine's cheerful voice came across with a hint of reverb, indicating she was on Bluetooth and probably driving.

"You don't need to worry. I'm on it! I'll get half of these done before lunch."

"Big promises. Are you feeling okay?"

"Not great, but I'll recover." She wondered what pics Raquel had posted. *How embarrassed should I be?*

Normally, Danica didn't drink much, and it hadn't been the spirit of Bacchus that had motivated her to get crazy either. Nor was it a pure desire to celebrate Raquel's happiness. Fact was, Raquel was marrying Danica's ex, and Danica wasn't 100 percent cool with it. But she'd experienced an extremely prideful need to prove that she was totally, completely fine with Raquel's nuptial plans——not at all upset over the fact that Danica had dated Darryl Kenwood for two years and the entire time he'd talked about how neither of them needed to make things official to be happy.

To exacerbate matters, four months after Darryl hooked up with Raquel, he proposed to her. And Raquel was as mundane as they came. *No need to be official, my ass, Darryl. Hard not to take that personally.* If Danica was an evil sort of witch, she would've hexed his cell phone to spam all his contacts with a link to the last porn video he watched. *You still could,* a little voice whispered.

Since Clem knew the whole backstory and had even broken up with her boyfriend in solidarity, it was no wonder she was worried. A thread of concern persisted in Clem's voice. "Why in the world did you go to Raquel's bachelorette party anyway? You've barely spoken since college."

"I was proving a point."

"The fact that you're pointlessly nice? Or that you're over him?"

"Maybe both? Look, she didn't steal him from me. *I* broke up with him, remember? I was tired of his crap, and I couldn't put up with it anymore, not even for Gram."

"Still—"

"Don't worry about me," she cut in. "I'm at work. The business is fine, and you can poke at my emotions when you get back."

"If you're sure. Darryl is a loser. I know why you were with him, but we're better off sticking to the pact. Don't let Gram pressure you into dating some random gene packet again, okay?"

She clenched her teeth, too grumpy for lectures at this hour. "I hear you."

"And don't get worked up," Clem added, like she needed that caution.

A witch with serious emotional issues trying to cast? All the machines might explode—extra bad for business.

"Drive safely," Danica muttered.

"Eat something! I'm off to learn how to make better use of our marketing dollars. Have a great day." With that, her cousin hung up.

Acknowledgments

First, I must thank my amazing editor, Christa Désir. I truly lack the words to express how I treasure working with her, and how I prize her creativity, support, and expertise. I can honestly say we're a perfect match. Together, we made the magic happen (a witch pun, you're welcome), and I hope everyone loves Clem and Gavin. And Benson, of course!

Next, I extend sincere gratitude to the whole team at Sourcebooks—with special thanks to Stefani Sloma. It's sheer joy partnering with such gifted and impassioned bibliophiles.

Thanks to my fabulous agent, Lucienne Diver. She improves my writing and my life, and I always feel like she has my back. I couldn't ask for anything more. Her joy and belief in my work gives me the power to go on, even when I start to doubt.

To the readers who've trusted me for over a decade, you are the heart and soul of my work. Your loyalty and trust mean the world to me.

Thank you to the friends who offer encouragement when

I'm struggling and never hesitate to lend an ear. I cherish you all, more than words can say—Bree, Donna, Courtney, Alyssa, Thea, Yasmine, Shawntelle, Lili—and the list goes on. I'm beyond blessed.

Finally, last but never least, thank you to my family for always believing in me. My husband, Andres, was my first fan, and he has remained in my corner through trials and tribulations. Thank you, my dear ones. Your love gives me wings.

Dear readers, I hope this story enchanted you.

About the Author

New York Times and *USA Today* bestselling author Ann Aguirre has been a clown, a clerk, a savior of stray kittens, and a voice actress, not necessarily in that order. She grew up in a yellow house across from a cornfield, but now she lives in Mexico with her family. She writes all kinds of genre fiction, but she has an eternal soft spot for a happily ever after.